THE STAR OF VALHALLA

SEEING NOTHING, KNOWING NOTHING BUT THAT HE HAD COME IN
TIME TO SAVE HER.——*Page 328.*

THE
STAR OF VALHALLA

A ROMANCE OF EARLY
CHRISTIANITY IN
NORWAY

BY

MYRA GROSS

With illustrations in colour by
ARCHIE GUNN

NEW YORK
FREDERICK A. STOKES COMPANY
PUBLISHERS

To the memory of my Mother
whose faith and perfection of soul
gave me a vision of the
City Beautiful

PREFACE

Unusual conditions will be found in this romance which is woven out of the weird sagas of the Northland, and the ever-interesting story of the growth of Christianity. A firmly-rooted heathenism which grew from and was fostered by natural conditions, battles with the somewhat distorted Christianity of the tenth century. It is only after bitter struggles that the " still, small voice " of truth conquers a heathenism strong enough to endure for almost a thousand years after the birth of Christ; and it conquers through the medium of a spiritual and beautiful love between man and maid.

Among the deep fjords, the rose-light of the low-swinging sun, and the shifting splendour of the northern skies, the struggles of the soul and heart become intense. Who could live among such scenes and not believe in Odin and Thor and Frey ?

Though dealing with and correctly portraying important historical characters and events, " The Star of Valhalla " is distinctly a romance. In a few minor instances the narrative deviates from the actual occurrences; but this deviation was intentional and for the purpose of accenting the momentous change which took place in Norway at the close of the tenth century.

*   *   *   *   *   *

A Glossary of old Norse terms will be found at the end of the book.

Myra Geraldine Gross.

CONTENTS

CONTENTS

ILLUSTRATIONS

xi

The Star of Valhalla

CHAPTER I

"I WILL NOT SERVE THY CHRIST!"

A DEEP blue sky over which the winds were swiftly driving the white clouds. Silhouetted against that blue sky, the figure of a man on horseback of such gigantic proportions that he seemed to have been created from the rocks and ruggedness around him.

His long hair and beard were almost white with age; but his shoulders were broad and straight, and his eyes were bright with spirit and energy. He wore a tunic of grey, drawn in at the waist by a belt of wrought silver. From this belt hung a tolle-kniv and an ornamented scabbard containing his sword. Above his leather boots, his grey hosur were held in place by lacings of silver cord. Massive chains of silver hung around his neck, and silver bracelets were on his arms. The horned helmet on his head was so heavy that it could not have been worn by a less herculean figure.

The grey horse, with its silver-trimmed bridle, was in keeping with the man's proportions and dress. Horse and rider seemed created to live and move among the sublime heights and unfathomable depths around them, — those unmeasurable Norwegian distances, — reaching to the roof of the sky and falling away beneath, down, down, through the dark waters of the Fjord to the uttermost recesses of its rocky bed.

The stony ledge on which the man had drawn rein was like a shelf which some giant had carved out of the side of the cliff. On the right, the edge ended abruptly. A misstep in that direction would have sent man and beast to sudden death upon the jagged rocks below, with a burial beneath the waves that lapped their base.

On the left, a rough path wound down the cliff until lost amid the sombre green of the pines and firs which had gained

a foothold among the rocks.   By this path the man had reached
the ledge.   Seemingly it stopped here; but keen eyes would
observe that in the rear of the horseman there was the faint
indication of its continuance, at least as a foot-path, high up
among the over-hanging rocks.

For some moments rider and horse were motionless, rigid,
— the man deep in thought, while the horse was restrained by
that powerful grip on his bridle that he knew so well.   But
the spirited animal soon began to paw the ground impatiently
and toss his head in the vain endeavour to slacken the tension
on his bit.

The man drew the rein tighter.

" Hist! Slöngvier.   Be still!   Dost thou, too, feel the
strange unquiet that is abroad in the very air to-day ? "

As he spoke, he glanced upward towards the scurrying clouds,
and then below into the little valley which wound its way from
the edge of the Fjord into the heart of the rugged hills, like a
fairy garden, wrested by enchantment from the grim powers
in the mountains.   There, on a peninsula cut from the shore
by the sinuous curves of the River Nid, stood a collection of
buildings of such extent that it was evident they were occupied
by no mean person.

When the old man's gaze rested on them, his powerful frame
quivered with suppressed emotion.   " Yea ! " he muttered to
himself, " a new King has come to Norge and the Thrandheim,
and would speak fair with Iron Beard concerning the religion
of the land !   So be it.   I come, O King; but I come in the
name of Odin and Thor and Frey ! "

He turned his horse abruptly, sprang from the saddle, and
making his way to where the underbrush was broken, he
stooped and parted the branches.   Taking a hammer-shaped
charm from the chain at his neck, he laid it carefully under a
broad, flat stone.   Then he pulled the bushes together again,
remounted, and urged his horse recklessly down the steep
slope.

Where the bridle path joined the wide road a group of
horsemen stood waiting for him.   He returned their salutation
with grave dignity.   After some orders given in few words,
the cavalcade formed into an escort, and rode swiftly down
towards the extremity of the peninsula.   Before reaching the
long, low buildings, they met and exchanged greetings with the

King's *gestir*, who took charge of their horses. A short distance beyond, they came upon a *hirdman* dressed in a bright suit of mail and carrying a long, silver-tipped spear. He lowered his lance before Iron Beard and said :

"Be well and happy. The King awaits the coming of the great Temple Godi."

Iron Beard bowed graciously.

"Thy greeting is returned, Jostern. Lead on into the presence of the King."

The attendants stopped, and Iron Beard and Jostern went on past the skali, or main building, to the málstofa where the King held all private conversations. This was a rectangular structure formed of massive logs, and built, as all Norwegian buildings are, to resist the furious onslaughts of the wild winter storms.

Jostern pushed back the heavy door and announced solemnly :

"The Temple Godi of Thrandheim enters to speak with the King of Norge."

Iron Beard passed in. Slowly the door swung to behind him. A log fire burned in the centre of the room ; for the afternoon was chilly, although it was only the end of August. The flickering light played hide and seek in the folds of the heavy tapestry which covered the walls, throwing diamond points of light upon the rich weapons and inlaid shields that hung around in reckless profusion. The dark shadows and the glancing lights served as a background to the central figure in the room.

Before the fire, reclining in a large, elaborately carved armchair, was a magnificent specimen of manhood. His fair complexion, blue eyes, regular, clear-cut features, and long hair sweeping his shoulders were evidences of pure Norse blood. His stately bearing, costly dress, and above all, the indomitable will which lurked in the cold depths of his eyes, marked him as one born to command, — a King.

He rose to greet his guest and said :

"Thou art welcome to my málstofa. Thy place is awaiting thee. Rest."

He waved his hand towards an empty chair opposite to his own. Iron Beard clasped his left wrist with his right hand and bowed rather stiffly.

"The King sent and I have come," he replied, as he accepted the indicated seat.

Hardly had the two men taken their places when a boy appeared, bearing a huge bowl of mead which he put on a low table in front of the King. Then taking two gold-mounted drinking horns from the wall, he filled, and passed them to the men.

The King raised his to his lips first.

"Skal!" he said.

"Skal!" replied Iron Beard.

Then both drained the contents to the last drop.

While the boy removed the mead not a word was spoken; but there was an interchange of looks, — a mysterious warfare waged in silence, — which made Iron Beard's eyes gleam like coals of fire under his bushy eyebrows, while the King's grew as steely blue as the blade of the Damascus sword at his side. Each measured the other's strength: each felt instinctively that the interview would be stormy: each determined to win.

Olaf spoke first:

"Norsemen use few words; therefore I say to thee plainly, Temple Godi, that I, the King of Norge, desire my people to forsake the heathen worship of Odin and accept the true God, Christ the White.

"As thou must have heard, I learned of this wonderful and great religion during my sojourn in distant lands. I believe he is the only God to whom men should bow. Believing this, it is my wish that the people over whom I rule should worship as I do. I desire the welfare of my people. I desire to see them prosperous and happy; and for this end, I think it necessary for them to abandon their cruel belief and follow the example of all the great nations of the earth.

"I have journeyed from the south of Norge, sending out in every district the Thing-token for the assembling of the people. When they gathered before me, I told them that they were to put aside their heathen worship and accept the Christ for their God. This have they done. Now I have come to the Thrandheim, and bring the same message to your jarls and bonder."

The King spoke smoothly; for he realized that he had personal and vital, as well as national interest, in making the interview as friendly as possible. He was in the heart of his newly acquired dominions; and nowhere was there such firm allegiance to the ancient faith as in the Thrandheim. Several kings preceding him had striven to pull up the old roots and plant the new seed; but those strong, heroic, and beautiful fibres of the Norse belief had wound themselves so firmly about the hearts of the people that they could not be removed, even though lives had been sacrificed in the fruitless effort to do so.

This Olaf knew; and though he had sworn to Christianize Norge or die, he did not repeat to Iron Beard all that had happened on his journey northward: did not tell him that hitherto he had commanded what he was now requesting; nor say that those who refused and openly rebelled were slain by his soldiers; nor spoke of altars and temples destroyed, of sacrificial stones shattered and broken, of desolate homes and orphaned children.

After a moment's pause, Olaf continued:

"I intend to send out the Thing-summons over the Thrandheim; but knowing that thou wert a great and powerful leader in this district, and that the people loved thee and trusted in thy judgment, I wished to see thee first and get thy opinion in this matter before I spoke openly to the bonder."

When the King ceased, neither man stirred from the position he had taken at the beginning of the interview.

Iron Beard listened in stony indifference to the King's first few sentences. As the King spoke of those who had accepted Christianity his eyes flashed scorn; but when he told of the sending out of the Thing-token in the Thrandheim, and the reasons for doing so, Iron Beard's lips set themselves tightly together, his eyes grew small and glittered dangerously, and his hand closed around the handle of the sword at his side. The flattering allusion to his position and power only increased the ominous grip on his sword handle; and as the deep, measured tones of Olaf's voice died away, they left a silence intense, and thick with evil foreboding.

Between Norsemen such a silence is sacred, only to be broken by the one addressed; so the King waited.

At last, slowly and decidedly Iron Beard spoke:

"Olaf Tryggvveson, hear the answer to thy words from the lips of the Temple Godi of the Thrandheim. I will not serve thy Christ! I will not help thee in any way to force thy worship upon my people. Who is this God of thine? We have heard of him before, and his teachings are not to our liking. A weak, sickly belief which has no feasts; which offers no reward to the warrior; dresses its priests in women's petticoats; and bids us bow down to the image of a man fastened to a cross! A dead thing, which ought to be buried out of sight among the gruesome inhabitants of the mounds.

"And what does this Christ offer to his worshippers? Forgiveness of sins? Bah! We Norsemen answer to ourselves for our misdoings. We ask not forgiveness from man nor god. Everlasting life after death? What for? To walk in a city of gold and play on harps like a lot of children! What cares the warrior for such a future? — a future that holds no promise of reward for his courage and bravery, no commendation for all those great and heroic deeds that Norsemen have been taught to love, and which they ever strive to achieve.

"Tell me, Olaf Tryggvveson, shall I give up my ancient belief, with its glorious feasts and battles? Shall I renounce Valhalla? Shall I close my eyes to the Valkyrias? Shall I drink no more to Odin and Thor for luck and victory? Shall I renounce all, all, to accept such uncertain, faintly defined benefits in return? No! Thou hast spoken to ears that hear thee not because the heart believes not!"

The man closed with a broad, sweeping gesture which seemed to throw the King's words to the winds, even as the waves cast high upon the shore the driftwood that burdens their crests.

But Olaf was not accustomed to having his requests violently hurled aside. He had not expected a direct refusal. A delayed answer, perhaps, or the statement of some objections, would not have surprised him; but open defiance and ridicule roused the tiger in him, — the tiger that creeps and crouches until its prey is within its grasp.

He answered with some effort to speak calmly:

"I do not blame one who has always worshipped the old gods of Norge for feeling as thou dost; but bear with me a little and perhaps thou wilt change thy opinion somewhat.

"It is now nearly a thousand winters since the Christ came to earth, and all great nations worship him save the Norse. I was once a heathen; but after a prophet of Christ had foretold many wonderful things about my future, all of which occurred just as he said, I allowed myself to be baptized. There are many warriors who are Christians; and though we have no Valhalla, yet there are great promises of happiness in the next world to those who help to spread the Christian belief.

"If my people obey me in this matter we will be able to stand with the strongest nations on the earth: we will have powerful allies in case of war: ships will enter our fjords with rich cargoes: men of influence and wealth will abide with us; and the years of my reign will be prosperous and happy.

"But if my people are determined to continue their sacrifices to Odin and Thor and Frey, the Christian nations will seek to wipe them from the earth: I shall not be able to secure allies in warfare: our cities will remain unvisited: we will be shunned and hated; and years of hardship will follow. Would such conditions be pleasing to thee and the Thrandheim? Would ye deliberately choose sorrow and suffering, rather than peace and plenty?

"Think well, O Temple Godi, before thou sayest thou wilt not worship my God. Dost thou not know that he is spoken of in the Norsemen's Edda? Listen to the words thou canst read there:

"'Then shall the Mighty One come from above, — he who ruleth over all, whose name man ceases not to utter. He cometh in his power to the great judgment seat. He shall appease all strife, and shall establish a holy place which shall endure eternally; but the foul Dragon, the venom-spotted Nidhöggu, flies away over the plains, and sinks out of sight bearing death upon his wings!'"

Iron Beard could scarcely control himself until Olaf had finished. Then, throwing aside the veil of courtesy to his King with which he had hidden his intense feelings, he turned upon him with the fury and rage of a man who has heard all that he held most sacred perverted to mean all that he most loathed and despised.

"Darest thou thus to use the prophecies which Odin will fulfill for thy strange god? Dost thou think that I am a wolf in the sanctuary, — a nithing-slayer, — to accept thy unholy interpretation of those holy words? They speak to me only of Odin, the Norseman's God! Odin, the God of Battles! the Manifold! the Much-knowing! the Father of Ages! And to him will I sacrifice in the future as in the past!

"It may be that thou hast persuaded the southerners to take thy Christ for Odin and Thor; but here in the Thrandheim the blood of the Vikings flows pure and strong, and cannot mingle with the dark, sluggish streams that must course through the veins of the Christian nations.   Therefore take warning that my answer to thee will be the answer of every jarl and bonde in this district.   Thou hast not one friend in this matter!

"Other kings have striven to make us bow down to this strange god, — this god who has no strength in battle, who loves not sacrifices, who bids us let our enemies kill without resistance, — and they failed, even as thou wilt.   I know my people; and blood, yea, the blood of kings, will be spilt if thou forcest thy god upon them!

"Say to me now that thou wilt not press this matter upon the people; else I warn thee with all earnestness that while in the Thrandheim thy life is but a pebble, tottering on the edge of an abyss into which it may be hurled at any moment.   Remember that thou didst receive the head of the last king of Norge from the hand of his servant who betrayed him.   Remember that he met his ignoble death because he trampled too heavily upon the rights and feelings of his people.   While we own willing allegiance to our lawful rulers, we are not footstools; and he who tries to use us as such will find himself treading upon red-hot plowshares."

Olaf rose and faced the Temple Godi, the red glow of the fire veiling the angry flush on his haughty face.   His first impulse was to hand the man before him over to the guard with his death sentence; but second thought proved how unwise such a move would be.   It would inflame the people, and make it not only impossible to continue his efforts to introduce Christianity, but even to remain in the Thrandheim.   So he smothered his anger; but the tiger in him crouched and crept as he replied:

"Olaf Tryggvveson has faced too many dangers to be afraid of his own countrymen.   I know, Temple Godi, that I am now among the bravest and best of my nation, — those who have never listened to the teachings of the new religion; whose lives and wealth are still laid at the feet of the ancient gods of Norge.   I see by thy speech that the old belief is even more firmly rooted than I thought; and though I fear not death for myself, I wish no blood to be spilt. I cannot worship Odin any more than thou canst worship Christ; but is there not some way to compromise? Thou art mistaken in thinking there are no feasts nor sacrifices in the Christian religion. At the Yule Feast I will celebrate the Birth of Christ on earth; and at the Victory Sacrifice in the spring, a feast to commemorate the wonderful death and coming to life again of my God. Then people and king will both be satisfied. It may be that in time one religion will suffice for all."

The words were blandly spoken; but Iron Beard was not deceived. He was keen enough to see that such a change from command to compromise was only one of a series of moves to entrap the bonder. What would come next? He doubted the King's sincerity; but was compelled to allow his anger to subside a little. Still, his forehead wrinkled into a fierce frown as he answered:

"King Olaf, I can give but one reply to thy unusual words. The smoke of the sacrifices I offer at Lladir to Odin and Thor can never mingle with the thin incense thou burnest to thy god. As for the people, let them speak for themselves. Thou wilt summon them to a Thing. There thou shalt hear their opinion."

For one instant a scornful smile followed the frown, then quickly vanished. The King eyed him suspiciously; but he saw that he could gain nothing further from the proud, defiant old man, and judged it wise to bring the interview to a close.

"So be it. While I grieve that thou hast so firmly and decidedly refused the Christ, I know that thou art only acting like a true Norseman, who does not change with the wind. We will say no more until we meet at the Thing; and time will adjust our different opinions as is wisest and best.

"Thou art Temple Godi in the Thrandheim, so I will send the Thing-token to thy skali first. Thou dost not need to be told further of thy duty as to forwarding it among the people. May Christ change thy mind and heart ere we meet again. Farewell."

Olaf bowed with kingly dignity and waved his guest towards the door. Iron Beard returned his bow with daring coolness; and swinging his sheathed sword backward with a heavy pressure upon the handle, passed out into the pale light of the autumn day.

CHAPTER II

THE STAR OF VALHALLA

A FEW moments later Iron Beard and his hirdmen were riding back over the rocky road. When they reached the place where the bridle-path led up the cliff, Iron Beard, telling his men to proceed without him, turned his horse's head towards the narrow ledge above. On reaching it he dismounted, and throwing the bridle-rein over a stunted pine, he strode to the edge of the cliff and looked down upon the dwellings he had just left.

"So," he muttered to himself, " the new King has dared to bring with him the hateful worship that the Norsemen twice before have driven from their shores. And they will do it again! Dost thou hear, Olaf Tryggvveson? I measured thy strength to-day as I would measure a man's sword in a holmganga, and thy new god has not won thy strength, though thou wouldst have me believe so. Thy heart dost not believe all that thy tongue sayeth. Thou art weak, yea, weak as a child before a Temple Godi of Odin! Thou talkest to Iron Beard of compromise, of changing the sacrifices gradually and leading the bonder to worship this Christ little by little! Thou hast been so long away from the Thrandheim, thou hast forgotten that our Norsemen are not led like dumb cattle. Better would I have liked thee hadst thou said: ' Let those who believe in Odin stand against those who believe in Christ, and the victors shall establish the worship of their god.'

"Then would Odin and Thor and Frey have crushed this Christ of thine as the ice-river crushes the rocks. But thou didst speak so cunningly that I had no cause to answer thee with blue steel as I had hoped. Yet I told thee there would be no compromise; for we will worship our ancient gods while breath is in us. Yea! and after breath leaves us! For then in Valhalla, the glorious Home of the Glad, shall we dwell forever! There shall we live with only the brave who gave themselves to Odin! There shall we measure swords with all the mighty Norsemen whose blood has reddened the battle-fields since Odin came from Asgard. Then, with the arisen slain shall we sit at feast and eat of the flesh that is never consumed and drink of the mead that flows forever! Glorious death that opens the door of Valhalla! Hail to Odin, the Father of the Slain! Never will the Norseman forget thy name. Never will thy temples be stripped of their treasures, nor the sacrifices cease to ascend unto thee! I, Iron Beard, defy all the Christian kings in the world, from Halgoaland to Micklegard! Yea, let them come! The *Star of Valhalla* shall still shine over Norge!"

The old man's eyes gleamed like live coals among the wind-swept masses of hair about his face. His right hand, raised in terrible energy, was clenched until the nails sank into the flesh. His whole frame trembled with passion; and so oblivious was he of his surroundings that he did not see a figure which seemed to rise out of the mists of the valley and stand at his side.

An uncanny voice answered his last words:

"Temple Godi of Thrandheim, the *Star of Valhalla* is fading already, — fading into the past, — and thou shalt see it vanish forever!"

The man turned in a frenzy —

"Who dares ——" but when he saw the apparition at his side he stopped with a sudden start. Then he bowed his head in reverence.

Beside him stood an old woman, bent with the burden of years until she seemed no longer human. Once she must have been tall, possibly even well formed; but the blighting touch of passing years had bowed the straight shoulders, and left but a frame-work of bones covered with wrinkled skin. A long, dark cloak that reached the ground hung around her shoulders. Where it parted slightly under its silver fibula there was a glimpse of scarlet and a shimmer of coloured light. Hairy shoes covered her feet, and white catskin gloves were drawn over her hands. She leaned heavily upon a knobbed staff, inlaid with gold and precious stones.

Altogether, she was like a dead tree clothed in its own dead leaves, on which some one had hung a few golden baubles. The only sign of life lay in her small eyes which peered from beneath her wrinkled brows with a wonderful intelligence.

They glinted and glanced as though lit by some internal fire ; and as the Norseman looked down into their unnatural depths they sent him a strange, weird message that he did not understand.

After a moment's silence he addressed her respectfully :

"I knew not that thou wast so near me, Mother, though I left the Hammer of Thor under the stone; for I wished to see thee soon. Thy words have not gladdened my heart; and surely, never would I have said that so dire a prophecy could have come from Heid's lips. What does it portend, Mother, that thou, the last of the Volvas, who can brew the witch's broth and who has worshipped our great gods more devoutly than any one in our district, shouldst declare that the *Star of Valhalla* is fading ? Did I not know full well thy sincerity and wisdom, I would hurl thee from yonder cliff for uttering such a prophecy. But many years thou hast dwelt among us; and great secrets the gods have told thee. Words have never lain lightly upon thy lips. I pray thee, explain this strange thought thou hast spoken.

"Are not the jarls and bonder of the Thrandheim as loyal to Odin as ever before ? Do not our sacrifices still redden the altar in our beautiful temple at Lladir ? Did we not reject the new faith when Hakon tried to force it upon us; and shall we take it more quietly from the hand of this King, who, though rich and a great warrior, has yet to learn that his countrymen hold firmly to their ancient worship ?"

The old woman listened in stony silence. Something of sympathy lit up her wrinkled features at his last words; but the light died out quickly — like a tiny flame kindled in the path of a rushing flood — leaving only the darkness of a sullen despair.

Then she spoke, solemnly and slowly, as one who is about to lift the veil from a mighty mystery :

"Iron Beard, when thou didst speak of the *Star of Valhalla*, thou didst utter words for which I have long been listening, — words which, to me, mean that the secret I have carried for many years may be shared with another.

"Whoever heard of the real *Star of Valhalla* ? Not even our most devout worshippers have ever thought or spoken of Odin's Light in the sky. Even thou, with thy burning words, spoke only by chance, though the Nornir directed thy tongue.

" But there *is* a *Star of Valhalla!* Look for thyself to-night when the light is dim. Over the Fjord to the north thou wilt see two stars. Long years ago, — long years before thou wert birth-sprinkled, — the greatest Volva of Norge told me that in those twinkling lights I·would read the fate of the gods of Norge.

" Wise was Snotra above all wisdom that ever has been known. She it was who taught me to understand the language of the ravens who bring messages from Odin. She it was who taught me to read men's dreams, to brew the witch's broth, and foretell the future. I was at her side when her spirit was about to pass over the Bridge of Asar. Wonderful were the visions she saw, and great were the secrets of the future which I then learned. Listen now to the strange story of the *Star of Valhalla* as I heard it long ago, — the great and awful secret of the Asar!

" I thought the Wise Woman had spoken for the last time; and I was waiting to perform the nabjargir, — to close her eyes and mouth after death, — when suddenly the life came back. She sat upright and pointed with one long hand out of the door of her cave to where two stars were shining in the northern sky.

" ' Seest thou, O Heid, those twin lights twinkling in the hall of the moon? Watch them diligently; for strange things shall come of them. Knowest thou that the brightest is the door of Valhalla? The time was when its light was marvellous to behold, — when no star could shine near it. But little by little I have beheld its brightness departing. Year by year have I watched it fading until I was filled with terrible forebodings, knowing no rest for thinking that Norge's gods were taking their light from her mountains and fjords.

" ' Then I spent all my wealth in offering sacrifices to appease Odin's anger and avert the unknown calamity that was threatening our land and nation. All in vain! My sacrifices reddened the temple until the Godi waded through blood. I went to the jarls when they returned from their vikings, and purchased the noblest captives, the fairest women and the most innocent children. All these I sent to Odin and Thor; but the *Star* only grew fainter and fainter.

" ' Then came a dark day when my wisdom was accounted as evil. Messengers arrived from King Harald forbidding me

to perform seid or foretell the future.   As I would not obey,
I fled to the mountains to escape death.   I spent one night in
the wildest spot upon this great Fjord.   There, high among
the clouds which wrapped me in their chilling cloaks, breast-
ing the strength of Egir's Brother, the Cloud-driver, crouching like a wolf among the rocks, I prayed for knowledge of
the great changes which seemed to be threatening all Norge.
That night, as I sang to Odin and Thor and Frey, the storm-
clouds were swept away from the upper world.   Behold! another star shone beside the door of Valhalla!   Faintly it
gleamed; and yet its steady rays struck such terror into my
soul that all consciousness left me.   For many hours I was
as one dead.

" ' The next night I stole down to the Temple Priest.
Together we went in the darkness to the temple to cast the
sacrificial chips and learn from them more of the future.
They told us a sad, terrible story.   The *Star of Valhalla*
would vanish from our sight, — put out by the Light I had
seen pierce the darkness at its side.'

" Here the great Snotra sank down upon the skins.   Long
did I labour to bring back the breath into her body.   When
she again opened her eyes there was a sadness in them so
great that it seemed to reflect all the sorrows of suffering souls
since Ymir was born.   She feebly raised herself on her arm,
and looking again towards the north, she used her last breath
in telling me the rest of the secret of the Asar:

" ' Since that awful night when I drew that knowledge from
above, the strange Light has been growing brighter and
brighter.   Now I tell thee that when thou art watching those
two lights, thou art watching a battle such as no human eye
ever looked upon!   A battle that rages between unknown
and terrible forces in the path of the moon with arrows of
lightning!   I cannot tell thee what it is that is driving Valhalla from Norge, — never have I been able to wrench that
secret from the skies, — but it may be that thou wilt get the
knowledge that was denied me.

" ' Now I lay this solemn charge upon thee.   Keep within
thy lips this secret I have told thee until thou hearest some one
speak of the *Star of Valhalla*.   Then the end is near.   Thou
mayest tell of what the Volva told thee on her death bed.' "

The old woman paused, and her bowed shoulders bent still

closer towards her staff, as if yielding to the increased weight of an already heavy burden. In low, broken tones she continued :

"Now thou knowest, O Priest, all I have to tell thee. Judge for thyself of the worth and reason of the words I first spoke."

Iron Beard had listened until his face was blanched with fear. To him, every sentence from her lips bore the stamp of unquestioned truth. Her weird revelations had struck through his heated feelings, leaving them chilled and numb. He did not speak ; but looked up the blue path of the wide Fjord to the grey cliffs in the distance, as though in their mist-crowned tops he recognized some dim resemblance to his own clouded mind. He was brought back to reality by Heid.

Suddenly she threw off her despair and sadness. She straightened her crooked form, raised her staff, and shook it violently over the valley in a wild burst of rage.

"What art thou, Olaf Tryggvveson, to betray thy country and its gods to the White Christ ? Thou who hast lived because thy mother was a Norsewoman ; and therefore strong and brave to hide thee from enemies who sought thy life even before thou wast born. Thou who wast redeemed from captivity because of thy Norse beauty, and saved from death because of thy Norse spirit. Thou who hast ruled the winds and waves as only a Norseman can, and who hast fought and conquered as only a Norseman fights and conquers. All that thou hast been and art and shalt be thou owest to the great Odin, the First of the Norsemen !

"Darest thou take this new god into thy bosom ? What has he done for thee ? How has he helped thee, save to let his own fly before thy Norse might like clouds before the storm-wind ? Thou hast come to thy native shores with treachery in thy heart, and I curse thee ! I curse thee, and tell thee thou shalt be punished with a terrible punishment ! From this White Christ shall come a sorrow which shall eat into thy vitals and cause thee such suffering as would never have come from Odin and Thor !

"Yea ! And thou shalt suffer unaided ; for thou hast driven the Wise Ones away. Listen to the groans and cries from Eyrind Kellda and his followers whom thou didst bind on the Skerry of Shrieks to be drowned like dogs ! Every shriek shalt thou answer in the agony of thy soul! And we who escaped thy clutches, we hide in the rocks like wild beasts, covering our red robes — once honoured far and near — with dark mantles, so that we may creep about among the crags and be unseen! Yea! So have I hidden my wisdom and my wealth!" — and with a quick movement she threw aside her cloak.

A singular, fantastic figure stood out with startling distinctness against the dark background of pines and firs. She wore a long, scarlet kyrtle of red brocade which fell around her feet in heavy folds. It was drawn in at the waist by a girdle of pure gold, from which hung a skin bag curiously wrought and ornamented. Around her neck were necklet rings of gold. Heavy chains of the same metal hung over her bosom down to her waist, and her wrists were covered with spiral bracelets. Red, green and white flashes from innumerable jewels on neck, dress, girdle, and wrists, enclosed her in a rainbow of light.

She turned to Iron Beard with all the stately pride and dignity her many years could command.

"Thou believest in me. Thou hast often visited me in my hole amongst the rocks where thou hast learned many things. To-day when I heard from thy lips the words for which Snotra bade me listen, my spirit was glad to know, at least, that the secret which had become the burden of my old age could be shared with thee.

"Now I ask thee, wilt thou see the door of Valhalla shut unless thy spirit enters first? Wilt thou let this strange god dwell in our beautiful Norge while thou art living? In the name of the glorious past let us fight to the death! Go out and battle for Odin and Thor and Frey. I have no mighty strength to wield a sword; but my wisdom is still wise to direct thy acts. We must tarry not; for I fear with a great fear that the Light that is destined to close the door of Valhalla, — the strange, white star which grows brighter every night, — is the religion of Christ the White!"

The Temple Priest tossed his head like an old war-horse scenting the battle from afar.

"Let the King send out his Thing-summons and offer the people his god. He shall have the hated name cast into his teeth. Yea, Mother, we shall fight to the death!"

Heid seized the sleeve of Iron Beard's tunic.

" Hist!   Does the King summon a Thing ? "

" Yea, so I told thee."

The old woman's clutch on his sleeve tightened.   Pulling him down to her, she said in a shrill whisper :

" Then the budstickke comes first to *thee!*   Dost thou know what to do ? "

She stopped, looked around, — up, down, beyond, — as if to detect a chance listener.   Only a solitary raven winged its way slowly over their heads.   She noted the omen.

" See ! " she said, " Odin's messenger flies o'er us !   This is what he tells thee to do."

Her little eyes twinkled cunningly and her thin lips parted in the withered remnant of a smile.   She breathed some words into Iron Beard's ear.

The old man started.   Then drawing his sword, he swung it slowly over the valley, — backward, forward, — saying as he did so:

" Thy words are indeed Odin's message.   I will obey. Odin, not the White Christ, shall rule the Thing ! "

Heid gave a low, satisfied chuckle.   Folding her long cloak closely about her, she turned and disappeared among the underbrush.

CHAPTER III

THE TEMPLE PRIEST'S DAUGHTER

IRON BEARD recovered his charm from beneath the stone where he had hidden it, vaulted into the saddle, and once more rode down the steep slope. When he reached the public road he turned his horse's head to the left and began ascending the hills.

The short Norwegian day was drawing to a close. A soft, autumnal haze hung over the landscape. Far below lay the Thrandheim Fjord, so hemmed in by its wild and rugged walls that it looked more like a lake than an arm of the sea. A rocky island dotted its surface, as if some mighty hand had torn a huge piece from the mountainside and hurled it into the midst of the blue waters.

The sun was low in the sky. It sent long, slanting rays of red light across mountains and fjord, crowning each prominent crag and far-off, snow-capped summit with warm rose colours, and lighting up the tiny crested waves with reflected, opalescent tints that broke into thousands of jewels as the waters rose and fell in perfect rhythm.

Among the dark green of the coniferous trees, the leaves of the aspen glowed crimson with the first touch of winter; and the tall, graceful mountain ash was loaded with its harvest of red berries. Colour everywhere, — rich, varied tints in sky, fjord, and forest, — and over all a stillness intensified by the echo of the horse's hoofs. Vidar, the Silent God, seemed reigning over the world. Yielding to the subtle influence, Iron Beard slackened his hold on the bridle and was soon lost in thought.

Winding in and out among the trees and rocks, he rode on for some time unconscious of his surroundings. He was suddenly aroused by the sound of merry laughter. Instantly his face was softly illumined with the light of fatherly love. He leaned eagerly forward to catch the first glimpse of the owner of that silvery laugh.

A bend in the road brought him before his own home, — the characteristic Norwegian dwelling with heavily carved door-posts and wide, over-hanging eaves ornamented with gargoyles. Many outbuildings told of wealth and a large following. Thralls were hurrying hither and thither, busily storing away the fruits of the harvest and preparing for the long, cold winter that was creeping down from the north. All were anxious to greet their master with loving respect; but he passed the upturned faces with scarcely a recognition.

His whole attention was riveted on the slight, girlish figure which stood in the doorway of his skali. He murmured softly to himself, " Sigrid, my daughter ! Light of my old age ! "

She was delicately though perfectly formed, and very fair. Her long kyrtle of pale blue silk, with its heavy border of silver embroidery, fell about her in graceful folds. Dainty chains of silver encircled her beautiful neck; many bracelets loaded her white arms; and a diadem set with diamonds held her long hair in place. The cloak that had been around her shoulders lay at her feet. She stood with her bare arms twined about the dark, weather-stained door-post. Her small head, with its glory of golden hair, rested against the carved surface.

Like the frail moon-flower clinging to the precipitous rock, and unfolding its chaste, white blossoms in the moonlight, so looked Sigrid the Pure, as she clung to the old column and raised her sweet eyes to her father with loving welcome.

He sprang from his horse, and clasping her in his arms, kissed her tenderly. Then stooping, he lifted her cloak from the ground and wrapped it around her, saying :

" Too cold, Little One, for those arms to be uncovered. Wilt thou never learn that winter is close at hand ? "

She laughed, — a merry burst of music that was a song for the birds to hear.

" What am I to do when my father leaves me alone so long ? Here I have been watching and waiting; but I forgot the cold when I heard Slöngvir's hoof-beats. Tell me now, where hast thou been, and what has happened to keep thee so long ? "

Across Iron Beard's face a shadow fell. Without answering, he drew her into the skali. He took his accustomed high-seat facing the south; while Sigrid curled herself upon a quaint stool at his feet. Resting her white elbows upon his knee, she anxiously waited for him to speak.

Patting her rosy cheek, he said smilingly :

" Nay, nay, my Sigrid, little need for those blue eyes to be clouded. I have heard that the new King is a Christian, that is all."

" But father," and the blue eyes did cloud over, "thou art not ! Thou art the Temple Godi of the Thrandheim ! Will he seek to harm thee ? "

" Child ! " The old man spoke almost fiercely. " Dost thou think thy father cannot defend himself if needs be ? But there ! Thou art a woman and hast a woman's foolish fears. So I say quickly that the King and thy father parted in peace. But the quiet of our district is threatened. I fear it will be necessary for me to be away from thee much during the coming weeks, instructing the bonder to be ready to stand with me for the maintenance of our loved gods."

Sigrid sighed ; but in a moment, with a Norse disregard of self, she said eagerly :

" Thou wilt soon have strong help, father, if all I heard to-day is true. Dost thou know that Jarl Rognvald and his son, Harald, the Blest of the Nornir, are returning from their summer viking ? Couriers from the coast passed here but a few hours since, saying they would enter the Fjord in three days."

Iron Beard arose, lifting Sigrid to her feet with a teasing laugh :

" So ! Trust to a woman's ears to hear all things ! They are like the Fjord which, in the end, gathers every rain-drop that falls on the hills for miles around ! But thy lips did speak good news, my Sigrid. Jarl Rognvald and Harald and Iron Beard, when hand in hand, can well afford to laugh in the face of any King who boasts that he can ride roughshod over the feelings and opinions of the Thrandheim bonder."

Then he kissed her forehead and said :

" Run to thy skemma now and continue thy weaving with thy women. Thy father is here. Thou needst not strain thy pretty eyes, nor let thy loom be idle because thou watchest for him. Run hither now, and dream, if thou wilt, of Harald Rognvaldson's return."

Sigrid clung to him a moment with smiles and blushes. Then she glided out of the door of the skali into the small building opposite, looking like a speck of the blue sky that had fallen to earth with some of the sun's golden rays clinging to it.

Iron Beard watched her until the last glimpse of blue had vanished behind the skemma door.   Then raising his arms and eyes towards heaven, he prayed in a voice broken with feeling :

"For myself I care not, — old trees must fall.   But to thy mercy, to thy protection, O Odin, Father of All, I give my child !   Let no harm come to her.   Shield her fair head from the terrible storms of life !   Remove all briars from the pathway over which her feet must tread !   Most of all, save her from this hated religion of the nations of the south, whose vileness I have seen and known !   Save her ! save her from this rank poison brewed in the hot atmosphere of falsehood and crime — CHRISTIANITY ! "

CHAPTER IV

THE VIKING OF HARALD ROGNVALDSON

THE tenth century was one of the darkest eras in the history of Christianity. During the earlier struggles with paganism, when to be a Christian was to be a martyr for faith and conscience, the purity, the holy beauty, the perfect simplicity of the teachings of the lowly Nazarene were retained.

The world rioted and danced unheeded above the Christians, as they sang hymns of faith amid the gloomy recesses of the catacombs. The followers of Christ had only Christ. He was their sole happiness, their wealth, their life, their eternity. Cruel persecutors gazed with dull amazement at their calm endurance of torture and death; wondered at their utter indifference to everything earthly; listened in strange bewilderment to their hymns that rose above the howling of the mob and the roar of the beasts.

While gazing, wondering, listening — the spark of spirituality, that lingers in the secret depths of sin-wearied souls, was fanned into a flame of faith and love. On, on crept that tongue of flame, in and out among hovels and palaces, in highways and byways, — melting the chains of the slave, anointing the crown of the King, and conquering the hitherto unconquerable. That wonderful fire burned the selfishness out of men's hearts and left only the love of Christ. Imperial Rome was conquered by the unarmed disciples of the Christian faith.

Then there came a time when the Christian was no longer an outcast from society; when Christ's name was reverenced above all names, and his banners floated above the ruins of the ancient temples.

But when Christianity was proclaimed as the religion of the Empire, it was also adopted as the fashion of a profligate society. The heroic age passed with the martyrs, and the Christian Church confronted peculiar difficulties and temptations with weakened forces. The vitality of its earlier principles was sapped by ideas foreign to Christ's teachings.

Men were untaught, and in their ignorance and superstition

made creeds to suit themselves, that had little affinity with the teachings of the Crucified. The rulers of the church, placed in high position by wealth or influence, wielded their power for personal benefit, not for the promulgation and welfare of the gospel. Infamous men and women stained the record of the church with dark and terrible deeds. Nine hundred years after the Great Tragedy on Calvary the Christian world was almost as cruel, as immoral, and as intolerant as ancient heathendom.

When this polluted Christianity attempted to roll its waves over the wild, majestic rocks of the Northland, is it strange that it was met by a fierce resistance that sent it back upon its southern shores? The Norsemen could not give up their weird faith, created amid the wild beauty of the midnight sun, the glittering seas of ice, and the tremulous gorgeousness of the Aurora Borealis, for what was offered them as Christianity.

At this momentous time, when the spirits of light and darkness were waging a terrible warfare for the possession of men's souls, it is wonderful to trace the perfect fulfillment of God's word — how the great truths of the gospel survived the battle, and laid the wounded and repentant world once more at the foot of the Cross.

Never could the flame kindled at the martyr's stake be entirely extinguished. Here and there it burned with as true and steady a light as ever, and was ready at the signal from above to burst forth in all its irresistible force and beauty. God had lit one of these Beacon Lights of heaven in a secluded spot on the sunny slopes of southern Italy. Here, on one of the many hillsides which descended in gentle incline to the blue waters of the Mediterranean, stood an old Roman villa, almost hidden in the dark foliage about it. But the silver moonlight hunted out the scarred and weather-stained columns, transforming them into pillars of whitest marble. The spirit of peace and quiet happiness was resting upon the old pile of stone, and the air was laden with the fragrance of late roses which bordered the garden walks, dropping their petals of white and gold at the feet of two persons, young man and maiden, who were walking slowly between them. As they passed from the deeper shadows into the moonlight, the girl looked up into her companion's face and said:

"Tell me more, my brother, of what thou didst see in Rome; for to me it is like a wonderful story."

The young man, with a touch of sadness in his musical voice replied:

"Yea, Persea, it is a wonderful story, — the story of Rome, its people, its exquisite works of art, its magnificent palaces, its sublime Basilica, its life, its religion. But, my little sister, I pray that thy pure, sweet eyes may never see Rome."

The girl looked at him in puzzled amazement.

"And why not, Tellus? Thou hast been there, and I know of no man more pure and good than thou art. Before our beloved mother fell asleep in Jesus," and the low, soft voice trembled with feeling, "I never cared to see or know much beyond our green hedges; but now I believe that I should go out into the world and learn what it is. Surely there must be much for me to know; and besides, God did not give me life without a purpose. I have some mission to accomplish for Christ before I die, and I would not be satisfied to stay here always. Yea, thou wilt some day take me to Rome."

She leaned her head lovingly against his shoulder. He wrapped her in a strong embrace with infinite tenderness, gathering her closer to him as if to shield her from approaching evil. He looked capable of protecting her from any harm as he bent over her in the full flush of manhood, — broad-chested, well proportioned, and with the ease, strength, and rapidity of motion of a perfect athlete hidden in the sinewy curves of his hardened muscles. He was not handsome; but he had a noble forehead crowned with a mass of dark hair, and his clear, open countenance would attract attention at once by its power of expression.

He soon released Persea, and they continued their walk to the brow of the hill. There they could see the scattered lights of the village below, and the fishing boats riding at anchor in the sheltered cove. On the water lay a broad path of moonlight leading out over the dancing waves until it reached the ball of silver sinking in the sea. The girl gave a slight exclamation at the beauty of the night.

"See! Is not that a mystic path beckoning us to follow its brightness until we reach the source of all light?"

" Yea," replied Tellus, " and sooner would I follow its treacherous guidance than to take thee to Rome. My visit was a necessity, and I have seen enough. The evil I saw so far obscured the good that I can think of Rome only as the vilest city in which I ever set foot; yet I have travelled far and wide, as thou knowest."

" But I do not understand," said Persea, earnestly. " Are not the people of Rome Christians? How can a Christian city be so full of evil as thou hast said ? "

Tellus hesitated. His sister had been reared under the tender, watchful care of a saintly mother. Far from the wrangling of the multitude, the clashing of creeds, and the jealousies of the church, she had listened to the pure teachings of God's word, and breathed in the sweetness of a life hallowed by his love, until she was as different from the Christian maidens of Rome as light is from darkness. He dreaded to tear the veil from her innocent eyes and reveal the hypocrisy and error that, in the name of Christianity, were stalking, unrebuked, in the glare of noontide. But he knew she was masterful. The question she had asked must be answered. Slowly he spoke :

" They call themselves Christians, and perhaps some of them may be; but they think not of sin as thou dost. The world has so persistently knocked at their doors that at last it has forced an entrance even into the Holy of Holies. Thou hast thought the priests were holy men ; but I have seen them participating in wild, drunken orgies that would bring a blush of shame to any cheek.

" The people drown their sorrows in the flashing cup that the world is always lifting to the lips of the despairing, — that cup of sin with which the Evil One deadens the feelings and conscience of those whom he would destroy.

" O my sister ! The world is not even yet truly repentant, though Christ gave himself a ransom for its sin. The human heart is vile beyond all conception, and I fear that ages must pass before the good conquers the evil, before the pure can purify the impure. Rome calls itself a Christian city ; but the old disciples of Christ would thunder condemnation upon the very heads of the Church ! "

Persea listened in pained bewilderment. She lifted her hand to her forehead, and slowly smoothing back the hair that clustered around her temples, she said in a voice that was filled with a new wisdom :

"This is the reason that mother would never talk to me of Rome. This is the reason she refused to go back to our old palace. This is the reason she always bade me look to God and the Bible, not to men, for guidance. But, my brother, it is not right for us to stay here in peace and quiet when souls are sinking into the grave in darkness and despair. Let us go and help to raise the Standard of the Cross above the sin and wickedness in yonder city !"

She stood there, bathed in moonlight, with her face uplifted to his. As he looked at her, and thought of the evil in that Rome he had just left, he shivered, for she was too beautiful.

The evening breeze had blown back the loose folds of her thin, silken drapery until it outlined the perfect curves of her form. Her hair, dark and luxuriant, was bound by bands of gold and then gathered into a coil on the back of her delicately poised head. Her face was beautiful with a loveliness almost unearthly in the silver moonlight. But no perfection of face nor form could compare with the crowning glory of her exquisite personality, — her wonderful eyes. Dark as midnight, yet luminous with a light that baffled description ; full of smiles, yet brimming with unshed tears ; clear as crystal, yet hiding strange secrets in their unfathomable depths. In them was most perfectly blended the spiritual and the beautiful. In them was mirrored a soul as pure, as perfect as the body in which it dwelt.

She seemed to Tellus to be a crowned spirit, awaiting the chariot of fire that was to bear her into the presence of the Omnipotent. As he gazed at her with awe and tenderness, almost forgetting that she had spoken, she clasped her hands tightly together and continued :

"Something stirs within me to-night that I have never felt before. Too long have I delayed going to labour in God's vineyard. There are souls crying to me for light, — crying for peace, for rest, for the knowledge of Christ's love and the gift of eternal life. Even now, out of the darkness I hear the *Voices* calling, and I must answer ! It seems to me that they come from the North, — it must be from Rome, — and they are the weary, fettered spirits who are worshipping images of God instead of God himself. I must go to them. I must help them; even though the way be dark and crowded with nameless horrors!'"

Tellus knew and felt that, in that moment, his sister had reached and passed an invisible line separating the peace of her past life from a future fraught with momentous events. He was alarmed to think that she, who had been reared amid the tenderest care, had spread her wings to brave the storms and temptations of the world. What would come next? What would be the end of it all? He did not dare to think. Wishing to stem the torrent of thoughts that was coursing through his brain and hers, he drew her to him and said:

" We will talk of this again; but now hear something more of what I saw in Rome, — something of the strange people of other lands who were thronging the market places. It seems to me that every nation in the world must have been represented in that motley crowd. Swarthy Arabs from the deserts; black men from the far south; yellow-skinned merchants from the east with rare spices and jewels such as thine eyes have never seen; soldiers of the Empire, gleaned from far and wide, — some dressed in brilliant armour and carrying silvertipped spears and shining shields; some clad only in skins with knotted clubs in their hands.

" But most strange to me were the fair-haired men from the North. There was a trading fleet of their long fantastic vessels in the harbour, and the market place was thronged with them. They are tall and very strong looking, with blue eyes and long, fair hair. They wear singular horned and winged helmets and sometimes coats of mail; though most of those I saw had on tunics of rich stuffs. All carry the finest of weapons and know well how to use them. They bought with a liberal hand and were peaceful enough; but the merchants whispered of their terrible might in battle, of their wonderfully strong vessels, and their cruel depredations on land and sea. ' They are called Norsemen,' they told me, ' and come here to trade; but the towns and villages on their way are not pleased to see them.' "

Persea had not listened at first; but gradually Tellus gained her attention. When he stopped, she asked with awakening interest:

" Didst thou talk with any of these foreigners?"

" Yea, I did; for I found their language was the same as

that of our old slave, Thorolf. He must have been one of this same nation. Dost thou remember him and his guttural speech ? "

" I remember," she said absently, looking intently at the brow of the hill on the opposite side of the village. Suddenly she caught his arm and exclaimed :

" Look ! What is that moving over the top of the hill ? I wish the moon had not gone down so soon ! What can it be ? "

Tellus strained his eyes in the direction she had pointed ; but could make out nothing in the darkness. He finally said :

" I think it is but the swaying of the bushes with the wind."

" It seemed to me a little unusual ; but go on with thy story. How didst thou come to speak with one of the Norsemen ? "

" Well," and Tellus brought his fist heavily down on his outstretched palm, " be the man heathen or not, he was certainly brave and merciful.

" I was standing at the bridge of Cestus watching the multitude passing by, when suddenly the street was choked with traffic. Arabs shouted to their camels ; drivers swore and tugged at their horses' reins ; men shrieked in terror as the tangled mass surged back and forth.

" Then down the street rode one of the most despised men of Rome ; although he is high in power in State and Church. He and his attendants were forcing their way through the crowd, — knocking, thrusting aside, and no doubt giving many a deadly blow with the flat of their swords. As they came opposite to me, an old man stumbled before the horse on which the nobleman sat. He leaned forward and raising his sword, struck the grey head a terrible blow which sent the man down under his horse's hoofs. Another moment, and the life would have been trampled out. I sprang to the old man's aid ; but another was quicker than I.

" A magnificently built Norseman, clad in gold-plated armour, leaped over the heads of those in front of him, seized the horse's bridle, and threw him back on his haunches so quickly that his rider was sent sprawling into the filth of the street. There was not room to do more ; but that giant of a man held the horse upon its haunches until I dragged the old man from beneath its hoofs. One of the attendants attacked him; but still holding the frightened horse, he tripped the fellow with the neatest twist of the ankle I ever saw, and he, too, rolled in the street.

" By this time the blockade was beginning to break. Throwing the horse's bridle to another of the escort, the Norseman came over to where I had borne the old man, and kneeled down beside him with a great pity in his blue eyes.

" The bedraggled nobleman swore and commanded his arrest; but the city guardsmen quickly disappeared. The man at my side paid no more attention to his vile language than I would to a dirty dog until he called him ' a beast from the North !' Then he arose, and I could see that he was intensely angry; but his self-control was perfect as he turned with withering contempt and answered the man in his own language :

" ' A beast from the North, am I ? Then it would be well for thee to make thy dwelling amongst the beasts until thou learnest to reverence grey hairs ! In my land even the wolves and the bears will protect their own. Go thou and hide thy coward's face in their darkest hole until thou learnest to strike a man only when he is thy equal foeman. Dost thou wish to try thy sword ? Come ! Thou hast said I was a beast ! Let me show thee my teeth !'

" He drew his blade and cut such rapid passes with it that the air seemed full of streaks of blue flame. The nobleman was a coward. Quickly he slunk away, anxious to leave the darkened faces and threatening murmurs that were closing him in.

" When he was gone, the Norseman turned to me. As he looked into my face, I knew he was evermore my friend.

" ' Thou wert quicker than I,' I said, ' or the old man would have been killed.'

" He looked me over a little critically and replied :

" ' Thou art well built. If thou hadst been born a Norseman thou wouldst have been able to reach his side as I did. We have met on common ground. Now we must see the old man made comfortable.'

" We took him to his poor home. The Norseman placed a bag of gold in the hand of the old man's daughter, and I gave her the contents of my purse. Then we departed, followed by blessings not often heard from the lips of the poor of Rome.

"We walked towards the wharves, talking of many things. I found myself charmed beyond measure with my new friend, who was very brilliant and entertaining. He told me his name was Harald Rognvaldson, and that he and his father commanded the fleet in the harbour.

"I asked him at what cities he traded, and I thought an amused smile flitted across his face; but he answered merely that they visited many places. Then I told him somewhat of myself, of you, and my journeyings with my father. He was pleased to think that I had ever been in the far north. We were now at a corner where our paths parted. He laid his hand on my arm and said solemnly :

" ' Tellus, yesterday we were strangers : to-day we are friends. Remember me when beside thy sister in thy southern home. As for me, — a Norseman never forgets. Some day we may meet again. May Odin keep thee ! Farewell ! ' and he walked rapidly away."

Persea's eyes were sparkling with interest as she asked quickly :

"And was that the only time thou didst see thy strange friend ? "

"Yea, the only time; though I often looked for his stalwart figure in its golden armour. But the fleet left the harbour soon after and is probably sailing towards its northern home with its brave commander. He may be a robber as well as a soldier; but that is because he is a heathen and knows no better. I am truly sure that he could never be cruel nor merciless."

Hardly had the words left his lips when lights suddenly flashed about the village. The narrow streets were filled with people, and cries of terror reached their startled ears.

Persea clung to her brother's arm in trembling alarm.

"O Tellus ! What can it mean ? What has happened ? "

He bent forward for one instant, looking and listening. Then throwing his arm about her, he urged her towards the house, saying with forced calmness :

"I know not, unless some dark-skinned Algerian pirates are

sacking the town. If so, Christ help them and us! We must get father, warn the servants, and fly to the hills!"

Persea did not need to be assisted in her flight. She seemed to be possessed of wings, so swiftly did she lessen the distance between them and the marble dwelling amongst the trees. Now they were in the garden. Tellus stopped for a second and listened again. Then he set his teeth grimly as he whispered to himself: "The priests who have hated us so long have told of the old palace and its rich treasures! They have found the path! Our time is short!" and he bounded after Persea, who had disappeared between the trees.

The servants occupied a building apart. He turned towards it, quickly rousing them with that cry which could strike such cold terror into the hearts of all dwellers on the Mediterranean, —"Pirates! Fly for your lives!" Then he made for the house with the frightened wailing of the servants ringing in his ears.

At the entrance stood Persea, clasping her hands in anguish as she said:

"O Tellus! Something is wrong with father! He is lying upon his couch and I cannot rouse him! I cannot get him to speak! O Christ! what shall we do?"

Tellus' face was white but masterful as he answered instantly:

"Run thou to the old arbour. They will hardly go that way for some time. If I do not come to thee in half a turn of the hour-glass, I will *never* come. Father and I will be with Christ! Quick! The torches are coming over the hill! Fly and pray!"

And she obeyed him; though the agony of that parting lingered in her dreams for many years, — that parting without a caress, without a loving word, nothing save that heart-rending sentence, "In half a turn of the hour-glass or never!"

How she found the arbour she never knew; but upon reaching it she dropped to the ground in utter exhaustion and terror, having only the strength to repeat again and again the prayer, "Christ God, help! Christ God, help!"

Then she felt the ground tremble with the trampling of many feet. She heard groans and cries from the servants' quarters, mingled with the clashing of swords and the glare of torches.   Every second seemed an eternity.   Tellus and her father — were they living or dead ?

Almost unconscious with fear and anxiety, she was given strength by feeling, rather than hearing, some one approaching her hiding-place.   She crept to one side where she could peer through the leaves.   As she did so, a great flame leaped into the sky, followed by another and another.   They had fired the old villa.   The glare became brighter and brighter, illumining the sky and earth until Persea could make out the dark forms beyond the trees rushing about between her and the burning building.   But those steps were coming closer! She could see a man's figure!   Was it Tellus?   Nearer it came.   Then she sank upon the ground in an agony of body and soul.

It was not Tellus; but a man dressed in armour.   He carried a large torch; every few steps he halted, and holding it above his head, peered into the darkest bushes and shadows. When he came near enough for Persea to see something of his face, she shrank back into the farthest corner, trying to hide her white draperies behind the leaves.   In that counte-nance there was something so vile, so sensuous that she felt she would rather meet death in any form than to know that those eyes had looked upon her.   All in vain did she shrink.

The next moment the man stood at the entrance to her hiding-place, and uttered a satisfied chuckle as the light fell upon her crouching figure.   Striding over to her, he roughly put aside her arms in which she had hidden her face, and forcibly turned her head towards the light.   He laughed when he saw her great beauty, — a laugh so fiendish, so cruel, so suggestive that it roused Persea from her paralyzed fright into resistance.

Springing towards the entrance, she gave a cry for help, — a cry such as might have been wrung from a pure soul that demons were dragging into the depths of hell.   But scarcely had she left the entrance when she was caught by an iron arm. Once again that cry rang out, so piercing, so far-reaching, that, with a terrible imprecation, the man closed his fingers about her throat.   The cry died in a strangled gurgle.   His brute force soon conquered her resistance and she lay ex-hausted in his arms.   Then he turned her face to his, and be-gan pressing her lips with kisses that were to her as coals of fire.

Suddenly the bushes were parted and a man leaped towards them. Persea was too far spent to know who or what he was; but the next moment the vile arms which held her were opened with herculean force and she sank to the ground. The arrival of some one who had released her from that scorching embrace hastened the return of her strength, and she raised herself upon her elbow. The dim light from the flickering torch, which was sticking in the ground, showed her a tall form in bright armour which stood over her protectingly, while a voice thundered out in fury:

" At thy nithing's deed again, thou son of Loki ! Canst thou never let thy captives alone ? Wilt thou never remember my command not to molest a woman against her will ? In answer to a cry like that I heard, Odin himself would descend from Valhalla ! Capture whom thou canst; but touch not without consent. The next time I catch thee at thy vile tricks I'll send thee to join thy evil father in Nifl-hel ! "

Taken unawares, Persea's tormentor at first shrank back; but he was balked of his prey, all his brutal anger and passions were roused ; and when his commander ceased his scathing rebuke he rushed upon him with drawn sword.

"Send me to Nifl-hel, wilt thou ? " he answered hoarsely. " Too long have I borne thy interference ! Go there thyself; for Thorstein's sword is at thy throat ! "

The man he attacked was ready for him. With sickening fear Persea watched the deadly conflict. Powerless to move, she was wild with terror, not only for herself, but also for her brave rescuer. Evidently the men were well matched; for though the clashes of sword upon sword were so rapid she could hardly separate the strokes in the one long ringing of metal ; yet she could not see that either had made a single telling thrust.

In their struggles they reached a spot just opposite to where the light of the torch shone from the arbour. Then Persea saw that her champion had long, fair hair, and was dressed in a complete suit of gold-plated armour. As its brilliance flashed upon her, so her brother's story of Harald, the Norseman, flashed through her brain.

Scarcely knowing what she did, she cried out :

" Harald ! my brother's friend ! Save thou me ! "

The sound of her voice was fatal.   Startled beyond measure
by her words, Harald's hand for one second lost its cunning.
He fell, pinned to the earth by a sword thrust through his
arm.   For the third time that night Persea tore the air in
shreds with her cry of terror and despair as Thorstein planted
his foot upon the prostrate form, and raising his sword, swung
it above his head with a yell of triumph before he turned its
point downward.

But that one second's delay, that one second's shout of triumph, was one of those mighty minims of time in which God
makes changes which affect the conditions of eternity.

Tellus, creeping back from the spot to which he had carried
the lifeless body of his father, heard Persea's cry.   Springing
to his feet he rushed through the bushes like a madman, reaching the spot just as the heavy sword swung downward.   He
saw his sister's agonized face in a sort of vision as, in obedience to her pointing hand, he threw himself upon the unknown owner of that uplifted sword.   His attack was so
violent that Thorstein's weapon was knocked from his grasp
and both men rolled on the ground.

Then began one of those awful struggles of human strength,
when men lose their humanity and are as beasts in the jungle.

But Tellus had the advantage; for he was clad only in his
every-day attire of belted tunic, while Thorstein was burdened
with his heavy armour.   Gradually the Roman felt his antagonist's
strength giving out : gradually he felt his resistance decreasing,
until seeing a small, sharp-edged rock near them, he made one
mighty effort.   Throwing his opponent upon it, he bent his
head back over its keen edge with sudden and terrible force.
A dull sound — a gush of blood from the thick lips.   Then
the arms loosened and fell heavily to the ground beside the
motionless body.

Exhausted by his struggle, Tellus lay beside his conquered
foe, breathing in short, panting breaths.   The next moment
Persea knelt beside him, holding up the torch so that the light
fell upon his face as she said in a strange, unnatural voice that
sounded far away :

" Tellus, speak to me !   Art thou wounded ?   Speak ! in
Christ's name ! "

Aroused by her words, he rose to a sitting position and managed to gasp :

" No, — nothing save — a few — bruises. Christ brought
me — just in time ! "

Persea's face was illumined with a spiritual radiance as she
sank upon her knees and clasping her hands, poured out her
prayer of thanks to that Providence which had saved her from
an awful fate. Tellus knelt with her.

Harald, who had risen to his feet and was trying to stanch
the blood that flowed from his wound, forgot his pain, forgot
what he was doing, and let his life-blood trickle unheeded to
the ground as he looked upon the kneeling figures and listened
to their prayer. He knew what prayer was. Had he not
often prayed to Odin and Thor for luck and victory ? But
this prayer was not merely one of thanks. Wonder of wonders ! She was praying for the soul of the man they had slain !
She was asking that his sins be not remembered, that his violence against her be forgiven !

" Father forgive him. Lay not this sin to his charge ; for
he knew thee not ; and knowing thee not, he knew not right
from wrong. Wash the stain of blood from our hands ; for
thou knowest it was not willingly we took that life which
thou gavest. Hear us, for Christ's sake."

" So," thought Harald, " they must be Christians ; but never
have I heard a prayer like that to any god of any nation.
These must be different from the Christians I have met
hitherto."

Tellus and Persea had now risen. Persea, with sweet
grace, turned towards Harald and said :

" See, Tellus, the man who saved me from the arms of him
who would have brought me to worse than death. Is he not
Harald, the Norseman, thy old friend ? "

Tellus sprang towards the open arms that were stretched
out to him. In that manly embrace, two souls were knit together with the cords of a strong, pure affection. The Roman
felt the warm, sticky blood upon the other's armour.

" Thou art wounded ! Quick, Persea, the light ! "

" It is nothing," said Harald, " just help me off with the
gauntlet. A twist of my belt will soon mend the hole in my
skin."

While they were assisting him, Persea asked her brother
anxiously :

" What of father ? "

Tellus' voice was choked with sorrow as he answered:

"He was dead when I reached him. He must have been seized with his old sickness and laid himself upon the couch. I do not think he suffered pain, and God must have taken him quickly. I carried his body to the little cave by the stream, and was creeping back to thee when I heard thee cry out. Thou knowest the rest."

Leaving her alone with her grief for a moment, as he knew was best, he addressed himself to Harald.

"I love thee for what thou hast done for my sister; but it seems to me that this is a strange night's work for thee."

Harald shrugged his shoulders.

"The Romans have taught the Norsemen to take all they can get. Yet, while we follow them in this thing, we are far less murderous and cruel. I will wager thee ten thousand aurar that the dead body over there is the only one thou canst find from the beach before which our vessels ride to the spot on which we stand. We capture and make slaves; but did not the Romans first steal our children and carry them into slavery? Where is the nation that loves not fighting and the taking of spoils? The world would rot with inaction if men did not amuse themselves in some way."

He would have said more; but at that moment the trampling of many feet was heard. An alarmed expression flashed across Harald's face. He was about to speak as he saw the brother and sister stand so trustingly at his side: about to tell them to fly for their freedom, when his eyes fell upon Persea's upturned face.

For the first time he saw her beauty, though all too faintly in the flickering light; saw the perfect form that swayed slightly towards him with a confidence which thrilled him with a new, sweet delight. The words he was about to speak died upon his lips; and when an instant later her eyes looked into his, he forgot himself, forgot Tellus, forgot his approaching comrades, forgot the position he was in, forgot the past, forgot everything save those eyes in whose depths he would fain have drowned himself forever. The only moment in which they could have escaped slipped by, unused, into that past which never returns.

At once they were surrounded by a great company of Norsemen with their hands filled with loot, who clamoured for

Harald. The foremost of them put his hand on the young man's shoulder with a sigh of relief.

"I feared thou hadst come to harm, my son, when we missed thee for so great a time. Why didst thou leave us?"

The man who spoke had passed the prime of life. His face was stern, yet void of any suggestion of evil. He had led an active life occupied with great responsibilities, which had been met with all the unbending force of an upright character in which heroism, honour, and sense of duty to his fellow men were as well developed as the condition of his country permitted.

Harald briefly told what had happened after he heard the woman's cry for help. Jarl Rognvald eyed Tellus and Persea curiously, and then said calmly:

"Well, then, this young man is thy prisoner; but thou knowest that according to our laws thou canst not claim this maiden because thou didst not first capture her. She will have to be accounted among the bulk of our spoils, to be drawn for by lot at the division of our property when we reach the Thrandheim."

Harald's face flushed with embarrassment, pain, and anger as he realized the unhappy conditions which confronted him; while Tellus looked from one to the other in startled surprise. The young Norseman saw that it was too late; that nothing could be done at that time but to accept the ruling of the regular law. He turned to Tellus and said earnestly:

"The meeting with thee and thy sweet sister made me forget the perils by which thou wast surrounded. Our laws are rigid, and these followers of mine know thee as my prisoner. I give thee thy freedom; but alas! thy dear one I cannot release now! Thou hast heard the reason; yet be not alarmed. If thou hast no ties to bind thee to this place, come with me. Be my brother, my Standard-bearer. Together we will watch over thy sister until she be restored to thee, unharmed. Trust to me. Harald Rognvaldson is not false to friend nor foe."

Tellus glanced towards the glowing embers that marked his home; thought of the cold, white body on the floor of the cave; and bowed his head in despair. But Persea's clinging arms around his neck aroused his manhood to a sense of the responsibilities which were yet his. Holding her close in a protecting embrace, he answered with calm and stately dignity, mingled with a trace of wounded and outraged feeling :

"We have met again, and our meeting is indeed remarkable. Thou art from a far-off country with beliefs and customs unlike those to which we have been used, so that the whole of this night's happenings is a terrible, unintelligible dream to me. In my eyes, and before my God, thou wast guilty of a most infamous deed when thou and thy rude followers didst land beyond the cove and descend like birds of prey upon yonder sleeping village.

"And now I stand before thee who hast sworn to be my friend, and hear that thy laws have decreed that my sister is a captive to this motley crowd ! I know not thy land, nor thy people, nor thy gods. I know not what awaits us in the future ; but the freedom thou gavest me is nothing if the only one left to me on earth, my sister, is a captive. I can but accept thy terms, and there is a ring of truth in thy voice which tells me to believe in thee until thou provest unworthy. Let me bury the precious form in which my father's soul once dwelt. Then I will follow my sister and thee. It is all there is for me to do."

Two hours later the fleet of long vessels, manned by banks of twenty to forty rowers, swept out from the shore and turned their prows westward towards Niorvasund.

On the little deck in the stern of the largest vessel stood three figures, two of whom were straining their eyes towards the land that was fast disappearing in the darkness. Now it is almost gone ! It *is* gone !

Tellus closed his fingers convulsively, and set his teeth to keep down the turbulent feelings which were raging within him. Persea hid her face in her hands, while her form shook with her passionate sobbing. Her brother gathered her tenderly in his arms, just as he had done once before in the early evening of that night. It seemed to him now, as he thought of it, that centuries had passed since they stood together in the moonlight on the brow of the hill, — that hill which they were fast leaving, probably forever.

When Persea had sobbed out the first great agony of grief, Tellus smoothed her hair back tenderly and said :

"Nay, my Little One, grieve not so bitterly. Much has been lost ; but father is happier beyond, and his departure only makes Heaven and Christ nearer to us. Still is the great Eye of the Infinite watching over us: still is his love descending upon us. While we have this knowledge and each other we have blessings untold. Be brave and true! God reigns in Heaven and doeth all things well.

"Think how strange it all is! See! The ship is gliding out over the waves, following the very direction of the mystic path of moonlight which thou didst think so alluring! *Thou hast answered the Voices thou didst hear calling to thee out of the North*, for behold! thy journey northward has begun!"

He spoke to take her thought from her present sorrow, hardly realizing, in his own tortured state of mind, just what he had said.

But his words brought back to Persea the remembrance of those wondrous, indefinite thoughts and desires that had floated down to her out of the beauty of the night and made her impatient to take part in the great conflict between good and evil. Somehow, the receding shores grew less precious; her wounded, quivering heart felt Christ's healing touch; her anxious, troubled soul heard the gentle, "It is I, be not afraid!"

Her tear-dimmed eyes grew clear and trustful as she lifted them to the star-sprinkled heavens and prayed that their lives, so rudely tossed upon life's stormy waves, would be safely guided into harbour by the One Great Pilot of the Deep.

Harald, standing apart in delicate respect for his friends' grief, knew instinctively that she was praying. So sacred, so precious, so pure did she seem to him that he almost feared she was a spirit from the skies who would vanish ere the dawn.

Then, catching something of the prayerful spirit that seemed to emanate from her, he placed his hand on the Hammer of Thor that hung about his neck, and in the weirdly beautiful words of the Northland vowed to all the gods he knew to honour, shield, and protect her at any cost, while life lasted.

CHAPTER V

"FOR PERSEA I WOULD BURN ALL ITALY"

THE ships of the Norsemen passed through the gates of Niorvasund, and swinging slowly around, pointed their prows towards the Northland. Then bulging sail and sweeping oar sent them swiftly onward. The waves of the Atlantic hastened to meet them.

The wind freshened, and Harald called the men from the oars. Thus relieved from duty, a group of them lounged upon the rowing seats near the centre of the boat. Said one, whom they called Wulfric:

" 'Tis now twenty days and nights since we left the shores of Italy. I wonder much what the dark-eyed maiden and her brother think of the company in which they find themselves."

The speaker looked ahead at the gleaming tent of pell over the forward deck, under which he knew the southland maiden was reclining. The eyes of his companions followed his with the same questioning interest. Finally, Snorro answered:

"It is a rare bird that Harald Rognvaldson has caught upon this voyage. That brother of hers is keen-eyed, and watches over her with untiring vigilance. At first he thought we were ready to devour his beautiful sister; but methinks he has found that Norsemen have some honour, and abide by laws as well, mayhap, as even his Roman friends. At least, he is easier in his ways than at first; and before this voyage is over, he will know well that Harald Rognvaldson's following, though fierce and warlike when needs be, are as harmless as a flock of doves. He knows not yet the greatness of the man whom we all love and obey, whose golden armour we would follow even into Nifl-hel! When he does know, then he will honour the day when he first saw the ' Blest of the Nornir.' "

The tanned and weather-beaten faces of the men reflected their belief in the truth of his words, as they said with one accord, "Yea! Yea!"

"But," said another, "do ye not think that Harald himself is blessing the attack on the village? Didst ever see the look upon his face that comes when he is near the maiden? She is counted as common property; but for once, the leader will ask of us a favour in the distribution of the spoils. See if it is not so. For my part, I could say now to him, 'Take my portion,' for Var has cast her spell upon him, and he will not be happy until she has heard his betrothal vows."

"Who would blame him?" said Wulfric. "When I look upon her, I remember the days of my youth, and the hot blood that scorched my heart when I first looked upon my Alfhild. Ah! those days of loving and being loved! Then, and then only, does a man know the joy of life. May Harald's love be blessed by all the gods of Norge. Great and noble is his heart, and great and noble will be the love he gives. Something tells me, too, that this maiden is worthy of him. She is beautiful, kind of heart, and gentle in her manner as a high-born woman should be."

"She is certainly an uncommon maiden," said Snorro. "Think of her conduct when the storm-waves rose, while we were on the inland water. Harald stationed Eindridi near her, and commanded him to save her if the storm sank the ship; for he himself must needs be above deck. Eindridi told me that never had he seen a woman so calm and fearless. She prayed, he said, to her God. Then she talked sweetly and quietly, only fearful that those on deck would be washed overboard or get broken bones. Now ye do all know that the storm was one that might have sent us all to Ran. 'Twas no small sign of mind-strength that the dark-eyed one showed no fear."

"There has been but one regret in my mind since that night," spoke Eindridi, slowly, "and that is because she is loved of Harald. She did pierce my heart with her great eyes and sweet voice. To none else than Harald Rognvaldson would I yield the first chance of winning her for my own. But I love him, as do ye all, and I know that he loves her. That is enough for Eindridi. His head will seek another bosom than the white one of the Roman maiden."

Several of the young men moved uneasily as Eindridi concluded. Said Wulfric:

"The son of Eric is plain spoken; but I know he is not alone in his feeling. Does he think the Norsemen know not beauty when they see it? And besides beauty, there is something else. I know not what it is; but it seizes even upon my old heart, and makes it tremble and burn; yet with no unholy desire. She is a wonder-maiden, of that there is no doubt."

"I think I know somewhat more of her gentle charm," said one great, muscular fellow, who played with the heavy oar as if it was a feather in his hands. "She saw blood upon my arm one day. I had not accounted it worthy of a thought; but she asked me, timidly, to let her bind the wound. More in amazement than need, I yielded to her touch. The women of Noregs-veldi are quick and ready with bandages and healing knowledge; but the southern maiden had something more. She touched the red skin with a tenderness that told me she felt the wound almost as much as I did. When it was finally bound, she lifted her eyes to mine, and I saw there a sweetness and pity that made me wish I had a hundred wounds for her to bind. Yet though my heart trembled, I felt no evil desire in my veins. Rather did she seem a holy spirit at whose feet I would gladly have worshipped. Methinks she has cast a spell upon us all."

"All save two," laughed a young fellow with large, coarse features and red hair, who lounged upon a pile of sail-cloth, displaying a great length of arm and limb well covered with hardened muscles.

"And who may they be?" asked Eindridi quickly.

"Thou art as near-sighted as if thou didst have the white blindness. Jarl Rognvald loves not the maiden; and neither have I fallen under her spell. What ye have called tenderness, I have seen only as a power that creates in me a desire to subdue. She is no easy prey, as even Harald Rognvaldson will discover. Mayhap even he will some day compel submission."

"Nay, thou art mad," said Wulfric, roughly. "Yea, mad and brain-foolish as ever. The maiden has power in her eyes that has chained the Blest of the Nornir; but he is not a beast like thyself. He is a man, with a man's honour and feelings; and he will woo until he wins. Hast thou not yet known the sweetness of lips that kiss again when they are kissed, that thou wouldst do that nithing's deed of which thou didst speak?"

The younger man laughed loudly.

"Ha! Ha! I thought I would set thy thin hairs to dancing! But be not fearful. Ulric has more thought for his head than to touch this captive maiden." He turned lazily over, while Wulfric muttered angrily.

Above them, and forward, Persea leaned upon silken cushions with dreamy, half-closed eyes. She could tell of no discomfort, even upon the narrow confines of the viking ship. By day, the deck with its tent, its cushions, and rich rugs; by night, the tiny cabin below, with every luxury that many treasure chests could give her. Costly apparel without limit had been lain at her feet; until Tellus, laughingly, told her she would be the envy of all Rome, could she be but seen. Very beautiful was she as she rested under her silken canopies, in her rich robes. Small wonder that the Norsemen caught their breath when they glanced her way.

During the first few days, she had clung almost pitifully to her brother. All was so suddenly new, so unusual. She felt as if a whirlwind had swept her out into the world. Many a sad hour was spent sobbing in the brave, comforting arms of her brother; but as the days went by, she grew more calm. The first bitterness of grief wept itself out, and she began to think of the future. She found that, even with all that had happened to disturb her thoughts of self and life, she had yet that sense of being needed somewhere. Then her prayers to Christ began to be prayers for resignation, patience, and strength. She began timidly to look about; to observe the personality of these strangers who were carrying her to their far-off land, — a captive. As she prayed and looked, peace came to her soul with the quiet assurance that God had willed all; therefore all was well. Now she could comfort Tellus, instead of receiving all comfort from him.

Her brother hovered constantly about her with utmost solicitude. He had sore misgivings as to the outcome of this voyage. He could not share his sister's spiritual exultation, so dimly defined was the future, so filled with dark possibilities. Harald's close friendship and many assurances could not dispel his anxiety. What sort of a land was it that could breed such remarkable men? Savage in their likes and dislikes, but who seemed never to break faith with a friend, nor forget an enemy; souls that gave faithful homage to their gods — wild and warlike as themselves — to whose names they drank huge horns of mead, and to whom they prayed for luck and victory. Here Tellus found the nearest reason for their mode of living. Worshipping gods who fought and feasted, how could they do aught but the same? There were good and evil among them, too, as among all men; but Harald Rognvaldson's magnetic personality ruled with a power that was undeniable. None questioned his skill, his wisdom, or his wish. Enough that it was his: that made it a law unto which they bowed willingly. How remarkable, thought Tellus, had been his acquaintance with this Norseman! First, a chance meeting on the streets of Rome; then the hillside by his burning villa; now, the open sea, with a vast unknown stretching northward: an unknown which had reached down and touched his life, and the life of his sister, and was fast drawing them into its mysterious depths. For himself it mattered little; but Persea, his pure, beloved sister, what would become of her? He drew a deep, troubled breath, and turned to look at her as she leaned upon her cushions, watching the circling of some strong-winged birds above her head.

As he looked, Harald touched his arm, and lifting his hand towards the swelling sails, said:

"See! The wings of the Raven are wide-spread, and they bear thee farther from thy Italy. I fear that this is no joy to thee; much as it is my heart's desire that all happiness shouldst be thine."

Tellus, speaking from his heart, replied:

"There is always a fear when we face the unknown. How can we know that the future thou hast promised will be as peaceful and safe as the past has been?"

"I know how thou must feel," said Harald, "and I cannot blame thee. I am strangely disturbed about this last viking of mine. In my heart new thoughts have been aroused; there is a condemning voice which tells me it was a nithing's deed to destroy thy home and carry thee off with me. When I look upon thee I feel troubled, as if my hand had been raised against a friend. But when I look upon thy sister, ah! maddening are the thoughts that do then course through my brain! For, although remorse gnaws at my heart when I think of thy ruined home; dost thou know that, even if Odin should turn back the days and give me again the opportunity of living over the events of that night, I would do all of it again? Nay! look not so reproachfully upon me! I could not help it; for only since that night have I known why Odin gave me life and a man's blood !' "

He stopped abruptly; and Tellus saw his forehead was veined with the rush of passionate feeling. Vaguely, the Roman understood what was coming. It was but the out-spoken trouble that had been buried in his heart. He could not reply : the words would not shape themselves.

Soon Harald spoke again :

"That night, in the light of thy burning home, I looked upon thy sister ; and to look upon her was to love her ! I saw nothing but her face ; heard nothing but her voice ; and I have seen and heard nothing since. To be with thee is a joy strong and great ; but to have, here upon my own ship, the presence of thy sister is an intoxicating delight for which I would burn all Italy, — yea ! a hundred times over ! When I am near her I have no strength ; while a madness rushes through my veins, almost making me cry out with the pain of loving so intensely. But I give oath to thee, my brother, that she has heard no word of love from my lips. To thee, in all honour, do I speak first. Give me thy permission to woo her during this voyage to Noregs-veldi. I love her ; but that is not enough. I must win her love ; and to do this, I must teach her to forget and forgive. Besides, she is a captive, and not as a captive would I tell her of my love. But she shall be free when we come to shore ; and then, after I have given her to thee, wilt thou be willing to let me speak honourable love unto her ? Wilt thou, O my brother, let her drink the wedding cup with me ? I cannot tell thee how I love her. Ask the flower why it thirsts for the dew ! Because without it comes torture, and withering stalk, and death. Nothing can take its place : nothing can give its gifts. So to me is Persea's love. Without her, life will be death ; but with her, death itself will be life. Wilt thou give me life or death ? "

Harald stopped ; his frame trembling, his voice broken. Tellus had drawn back and half raised his hand, as if to ward off some invisible blow. Then slowly his arm sank until it hung at his side. His face was white and troubled.

"Thou hast asked for much ! "

Harald's tall form seemed to shrink to half its size in the humility with which he bowed his head. Sadly, pleadingly he spoke :

" Yea, know I not that? Have I not lain night after night, and looking up towards the stars, have I not wondered whether, on all the earth, they shone upon a more tortured heart than mine? Through me thou didst lose thy home, mayhap even thy father; and now I ask thee for all that is left to thee. But think not that I am cruel or unfeeling. I know that I must appear selfish and brutal; but be kind, my brother. Give me time to prove my love for thee and thine. The past is gone; and if perchance it has brought an influence which shall shape and fashion the future, can we change that past? Can we sweep aside its effects? Though I know that all thy lost wealth is naught beside the gift I ask of thee, yet I must ask. I can keep my secret no longer. It has grown beyond my control: it has encircled my life as the sun encircles the heavens. Speak to me, Tellus! Tell me that thou dost not hate me: tell me that thou wilt not forbid me to hope for this great joy!"

Tellus' face was still white and drawn; but he spoke with quiet calmness, — that calmness which comes to the soul, when, in the blinding whirl of the world, it reaches out to touch the hand of God and be led through darkness into light.

" Thou knowest she is all I have. Thou knowest I live but to protect and care for her. I do not blame thee for loving her. I have learned to trust thee, and surely thou hast dealt most honourably in this matter. If thou art worthy of her; if thou canst win her love, and adapt thy strangeness of race and living so as to bring happiness to her, why should I refuse to see her happy with thee? She is the one to decide, and I do not fear to trust all to her wisdom. But be not over sanguine nor rash in thy wooing. There are many obstacles in thy path which thou canst not understand until thou knowest more of Persea than thou canst see in her face and form; but if thou dost win her heart, her brother will not hold her from thee."

Harald seized his hand in a pressure that told of love and gratitude too deep for lips to express. In the eyes of the brother the tears gathered as he said:

" Go now and begin thy wooing; but remember how precious she is; remember she is all I have!"

The answering film dimmed Harald's vision.

"Only the gods can understand thy generous heart, — thy kindness to me. I will remember, and yet remember — always, eternally!"

Tellus turned abruptly away and descended into the cabin. Harald remained where he was for a few moments. When the rush of feeling had subsided, he crossed the deck and threw himself upon the rug at Persea's feet.

She had clasped her hands behind her head, and was looking beyond into the blue of the northern sky with a dreamy mistiness in her eyes. She did not notice his approach; and he lay and feasted his eyes upon her beauty, — that beauty which Tellus had given into his keeping if only he could win. Could it be possible he might not win? He felt a spasm of pain as he thought that she might never learn to love him. Why should she? What had he done to bring love into her heart? A bitterness stole into his soul born of the knowledge that he was responsible for so much sorrow in her life. He groaned aloud.

Persea, recalled to the present, turned her face towards him and said:

"Why is the heart of Harald Rognvaldson so troubled?"

In the bitterness of his soul he answered:

"I saw a great sadness upon thy face, and a longing in thine eyes. Dost thou think that I am a dog, that I know not why sorrow abides with thee? Thou didst dwell in a beautiful home in a beautiful land. One night, violent men burned thy house, all but dishonoured thee, and finally carried thee off towards an unknown land, a captive! Is it strange that sadness comes upon thee? Yet that look upon thy face is worse than a knife-thrust through my heart; for I did the deed. I, who — who would save thee from all sorrow; *I* brought this pain and loss into thy life. How canst thou ever think of me as thy friend? How can I ever ask thee to smile upon me, or to do aught but hate me with a hatred that comes from causes which cannot be forgotten or forgiven?"

A slight tremor passed through Persea's form. A faint flush crept up from her neck and mantled her face in a warm light. There was something hidden in those words she had heard that played upon her heart strings with a new touch. It was something she hardly understood; but it was strong and masterful. He had ever been considerate and tender; but

she had never heard this tone before. What did he mean?
His last sentence gave her thought to reply:

"Nay, I do not hate thee. I have already forgiven; and
some day, I trust I shall even forget."

Harald raised his face from his hands and leaned eagerly towards her.

"Can this be true? O Persea! mock me not!"

She flushed again at that note of power that thrilled in his
voice.

"I have no thought of mocking thee. I forgive thee."

A passionate colour crossed Harald's face. He grasped her
robe almost roughly.

"Thou dost forgive me! Wilt thou tell me why?"

He knew not what was in her mind. He was judging from
his standpoint. Quickly, innocently she replied:

"Because my God tells me to forgive all wrong. It would
not be Christlike for me to carry hatred in my heart towards
any one. Besides, didst thou not save me from a terrible
fate? Have I not much to thank thee for, after all?"

"Nay, speak not of thanks to me. But thy words cause
me to wonder much. Thy God says to forgive such a
wrong? Truly thy religion is a strange one; yet if it leadeth
thee to count me as thy friend, I will drink a horn to thy
Christ at the next feast. Say again those thrice blessed
words, 'I forgive thee.'"

He leaned close to her. She felt the warmth of his great
form and saw the trembling of his hand as it rested on the
fold of her robe. She could not look into his face; she was
almost frightened at the something that she knew was there.
A trembling seized her, with such a thrill of strange joy that
she knew not what to do. Then she heard his voice again;
this time a gentle, pleading voice:

"Let me hear once more those blessed words. Grant me
this. Tell me again that thou dost forgive me, that I may
truly believe and rejoice."

Her head drooped so that he could not see her eyes; but his
quick ear heard the softly spoken words:

"I forgive thee."

He caught her hand and carried it to his lips. Just as he
did so, the form of Jarl Rognvald appeared above deck.
He saw his son's action and frowned heavily; but Harald, all

"I WILL DRINK A HORN TO THY CHRIST AT THE NEXT
FEAST."—*Page 48.*

unconscious of his frowns, gazed into the half-frightened face above him and said :

" Now I shall sit at thy side and lend my poor art towards making this long voyage less burdensome to thee.   I have not ventured to come near thee, lest my presence should only increase thy sorrow ; but thou hast forgiven me and joy is mine. I shall tell thee of my life, my home, and my mother who waits for me in a country that will be strange and weird to thee ; but whose beauty is wonderful, surpassing in many ways thine own Italy.   I shall tell thee of our nation and our people and our gods, and ——"

Persea interrupted him —

" And I shall tell thee of *my* God, and his religion of love."

" Yea, tell me what thou wilt.   Only let me lie at thy feet, and listen to thy voice, and behold thy beauty.   Dost thou know, O sister of my Tellus, that Harald's eyes have never seen beauty so rare as thine ? "

Persea grew rosy red at his warm words.   This imperative, commanding admiration was very new to her ; but she was not entirely displeased.   The power which made him a leader of men she did not really fear ; rather did it rest and protect her.

That night she sank to rest with a new peace and sense of security hovering about her.   As the dream-ship drifted silently above her pillow she had visions, not only of her brother who was ever watching over her, — but beyond, just beyond, there was another, a brighter vision in glittering armour, that raised over her a golden shield and whispered, " Sleep, and fear not ! "

CHAPTER VI

"ALMOST IS HE A CHRISTIAN"

AFTER the day when Harald opened his heart to Tellus, the journey towards the North was one long dream of happiness to Persea and the fair-haired Norseman. For hours he sat by her side or lay at her feet; while her beauty filled his brain as her soul did his heart.

Oh, those long, dreamy days and those clear, starry nights, during which the rhythmic beat of the oars was ever sending them northward! On they swept, past vine-clad hills, past low, mist covered shores, past high, chalk cliffs, over the wild North Sea, to finally shoot in among the countless islands that fringe the coast of the Northland, and say, "Stand off!" to the storm billows ever lurking under the surface of that treacherous sea. When Harald's vessels reached those sheltered paths, he knew all perils were past; for neither foe nor storm-wave dare follow them further.

He stood upon the deck, his brain bursting with thoughts. Soon Persea would belong only to Tellus, and then, — yes, he had seen love in her eyes, — then she would belong only to him! Oh, the joy of life and love! the beauty and purity of this maiden who owned his heart! the calm depths of those dark eyes where reigned a peace that her Christ had given her, a peace impossible to disturb. Why did not Odin give this strength to his followers? Odin's might was the might of the sword, and it was well enough for a warrior; but this love for mankind, this forgiveness for sin, and the memory of a Christ who had suffered death; ah, this was a creed of love — and a mighty creed. Warrior as he was, it touched his heart and conscience. But then, would he not love anything that Persea loved? Was not any god that she reverenced worthy of his respect and thought? As he watched the familiar opening to the Thrandheim Fjord draw nearer, the waters were bluer, the skies clearer, the hills more beautiful than ever before. Upon them all a soft radiance rested. Was it the reflection of the love that burned in his heart? Or was it the faint

glow of the God-love that Persea had brought to his native
land? Whatever the source, it was surely the light of love;
and love was life. He had learned a grand, new lesson on
this viking. Life was not the glory of successful battles, nor
the taking of spoils, nor the defeat of an enemy, nor feasting,
nor idróttir, nor any of those things in which he had found
pleasure in former times. They were all nothing, nothing
beside love; and soon that priceless life of loving would be
his.

While he thought his warm, glad thoughts, Persea clung to
her brother, and watched, with anxious eyes, the approach of
that shore behind which Harald had told her his home lay.
Tellus felt her hand tremble. He clasped it strongly in his
own, and said:

"Why so fearful, little sister? Dost thou shrink from
what awaits thee behind yonder mighty hills?"

He watched closely the effect of his words; but her face
gave no sign that he could interpret as she replied:

"Yea and nay. My spirit shrinks from nothing that
Christ has put into our lives; but, mingled with the Voices
that call me onward, I hear minor strains, notes of sadness,
wails of human anguish, which sink into my heart and make
the weak, the mortal in me to tremble with fear. Life is not
all peace, and hope, and love. There are some things which
I feel will happen behind those rocky walls which shall bring
much pain and sorrow to us."

"And so little of gladness? Thou art indifferent to the
friendship of Harald Rognvaldson. He would be pained, did
he hear thy troubled speech."

"Nay, I meant not him. He is noble, and tender, and
true. Is it not so, Tellus? He will not fail us, — never!
But there is another who loves us not; at least, he loves not
me, and I fear him."

Tellus turned quickly.

"Who is this? Has any one dared to ——"

"Nay," she interrupted, "not that. It is Jarl Rognvald.
He loves not me; yet he is the father of Harald."

Tellus drew her tenderly to him as he said:

"Fear not, Little One. Thy brother is neither a fool nor a
weakling. Thou shalt be safe with him as long as thou dost
wish to stay within his arms. But other arms are reaching

out for thee, Persea, — arms that I believe are as strong and brave as mine. Some day, maybe, thou wilt leave me to go to that other embrace. Nay, hide not thy face upon my breast. If thou dost love, thou dost love worthily ; else God would not have permitted it. Thou needst fear no earthly man, for Harald Rognvaldson is not the one to let even his father trifle with his love and his honour. There is only one thing thy brother would wish for thee. Would to God thy lover were a Christian."

Persea lifted her blushing face, and said, with a glad light in her tear-wet eyes :

" Almost is he a follower of Christ. Almost does he believe. Pray for him as I have prayed, my brother, and thou wilt soon know thy friend as all that he must be ere I trust him to the uttermost, — a Christian ! "

CHAPTER VII

THE LANDING OF THE VIKING

A FAR-OFF, faint, melodious blast, borne by the wind up the Fjord, echoed and reëchoed from crag to crag. At the sound, a great shout went up from the crowd of gaily dressed men and women who had gathered on the Nid peninsula to welcome Jarl Rognvald and Harald. Foremost among them stood Iron Beard in his suit of grey and silver, his great, bushy head towering above his companions as the one snow-crowned peak in the distance towered above all others. Near him stood a tall, stately woman, with a pure face that was illumined with happiness. This was Brynhild, wife and mother of the returning Norsemen. Close around them were many friends, laughing, talking, in excitement and anticipation.

Off to one side, as if not quite within the confidence circle of friends, stood King Olaf with a large retinue of soldiers and hirdmen. Beside him was an uncovered carriage in which sat two women, Ingiborg and Astrid. Ingiborg was his sister; but Astrid was a distant relative, an orphan, whom he had taken into his household since the marriage of his sister who bore the same name. Ingiborg was small in stature, with little beauty of face or form; but she had a thoughtful, tender expression which made her features far from unattractive.

Astrid was a glorious picture of almost defiant loveliness. Well did she deserve the title of "Astrid the Peerless." Flashing, brilliant, overflowing with pride and conscious beauty, she was the personification of a Norse King's daughter. One imagined her standing at the gilded prow of a dragon-ship, clad in golden-linked armour, her long hair floating in the wind, and her white hands grasping sword and shield. Then she would be perfectly happy; and wherever she went, whatever she did, she would conquer, though the sun turned black, and the stars fell! Never was an unconquerable will so plainly visible in bearing and expression. Even Olaf had known the force of a "No" from her lips, and had been compelled to bow to her decision as he had to none else in the world. Her lovers were as numerous as clouds in an April sky; and she treated them as the clouds are treated by the April wind — lulling them to fancied rest and security one moment, and then sending them forth in a violent rage to dash themselves against each other with mad hatred, until they vanished beneath her horizon. Many a holmganga had been fought on her account; but if a valiant life went out on the field, it went unmourned; and the victor was no nearer the coveted reward than his vanquished rival. Her imperious will refused to surrender her heart, until she herself had begun to wonder if it ever would be conquered.

Olaf turned to Thorkel Nefia and said:

"So thou dost think it very necessary to gain the goodwill, as well as the allegiance, of these returning Norsemen?"

Thorkel replied with the greatest earnestness:

"Thou knowest, King Olaf, that these Thrandheim jarls and bonder have always been counted as the best of Norge's sons; but they acknowledge no man king unless he pleases them. Although thou hast been crowned, it behooves thee to win this powerful Rognvald and his son to thy standard. Rognvald is wise in all law matters, and so just and brave that he is beloved throughout the Thrandheim. Much would his words of approval strengthen thy kingdom and further thy ends. But shouldst thou offend these men, they can wield a mighty influence against thee. Moreover, there is a strange story about this Harald that thou wouldst do well to silence by absorbing him into thy following. Thou knowest that when a child is born, its father sprinkles it with water, and gives it a name and birthgift; or else orders it to be exposed to die. Rognvald and his wife quarrelled bitterly just before Harald was born, and Rognvald vowed that the child should be exposed. On the birth-night he was standing a spear's length from the skemma, when suddenly there shone above it a soft radiance, from which descended a bright spirit who said to him, 'Destroy not this child just born to thee, lest thou destroy Noregs-veldi. Strong and courageous shall he be; and a wonderful blessing shall he bring to his country.' Of course, Rognvald birth-sprinkled the child and became reconciled to Brynhild. Then they inquired of the Volva what this strange revelation meant. The old woman told them they had received a message from one of the Nornir, Skuld the Future. Now Harald is a great warrior, strong and valorous, and has won honour and wealth by his victories on land and sea; so the people are beginning to revive the story of his birth, and to look for some sign of the fulfillment of Skuld's prophecy."

Olaf adjusted the sword at his side without making a comment, or asking a question about what he had just heard. Thorkel was annoyed to think his words of interest and warning should have had so little effect upon the King. "So he cares not to speak; he thinks it all of little consequence," he muttered to himself. "Well, so be it. If he wills to be silent 't would be easier to empty the Fjord than to draw one word from his lips; but he had best listen."

However, Olaf was disturbed, though his face was expressionless. He gave no one his inmost thoughts, especially when they were not entirely pleasant to him. The newly-chosen King found himself already disliking this man whose birth was so unnaturally protected. What was the blessing he should bring to his country? Could the spirit have meant that Harald would be king? No! It should not be! Had he lived his restless, wandering life of exile and danger by land and sea, only to have his kingdom snatched from his grasp at the final moment? Should a woman's tale of heathen spirits and prophecies shake his throne? If Skuld meant that this Harald should rule over Norge, she knew not that Olaf holds what he wills to hold. The son of Rognvald had best not cross his path.

Just then Astrid's voice reached his ear. "It is certainly true," she was saying, "that we would look far to find another such sheltered, beautiful valley. The hills invite us to take up our abode within their protecting arms."

Olaf laughed, and said teasingly:

"A pretty speech; but when thou speakest of arms, we warriors prefer the warm, white ones a fair maiden can twine about our necks. Am I not right, Ivar?"

The young man flushed, and said quickly:

"I would willingly give myself to Odin for one moment of such intoxicating delight with the one who owns my heart."

Olaf threw back his head with a hearty laugh, while Astrid looked annoyed. But her foster-brother did not spare her.

"Never fear, my brave friend. Thou shalt yet speak thy betrothal vows; mayhap even with Astrid the Peerless!"

Then to himself, he said, " Ah! he is still young. A man only loves once as he loves; and I fear that I have forever missed that priceless experience. I cannot understand this perfect love that cares for nothing but the society and happiness of the loved one: this love which can sacrifice everything for love only. I acknowledge it is pleasant to spend the winters in love-making; but when the month of Thori comes, I long to board the steed of the breeze, and go forth on the sea-king's road. The kiss of woman and the fire of battle are equally sweet to me. And Astrid, is she like me? But some one will conquer her at last; for I have seen a bold man win victory with a blunt sword."

His thoughts were interrupted by the notes of the war-horn. Once, twice, thrice, that clear, far-reaching blast cut the air. Shouts arose from the shore, " The signal horn! The lur! They are nearing the bend!" Clearer and clearer sounded the war-horn, answered by sentinels and friends on the cliffs and shores; until, amid the greatest excitement, a fleet of vessels swept around the cliff and moved grandly up the Fjord. They were led by two large dragon ships, flying war pennants of white upon which were embroidered black ravens, Odin's messengers. Their small decks, fore and aft, were crowded with men in glittering armour. The bows and sterns, which stood high out of the water, were shaped like dragon heads and brilliantly gilded. The sides were covered with round shields painted red and white; and from the masts hung sails of pell stripped with many colours. These had been hoisted more for appearance than propelling power; for the wind had only strength enough to spread their heavy folds in wave-like expansions which grew less and less broad as the boats swept under the lee of the cliffs. On they came, leaping forward in response to the regular beat of many oars. Under that clear sky, surrounded by those stern, unscalable walls that towered above them to dizzy heights, the approaching vessels seemed like veritable monsters, winged and scaly, who were returning, gorged with prey, to some gloomy fastness within those mighty walls. Small wonder that the appearance of the Norsemen's vessels before a southern village or city was the signal for a wail of terror from its luckless inhabitants. They rode forth to conquer; and they conquered in spirit before a prow grated on the sand.

Following the war vessels came several transports laden with captives and spoils. A murmur of astonishment and delight went up from the waiting crowd at such plain evidence of an unusually successful viking. The standard bearers on the high decks once more raised the long, graceful lurs, and one final, triumphant blast rang out, filling the air with vibrating waves of sound. The rowers, bending their supple bodies far forward, put all their strength into the rush for the beach. Gangplanks were thrown out; and the next moment Rognvald and Harald stood upon their native soil once more. The cliffs rang with the blowing of horns and the shouts of welcome. All was noise and confusion, — cries of joy, gay bursts of laughter, hoarse commands to thralls and sailors, the creaking of cordage and plank, — a bedlam of sound which grew wilder as the boats discharged their armour-clad crews. What mattered it if some who were waiting heard that which struck the light from their life, and sent them stealing away with white, drawn faces and a deadly pain in their hearts? They were but few, and they were not missed.

Rognvald and Harald were almost overwhelmed with glad greetings. First, the loving welcome of wife and mother; then the rush of friends and relatives, among whom Iron Beard was foremost. The close friendship between him and Rognvald was very evident; and as soon as the tension of welcome had relaxed, the old man turned to his two friends and said:

"A word of surprise to ye. We have crowned a new king since ye didst leave Norge. Hist! 'T is no time for explanations; but look for me to-morrow when the sun hangs low and red in the southern sky. Then I will tell ye all. He seems fair in all ways but one; and we will speedily check him there by building a wall he can neither get over nor under. Meanwhile come, let me present ye both. If ye care for my advice, I would say, 'Let your words be few but fair.'"

During this terse communication, Rognvald and Harald had followed the direction of Iron Beard's gaze, and seen the imposing figure of Olaf with his gay crowd of retainers. Every inch a king, with the sun's slanting rays shining on rich velvets and furs, flashing armour and jewelled ornaments, the Norsemen saw this was no ordinary man. They accepted the situation with no further display of curiosity. Among the fjords of Norge men were schooled to changes; so, though their

minds were busy with conjectures, they merely signified their
readiness to be taken into the presence of their new ruler.
Iron Beard preceded them, and upon reaching Olaf, bowed
low; and perhaps there was a trace of sarcasm, of challenge in
his words as he said:

"I am most happy, O King Olaf, to bring to thee two of
our strong men of Thrandheim, — Jarl Rognvald and Harald,
his son. They are loved by friends and feared by foes. They
knew not that Norge had crowned another king while they
were roaming over the home of Egir's Daughters."

The two men were about to yield homage to their King,
when Olaf spoke quickly, with rare tact and diplomacy:

"My gallant warriors, bright is this day, since mine eyes
have now looked upon those two brave sons of Norge whose
valour has been praised by all, both far and near. Yea, I have
been crowned King of thy country; and proud am I of the
honour which has come to me after so many years of
peril and waiting. But I ask ye not to render allegiance
to an unknown ruler. I ask only for your friendship now.
Later, when ye have heard my claim to the throne, ye may
judge my cause. If it be worthy and right in your minds,
't will be my highest pleasure to count such renowned warriors
amongst my subjects."

It was a wise, opportune speech. Rognvald and Harald
were plainly pleased; but Iron Beard frowned. He knew the
stakes for which Olaf was playing; he knew the game was
one which would require all the keen wit and discretion the
King could command. In this first move he saw that his
enemy was strong in wisdom and caution, yea, stronger than
he had believed. He realized that a more deadly conflict was
before him than he had at first imagined. He must be quick.
He must draw in the net he had spread, or this man would not
only escape, but be able to turn and entangle all Norge in the
trap laid for himself. While these thoughts had been shooting through Iron Beard's brain like stars through the sky,
Rognvald had replied to the King's gracious words:

"Most noble stranger, whoever thou art, thou art wise
enough to have taken a drink from Mimir's Well. We thank
thee for thy words, and tell thee that Rognvald and his son are
thy friends until thou provest thyself unworthy of their trust.
Yea, I give thee a token thereof. When the vessels have

landed the spoils of our viking, do thou take therefrom anything that pleases thee most. It shall be a friendship gift from us."

As he finished, Harald said briefly :

"As the father speaks, so does the son. We are friends, O King."

Though the words he said were few, Harald's full, rich, musical voice had a most strange effect upon Astrid the Peerless. It took from her the present; her eyes saw not the gay crowd, the blue waters, nor the cliffs with their green belts of foliage. She seemed to herself to be lost, — lost in a vast, wonderful forest. Life was all around her. The trees twined their branches together and whispered to each other; flower nodded towards flower; vine clung to vine; only she stood alone. Suddenly, as a bird hears far off in the dim aisles of the wood the clear, sweet call of its own, her heart heard a voice that answered to its voice; and even as a bird lifts itself on joyful wing to seek that hidden song and singer, so her heart leaped out towards that full, rich, musical voice. She could no longer stand alone ! What if the bird sought in vain ? Was the call less sweet, or the wing less swift in the seeking ?

She was called to a consciousness of her surroundings by her foster-brother's words :

"Thanks to ye both. Your words are more pleasant than any gift could be. But I see impatient glances around me. I have kept my new friends too long to myself."

Then followed the succession of presentations to the hirdmen and royal family. Low did the men bow before the two women. Ingiborg's face was sunny with smiles as she greeted them sweetly; but Astrid had lost her self-control and, try as she would, her brilliant wit had forsaken her. She responded to their polite words with only an inclination of her beautiful head. Both men noticed her striking beauty and personality. Ivar scanned Harald's face with fierce jealousy for a sign of any deeper interest; but even a lover's eye could see that the noble countenance expressed nothing beyond a passing homage to beauty. The three men soon after returned to the shore. Astrid, vexed beyond measure at her discomfiture, immediately devoted herself to Ivar, stubbornly endeavouring to not even glance at the lately arrived heroes. But the golden helmet flashed again and again before her eyes, until she could see or think of nothing else. She finally subsided into a petulant silence, under cover of which she cunningly hid her interest in the surrounding scenes.

Meanwhile, the warriors had all landed, and now the spoils were to be spread out and distributed. A large field had been cleared, on one side of which stood the two leaders, with their personal guard and following. Harald was speaking with great earnestness to the man at his side:

"Nay, Tellus, be not so concerned. Have I not planned everything so that Persea must receive her freedom? If my father forestalled me first, I have forestalled him now, which is better. I have the promise of every warrior that I shall have the first choice of the captives. They were willing enough to grant it, because it was the first request I have ever made. Besides, I have paid them well. Fear not, Persea will soon be placed in thine arms."

To himself he continued: "And may Odin speedily give her beloved form to mine. O my love! my life! my all!"

Now all attention was centred on the landing of the spoils. In the middle of the open field before the warriors a tall pole had been planted; a line of thralls was busy unloading the transports, and stacking the treasures around this pole. Here, under the cold northern sky, man's conquering arm had brought the best and richest treasures of far distant civilizations. Loads of costly silks, velvets, gold brocades, and foreign stuffs of many kinds; all captured from vessels journeying from Micklegard, the Gateway of the Orient; exquisite Venetian ware, and groups of Greek statuary from the shores of the inland sea; bags of foreign coins, beautifully wrought gold and silver ornaments of every description, swords from Damascus, scabbards, inlaid shields, coats of mail, all sorts of war-like accoutrements; finally, large chests filled with jewels, which sent out scintillating rainbow flashes of light in every direction. All climes, all conditions of men had laboured to acquire this vast wealth, only to pour it at the feet of the conquering Norseman.

Native to a bleak and rugged country, whose rocky cliffs grudged even the small patches of earth which yielded the little handfuls of grain so carefully cultivated, and upon which so much depended, the viking heroes were pushed out from the land. Accepting the inevitable, they built those vessels whose strength and seaworthiness were the marvels of their own and future ages; and in them, sailed forth to reap the boundless ocean.

The captives were now being landed. King Olaf and Thorkel pressed forward in the crowd.

" Surely Thorkel, these must indeed be valiant men; for seldom have I seen such great wealth brought back from one expedition. They have a large following; but I think each will be well repaid for his services."

Thorkel answered with much emphasis :

" Thou seest I have spoken the truth. These men are always successful, and so just in the division of spoils that all the bonder are anxious to go out under their leadership."

Meanwhile, the captives had been passing; and a glance at their varied features showed the distance which the Norsemen's ships had travelled. Suddenly, Olaf grasped Thorkel's arm.

" By all that moves and breathes, look at that form approaching! Has she fallen from the skies? Have they captured the spirit of the beautiful? "

Thorkel looked and exclaimed. It was Persea who was nearing them. With eyes downcast, she might have been taken for some masterpiece of art; but when she came opposite to the King, the long sweeping lashes were lifted from her cheeks. Olaf looked into the luminous depths of those dark eyes and trembled. Through his brain flashed the thought, " I have seen her soul ! " That light in her eyes was too deep, too rare, too intense for comprehension. As she passed, Olaf turned to Thorkel, trembling with excitement so that he could scarcely speak.

" The friendship token he offered ! I will accept his gift ! Go, fly to Jarl Rognvald, and tell him I have taken him at his word. Tell him that I choose yonder maiden as a companion and maid for Ingiborg. Dost thou hear me ? Hasten ! I would sooner lose my throne than her ! "

Thorkel attempted to stay his passion.

" My King, be careful. She can be no ordinary captive. Thou mightest offend by asking for her. Do nothing rash. Remember Hakon's fate."

But Olaf was deaf to remonstrances.

"I tell thee, go! Am I a beast? Have I ever forced a maiden to receive my embraces? But she must be in my house; she must belong to me. Go!"

Thorkel could only obey. As he neared Rognvald he noticed that he, too, was looking at the dark-haired maiden, and with some perplexity, as if she was a problem he was trying to solve. When he saw Thorkel, he said pleasantly:

"And what thinks the King of our good fortune on this viking?"

Thorkel replied somewhat bluntly:

"I bear his congratulations to thee. He also told me to tell thee that his choice of gift for a friendship token is that maiden yonder, whom he desires as a companion for his sister Ingiborg."

Rognvald uttered a startled exclamation, almost as if he would refuse the gift.

"A Norseman is ever true to his word. I will bring the maiden to the King; but tell him she must not be offended, for she is of noble birth, sister to Tellus, Harald's standard-bearer. I yield her to him only because what I have said, I have said. I expect him to treat her as her rank demands."

Thorkel did not think it wise to prolong so delicate a conversation. He bowed his thanks and withdrew.

After the King's messenger left him, Rognvald recovered his self-possession and thought to himself, "It is not so bad after all; for it will not be quite so easy now for Harald to take the marriage vows with her; as I am afraid he would speedily have done, in spite of all I could say. She is very beautiful; but I like not these foreign women. Besides, she has a power in her face that I cannot fathom, nor hardly resist. I care not to see Harald entangled in its mysterious coils."

Meanwhile Olaf received the answer to his request. "So," he muttered under his breath, "she happened to be the rarest of his treasures, after all. It matters not to me, just so he kept his word. 'T is well he did; for never have I desired anything as I do this maiden. If she is as pure as she looks, I will have to place her beside the high seat as my wife; but yield to me she shall."

Now began the division of spoils. Harald, bowing low before Persea, was about to claim her as his, when Rognvald stepped up. Laying his hand heavily upon his son's arm, he said with a distress that was real, in spite of his effort to believe all had happened for the best :

" My son, didst thou hear me tell King Olaf to choose from our new possessions that which pleased him most ? I see now that it was a rash speech ; but Rognvald must keep his word, and Olaf has asked for Persea as a companion for Ingiborg, his sister."

Harald's face was livid. His breath came in short, quick gasps. For a moment he was blinded, stunned by the terrible words he had heard. Persea to be given to the King ! Earth and sky rocked and reeled before him : an awful gulf yawned at his feet. He drew his sword, and would have rushed upon Olaf, had not Rognvald arrested him sternly.

" Is the word of thy father nothing to thee ? "

At that rebuke, at that reminder of the family honour which was held sacred beyond life itself, Harald's rage was checked. His sword slipped back into its scabbard ; but on his brow the veins stood out like whip-cords.

" Forgive me, my father," he said brokenly, " but Persea ! Persea ! How can I endure that she should be given, a captive, into a stranger's hand ? "

Rognvald was silent. He knew he had said the only thing that would be heeded. In his heart, which was not void of tenderness, he felt a sorrow for the trouble which had come to his son.

Fiercely now spoke Harald :

" How can I prevent it ? Is there no way of escape ? Art thou sure that Olaf wants Persea as a companion for his sister ? For by Odin, if there is a dark deed behind his words, I will kill her and thee and myself ! "

His eyes glared like a wild beast's ; and Rognvald hastened to quiet his terrible suspicions. He told him all that he had said to Thorkel, and then continued :

" So be easy on this score. She will not be violated. The King would not dare to do so."

Harald breathed easier ; but still his hands were clenched, and still his veins were like ropes across his forehead.

" What shall I say to Tellus now ? What cruel thing is this I must tell my brother, the one who saved my life ? "

Rognvald was silent again, troubled by his son's anguish of

mind, but thinking not once of the maiden who had drawn
closer to them during the stormy interview. He had no
thought for her; and when, in answer to Harald's last piteous
questions, she laid her little white hand on his arm, Rognvald
was startled at her calmness. Her face was pale with emotion; but that emotion was not fear. Not one sign of fear;
but lo! instead she was strong and full of courage. She, a
woman, a captive, who had heard that she was to be taken
from her only friend and brother, and given to a strange person in a strange land, — she alone was calm.

"I have heard and understood. Thou art not to blame.
Thou canst do nothing now. Let me go quietly to the King's
household. I am not afraid. Have I not been in great perils
before? Yet the God I worship has always protected and
cared for me, and he is with me still. This strange twisting
of circumstances must be for the best; for he doeth all things
well. I am willing to go. Let not thy hand be lifted to shed
blood."

Harald could scarcely endure the agony of her presence so
near him, her hand on his arm, and her low, sweet voice in
his ear, knowing how irrevocably that presence, that hand, and
that voice, were slipping from him. If he could only clasp
her once in his arms ere she departed; if he could only press
his lips upon hers! His voice was thick as he replied, with
teeth set in passion:

"Thou dost not know, thou canst not understand the dangers that threaten thee. Yet I see no way to save thee now."

"But I tell thee that my God will not let harm befall me.
Comfort my brother by saying that this new sorrow will not
crush me; for even now do I hear the Voices calling; and I
believe in them. He will know and understand. Grieve not;
for some time, somewhere, all will yet be well. Very kind
hast thou been; and much have we learned to prize thy
friendship. May God keep thee, and bless thee."

For the first time her voice trembled, and tears gathered in
her eyes. Her love and trust in God gave her courage; but
when she instinctively felt, very close to her, the presence of
a mighty earthly love, she faltered.

Harald, with a supreme effort, rallied his scattered senses,
and replied as calmly as he could:

"Thy words are wonderful to me. Thou dost not understand our ways; and no one would blame thee if thou didst accuse me of the basest treachery. Instead, thou acceptest this strange disposal of thyself with a courage and trust which is beyond the mind to conceive. If Christ the White dost give thee thy strength, then is he mightier than Odin, or Thor, or Frey; for they cannot breathe a warrior's spirit into a woman's soul. But I know not whether it is a God, or only thee thyself; for to me thou art a goddess."

Her beautiful head drooped, and her eyes were still hidden. Not daring to trust himself longer in her presence, Harald concluded hastily:

"And now, let me say to thee that thy captivity shall not be for long; and I doubt not that thou wilt receive the kindest treatment in the King's household. Our skali is not far distant. Thou canst see it from Olaf's court-yard. We will be with thee often, and watch over thee carefully, ever planning for thy release. If everything else should fail, there remains the war-token. Farewell! I cannot stay to see thee given to the King."

He touched her hand with a quick, passionate movement, waiting a second for her to raise her head; but she only murmured a faint " Farewell," still hiding the light of her eyes from his burning gaze. He saw not the new, sweet joy that leaped and shone in their dark depths.

The next instant Harald was gone. Rognvald, taking her hand with respectful reverence, led her away. Olaf received her with a calm exterior, giving her to Ingiborg's keeping with scarcely a glance; but his feelings were running riot, and his heart was sending the blood rushing madly through his veins.

The two women knew well that she was beautiful; for womenkind are never blind to each other's attractions. But how differently they were affected by it! Ingiborg showed her sweetness and lack of jealousy by the open admiration in her face. Astrid, with her long undisputed reign as beauty of the North, did not consider that Persea's dark loveliness was comparable to her fair, golden self. But the longer she looked the more she was convinced that this girl's beauty was indeed dangerous. She began to rejoice that this stranger was a slave, and so unable to occupy a position where she could display her charms on a level with her own.

All this time, Tellus had been watching these incomprehensible actions with growing alarm. Something had surely happened. Something was surely wrong. Harald was returning to him alone; while Rognvald had taken Persea to the King. When the two men met, Tellus' lips could form but one word, "Persea!" Only his Norse pride in the presence of others kept Harald from complete collapse. He grasped his standard-bearer's arm, and said hoarsely:

"Would that thou hadst let Thorstein's sword bury itself in my heart, than that I should have lived to see this day. Upon me the skies have fallen, and the sun has ceased to shine. Wild storms are raging in my heart; and the life-blood has frozen in my veins. Some evil spirit, some fiend of darkness, has crossed my path. I cannot place thy sister in thy arms; for she is claimed by the King!"

"How comes this? How dares the King? Why didst thou allow this terrible thing to take place? Why couldst thou not save her? Speak, for I am her brother."

Harald raised his hand to ward off the words that pierced his heart like keen knives.

"On my honour, I can do nothing now. Listen to me. We have a new King, crowned during our absence. He spoke fair with us; and my father, with a generous courtesy befitting his rank, offered him, as a token of friendship, any gift from the spoils which pleased him most. Rognvald thought only of gold and jewels; but Olaf took him at his word, and chose Persea. A Norseman would not dare to appear before Odin if he refused to give such a gift; therefore Persea has been placed in the King's keeping. Kill me if thou wishest; for death would be sweet in comparison to the anguish I am enduring."

Tellus had listened while anger, pain, brotherly love, and despair, passed over his face in passionate waves of feeling.

"Harald! Harald! he must not, he shall not have her. Let me go; let me snatch her away, and fly to the Southland once more. What wants this King of my sister? Dost thou think I can stand by and see her perish?"

"But she will not perish, my brother; neither is she in any immediate danger. The King dares not to touch her; for she was sent to him with my father's express commands that she be treated as became her rank. The King gives her to his sister as a companion; and she will be well cared for. Truly,

the future is thick with trouble ; but we will meet it as men.
Ere its dark clouds descend upon us, we must hurl upon them
such arrows of lightning as shall pierce and shatter their
murky darkness.   Fear not.   Persea shall be saved to thee as
pure as the dew from the sea of mist.   Yea, even if human
arm and mind fail, she need fear not ; for the heavens themselves would open and receive her if she prayed to them.
Come with me now.   Let me give thee her message ; stranger
to me than the flashing of the lights in the upper world."

CHAPTER VIII

"WATCHMAN, WHAT OF THE NIGHT?"

THAT night, long after Persea's eyes had closed amid their unusual surroundings, Harald was pacing the edge of the cliff, vainly endeavouring to devise some plan to obtain her freedom. He knew that the King must be enamoured of her great beauty, and that he would undoubtedly refuse all offers of purchase. She was safe from present violence; but suppose the King should wish to marry her! He was not perfectly sure that Persea returned his love. What if this handsome, wealthy King should succeed in winning her heart? A groan escaped his lips; and faster and more furiously did he pace the narrow pathway. Why had he not spoken of his love before? He had been waiting, with delicate courtesy, until she was restored to her brother's care and protection; but now he wished mightily that he had been less considerate. Now, when his love was powerless to redeem her from captivity, he felt as if it would be almost mockery to speak. Meanwhile, what complications might arise! One thing was certain: he would know to-morrow how this man came to be acknowledged King. If there was any flaw in his claim he would soon lead a revolt against him. More than one stanch bonder had whispered words of praise, and hints of future honours in store for him. To-night, for the first time, he rejoiced in their veiled meaning.

Then, wearied in wrestling with the present and future, his thoughts flew back to the past, — to the exciting scenes during which he first saw the girl he so passionately loved. But now, when would come the realization of those hopes which had gathered strength on the journey northward? When would he be able to fold Persea in his arms, as his alone and forever?

The clouds began to gather in the north. From the white-crowned mountains blew cold winds, armed with their stinging lash of mist; but the lonely figure on the cliff felt nothing, knew nothing, save that a cup of intoxicating happiness had been lifted to his lips, only to be dashed to the ground just as he was about to drain its sweetness.

CHAPTER IX

"AH ! he is a gay and gallant King, I can tell thee; and he has true Norse blood in him."

Iron Beard had spoken. He was sitting on a long, carved bench in Rognvald's skali, with the red light from the huge fire lighting up his rugged features, as he leaned forward with his head on his hands, and looked at the burning logs. Rognvald was beside him in his high seat of honour, — a massive piece of furniture, completely covered with deep carvings of runes and scenes from the old sagas; while the corners of the great back and the ends of the arms were ornamented with huge, open-mouthed serpents' heads. Harald sat on the opposite side of his father, his face anxious and troubled.

Iron Beard laughed a short, mirthless laugh after he made his remark, and then continued:

"So he trapped thee on thy gift offer, and took that which thou didst not wish to give? 'T is only to be hoped he will not so treat the country over which he rules. But I am putting the spear head on the wrong end of the lance. Listen to Olaf Tryggvveson's story; for it is as strange as any tale in the Sagas."

Harald and Rognvald leaned forward expectantly, and the old man commenced:

"Thorkel Nefia is his stepbrother ——"

"What !" exclaimed both his listeners; and Harald added:

"Why then, have we not heard of this Olaf long ago?"

"Hist ! hist !" said the old man, impatiently. "When I finish, thou wilt know that he knew no more of Olaf than we did. As thou knowest, Olaf Tryggvveson's name tells us he was a son of Tryggvve, who ruled over Viken twenty winters ago; but it was just this that troubled me; for I remembered not that Tryggvve left a son. I feared that this bold stranger was an impostor."

Harald's eyes flashed in the firelight.

" I only wish that he was. Tell me, is there no evidence of treachery ? "

Iron Beard shook his head ; but, looking keenly at the handsome young man, he said to himself, " So, thou lovest him not ? It is well." And then aloud :

" Nay, his claim to royalty is supported by undeniable evidence."

Harald was bitterly disappointed. To his active, fiery nature, worked into a fever of excitement by the thoughts of the past twenty-four hours, there had been only one real, tangible plan of action. That was based upon the hope which Iron Beard's words had destroyed. If Olaf's claim was unquestionable, the dark chasm which separated him from Persea was widening. His best hope was gone. But the invincible strength of his love soon forced back the tide of despair. He faced his disappointment with a courage undaunted, and a purpose only delayed, not thwarted. Meanwhile, his thoughts had not kept him from hearing Iron Beard's deep voice, as he kept on with his story :

" Thou knowest how Tryggvve was treacherously slain by Gudrod, who coveted his possessions. When Tryggvve's wife, Astrid, heard of her husband's death, she fled to escape the same fate; and in hiding, gave birth to a son whom she named Olaf. With him, she journeyed to Sweden, where the King, Hakon Gamle, gave her kindly welcome. When news reached Norge that Astrid was safe in Sweden with her son, her enemies sent messengers to take them ; but Hakon refused to give them up without their consent. Then, for further safety, Astrid determined to journey to her brother Sigurd, who was high in honour with Valdemar, King of Russia. On the voyage the vessel was captured by pirates; and mother and son were separated and sold into slavery. After having been in captivity over six years Olaf was again exposed for sale, this time in the market place of Novgorod, where the Nornir directed that his unusual beauty should draw the attention of his uncle, Sigurd. He questioned the lad, and discovering his parentage, purchased him. He became a great favourite at the Russian court, where he was instructed in all exercises and idróttir as became his rank. Finally he was made chief over the men-at-arms ; but here he gained so much renown that jealous enemies arose, who endeavoured to poison the minds of the King and Queen with evil stories concerning him.

" Seeing this, Olaf wisely determined to leave Russia, with the intent of finally coming back to his own land. Commanding a large fleet of war vessels, manned with mighty men of valour, he cruised over many seas for many years, making great conquests, and acquiring immense wealth. Finally he went ashore at Dublin. While here, he inquired concerning his native land. Learning that the jarls and bonder were much displeased with Earl Hakon, he journeyed hither to lay claim to the throne."

Here Harald interrupted him.

" I have been thinking ever of Olaf's mother, who suffered so much for him. Dost thou know what became of her ? "

" Yea, it is an uncommon story ; for she was also discovered in her captivity by Lodin, a Norse sea-king, who offered to purchase her if she would become his wife. This she did ; and Thorkel Nefia is the son of this union. Ingiborg is Olaf's own sister, who was left in care of Astrid's brother when their mother fled from Norge. But now I will return to Olaf's history.

" Thou knowest that Hakon was very loose in his conduct with the wives and daughters of our Norsemen. Just after thy departure, he had the great daring to send messengers to the powerful Orm Lyrgia requesting that Gudrun be given him."

" What ! " said Rognvald in anger. " Dared he go thus far in his vileness ? He must have lost his senses when he aspired to the possession of Gudrun, the Lundi-Sun ! "

" Yea," Iron Beard said grimly, " he had not measured the strength of the bear whose den he attempted to violate. Orm defied the messengers, and sent the war-token to the bonder. We assembled in great numbers to avenge his insult, and Hakon was compelled to fly for his life.

" Just at this opportune time, Olaf Tryggvveson arrived on our coast. Thou canst see how gladly the people welcomed as their King a man at once so filled with royal blood, and so brave. Earl Hakon was slain by his thrall Kark, who brought his head to Olaf ; but the newly acknowledged King gained further praise from the people by denouncing this treacherous murder, and having the thrall beheaded at once.

" Now thou seest this is no ordinary man who has come among us. He is certainly of pure Norse blood, with kingly appearance, great wisdom, expertness in all idróttir and exercises we hold of account, wide experience in warfare on land and sea, and possessed of immense wealth. Could we ask for more ? "

He ceased; waiting, wondering, if they would think of that one vital question which had been lying so near his heart since that never-to-be-forgotten interview with the King. But he had not misjudged his friend's sagacity. Harald, to be sure, was silent. He was thinking of other things. But Rognvald, in a clear, measured tone, said slowly :

" This is all very favourable. The King appears to be kingly enough. But, Iron Beard, Temple Priest of Thrandheim, does the King worship our gods ? "

Iron Beard dropped the mask from his voice and thoughts. Starting to his feet, he raised his clenched fist and brought it down on the broad arm of Rognvald's high seat with a violence that vibrated through the whole of that immense hall, while he thundered out :

" No ! by Odin, he does not ! And more yet, he sent for me, and said he was determined to make his subjects worship the Christian God. Yea, he dared to speak thus to me, who wears the stalla-ring on his arm. First boldly, and then cunningly, ah ! how very cunningly ! Thou knowest that the Thrandheim jarls and bonder hate the White Christ ; and thou knowest how the blood boiled within me while he spoke of his desire to make our land a Christian one. Bah ! " and the great grey head shook with disgust until the thick masses of hair tumbled about his face in wild disorder.

His words had sounded ominously in Harald's ears. At the first mention of Olaf's Christian belief, a look almost of fear had swept across his face. The king a Christian ! What might this bring to Persea and to him ? Here was something that Olaf had that he had not. Yet, how could the king deny Tellus the possession of his sister, if he followed the teachings of the White Christ ? But Olaf was a man, and Persea was beautiful. He would keep her until he taught her to love him ; and then he would send her back to her brother, only to take her again, — even as he himself had thought to do. And it would all be because of the power of the White Christ.

Harald trembled; for a hand from the invisible world had touched his life. He felt helpless, crushed; but not long did this despair lie upon him. She had loved him once, and he would win her yet, though a thousand gods opposed him. Still, even as the strength of his love and will sought to count as naught the King's Christianity, something within him refused to answer to the call for courage, and whispered, " Ye worship Odin, and the Christ power is not with ye."

While Harald was almost stunned by Iron Beard's communication, Rognvald did not seem at all surprised. He nodded his head in quiet affirmation.

" I thought as much. I followed thee closely; and I wondered what belief this man could have adopted during his unusual, wandering life. One must live among Norge's rocks to believe in Odin and Thor rightly. He may, perchance, be a kingly man; but no man, however kingly, can fasten this thrice-defeated belief upon us. Fear not, Temple Priest of Lladir, the sacrifices shall still be offered to Odin and Thor and Frey. But what dost thou think this King intends to do ? "

Iron Beard laughed.

" He will summon the people to a Thing, and order them to worship Christ. The Thing-token comes first to me."

Harald spoke now.

" But," he said, " the people will refuse, and what then ? Will he dare command ? "

Iron Beard answered slowly, with decision and emphasis :

" No, he will not dare command. The people will command him. We will make him eat his words over a horn dedicated to Thor. Come close to me."

He whispered something to them. Rognvald slapped his hand upon his friend's knee.

" Thou hast planned well. Rognvald and Harald will stand by thy side, and we shall win."

Harald said earnestly, thinking far more of love than hate :

" A quarrel like this may help to release Persea."

Iron Beard looked around with the same piercing glance he had given him once before that evening.

" Ah ! the maiden is yet on thy mind. I was young once myself, and I have not forgotten. Thou art not willing for her to remain under the King's protection. If thou desirest her, thou mayest well be unwilling; for if he is as smooth-tongued with women as he is with warriors, thou wilt have to have keen wits and a sharp sword to pluck the flower before he sips the honey."

He spoke lightly, little dreaming of the depth and intensity of Harald's feelings. His words struck on the young man's heart like a heavy sledge on red-hot iron, sending out fiery sparks of passion and rage. Springing to his feet, he cried:

"While I live, no wisdom nor strength known to men or gods shall ever give Olaf Tryggvveson one touch of her hand!"

He strode angrily from the room. Iron Beard looked after him curiously; and Rognvald, anxious to explain, told the whole story. Yet he spoke far more of Tellus than of Persea; for he remembered Sigrid. When he finished, Iron Beard said quietly:

"'T is hard for him, certainly; but it will make it harder for Olaf to win in the game we are playing. Well, we have spoken together of many things, and we have agreed. Now I must journey back to my bird; or she will be flying over the hills to seek me."

He smiled that bright, sweet smile which could ever soften the rugged features, and bring infinite tenderness into the eyes so often glinting in violent anger.

Rognvald spoke quickly:

"And I have not yet asked of thy Sigrid. How fares she? Why didst thou not bring her with thee? Brynhild would have welcomed her gladly."

"She wished to come," answered the old man, "but somehow, she is so small and slight that I feared to let her breast the threatening storm. She is brave, and would often go forth with me; but I cannot think she should. Strange little woman she is, with her mother's tiny frame, and her father's reckless daring. She is a true Norseman's daughter;" and he smiled again. "But Brynhild will see her soon; for the King gives a feast, and I know my jewel will want to shine there. After all, she is a woman."

The two men laughed lightly. Iron Beard emptied a huge horn of mead with Rognvald, in which they pledged themselves to stand by their ancient gods forever. Then he wrapped his cloak about him, and departed.

Soon after Harald reëntered, somewhat calmer than when he left; and threw himself at full length upon the bench before the fire. His symmetrical form was displayed to its greatest advantage, and was a fit setting for the noble soul which looked out of the fearless, blue eyes. His costly dress and flashing jewels gave a kingly touch to his appearance.

Rognvald looked at the outstretched figure as one might gaze upon a canvas, whereon a master hand had given form and colour to some cherished hope that lay deeply hidden in the inner courts of the soul. The father's whole being was wrapped up in the handsome son. The vision that had appeared to Rognvald wielded an enormous influence over his usually matter-of-fact nature. With the old prophecy ringing in his ears, he had guided every step that Harald took towards manhood, in the hope of assisting its fulfillment. So he had viewed with disfavour the growing attachment between Harald and Persea. How would a marriage to a foreigner with new ideas and ways influence his great destiny? How could she assist him to fulfill the spirit's prophecy? No! it should never be! Harald must look among his native cliffs and fjords, for a woman fitted for a Norse King's bride! Persea moved and breathed as a queen among women; and Rognvald himself, as he instinctively did her homage when she passed, knew that she could never be won save as an honoured wife.

He did not see how he could prevent her restoration to freedom; and what would become of her then? Would the two return to their native land? He had learned from Harald that they had no especial ties binding them to the Southland. On the other hand, Tellus and Harald were almost inseparable. Suppose then, that the Romans decided to remain in Norge, even if only for a season? In that case, he felt that his son was lost to this beautiful girl.

Thus had Olaf relieved him of a wearisome burden, when he made so unexpected a choice in response to his offer. To Rognvald it was a perfectly honourable transaction. As he had in no way planned it, the whole thing seemed to him to be sent from the gods to avert the disaster which threatened Harald.

Following this, he was not displeased when Iron Beard had proved Olaf's right to the throne. He knew there would be immediate trouble between Harald and the King if any excuse could be found for it. He reasoned that Persea was probably as well off in the King's household as anywhere. Of course, her beauty would expose her to some perils; but he trusted that her close proximity to powerful friends would save her from violence.

Now that she could not become his without the King's sanction, Harald might become reconciled to his loss. Youth was not inconsolable; and there were other beautiful women near by. Many times had Rognvald thought, in the past, that Harald would mate with his playmate of childhood,—Sigrid, daughter of the Temple Priest. But to-day a vision of Astrid, with her radiant loveliness, rose before him. "Ah! my bright beauty, thou dost not dream that the eyes of Rognvald have guessed thy secret already. Perhaps thou dost not know that thou hast a secret; but I know. That wild and passionate Ivar never saw the light that shone in thine eyes when Harald stood before thee. And thou wouldst be the true wife for my bold Norseman."

Yea, here was a woman already close to the throne, beautiful, brilliant, and evidently much pleased with Harald. Surely she was to be his real bride. Dreaming such dreams of a brilliant future for his idolized son, Rognvald continued to gaze in silent abstraction at the recumbent figure on the bench.

It was Harald who broke the stillness:

"Well, it is certain that we have no excuse for refusing to acknowledge the bonder's choice as King; but I will discover some other means by which the sister of Tellus shall be released. My heart burns with shame and grief when I think of her position; and when am I not so thinking?"

"It was certainly an unforeseen conclusion to my speech to the King; but after all, my son, 'tis not so trying for the girl. I have inquired as to her treatment and position. Persea lacks for nothing."

Harald rose, and paced rapidly back and forth over the rush-strewn floor.

"And canst thou believe, for one instant, that I would let my sword rest by my side if I thought she lacked for one comfort or luxury? Let me hear that she does, and Olaf shall meet me on the skin, though Odin himself held his shield."

Rognvald's face grew serious as he watched his son stride

to and fro; but still he refused to acknowledge by word or sign that he understood the reason of his strong words.

"Nay, Harald, be not so inflamed. The girl is in good hands. Tellus will see her as often as he desires; and the King will, no doubt, allow him to purchase her when he tires of her beauty."

Harald stopped before Rognvald, so choked with indignation at his words, rage towards the King, and love and fear for Persea, that his tongue refused to obey his will. Then his pent-up feelings burst the barrier of composure which his self-control had erected. In a hoarse voice, trembling with passion, he replied:

"Knowest thou that such words are as hot irons through my heart? Learn, my father, that while Tellus owns my life and our friendship is as deep and lasting as the sea, 't is not for Tellus that I would rescue Persea. 'T is for myself. I love, her. Dost thou remember what those words meant to thee when life was young, and the red blood rushed furiously through thy veins? I tell thee that words are as fitful gusts beside the wildest storms, when I attempt to describe this love that has taken possession of me. I know nothing, feel nothing, see nothing but Persea; and now Persea is being unconsciously led towards a terrible precipice. If I save her not, she will soon step over the brink and be lost to me forever. Thou hast acknowledged that the King must have selected her for her beauty. Why? Dost thou wonder that I am seized with the berserk-rage? This moment is fire coursing through my veins instead of blood."

Never before had Rognvald seen Harald so violently aroused. He was alarmed at the depth of his passion for Persea, and angry that he had so openly acknowledged it. Those words sounded in his ears like the distant rumble of the ice-pack, ere it starts on its death-dealing slide to the valley. It foreboded trouble. He answered him angrily, sternly:

"Thou hast been hasty, my son, in saying that thou lovest this maiden. Norsemen boast not of battles unfought, nor of loves whose desires are unsatisfied. Art thou sure this maiden would yield to thee? Thou art no fairer nor braver than Olaf, and he is of her belief. May she not prefer to stay with him? Wait awhile, ere thou declarest so vehemently the secrets of thine heart."

Harald's face flushed with anger and passion.   Those were
uncommon words his father had spoken.   Then the red died
away, and a pallor took its place that showed deathly white,
even in the ruddy flame-light.   Straightening his tall form until his golden helmet seemed almost to touch the smoky rafters,
he answered with quiet decision, ominous in its very calmness :

" It may be that I have not spoken wisely ; but I have
spoken the truth.   We will talk no more of this matter.
Thou knowest why this maiden's fate is of such moment to
me ; and why it is impossible for me to calmly wait until Olaf
tires of her beauty, as thou hast said.   She may indeed prefer
to remain with the King ; but unless she herself forbids, something must be, shall be done."

He left the skali quickly, and plunged into the sombre stillness of the pine forest.   After walking until he had left all
signs of men far behind him, he threw himself upon the soft,
pungent carpet of the wilderness.   Burying his face in his
hands, he prayed fervently to his gods for help ; but his prayers
brought him no comfort.

Finally, desperate with the torture of brain and heart, he
timidly, fearfully, offered an unspoken petition to Persea's
Christ.

CHAPTER X

A NORSE homestead consisted of a collection of low buildings, varying in number with the wealth and importance of the owner. They were all built of heavy timbers, with slanting roofs ornamented with massive carvings and gargoyles. The buildings were grouped together in the form of a rectangle, the whole enclosed by a fence having a gateway which was usually guarded. The skali was the largest building, and was used for general living purposes and feasts. This was oblong in shape, always lying east and west, with the main entrance in the eastern gable end. Before the huge, carved door was an open vestibule, wide enough for several persons to enter abreast.

Inside, long benches stretched along the northern and southern walls, in the centre of which were the high seats of honour. The high seat on the northern side was considered the most honourable, and was always occupied by the master of the house. The other positions decreased in importance as they left the high seats. The huge fire blazed upon the earthen floor; and between the fire and the benches long rows of tables were set at mealtime. The walls were carved, panelled, or hung with rich tapestry; and were adorned with beautiful shields and weapons.

To the north of the skali stood the dyneyja, a small structure where the women gathered during the day to sew and embroider; and to the south was the gestahaus for the entertainment of visitors. Opposite the skali stood the skemma, usually seen only on the lands of the wealthy; for it was a separate apartment for women of quality for day and night use. It was distinguished from the other buildings by its upper story, which contained the sleeping apartments. This was surrounded by a balcony, from which a staircase descended to the ground, there being no communication inside between the first and second floors. Besides these main buildings, there was the málstofa for conferences; and beyond, and to the rear, were numerous outbuildings for the maintenance of the servants, thralls and cattle.

Persea stood upon the balcony of the skemma one morning, looking out with wondering reverence upon the grand, wild scenery so new to her. The autumnal sun slowly rose, heralding its coming by a blaze of golden fire that spread out in a widening fan over the sky, shedding its beams across fjeld, mountain and fjord with a radiance so pure and soft that it seemed to have escaped from the half-opened portals of heaven.

The waters of the Fjord lay as smooth as glass; reflecting every rugged crag, towering precipice, and dark belt of pines and firs. Flocks of wild fowl rose from their haunts among the rocks, and soared across the sky, uttering faint, far-off cries. Light breezes began to float down from the mountains, rippling the waters of the Fjord, and breaking the clear reflections into thousands of glittering fragments. Mists rose from the dew-laden valleys and chill streams; and another pale, cold day was sweeping low across the Norsemen's home.

Persea was awed and fascinated by the phenomena about her, to which she had not grown accustomed since the landing of the viking. Even her long journey northward upon the Norseman's ship had not prepared her for the strangeness of her present life and surroundings. To her there was ever present a peculiar sense of the unreal, as if she had died, and her spirit was inhabiting another world. A short time since, she had lived in a marble palace, under blue skies that were warm and sunny. Now, she saw about her a collection of low, rough buildings, under a flaming sky, amid wild, unknown scenery; and she knew that those who inhabited the dwellings were of foreign nationality and heathen belief. Moreover, she was held as captive to the one who was their King!

Only the frequent visits of Tellus enabled her to realize how the stupendous changes had come into her life. Not a day passed without a meeting of brother and sister; for Tellus' mind was filled with apprehension lest harm should fall upon his sister as a bolt from a clear sky. But all was well with Persea. To his anxious questioning she gave no unhappy reply. While her life was new and unusual, she could not speak of neglect or insult. Every luxury that Olaf could command was given her. She had soon discovered that only in name was she a waiting woman to Ingiborg. Not a duty was hers; not a wish was ungranted, save the wish for restoration to her brother's care and protection. She had been given a place of honour at the King's table; she came and went about the boer at will; but if she approached the gateway, a hirdman barred her path.

During her moments in the skemma, before the embroidery frame, Persea had begun to know Ingiborg as a real friend. From the first, the King's sister had felt a great pity for this captive. When she knew her story, when she understood, as far as she could, the purity of her soul and mind, she had great sympathy for her. This, Persea soon felt, and in her loneliness was drawn towards Ingiborg; but she felt no affinity for the King's foster-sister, Astrid. She was too proud and cold, and moved about as a queen, with scarcely an eye for anything beyond her own beauty and its adornment.

As for the King, Persea avoided him at every possible opportunity. Tellus had made known to her all that had happened on the eventful day of the landing of the viking; and she was warned of the possible danger which threatened her. So, though the King was handsome and brave, and had ever been kind to her, she soon noted the persistency with which he sought her presence; and she dreaded the consequence; dreaded even a chance conversation with him. Deeply hidden in her heart was the image of another man — one who had sat by her side during the long days of the journey northward; one who had been gentle with all his strength, tender with all his bravery, and lovable because his own love was so great, so masterful. If only he were a Christian! That had ever been a barrier between them; for when she knew the weird religion in which he believed, she shrank from him, lest Christ should be offended and withhold his blessing. Still, at every thought of Harald her heart beat faster, and her brain was in a whirl. She knew he was laying plans for securing her freedom; but she had not seen him since she had been an inmate of the King's boer. That Harald could not trust himself in her presence she understood by the heart's intuition; but the knowledge made her tremble with mingled pleasure and pain.

In the King's household she held a strange position. The

warriors and hirdmen of the King's guard, taking their cue
from the deference paid her by the King, the honourable seat
which was hers at the King's table, and her personal beauty,
bowed low as she passed. If perchance they could do aught
which would win them recognition, they considered themselves
fortunate. Many who had thus received a glance from her
had felt their pulses quicken, and wondered not that the King
looked favourably upon her. More than one wished that he
was the King.

She had not been long within the boer, yet she was to the
thralls a revelation. Accustomed only to harsh command
and the degraded condition of the slave — though many of
them were born to better things in far-off homes from which
they had been captured — her unwonted kindness overwhelmed
them. Deep in their deadened selves awoke an echo of something forgotten, but wondrously sweet. To those who came
not into her presence was told the story of her gentleness, until
there was not a thrall in the great boer who did not secretly
worship her.

But Persea was unconscious of the influence which had gone
out from her. Saving Ingiborg, she felt utterly alone in a
strange abode. As she stood upon the balcony, realizing the
intense loneliness of her present state, her heart grew faint
and weary, and tears began to gather in her eyes. As she felt
her courage departing and her strength failing, she turned to
God for help. There upon the balcony, she clasped her hands
and raised her eyes to heaven, breathing a prayer to the Eternal
Comforter for strength and faith.

She neither saw nor heard the King as he came out of the
skali, and crossing the paved court-yard, stood gazing at her
profile, so perfect against the clear sky. He drank in all the
beauty of her face and figure ; not the smallest detail escaped
him, — from her tiny foot, just visible over the edge of the
balcony, to the touch of gold the sun left on her hair. Even
as he looked, there surged through him a mighty torrent of
love and desire that he was unable to check or subdue. Turning from the door of the málstofa, he sprang up the stairway,
and stood at her side.

" So thou art not indifferent to the wild beauty of our wild
home ? "

Persea was startled, and dropped her hands upon the railing.

The King had never before intruded into the sanctity of the skemma. She was vaguely frightened.

"I was praying," she answered, as one who takes refuge behind an impregnable wall.

"Ah! and may I ask to whom?"

Olaf was in a mood to be madly jealous of even her gods.

"I was praying to the only God of the Universe. I have heard thy people call him the White Christ."

"So, a Christian art thou? Then we have a binding tie in this heathen land; for I and my followers in the boer also worship Christ."

Persea's face grew bright, and she clasped her hands in the quick, earnest way natural to her. Lifting her eyes to his with more confidence than he had ever before seen, she said:

"A Christian! O most gracious King! Thou knowest not how thy words cheer my heart."

Olaf gazed upon that beautiful face, and quivered with suppressed passion. He was glad that he was a Christian if it brought such a look from her; but if she had wished him to be a pagan, he would have thrown his priests and cross to the winds. Then he said:

"And has thy heart, then, been sad? I did not take thee to wrap thy beauteous form in sorrow. Has our rude home been so entirely repulsive to the Roman goddess who has made it her present shrine? If thou hast missed thy worshippers, behold! Olaf himself is at thy feet."

The King dropped on one knee, and tried to take the hands so tightly clasped.

The tone, low and exquisite, the action, the words, were tinged with an unmistakable something which Persea felt was intolerable to her. She snatched away her hands, and tried to speak; but could not. Her heart beat wildly. She felt as if enveloped in an atmosphere charged with danger. She wished to escape, but could not.

The King appeared to be unconscious of her agitation; or if he was not, he did not ascribe it to displeasure with him. It was only a little maidenly confusion and alarm at his first warm words; something which made her more beautiful and attractive to him. So, while she stood trembling like a frightened bird, he did not seek again to touch her, but continued to speak of her beauty, his desire to surround her with every luxury, and to see her happy in his Norse home. He would grant her slightest wish, go to any lengths to please her, asking only that she bestow upon him her glances and smiles. He had not chosen her as his gift-token by mere chance or trick of fortune; and he wished to make her happy. When he had done this, then happiness would come to him.

He ceased, and his voice, persuasive and gentle, threw around her its powerful magnetism, holding her captive against her will. But she felt the unspoken passion in his words; and when he finished, her inner consciousness threw out instinctive danger signals. She recognized its warning, and replied coldly:

"Arise. It is not seemly for thee to speak and act thus towards a captive. I have lacked for nothing. I wish nothing more of jewels or raiment; for a captive needs not such adornment. Thou didst take me as a waiting-woman to thy sister. I go to my place beside her."

She had recovered her self-possession; and the last words were spoken with a calm dignity that it seemed impossible to oppose. But Olaf was not to be foiled. He had come expressly to have an interview with his lovely captive. She must see that she could not slip through his fingers like that. She had managed to elude him until he was angry with himself and her. Now he was determined that she should hear and understand something of what the future had in store for her. He stopped her with a slight gesture.

"Nay my fairest one, thou hast been too closely confined among the women. Do not think thy place in the royal household is so obscure. Norsemen value beauty such as thine far too highly to allow it to bloom unnoticed. Thou art no thrall, no slave. No bonds are thine, save the bonds which my jealous care and tenderness towards thee would lead me to throw about thee, so that I may ever keep thee near me. I shall come often to see thee, to enquire of thy welfare, to gratify thy slightest wish, to kneel at thy feet and beg for a smile, a glance, from thine eyes, that are to me the brightest stars that ever shone in the sky of my life."

Persea's voice was tinged with indignation as she turned and answered him quickly:

"If my wishes are to be gratified, grant me my freedom. That is all I shall ever ask or take from thee."

Olaf smiled. How little she understood him! How far she was from fathoming the iron will which had already claimed her as his own! He answered:

"When a beautiful bird happens to stray to our shores, we would keep it to continually delight us with its sweet presence and song. We would be cruel to put it out under our cold skies; even though at first it fluttered in our grasp."

The tone was soft, and meant to be soothing; but Persea shivered. She felt as if she had heard her death sentence. She began to understand, to detect the relentless will. Then her own rose in rebellion, and she replied:

"Thou art not speaking as a Christian should speak. Thou dost not restore me to my brother; yet thou askest me to be glad and gay when my heart is sore and sad. I am thy captive; but ask not a captive to sing."

Ere he recovered from her brave, haughty reply, she had slipped past him and was gone. So quickly did she move and speak that Olaf had no chance to detain her. He stood looking in annoyed amazement towards the staircase down which she had vanished. Never before had he known a maiden to really desire to leave his presence. Wounded pride, anger, and thwarted will surged mightily within him. He started forward to give command that she be brought to him, with the intention of humbling her high spirit, and showing her something of what his displeasure would mean. But ere he reached the staircase, he stopped. He remembered that, for the first time in his life, he did not dare to please himself. To be severe, now, might mean the loss of many things. It would not do. He must abide his time. He felt perfectly confident of making her love him in the end; it would be something new to tame such a spirit, and bring from those eyes the fire of love and passion, instead of the flashing scorn he had just seen.

As he turned to depart, Ingiborg stood in the doorway. He wondered how long she had been there; but he did not care. She, — every one, — would soon know that Persea was his love. If necessary, he was powerful enough to place even a captive on the Queen's seat. He said to Ingiborg:

"This Persea is very beautiful; and thou shalt arrange that

I see her more frequently. Have her wear my jewels and the robes I send her; for she is a valuable captive, and I want her to be satisfied with her home. Her brother and Harald Rognvaldson wish to purchase her. I speak smoothly to them, for it is not my wish to make enemies in the Thrandheim at present; but it will not be my fault if Persea does not rather stay when they ask her to go. She must stay; she shall stay; and thou art of a nature to help me much in getting my desire with this maiden."

Ingiborg's gentle face grew troubled.

"Olaf, I beg of thee, be not unkind to this thy captive. She is very beautiful in face and form; but I know also that she is singularly pure and beautiful in her mind. She is unlike any woman I have ever known. She knows not the world. She is a Christian of a different kind from that of Thangbrand. I have learned to love her as a sister; and I would not see harm come to her."

Olaf frowned.

"Did I say I would harm her? But I wish her to be satisfied with her present state. Use thy influence to make her happy and contented in my household. I will speak no riddles unto thee. I love her. I shall not rest until I have won her; and I have a mighty rival in this Harald Rognvaldson, who has already had time to do his love-making with her. I shall not harm her; but I do not intend to sell her at any price to any one. She must be mine. If she is as pure as thou sayest, I shall drink the wedding cup with her; but mine she is in right, and mine she shall be, body and soul. Treat her as though she was a member of my royal house. When we ride to the Thing, all people shall see and render respect unto her, even as they would unto thee and Astrid. There must be no difference between her rank and thine."

Ingiborg hastened to reply:

"I am nothing loth to give Persea rank with me; for royal is she from the crown of her head to her shapely foot; and she is pure and wise also. To look upon her as my sister will give me pleasure untold; and if thou canst win her heart, thou couldst find no worthier bride. I will try to make her happy; but I know her heart is sad because she pines for her freedom. I pray thee to be patient with her, and compel her not."

Olaf turned upon her almost fiercely.

"Did I not tell thee I would not harm her? Never yet have I compelled a woman, — they were always ready to yield, sooner or later. Persea knows not how Olaf can woo when he loves. She, too, will come to me, and be content to abide. Thou art commanded but to do as I have said."

He turned, and passed down the stairway, leaving a great trouble in Ingiborg's face. As she watched him stride across the court-yard, she whispered to herself: "Poor Persea! Thou hast a dark storm gathering over thy head. Olaf will never give thee up; yet I know thou lovest him not; and I fear thou never wilt love him. Thou art so pure, so gentle that he will crush thee, overwhelm thee with his mighty passion. My heart aches for thee; and I will shield thee as long as I may; but little can Ingiborg do when Olaf speaks."

Then she sought the dyneyja, where the women were embroidering. She looked in vain for Persea. Astrid, who was reclining in a large chair, with a strange expression upon her face, noted the enquiring glance, and said:

"If thou seekest for Persea, she has just been summoned to the skali to see Harald Rognvaldson, who came to enquire of her welfare. 'T is not often a captive receives such noble visitors."

"No," replied Ingiborg. "Yet this girl is considered by no one to be an ordinary thrall. Dost thou know that she is to have rank with us, and ride to the Thing?"

Astrid sprang to her feet in a violent rage.

"What! she, a slave, to be placed on an equality with *me*! Who has said this?"

"Thy foster-brother, Olaf Tryggvveson."

For a moment, Astrid was speechless. Then she struck her foot upon the floor in passion, and said:

"Does Olaf Tryggvveson think that I will allow this thing? What means he thus to insult the women of his royal household?"

Ingiborg was surprised at the fierceness and bitterness in Astrid's voice. She had expected amazement and questionings; but not this outburst of anger. She replied:

"I know not that he has hurt us by thus acknowledging Persea's beauty. As for his reason, why does any man so honour beauty in woman? Hast thou been so blind as to think that Olaf was indifferent to this extraordinary maiden?"

Astrid turned suddenly and looked at Ingiborg. Then a calmer expression, almost of relief, came into her face as she said :

" Ah ! is that it ?   I hope he may be paid for his trouble ; but at the same time, I like not to see this woman, this slave, sharing with me the honour of belonging to the King's family. But I suppose I must endure, if Olaf has spoken."

As she finished, she threw herself back into the chair and stared fixedly into the fire.   Ingiborg turned away with a sigh. She would like to have spoken more about Persea ; but Astrid was evidently in no humour to talk.   She knew by sad experience, that Astrid did only what she wanted to do ; and that now she wanted to be let alone.   She could not know that her foster-sister was madly jealous of the beauty which she feared was likely to rival her own in the eyes of the one man for whom she had ever felt a real heart-throb.

Several times since that memorable day of the sea kings' return had Astrid seen and spoken with Harald.   Each time had her heart beat painfully with the desire to be pleasing in his sight ; but the knowledge of her own attractions had made her confident of success.   Though she would scarcely own it to herself, she was already dreaming of the realization of her heart's desire, and the intense happiness which would come to her with this man's love.   But the last time they had met, she could not fail to observe how much he spoke of Persea, how anxiously he inquired about her.   That gave her many jealous doubts ; and when, finally, Harald had come out plainly, and asked her to persuade the King to sell Persea to him, the poisoned arrow pierced her heart.   Then she knew, beyond all doubt, how passionately she loved this man pleading for another whom she hated.

Little did Harald know whose sympathy he had tried to enlist, or into what a tangle the Fates were weaving his web of happiness.   All unconscious of evil, he sat by Persea's side, intoxicated with the sense of nearness, and noting, with a lover's keen sight, the mounting colour in her cheeks as his voice grew low and passionate, breathing a subtle knowledge into her soul which he could not express in words.

CHAPTER XI

THANGBRAND

A PARTY of Olaf's followers had wandered to the shore of the Fjord, and were amusing themselves in various ways. Some were gaming with small chips; some repairing weapons, or carving; some lay at full length, basking in the sunlight. Among them sat a number of the Thrandheim warriors, who were finding pleasure and companionship among their new King's retinue. From time to time loud bursts of laughter came from the largest group, which centred about one man who was providing great entertainment.

He was seated in a comfortable position, leaning heavily against a large rock. He was a short, thick-set fellow, with red hair and beard, and a face which was an odd mixture of wisdom and wit, cruelty and sensuousness. His dress was half priestly, half a warrior's. He wore a long, hooded monk's robe of coarse black cloth; but instead of the rope at his waist, there was a gold belt with scabbard and sword attached. Upon his shaven head a winged helmet of brass sat oddly enough. A golden chain and crucifix hung around his neck. Jewels loaded his fingers; and the loose sleeve of his coarse robe showed a silken tunic underneath.

He had just ended a tale which had called forth loud laughter; but several of the Thrandheim men looked at each other with inquiring glances, as if something had happened that they could not understand.

The man with the red beard said:

" It is in my mind that some one has given King Olaf a sleep drink since we came to the Thrandheim. We had other sport besides telling tales while we were in the southern districts," and he winked slyly at his nearer neighbours.

One of then glanced towards the Thrandheim warriors and whispered:

" Hist! thou art careless with thy jokes ! "

But the priest scowled angrily, and said:

" Bah! Wherefore is the King afraid ? I would that he

give me the power. Then all would soon be finished. A pan of hot coals would do much towards warming the hearts of the bonder to Christianity. If I have not some speedy use of my muscles, I will rot like a stuck boar. I would much enjoy some weapon-swinging," and he stretched his great limbs lazily.

A man on the outside of the group, — one who had not laughed much at Thangbrand's coarse tales, — looked up quickly.

"Listen to Thangbrand. Since he speaks of it, I will acknowledge that he has some likeness to a boar, save that his snout is not so long."

A laugh greeted this sally, in which Thangbrand did not heartily join. But he pulled out his tolle-kniv, and placing the end of the handle on his nose, he gave reply :

"There, has that lengthened it enough for thee? I will measure it in thy hide to prove the finger distances."

This time, the laugh sided with the priest ; but Karlson shook his head, and said :

"Nay, I wish not a pig's snout rooting in my skin. 'T would tickle me too much."

"That is so," quickly answered Thangbrand, "and then thou wouldst have to laugh. Thou wert ever afraid of laughing, lest thy mouth open so wide that thou swallowest thy brains."

Karlson replied to this thrust with a shrug of his shoulders, and the words :

"Never do I care for that. If thou couldst once kiss a maiden with my mouth, thou wouldst wish for no smaller one. It can gather twice as much sweetness as the slit in thy face."

"And by the Holy Cross," retorted Thangbrand, " 't is well for thee that it does ; for no maiden would be kissed twice by thee ! "

"None but Kathleen, the Blue-eyed," said Karlson, in a tone that implied there was much more that might be told.

"Hear ! hear ! " cried several voices. "Give way, Thangbrand, for he has thee now. He won where thou didst lose."

Thangbrand waved his hand towards his antagonist, and said, with mock reproachfulness :

"Why wilt thou remind a man, who may not marry, of the enjoyments he has missed in life ? Ah ! Kathleen in far-off

Ireland, had I been a warrior, instead of a priest, thou wouldst not have been a virgin, — so long ! "

The priest leaned back and laughed loudly.

The men now began calling for more entertainment; and Thangbrand was speedily holding their attention with stories of adventure in many lands, stories in which he played a great part; bloody struggles, feasting, love-making, — all interspersed with pilgrimages, vows, and penances. Finally he said that he would tell no more, since he must return to the King. As he rose to go, one of the Thrandheim men addressed him:

" Stay a moment, priest of the White Christ, for I have a question to ask thee. Thou hast said that thy priesthood forbids marriage; yet from the words of thine own lips, I know that thou dost not lose pleasure thereby. Would not lawful marriage be better than thy license ? "

Thangbrand moved uneasily, and did not immediately reply. The silence was broken by one of Olaf's men.

" By all that breathes, what difference does a man's gods make in his actions ? If he be an honourable warrior, so will he remain; whether he sacrifice to Odin or say mass to Christ. If he be a nithing, a nithing will he remain; though he worship all the gods in the heavens. For my part, I see no difference in worshipping Christ or Odin; save that Valhalla is Heaven, and the manners of worship are unlike. Can vows make a man perfect in his life ? Thangbrand has made many vows. Let him say whether they have kept him from evil."

Every one looked to see the priest's mad temper rise; but he only fixed his eyes on Hilmir and said:

" So, thou seest no difference between Odin and Christ ? Then thou art almost an unbeliever. Keep on with thy speeches, and some day thou wilt be one. Then I will show thee which of my vows I do keep. Thou shalt squirm under my zealous care; and fain wilt thou wish that I had never kept one vow. Thou wilt find it easier to believe in Christ than to have thy muscles crack, or to sit upon a stake. Teach thy tongue better words, ere it be too late."

The priest walked away. When he was beyond hearing distance, one of the men spoke:

" Hilmir, thou art surely mind-empty to risk these quarrels with the priest. Thou dost know his evil temper. Why wilt thou anger him so ? "

Hilmir pushed his hair back with a swift movement of both his hands, and said impatiently :

" I care not an aurar for his tongue, nor his temper ; no, nor for his teeth.   Let him bite if he can.   I am altogether weary of his long prayers, and his masses, and his holy water.   In what ways are we better than when we believed in Odin ?   As for the priest, ye do all know that Iron Beard, the Temple Godi of the Thrandheim, is as much better than this foul-mouthed Thangbrand as day is better than night.   I have tried to believe in this Christianity ; but it sticks uneasily in my mind.   We can do evil that is blacker than the storm-cloud ; yet Thangbrand says he can hear, give penance, and wipe out the stain !   Does this belief make better men than the religion of Odin ?   There, if a man offends, he cannot buy off his offense.   He is shut out of Valhalla, and sent to dwell forever with Nidhöggu in Helga Pool.   I speak to ye as men who have minds to think, not as followers of King Olaf ; and in your hearts ye do all say as I do, — that this Christianity is weaker than Odin's belief.   I have no thought of being false to Olaf Tryggvveson ; but I say fairly and openly that if Thangbrand has told us all there is to know of Christ, and if he is the best that Christianity can boast of, then the religion of Odin is better and makes better men."

No one answered Hilmir's words ; but many different expressions came upon the men's faces.   Some looked anxiously in the direction Thangbrand had disappeared, fearful lest he had heard the bold words.   Some cast down their eyes, evidently to hide their real thoughts.   Some looked open approval.   Then from out the group of Thrandheim men came a clear, quiet voice :

" This ill-tempered Thangbrand knows no more of the White Christ than the wolves that prowl upon the fjelds.   He is not the best that Christianity can boast of ; and he has not told all there is to know of the White Christ.   But there lives, under the King's roof, one who is the best, and who can tell thee strange stories of the Christ ; stories that seem like women's tales of submission and sorrow ; yet they have the strength and power of an all-conquering warrior.   I mean Persea, the dark-eyed woman from the South.   Wouldst thou know what Christianity is ?   Then go to her ; for she can tell thee ; even as she told me."

The men stared in open-mouthed wonder at the speaker. The one next to him leaned over, and said :

" Be careful, Eindridi, there is no lack of wisdom in silence."

But the man addressed only straightened his shoulders and continued :

" That evil priest could never be aught but evil, let him worship whom he pleases. His stories were only black filth, drawn from a filthy mind. The God that the dark-eyed worships *must* be a good God. Mayhap he is not to us as Odin ; but he stands for such purity and conduct as becomes men and women, not for the vileness of yonder priest. Thangbrand loves power, hence he will teach such belief as will bring him power. Blame the man who has distorted a worship so as to aid his own purpose, but blame not the White Christ. Dost thou remember, Wulfric, the day when she told us the Christ story, while we were waiting for the wind to fill the sails ? And if we do worship Odin, we reverence the White Christ for the sake of the pure maiden who spoke to us of him."

A long silence fell upon the noisy groups. Through many a mind distracting thoughts were straying ; and more than one man secretly wished that he, too, could hear the Christ story from the lips of the Southland maiden. The unconscious homage which they all paid to her beauty, gentleness, and purity, only intensified their desire to know what she had told Eindridi. What was her story of the White Christ ?

Old Wulfric shook his head slowly as he thought : " Odin has only half the heart of Eindridi. Iron Beard has arrayed the bonder against Olaf's Christianity ; but all unknown to him, there has been seed dropped by another hand that has far more strength than Olaf's sowing. It has fallen into great, strong hearts, and the end is not yet. We hate Thangbrand ; but we hate not Persea's Christ."

CHAPTER XII

"OLAF SHALL PAY FOR THIS"

AT the King's command the bearer of the Thing-summons rode forth with the Thing-bod. The bonder hastened to their doors to receive it, and set their teeth grimly as they saw the war-arrow that Iron Beard had substituted for the bud-stikke. Then quick orders were given, and a fresh horse and rider were soon speeding to the next boer with the momentous summons. On the tidings swept, calling upon the men of the Thrandheim to rise in the defense of their honour and religion. Over valley, crag, and fjord, rose the low rumble of the approaching storm; all unheard by Olaf as he sat in his málstofa, and planned for a grand pageant of wealth and beauty at the Thing which should change these heathen to holy Christians. More than ever he desired to do this, since Persea was a Christian.

This girl was a puzzle to him. Try as he would to be with her, she ever eluded him, until he became annoyed and angry with himself and her. He had sent unto her rich jewels and robes; but his jewels were returned, and the robes were never worn. She appeared always in the coarse, white vadmal that told she was a slave. This angered him, and yet increased her charm to him; angered him, because he would fain have seen her decked in beautiful attire which he had provided; made her more desired, because he saw in her refusal only a hauteur and independence which were new and delightful to him. From Ingiborg he had heard all her story. Deep in his soul there was a great bitterness, a fear, and a pain; for he trembled lest Harald Rognvaldson had won her love. But this fear of a rival made him determined never to give her freedom until she had consented to be his. He had read the young viking's heart only too well in his vehement and persistent efforts to free Persea. However, the King noticed that his plea was ever on honour's account. He spoke only of the debt of his word to Tellus; and his stained honour until he had redeemed his promise. Olaf began to be quite sure that

Harald's love was, as yet, undeclared. If so, he had only to keep them apart, and the prize was his.

He found great joy in dreaming of the happiness that seemed so sure. Some day he would clasp her in his arms, and see in her eyes the reflection of his own great passion. Some day he would feel her form close to his, yielding willingly to the pressure of his arms. Some day he would feel the weight of her head on his breast, and the touch of her lips on his.

His dreaming was suddenly interrupted. The door of the málstofa swung violently open, and Thangbrand stalked into the room with but little regard for the King's presence. He threw himself into a chair with a rage that was neither concealed nor controlled.

The King had started, and instinctively put his hand on his sword; but at the sight of his unannounced visitor he recovered his composure, saying:

"What now? Was the mead sour; or has some unruly one refused to pay the price of his sins?"

The priest deigned only a half grunt as a reply. The King said no more; but sat watching him as the purple gradually died out of his coarse face. Finally Thangbrand spoke:

"My anger was so great that my tongue was twisted, and the words stuck in my throat. Dost thou know, King Olaf, that there is heresy breeding in thy following? Dost thou know that there are men and women within thy boer who dare to speak evil of the Priest of Christ whom thou hast set to save their souls? To-day, one did foul me to my face. Afterwards, I listened, — yea — and I found others were with him. But best of all, I found out the source of all this unruliness. Thou hast a child of the devil in thy boer."

"Upon whom has thy present displeasure fallen? If evil has been said or done, tell me, that I may punish fitly. I brook not dissension or unbelief among my following."

The King was scowling. It was not pleasant to hear of such things when he was on the eve of a great religious struggle.

Thangbrand answered guardedly:

"Thou must get rid of the heretic, lest the wrath of God descend upon thee. If we were with thine army, where the men of the Thrandheim could not interfere, I would say, 'Burn!' So does the Holy Father purge the Church of those who are worse than heathen.   Within me is rage, because I know it would not be wise for thee to burn; but thou canst pluck the thorn out of thy flesh and cast it from thee, ere thou art accursed."

But the King was growing weary of the indefinite, and said impatiently :

"Thou dost speak in riddles.   I know not of whom thou dost rave so madly."

"Know not?" said Thangbrand.   "Thou hast honoured her enough to know.   Yea, and thou didst tell me she was a Christian.   Sooth, for her the fire is waiting; and I would be the first to touch the faggots with flame.   I speak of the she-devil thou didst take from Jarl Rognvald.   She it is who is filling the minds of the people with evil thoughts."

Olaf leaped towards the priest as if to take him by the throat.

"Take care of thy words!   Name her but once again as thou hast, and thou shalt feel Olaf's sword!"

But Thangbrand eluded him with ready alertness, and lifting the golden crucifix to the King's gaze, he said sternly :

"I am the Priest of the Christ thou hast sworn to worship as thy God; and by this Holy Cross I command thee to calm thyself."

Olaf's hands opened and closed convulsively; but the symbol conquered.   Slowly he sank into his chair, though the dangerous light still glittered in his eyes.   The priest stood a moment longer, fixed, immovable.   Then he lowered the crucifix, and said :

"Thangbrand speaks not without good cause.   The breath of rebellion against me, and so against thee and Christ, is fostered and strengthened by this woman thou hast taken into thy boer.   Thou didst tell me she was a Christian; but she has attended no masses, nor has she asked for a priest's blessing.   After I heard these rumours of the evil she had done, I did seek her presence to prove their truth.   And by the Holy Cross, she did count me as dirt under her feet!   She did say that she had no need of masses nor confession, since she prayed to Christ for herself!   She did dare to refuse my blessing, — yea, and more, — she did dare to tell me that I was no fit priest of Christ : that I was evil, and did evil when I taught men that I absolved their sins and could give in-

dulgences! Many a person has been roasted in Rome for
saying less. The girl is a menace to thy cherished plans.
Get ye rid of her. Send her away, or — give her to me. I
will see that her soul is made as pure as mine!"

The priest laughed; and with half-closed eyes, seemed to
gloat over some mind-vision.

Olaf ground his teeth. The look upon Thangbrand's face
destroyed all effect that his words might have had; for it gave
to the King a reason for his condemnation of Persea. He
felt disgust himself towards the holder of the holy office. He
was the master once more. He arose, and answered in a tone
that Thangbrand had learned meant obedience, instant and
unconditional.

"When gave I thee permission to approach the Roman
maiden? Thou art less than dirt under her feet; and she did
well to count thee so. Thou art more fit to understand the
minds of the swine than this maiden's thoughts. I will be
responsible for any evil she may do. Let her think and act
even as she wills: 't would not be many sins she could confess
unto thee. As for removing her from my sight, or bringing
harm to her, if thou dost ever breathe such vileness into mine
ears again, I will command that the blood-eagle be cut upon
thy back! Go!"

The priest shivered; and a sickly pallor spread across his
face. He knew Olaf made no idle threats. He silently rose
and left the King's presence.

But once outside, he pulled his monk's hood over his head;
and under its protecting shadow his lips muttered curses and
vows of vengeance. "He shall pay for this! Yea, if I cannot convert these swine in mine own way, then he shall have
no victory over them. And the blood-eagle! Thangbrand
forgets not those words!"

CHAPTER XIII

THE VERDICT OF THE PEOPLE

BEAUTIFUL was the Thing-plain of Lladir on the morning of the day before the Autumn Sacrifice. The summer lingered. The month of Goi was half gone; and yet the Snow King had only let the fringe of his white robes sweep over the land. The sun rose far to the south; its rays had lost their warmth, and begun to shine upon the rugged face of the earth with a chilling light, the frost-breath of the coming winter.

Bathed in that cold sunlight lay the wide Thing-plain, the gorgeous temple, and the solemn dom-ring, its sacrificial stone sacredly guarded by twelve majestic rock fragments. Around them rose a forest of dark pines that pointed their needle tips to the sky, calling upon the assembled multitude to look towards the upper world for wisdom in their verdicts.

For twelve hours the people had been gathering to answer the King's summons. The broad plain surged with a mass of humanity, whose multi-coloured cloaks gave a bright touch of colour to the picture in its sombre frame of grey crags and cold skies. There was no confusion, no display of passion as these stalwart men talked together in groups or pairs, ever keeping their long cloaks well wrapped about them.

In the distance stood the temple, its gilded roof reflecting the cold sunlight; and on every side were rude booths and tents that the people had erected for their shelter during the feasts and sacrifice days. The moments went by, and the people began to be restless and impatient. At last a murmur arose, sweeping over the Thing-plain with swelling force until it broke into far-reaching shouts, " The King! The King ! ''

Amid the blare of trumpets, the wild cry of the lurs, the floating of banners, and the snorting of war-horses, Olaf rode into the midst of the people. Behind him, in carriages glittering with costly ornamentation, rode Ingiborg, Astrid, and Persea. The people stared in open-mouthed wonder at the

three women and their equipages; for even the wealthy
Thrandheim jarls could not clothe their women in the
magnificent robes and jewels that Ingiborg and Astrid wore.

But amid this barbaric splendour, amid the shimmer of
brocades, the rich darkness of velvets, and the flashing of
rarest gems, Persea sat clad in the thick, white vadmal. Its
coarseness, its whiteness, only enhanced her loveliness; and
the eyes of the people passed quickly over all the pageant of
wealth to look upon, and marvel at, this strange and beautiful
maiden who occupied a place of highest honour, and yet wore
the slave's garb. Who was she? In what relation did she
stand to the King? All tongues were busy with questionings.
Astrid felt a fiercer jealousy as she realized that Persea was
claiming more attention than she. Everywhere did this
southern maiden cross her path!

The King had been bitterly disappointed when Persea entered the carriage at the last moment, still clad in the hateful
white. He had given Ingiborg such positive commands, and
had sent such an imperative request to Persea to dress as became one of his household, that he could not believe he had
been understood. He inwardly blamed Ingiborg for negligence
in carrying out his wishes.

After the people had satisfied their first curiosity, they noted
the King's retinue with anxious eyes. Ah! Barely a hundred men in his guard, and no weapons. They looked into
each other's faces with relief and satisfaction. The gods had
favoured them.

Olaf dismounted when he reached the law-hill, and, beckoning to Thangbrand, who carried a large crucifix, he turned
and stood facing the jarls and bonder who were seated on the
law-benches to receive him.

A hush fell upon the assembled crowd. There was a lull,
an instant of dead silence. Olaf felt vaguely uneasy. An indefinite something in the way the lawmen received him was
faintly suggestive of mockery. Iron Beard, especially, was
too deferential in his greeting. But the momentary feeling of
unrest did not make itself apparent as he returned their salutation, and then addressed them in a clear, commanding voice
that reached every ear.

"Jarls and bonder of Thrandheim, noblest sons of Norge,
I, your chosen King, have summoned you hither to pass judg-

ment on a question of such vital importance that the very hills
are bending to listen to what shall be said here to-day.   For
centuries ye men of Norge have worshipped strange gods, unheard of beyond the shores of your own land.   Ye serve them
well, but ye are worshipping in ignorance.   Know that your
gods are but mere fables which have been passed down from
the time when men were as children.

"I believe in Christ the White.   He is the great God of
all nations; and the God I desire my people to worship.   All
the southern districts have given up their bloody sacrifices,
and been baptized in the name of Jesus Christ.   Now I stand
before ye with this priest of my God and say, 'Accept this
Christianity, men of Thrandheim.   Put aside your heathen
sacrifices, and be sprinkled with the holy water of baptism.
Then ye will be considered a Christian people, and will be in
favour with the world and your King.'"

Low mutterings had greeted his first words, growing, swelling in volume and intensity, until, when he ceased, a great
roar of fury rolled over the multitude.   The lawmen sprang
to their feet, the crowd surged and swayed; and suddenly, at
a signal from Iron Beard, all cloaks were thrown aside, and
lo! a threatening army ready for conflict, with bright coats of
mail and drawn weapons flashing in the sunlight!

Olaf instinctively drew back at the unexpected transforma-
tion, and the ominous sea of dark, lowering faces.   As he did
so, Iron Beard sprang in front of him with naked sword.

"Christianize Norge, sayest thou?   In thy teeth I cast thy
words.   Never!   So did I tell thee in thine own málstofa;
and so will I tell thee now, before all Thrandheim.   We hate
thy Christ!   We despise his teaching, which has no affinity
for the brave Norseman's heart.   We will not be sprinkled
with water by yonder dirty priest of thine, whom Odin would
shut from Valhalla because of his evil doings.   Look upon the
faces about thee, and see if there is one whom thou canst persuade to thy belief.   We men of Thrandheim have a mind, a
will, yea, and an arm of our own; and thou dost see our
answer!"

He swept his sword towards the warriors, who stood with
hands upon the hilts of their weapons, waiting only for the
word to draw them upon the King and his following.

The moment was critical.   An unguarded movement, an

unwise word would be fatal. Olaf knew this, and slowly raised his hand to quell the tumult. Gradually the howls of rage grew lower and lower, until they were like the distant rumbling of thunder. Then the King spoke:

"My people have dealt treacherously with me. Why has the sanctity of the Thing-plain been violated by the presence of weapons?"

Now Rognvald arose. The low murmurs ceased entirely; for the people loved and reverenced their wise lawman; and all wanted to hear his words.

"Nay, O King. Turn thy speech to thyself; for thou hast dealt treacherously with us. We did choose thee as our King; we did promise to help and sustain thee; and thou, on thy part, didst swear to uphold the laws and rights of the land. Now thou preachest such lawlessness as that no one should believe in Odin, and Thor, and Frey, and all the ancient gods we love. We will not let thee break our laws. Thou hast used strong words to us, and we have replied with weapons. Choose now. Worship with us at our Vetrablót to-morrow; or be swept from thy throne to thy grave. We drove away Hakon, foster son of Athelstan, when he brought us the same message; and we held him in quite as much respect as we hold thee."

While he was speaking, Olaf swept keen glances over the sea of upturned faces. In the foremost row stood a young man in golden-linked armour, whose sword was half drawn to strike. Had the word been given, he would have been the first to reach Olaf's heart. All this Olaf noted, and put the memory aside. Some day, revenge! Then he turned suavely, and bowed low before Rognvald and the lawmen. He was wise enough to know that his first shot had gone wild. He must submit for the present.

With persuasive words he calmed the angry crowd, saying that he had no thought of breaking their laws, and that he supposed they were all long since weary of their old gods. He would recall his words, since they had given such offense. He concluded by saying:

"I wish only to be in good understanding with you as of old. I will come to where ye hold your greatest sacrifice-festival and see your customs. Thereafter we will consider which to hold by."

The threatening murmurs changed to shouts of joy and delight, as the bonder listened and believed that they had won the victory. The weapons were replaced in their scabbards; and the air rang with "Hail to Odin! Health and long life to the King!" Only Iron Beard murmured to himself: "All doorways, before one goes forth, should be looked over."

Persea had known the reason of the journey and the assembling of the people; and she had listened breathlessly to the speech of the King. Her heart beat with anguish as she heard the harsh, cold words in which he addressed the people on this subject so dear to her. How could he expect them to accept the worship he offered? What had he done, save to offer them a new name for a God, with no reason except his command? Was this the Christianity that was abroad in the world? Into her mind crept a resolve, and with it, a sudden knowledge. Here were the Voices she had heard calling to her out of the North; here were the souls of a grand people chained down by superstition and ignorance. Better if they had never heard of the Christ which Olaf had preached to them. She must try to bring them the truth, she must try to do her part. Tellus would help her, and perhaps, — Harald! God would give her the strength. She would speak now! She half rose in the carriage; but lo! the Thing was dissolved, the King descended from the law-hill, the lawmen followed, and all the assembly began to disperse. Her opportunity was gone.

The King rode quickly up to her, and whispered:

"Be not dismayed, my fair one. I will yet baptize these beasts. I will lay a greater trap for them than they have for me."

Persea answered him with sadness and reproof in look and tone :

"Strange to my ears wast thy espousal of the cause of Christ. Why dost thou talk of violence when he was all meekness? Why dost thou use command when he used only love and tenderness? Why dost thou promise only forms and ceremonies when thou hast his great and wonderful promises for all time and eternity? No wonder thou didst fail; and thou art no Christian, according to God's wish, for I heard thee say thou wouldst attend their heathen sacrifices. Better die first. Death has less terrors for a Christian than a denial of Christ."

Olaf did not understand what she was saying to him, for he could not. He had never known of the Christ Persea worshipped. He only saw how radiantly beautiful she was. He only felt the blood tingling in his veins as her dark eyes flashed rebuke into his. He only knew that she was displeased with what he had done, and dared to condemn him. His passion became cruel and savage; and at that moment it would have been a keen delight to him to have humbled her before all Thrandheim. He would make her suffer for her haughtiness. All in time, in time. But now he turned from her with pretended indifference, and wreaked his rage upon Ingiborg.

"Did I not give command to thee to clothe Persea in rich robes and precious jewels? Why then, wears she this white vadmal? 'T would be well if I stripped thee of thy robes and gave thee the slave's garb."

Ingiborg shrank back, terrified at his hoarse, passion-strained voice, and his insulting threat. Never had Olaf so spoken to her; and this was before many people. She was crushed in spirit, mortified beyond conception, and could not reply for trembling.

But Persea spoke for her, laying her firm hand on Ingiborg's arm with the touch of sympathy and love. She said:

"Blame not the noble Ingiborg. She obeyed thy commands. She gave me thy message. She laid before me the costliest robes in thy great chest, and flashing jewels of untold value; but I refused to wear them."

"Thou didst refuse?"

"Yea, I refused. I am thy slave, and so will wear the dress of a slave. Thy jewels are for thy kinswomen. Give me, if thou wilt, the one jewel of my freedom; but seek not to blind mine eyes to my sorrow by the flashes of thy costly gems. Their glittering fire is but an impassable barrier which thou wouldst fain erect between me and my brother. Spare thy gentle sister thy reproaches; for never will I take thy gifts."

Olaf was speechless. Anger and amazement ran riot in his brain. Here was some one refusing to obey his express commands, when those commands meant only the adornment of beauty! Again that undefinable mystery about this slave girl, something more wonderful than even her wonderful beauty. She possessed a courage, a power, which made her reach heights of womanhood unknown to him. She was in an unusual position to be so absolutely fearless of him. He writhed and stormed at the unknown power that emanated from her and compelled his self-control. He wished to command her; yet she had ever commanded him.

His mind was distorted by conflicting thoughts; but out of the chaos there rose one truth, unquestioned and supreme. He loved her: the first, the only woman of his heart. Without her he could not live, could not breathe. Unless he could some day hold her to him and press those lips with his — there was still the precipice! They would go over together. He would hold her in a clasp that death could not sever; and at the bottom of the Fjord she would lie quietly in his arms through all eternity. Such strange, confused thoughts as these flashed through his brain; but finally, with an attempt to ignore her decision as to his gifts, he leaned towards her and spoke in a tone that only her ears could hear:

"Thy beauty must be adorned, and I offer no mean gifts to thee. But thou art cold; and in my jewel chest are red rubies that glow with fire and warmth. They will suit thy dark beauty, and thou shalt wear them. They will throw around thee the light of my love, yea, the red burning of my passionate love. Mayhap thy heart will feel an answering glow."

He had spoken the words! They had burst from his lips as the molten rock tears through the crust of the earth. Nothing human could have stopped them. Then, even as the red rock loses its fiery glowing, and stands still at the touch of the chill wind, so Olaf grew white and stood motionless. For Persea had not even heard him. She was looking past him, to where Harald and Jarl Rognvald were approaching the royal group. In her cheeks, the ruby love flush was slowly, faintly rising; in her dark eyes the dawn of love was glowing. Olaf saw, and understood now that the fire was already burning; but it was not burning for him. He set his teeth in mad, jealous rage, and half drew his tolle-kniv with a frenzied movement that brought Persea's gaze quickly upon him. She trembled at the glance he gave her; but he made one mighty effort to regain his self-control, and then strode rapidly away.

Astrid was standing just in front of the royal carriage. Harald would have passed her by with only a courteous recognition; but Rognvald stopped when he saw her.

"Nay, gracious lady, wilt thou not vouchsafe to us more than a smile ? We have seen nothing for many days so priceless as thy beauty; and thy voice would be far sweeter than the whispering of Egir's Brother, as he wafted us over the land of the ships."

Astrid laughed merrily as she replied :

"'T is well thou didst not make so rash a speech when thou wert on the glittering home, else the jealous Wind God might have sent thee to Ran. To-morrow thou hadst better offer a sacrifice to appease the God's anger, lest thou yet feel his wrath."

Turning to Harald, she continued :

"And thou, Blest of the Nornir, what dost thou think of thy country-women in comparison to the southern beauties, to whom thou must have whispered soft words during thy long absence ? Are we as fair as our sisters who bathe in the dew and recline on beds of roses, while we face wild storms under our cold, northern skies ? "

It was a bold challenge, flung down as only Astrid the Peerless would dare to do. Would he venture to take up the gauntlet ? Would he tell her to her face that the southern women were beautiful, — that Persea was beautiful ?

For a short space of time, Harald was silent. This was a brilliant woman who had so graciously honoured him by reference to his peculiar birth. She stood close by. The wind from the Fjord caught her long hair, and tossed it boldly towards him, until some of the golden meshes lay against his breast. There was a faint, subtile essence and sting wafted from its glittering waves that affected him strangely. When he looked into her bold, fair face, his passionate manhood felt the magnetism of her beauty ; and he would have wished her long hair to draw him closer to it. She saw this in his face, and answered it with a glance like a flash of lightning, expecting to increase the spell her beauty had cast upon him. But it only blinded him for a second; and in that second he saw Persea's dark eyes gazing into his. The danger was past.

He gave Astrid merely an outspoken glance of admiration, that brought a faint increase of colour to her cheeks, and replied gaily :

"Does Astrid the Peerless wish me to compare light to darkness, that she asks such a question ? Does one who is known as the most beautiful woman in Norge, think that any southern flower would not pale before a diamond of the hills ? "

But in a new, quiet tone he continued :

" I know of only one in the world who is worthy to stand with thee, — a perfect woman born of the sunshine and flowers, as thou art of the winds and waves."

Ah ! he was loyal to his heart and love. Astrid's smile grew chilly as she asked, searchingly :

" I would that this one of whom thou speakest could be seen by mine eyes."

She was not sparing him. She would drive him to the wall. But his love was more to him than this woman's good-will; though he recognized her wish to be undisputed queen of beauty. Was that all over which she wished to reign ?

Quietly Harald answered :

" Thou canst see her now. I mean the sister of my beloved Standard-bearer. Yonder she sits beside Ingiborg, — Persea, the Roman."

Astrid started, feigning surprise.

" What ! a slave and a Christian, too ? "

The King's voice broke upon their ears.

" Yet still she is beautiful."

There was a bitterness in his tone; and upon both Astrid and Harald his words grated and jarred, though for vastly different reasons.

Only Rognvald was undisturbed. He answered :

" Well, a slave and a Christian can never be compared to a beauty of Norge. I judge by thy words, fair lady, that thy brother has not changed thy faith in thy country's gods."

Astrid tossed her head proudly as she replied :

" All gods are strange to me. I know not in whom I believe," and she turned away.

Divining Harald's wish to speak with Persea, Olaf detained the father and son with remarks about the events of the day, ever toying with the sharp-edged weapon in his hand. At last he saw that Ingiborg and her attendants had withdrawn into the royal enclosure. Then he bade them farewell, and began mingling, unattended, with the groups which were scattered about, strengthening everywhere the people's allegiance to him by his graciousness and willingness to comply with their requests.

When the sun began to grow red he turned towards the gorgeous tent of pell and brocade, beneath which he would find the women of his household, leaving a spirit of rest and relief upon the bonder's faces. They believed they had conquered him completely. Solemnly they laid aside their weapons, and made ready for the great sacrifice and feast on the morrow.

CHAPTER XIV

"I WILL NOT PROMISE"

WHEN Olaf left Persea and Ingiborg, the latter realized that it was best for them to retire into the privacy of their tent. She had seen all that Olaf had seen in Persea's face; and she had, like Persea, trembled at the sudden change in the King's countenance when jealousy leaped at his throat. The girl must be led out of his sight, lest harm should come to her.

Once within the tent, Ingiborg sat down upon the fur-covered couch and drew Persea towards her. The Roman maiden, quivering with the fierceness of the last glance that Olaf had given her, sank upon the floor and buried her head in the soft furs. Ingiborg stroked the dark hair tenderly as she said:

"Tremble not so. We are alone. No one can harm thee."

From the furs the beautiful face was slowly lifted. There was anguish written across the white forehead; and there was a dull pain in the great eyes. Quietly she rose, and turned away, saying:

"I will pray for strength and help. Then I shall not tremble."

She disappeared. Ingiborg leaned her head upon her hand and waited for her return. Ten, twenty minutes went by before the curtain was lifted and Persea reëntered. Ingiborg glanced up, and breathed a deep breath as she looked upon her. All anguish was gone from the white forehead; all pain had left the great eyes. Where Ingiborg had seen weakness, there was now strength; where she had seen sorrow, there was now the soft light of wonderful joy and peace. She gazed at the smiling face turned towards her; and she knew that Persea had indeed been talking to God. But she, too, prayed to Christ; yet never to her came such a spirit blessing. Why not? Oh! why not?

With a woman's heart-cry of longing, she sprang to her feet and held out beseeching hands to Persea.

"Tell me whence comes that comfort which Christ has sent thee. Tell me, teach me how to pray to him, so that I, too, may know the peace that shines in thy face! Ever since thou hast been with me my soul has longed for something, I know not what, that was in thee; something which would satisfy my heart-yearnings, — the cravings of my inner soul. It is in thy face now. It has taken away thy trouble and thy fear. Teach me thy prayer. Lead me to love the Christ as thou lovest him, that I may receive his blessing."

Swiftly the Roman girl glided forward and folded the King's sister in her arms. Then she led her to the couch, and they knelt in prayer together. When they arose, the soul-light was shining in Ingiborg's blue eyes. She had found Persea's Christ.

Just then a summons came for Persea, who was wanted without by her brother. Ingiborg smiled upon her, and said softly :

"Go, my sister. Leave me with my new-found joy."

Hardly had Persea left the tent when Olaf strode into Ingiborg's presence. He found her reclining on the fur-covered couch.

"Where is Persea ? " he said shortly.

"She has gone forth to speak with her brother."

The King almost snorted in his ill-temper as he turned upon her and demanded :

"Why didst thou allow her to go ? I wish to speak with her myself."

Ingiborg looked up at him. Vaguely he felt that there was something different about her. She had not the expression he expected to see. She was calm, though tearful. She replied gently :

"My brother, how could I know thy wishes when thou wert absent ? Besides, wouldst thou refuse to let her see her brother ? He has powerful friends ; and I do not think that thou dost wish to offend them. I am sorry she is not here ; but I have only done what was right."

Olaf did not answer immediately. He had come in, steeled against a torrent of tears and bitter reproaches because of his public insult that morning ; for Norse women were proud, and Olaf knew that he had wounded deeply. He had determined to hear no woman's complaints. He had told Ingiborg to

dress Persea in royal robes; and she had not done so.   His
wishes must be obeyed.   He intended to take no excuses; but
he was hearing none.   His sister was calm and uncomplaining.
" After all," he thought, " she is no fool."   Finally he said:
   " Very well.   But I wish to tell thee again that Persea must
be persuaded to wear something besides that coarse raiment.
See that she does, else worse things will happen than have hap-
pened.   At the feast I soon give, she sits at my right hand.
Thou must see that she brings me the night-drink."
   Ingiborg arose with royal dignity.
   " My brother, does the girl know the meaning of this as I
know it, — knowing thy love for her ? "
   Olaf laughed shortly.
   "Am I a fool, to fling away that which I most desire ?
She knows nothing."
   " Then dost thou do her a cruel wrong to lead her into so
great a danger without her knowledge.   Suppose that Persea
refuses even to sit with thee at thy feast ? "
   " She will not do that, because she will not realize her true
position until the feast has begun."   He turned fiercely upon
her.   "And thou shalt see that she knows not, else I will ban-
ish thee from my court forever."
   Ingiborg grew white, but she did not reply.   Olaf looked at
her, and said sternly, commandingly :
   " Promise me thou wilt not tell her."
   The Norsewoman trembled from head to foot at those
words, spoken in that tone.   She knew the danger of refusal ;
yet she answered firmly :
   " Olaf, what is this thou art asking of me ?   Where is thy
Norse honour ?   This is a pure maiden.   Pure, said I ?   Nay,
there must be some other word, some stronger language that
would describe her purity.   Thou sayest thou art a Christian ;
but thou knowest not the Christianity that this girl knows ;
else thou wouldst not plan so evil a deed.   Nay, speak not.   I
know thou wilt say that it is a Norse custom ; but 't is not like
thee to ask such a one as she to keep these customs with thee.
Thou knowest in thy heart that thou seekest to entrap her ;
and I tell thee that this is a great wrong.   To-day I have
heard strange things that I cannot yet understand ; but I love
Persea for what she is, and for what she has done for me.   I
know, too, that she will never be thy mistress or thy wife.

Thou hast asked me to help thee to lead her into a dreadful snare. I tell thee now, I will not."

Olaf caught her roughly by the arm.

"Darest thou say this, — and to me?"

Straight into his eyes looked Ingiborg as she answered fearlessly:

"I am sorry to displease thee; but the deed is evil. I will not help thee," and she rose from the couch, facing him with something more than refusal in her face, "nor will I promise not to warn her of her danger."

Olaf's face grew purple; yet Ingiborg neither trembled nor shrank from him when he seized her by the arm. Her weakness had turned to a strength that was stronger than death. She leaned nearer to him as she said:

"I cannot deceive Persea."

With dreadful words, Olaf flung her upon the long couch. Rage so possessed him that he was a madman. Drawing his tolle-kniv, he held it over her heart, and hissed between set teeth:

"Dost thou see this? Promise."

"I cannot."

Lower sank the uplifted blade, wilder grew the fury in his face.

"Promise."

"I will not."

The deadly point now touched the blue brocade of her kirtle. His voice was absolutely merciless.

"For the last time I command thee. Promise."

Ingiborg lay calmly beneath his knife. She even raised her hand, and laid it lovingly, tenderly upon the clenched fingers that held death over her heart.

"My brother, I love thee. When this hand brings death, 't will still be dear to me. But I will not do this great wrong. I will not promise."

Olaf felt a second's thrill of wonder at her courage. Then his untamed nature broke forth anew; fury possessed him like a raging tempest, and raising the knife, he shouted hoarsely:

"Then die!"

At that instant, Astrid's hand parted the curtains. She saw the uplifted knife. With a shriek of terror she sprang towards the King:

"Olaf! Olaf! art thou mad?"

The cry startled him; and the knife dropped swiftly from his hand, sinking its long, sharp point deeply into Ingiborg's shoulder. Red gushed from the wound; and she lay as dead. Astrid knelt beside the couch, and withdrawing the knife, vainly tried to stay the rush of blood. She turned to Olaf.

"Quick! go for help. She will bleed to death!"

Olaf gave one glance at the white face, and at the crimson stream that was spreading over the couch and trickling to the floor. His mad rage left him. He sprang towards the entrance, only to meet Persea. She saw at once that something was wrong. She spoke to the King:

"What has happened? What ails the noble Ingiborg?"

He barred her nearer approach.

"She has been injured. Send Helga hither."

A moan came from the King's sister. With a low cry Persea burst past Olaf and knelt beside the couch. Persea tore the kerchief from her neck, twisted it above the wound, and soon stopped the terrible flow of blood. Then she asked for sundry cloths and ointments and ere long the wound was safely dressed.

Olaf had left the apartment; but shortly after Thorkel appeared, and stood silently on guard until Persea had finished. Then he saluted her respectfully, and said:

"Lady, it is the King's command to take thee to other quarters while the noble Ingiborg is ill. Come now with me."

Persea looked from Ingiborg to Astrid for a solution of this problem. Seeing her hesitate, Thorkel spoke again:

"Others have been appointed to attend the King's sister. Come."

Feeling a strange sense of unrest and impending peril, Persea bent over Ingiborg for a parting look. Slowly the blue eyes opened. The white lips moved; and Persea, leaning close, heard the faintly whispered words:

"I did it for thy sake and Christ's. Beware the King!"

She tried to say more; but no sound came from the moving lips. Persea was forced to leave her, feeling as though the only friend she had in that whole royal home was the weak woman upon the bloody couch.

Astrid had stood aside, and watched Persea's skillful fingers

with a growing hatred.   Even her sister preferred their touch
to hers.   This girl was turning all heads.   Her jealousy grew
fierce and cruel, eating out of her heart all womanly tenderness, all the natural instincts that save a woman from those
deeds of darkness and crime which brutal men may commit
rarely, but of which a woman cannot even think without first
becoming a devil incarnate.

To this accursed state Astrid was fast approaching.

CHAPTER XV

THE AUTUMN SACRIFICE

THE solemn ceremony of slaying the animals offered in sacrifice was just ended. In the great temple, with its dark panelled walls and gorgeous furnishings, the people stood with worshipful silence as the Temple Priest drew the long knife from the neck of the last victim, and held the hlaut-bolli to catch the streaming blood.

The altars of the gods were piled high with offerings, especially that of the great Thor, who sat in his magnificent chariot, all ablaze with gold and precious stones, looking out over the heads of the people with his never-ending stare.

Next would come the dipping of the hlaut-tein into the huge copper bowl; and the reddening of the temple, idols, and people with the sacred blood. For this they were expectantly waiting.

Iron Beard bent low over the hlaut-bolli, and eagerly scanned its contents. Suddenly he lifted it high above his head, and turned and faced the people. There was something dark and terrible in his face, — something that made him frightful to look upon as he stood before the altar in blood-stained robes, with upraised, giant arms down which red drops were trickling. Slowly, in an unnatural, hollow voice he spoke:

" Men of Thrandheim, the gods have not accepted our sacrifices. Beast after beast have I slain; and yet the hlaut-bolli will not fill with blood. The great Thor is offended; and by holding the red life in the veins, would tell us that our offering is too small to win his favour. Woe unto us! for our gods hide their faces from us. Woe unto us! that we have so mightily offended the Asar. They have heard too often the name of the White Christ; and they reject our sacrifices! Woe! Woe! Woe!"

The wild wail of despair was taken up by the startled multitude, and prolonged until the very rafters trembled with the fear.

Then Iron Beard's demeanour changed.   He placed the hlaut-bolli upon the altar, and lifted his hand to command silence.   When he spoke this time, his voice was bold and imperative.

"If the gods be so angry that our usual sacrifices please them not, then must we lay greater offerings at their feet. Long nights have passed since the sharp stone in the dom-ring has broken the back of man, woman, or child.   In time past, when the Asar smiled upon Norge, our fathers sent many thralls and captives to Odin in sacrifice.   But we have grown cold in our worship, and have given only the life of beasts.   Men of Thrandheim, the gods want richer blood to fill the sacred bowl.   Give me a human sacrifice to offer upon the stone!"

For a moment the people were dumb.   Then they caught the fever in his words.

"A human sacrifice!   A human sacrifice!"

The demon of blood, called from the depths of hell by the cruel words of their fanatical priest, took possession of them, soul and body.   They yelled, and struggled, and shouted, until that terrible cry, "A human sacrifice!" grew to such stupendous proportions that it rolled out of the temple in great waves of sound, farther and farther, until it reached the outer tents on the Thing-plain, — even the royal tents, where Persea, reclining on her low couch, started up and listened.

The cry grew hoarser and more imperative.   Iron Beard was only waiting for the victim.   Who would it be?   He scanned the multitude anxiously.   Many captives were held as thralls by the men before him ; but who would give a life to the Asar?   Through the excited multitude strode one of Olaf's warriors.   He held by the shoulder a swarthy Arab boy of about fifteen years.   When he reached the altar, he flung the boy at the feet of the blood-stained priest, crying out to the people :

"'T is for me to give the great offering to Thor.   The lad is unruly and disobedient, so take him.   Take the thrall Hassan to be broken upon the rock.   Out to the dom-ring to sacrifice to the Almighty Asar!"

The feelings of priest and people burst all bounds as they beheld a member of the King's following leading in the most extreme rite of their religion. They were now like a half-frenzied pack of wolves, scenting blood in the air. They took up those last words, " Out to the dom-ring ! Out to the dom-ring !" and surged forth upon the Thing-plain, carrying in their midst the Temple Priest and the dark-skinned boy. At the ring of great rocks that guarded the sacrificial stone the people paused, and made way for the passage of Iron Beard and his victim.

The boy held his head proudly erect. He remembered that he was a sheik's son ; and he did not flinch or cower as he looked into the pitiless faces around him. There was even a flash of something like scorn as he met, last of all, the cruel scrutiny of his master.

Now merciless hands bound him. Another moment, — then the stone and death. Only one moment to breathe God's air, to gaze upon his beautiful world, to rejoice in the joy of life, so precious to youth. The faces about him were so dark and inhuman that he looked beyond them, — out, upward, into the infinitude of sky above. Was the arching heaven, with its gorgeous tints of orange, saffron, and rose pulsating in great sobs of sympathy for him ? He felt that he could see the bosom of heaven heave with compassion, as the declining sun threw out wide, flaming banners of red, tinging all things with the colour of passion and riot — a fiery background, against which the sacrificial stone stood sharply outlined, awaiting its baptism of blood.

Iron Beard's eyes looked like small apertures, through which could be seen the lurid glow of a volcano's seething furnace, as he lifted the slight body and gathered his gigantic strength to hurl it downwards, — but upon the dark rock stood Persea.

Dressed in her white garments, without jewel or ornament except the golden bands in her hair, beautiful, pure, and fearless, she appeared among those fierce men unheralded and alone ; even as the spirit of truth descends into the darkest depths of sin and ignorance.

Iron Beard's victim fell heavily to the ground ; and before the mystery and power of her presence, the howling, swaying mob grew strangely still, frozen with astonishment. Then she spoke ; and her clear, sweet voice, holding in its depths an indescribable tenderness and pathos, filled the passion-warped brains of those before her with new, unusual thoughts.

"What dark deed is this my brethren would do? Is not life sweet to all? Think every man within himself — would ye love and believe in your gods if ye, or one ye did love, wert bound for sacrifice? Can any God be good who glories in the destruction of the work of his own hands?

"Men of Norge, I have been told of Baldr the Good, and his death which brought upon the earth the Twilight of the Gods. During this Twilight ye have become cruel and bloodthirsty. Ye have forgotten that ye can be brave and yet merciful; strong, and yet not cruel. Ye believe that Baldr will yet arise; that darkness and doubt will depart. Ye believe that there shall be a new earth, purified from sin and sorrow; and that the God of innocence and purity shall reign; and all the good shall dwell in happiness forever. Think ye that the sacrifice of yonder lad will hasten this time? Nay, rather will all things on earth weep as they wept at Baldr's death; and the mist from their tears will dim the light of the approaching dawn."

Not a man or a woman moved. Under the magnetic influence of her voice, all else was momentarily forgotten. The people only wished to hear every word that dropped from her lips.

When she rushed impetuously from the tent, Persea thought only of saving life; but when she saw the silent sea of faces about her, when she looked upon the great, discoloured rocks and thought of the deeds of cruelty and ignorance they had witnessed for ages untold, then the air seemed filled with innumerable spirits of the sacrificed, floating past in sad procession and breathing a prayer to her to lift the dark curse from this temple of nature. A powerful, a divine inspiration seized her.

A glance upward, a prayer that flashed through heaven's gates like a shaft of lightning; and then, with Christlike tenderness and heart-yearning, she began to tell this wild and warlike people the sweet and wonderful Story of the Cross. Wisely she spoke and well, not naming the name of Christ; but speaking in simple, childlike words the message of love Christ brought to the earth.

Never before had the men of Norge heard the beautiful

story.   They listened in wonder as she spoke of God as One. Their hearts were unconsciously stirred with a new feeling when she proclaimed God as our Father, and told of his infinite love.   Then she spoke of the wickedness and sins of mankind, of their hatred and malice and strife, of their false-hood and crime; until many a dulled conscience stirred un-easily.   Still the silence was unbroken, save by her voice.

"If man has sinned so terribly against the goodness and love of the great All-Father, can atonement ever be made ? Not by us; for we are too poor, too weak.   We have no power, no wealth, no gift that could appease the God whose laws we have disobeyed.   What are your sacrifices to the One who owns the earth, sky and sea; who gave ye breath, and who appoints your death ?   Call God by whatsoever name ye will; still God must be good; and your cruel and bloody worship cannot be acceptable to him."

And yet the people listened, looking upon her with won-dering gaze and bated breath, spellbound by her beauty and the strange words she was speaking unto them.   At their feet, their human victim lay unnoticed.

On, on she carried them upon the wings of thought; showed them how the world had longed and striven for power and wealth; and how utterly power and wealth had failed to bring happiness into men's souls.   She spoke again of their efforts to make atonement for the sins committed in the struggle for earthly gain; and the utter unworthiness of any sacrifice that was within human power to offer to appease the wrath of God.   Thus she led on to the story of Christ's sacrifice   for   them.   Standing   where   so   many   unavailing sacrifices had been offered, she told of the birth, life, and death of the Son of God, — the One Great Sacrifice for all time and all people.   She proclaimed the doctrine of truth and love.   She   gave   them   the   heavenly   message,   " Peace   on earth, goodwill towards men."

"What think ye ?   Is it not easier to draw the sword and kill than to forgive ?   Ye love strength and power of endur-ance; and I ask ye all, 'Does it take more strength, more will to do battle with thine enemy than to endure his taunts ?' Nay, the man who bears pain, or goes forth to do battle, knows not the strength of the man who follows in the foot-steps of Christ.   In the name of the Great God who has

made atonement in his blood for your sins, in the name of all
love and pity, I plead for the life of this lad. Wet not your
hands in his innocent blood; for the Christ who gave himself
to be sacrificed for your sakes has commanded ye to love and
not to slay."

The moment she spoke the name of Christ, the spell of her
voice and presence was broken. A murmur arose; faces
grew dark; and the crowd surged forward. Iron Beard, maddened beyond measure at her daring interference with the
offering of the sacrifice he deemed would be mighty enough to
secure all favours from the gods, thundered out:

"The tale of the Cross! She speaks of the White Christ!
Down with the Christian who dares to name the hated name,
even upon our sacred stone! Let her die! Send her to
Odin!"

The revulsion of feeling that swept over the people, as they
realized the meaning of the words to which they had so
quietly listened, was swift and frightful. They howled and
shrieked with a fury that made Persea's bosom heave with
deep drawn breaths; though there was no fear in her dark
eyes.

The mob was closing in upon her; already Iron Beard's
hand had grasped her white robe, when, through the surging
crowd plunged a black horse, bearing a rider clad in golden-
linked armour. With impetuous onrush, he forced a pathway
to the dom-ring, and leaping upon the stone, caught Persea in
his arms. To the angry crowd he turned and shouted
hoarsely:

"Back! and be still!"

They obeyed. Was he not Harald Rognvaldson, their
idol? Older warriors were amongst them; but to none was
yielded such homage and obedience as to the Blest of the
Nornir. They would listen to him.

"Have ye warriors of Thrandheim grown weak and old
that ye clamour for the blood of women, — a maiden who
stands alone in your midst, like a lamb among a pack of
wolves? If ye thirst for blood, find it in the veins of warriors. Touch not a weak woman, a woman born under the
warm, southern skies; in whose eyes our wild, rough customs
must be strange and cruel. She has spoken well. She has
shown that great courage may dwell even in the heart of a

woman. Love we not courage? Has she not courage of which a warrior might boast? Shame on ye, to crave the blood of such a maiden."

An expression of approval was faintly heard, when Iron Beard's voice broke out with a sinister question:

"And thou, Harald Rognvaldson, thou who protectest the Christian, why hast thou not attended the Vetrarblót? Thy place has been vacant; thou hast offered no sacrifices; thou hast drunk no horns to Odin and Thor. Why hast thou neglected the sacred rites of the religion of thy fathers? Art *thou* a Christian?"

All nature, all life, seemed to listen breathlessly for that answer. It was as if the trees stopped swaying their branches, the long banners of red across the sky ceased to quiver, and the wind stood still. Not a sound from that great multitude; not a voice, save the still, small Voice that was whispering to the hearts of the people, "God is love!"

Harald stood erect, but silent. Every eye was fastened upon him. It was true. He had not attended the sacrifice. Why? His heart was beating so violently that Persea felt its great pulse. He looked towards the blood-stained priest, the crowd of humanity, and then down to the beautiful face upon his breast. It leaned closer to him. The dark eyes pleaded for the acknowledgment of the truth that she knew was in his heart, as she whispered: "Choose this day whom thou wilt serve."

Swiftly came the answer: strong with the strength of right, sure with the surety of truth:

"Hear, men of Thrandheim. I, Harald Rognvaldson, do renounce Odin, and Thor, and Frey, and do proclaim that I believe in Christ the White! Not the Christ the King would bring to Norge; but the Christ of love and light: the Christ who teaches us to be brave, yet not cruel; the Christ who loves the world, and would rule the world by love. I brought to Norge this maiden who has told of the Christ love. Is it the fulfillment of the spirit's prophecy at my birth? I know not; but out of the blackness and cruelty of the past a new day is springing. The son of love is rising over our fjelds and fjords; and she who has proved that Christians can be grand in spirit and deed is the Angel of the Dawn. Go your ways. Worship the old gods of war and blood until your hearts are weary of the unanswered prayers, and your hands shrink from the stain of bloody sacrifices. The time cometh, and cometh soon, when the true spirit of Christ love shall fill your hearts; and ye shall believe, even as I believe, in the One God of the Universe."

Upon the broad Thing-plain, truth and error were playing a desperate game. Having spoken for truth, Harald Rognvaldson stood grandly before his countrymen, holding the white-robed form close to his breast while he waited for that uncertain reply, — the verdict of a multitude, — which, since time began, has swept thousands of human souls into heaven or hell without a moment's respite.

Death stood ready to open the gates of eternity; but to Harald and Persea it was only an eternity of love.

The minds of the multitude were torn by conflicting emotions. What they had heard was so unexpected, so far-reaching in its effects, that even the tempest in the soul of the priest was stilled for the moment, and his powerful will delayed in its action.

Out of that moment's hush, from far back in the crowd, came a clear, bell-like voice:

"Let us honour to-day the courage of women. Let us honour the Valkyrias, the Glittering Maidens, by giving the lad to her who was brave enough to face the wrath of all Thrandheim to save him. Behold my beautiful steed, Hrafn the Raven. Ye know well how I love him. Ye know that there is none like him in all Norge. Many men would give gold rings without number to possess him. Think ye now, if ye must shed precious blood, is he not more precious to me, is he not more costly, more beautiful than yonder frail lad, puny and dark of skin, one whom the gods would spurn and spit upon? Take him, and fill the hlaut-bolli with his blood. He will satisfy the gods; and the Valkyrias will appear before you and shower success upon your vikings for the honour ye wilt do them. As for Harald, the Blest of the Nornir, let him walk in the path he has chosen, while we watch and wait."

At the first sound of that voice, Iron Beard started, looked, listened. The cold perspiration gathered on his forehead: a madness gleamed in his eyes. When the voice ceased, he gave one agonized shriek; and then, tearing through the crowd like an infuriated beast, he disappeared into the gloom of the forest.

The voice was the voice of Sigrid.

With him seemed to go the thirst for human blood that had so possessed the people. They looked upon that exquisitely beautiful couple before them, — the man, their idol, in all his perfect manhood and kingly attire, holding, as only a lover can, the strange, brave girl with her marvellous beauty, — and as they looked, the spirits of love and light found entrance into their rude minds. Not one but thought he saw all the reason for Harald's interference and conversion to Christianity; and they blamed him not. Such a prize was worth any cost.

Thus it was that sympathy with their idol's love, mingled with real admiration for his beloved, and the memory of her new, sweet story of a merciful God, surged mightily through their excited brains. From all sides rose the shout:

" Give over the boy! Honour the Valkyrias! Great is the courage of the Christ Maiden! Great is the courage of the Blest of the Nornir! "

The desperate game was ended; and truth and right had won. The bloodthirsty mob, which had rushed out of the temple with such violence and cruelty, now cut the thongs which bound their victim. Then they swept back to complete their religious rites, leaving their prey in the midst of the dom-ring, with Persea, Harald, and — the King.

Persea drew away from Harald, and stood between him and the King. Now there was fear in her eyes as she saw the overpowering hatred with which they glared at each other.

Olaf's mind was filled with every evil passion and thought. He had urged his warrior to offer the boy for sacrifice; but his diplomacy, his iron will, his influence, — all had been as naught before this man and this woman. To them the people had listened; and by them the people had been led. They had greater power than even he, the King of Norge. Olaf Tryggvveson, who had never known defeat, stood face to face with the two greatest disappointments of life, — an unsatisfied love, and a power that outpowered his. His hatred of Harald was so intense that he was only prevented from closing with him in a death struggle, by the presence of Persea; for the possession of whom his passions were driving him mad. He knew she was far from won yet; and he dared not, — he who had never known fear, — he dared not, lest he should offend her. Therefore he feigned indifference. Pointing to the lad, he said to Persea:

"The boy is thine. Take him with thee to thy bower; and know that the King would fain change places with him for the joy of being thy slave."

Persea hesitated; but she saw that her presence would only inflame the men still more. She gently touched the crouching figure; and with one glad look towards Harald, she turned, and followed by the lad, passed up through the rose-light into the shadow of the tent.

The men were now alone. The King, sullen and angry. Harald, glad with the gladness of truth; yet stern and determined for Persea's sake. He spoke first.

"Olaf Tryggvveson, the maiden who has moved all hearts to-day is lawfully thine; but thy possession of her is one of those tricks of fortune with which evil spirits plague the hearts of men. I have told thee, many times, why I wished to restore her to her brother; but thou hast ever evaded my anxious questioning. Now I desire a Norseman's word from thee as to thy intentions in this matter. I will wait no longer. Name what price thou wilt, what conditions that please thee; but name as thy part of the transaction, the freedom of this maiden."

The King bit his lip. This man to dare to command him! Did he think that Olaf was afraid to give a Norseman's word concerning the girl? With drawn brows, he replied:

"Harald Rognvaldson has asked for the price I put upon Persea, the Roman. Such beauty, such perfection has no price. Though the world be turned to gold, 't would not avail to purchase this marvel of womanhood. She came as a gift to me; and only as a gift will she ever go from me. That is her price. As for thy second demand, a Norseman's word, I will never yield her to any power, save death!"

Almost did Harald spring at King Olaf's throat. The two men faced each other with hands upon swords and muscles tense for the stroke. But the King did not wish to strike. His cause would be injured thereby. Besides, he had the girl; and 't was possible to restrain his fighting humour. Harald hesitated because other plans were in his mind, plans that bloodshed now would render useless. Gradually the men drew away from each other and let their hands slip from their sword handles; just as tigers withdraw, inch by inch, from the foe they do not wish to meet.

Harald broke the ominous silence.

"Thou didst speak most truly when thou didst say that Persea had no value in gold; but there is one thing that can purchase even one as perfect as she. It is love. I love her. I would seat her beside the high seat as my wife. I make one last appeal to thee in the name of my great love, which dared to think of happiness with the loved one long ere thou didst see her form. Grant her to me, for my love's sake."

The King laughed long and loud, laughed him to scorn, as he said:

"So! thou wouldst place her beside thee as thy wife. Hast thou asked the maiden if this would be pleasing to her?"

Harald was silent. He had not asked; but could he acknowledge it when he was so sure of his answer? Did he not remember how trustfully she had yielded to his embrace not an hour ago?

The King saw his hesitation, and said tauntingly:

"Ah! not sure. Then keep thine eyes open. Mayhap ere thou *art* sure, thou wilt see her beside the high seat of the King's skali. Is my riddle hard to read?"

With a mocking bow, the King turned to depart; but Harald stopped him with a quick, forcible gesture.

"Nay, go not. Harald Rognvaldson has not yet finished speech with thee. He will offer thee another law to settle this matter, namely; that for the possession of this maiden thou shalt strive with him in weapon-crossing or ordeal. All choice of time, place, and manner of strife is thine; but man to man shall this thing be decided."

The King laughed again, this time a deadly laugh. Then placing his hand on his sword in token of acceptance, he said scornfully:

"'T is less trouble to use skill and strength for a maiden than to win her by love-making. I will send my shield-bearer to thee with the time and place of meeting. Olaf Tryggvveson will give thee thy fill of strife, and then take his fill of something else."

He turned the second time, and strode rapidly away. Harald folded his arms and watched him as he disappeared from view. Then he drew a deep breath, and involuntarily looked upward. From somewhere far above, he felt he could draw the strength he needed for the future, strength to wait and win from the King the person of his love : strength to meet the condemnation that his confession of Christianity would bring upon his head. Yet, when he remembered the faces about him at the time of his acknowledgment of Christ, he could recall no great disapproval. He recognized the reason. It was Persea's Christ, not Olaf's, he had accepted.

He had also the memory of the look Persea had given him, — the glorious message he had received from her dark eyes. She loved him ! That look he had never seen before ; but he knew now why she had kept it hidden for so long.

His arms fell to his side, and he walked away in a reverie. Though Persea was a captive, and he knew the King's mind towards her ; though Olaf had muttered the direst threats ; though a momentous meeting with the most renowned athlete of Norge awaited him ; yet his heart sang and leaped for joy, and his soul was thrilled with the melody of God's peace.

He feared nothing, he knew no sorrow since Christ and Persea were his. Christ and Persea ! Christ would strengthen his arm, and give him all quickness and skill to win in any conflict. And Persea, if he could but see her alone, would listen to all the burning words that had been trembling on his lips so long. Now that he had challenged the King for her sake, he need let no false sense of honour deprive him of that great joy.

CHAPTER XVI

THE ANGEL OF THE DAWN

It was late. The moon was reigning over Old Norway; but in the farthest tent, Hassan still crouched at Persea's feet. In vain had she offered him a seat beside her. He would not move, except to touch his lips to the folds of her dress. After a long interval, he gained courage to look up. Then Persea saw that the swarthy Arabic features, wise with a wisdom beyond his boyish years, were glowing with an unspeakable adoration that moved her deeply.

The curtain at the entrance parted, and Thorkel appeared.

"Thy request, lady, is granted. The boy sleeps in the outer tent."

Persea thanked him sweetly, and dismissed the lad. He once more touched her dress with his lips, then rose and passed beyond the curtain. As soon as he found himself alone, he swiftly explored every nook and corner. Upon the walls hung several shields and various weapons. Choosing a long, keen-bladed knife, he concealed it in his bosom. Then, ignoring the couch of skins upon which he was supposed to spend the night, he lay down on the rushes before the heavy curtains that guarded Persea's apartment, murmuring to himself: "My beautiful One, my Moon of the Desert, is shadowed by an evil eye in this dark land; but Hassan sleeps ever at the fold of her tent. While he lives, no harm shall befall her."

Left alone, Persea was soon lost in thought. The memories of that day just past! Ingiborg's strange warning, the fierce mob, the blood-stained priest, those moments of peril, and — Harald!

She buried her face in the velvet cushions to hide from even the tiny ancient lamp the rich flush that rose to her cheeks. Still could she feel those strong arms about her. Still could she feel that breath upon her cheek, that great heart beating so near her own. Still could she hear those words that saved her from death, and told her that he was a Christian.

Then upon her dreamy consciousness there broke a vision of

the King; and she remembered where and what she was. The warm flush died away from her neck and face. Wearily she rose to prepare for sleep. As she was about to lay aside her outer garment, she noticed a dark stain upon it. She looked closely, and behold! a bloody hand outlined with startling distinctness upon its pure white. It was the imprint of the Temple Priest's murderous grasp. She shivered with an undefinable fear. The air seemed heavy and oppressive; and she suddenly felt an overwhelming desire to slip out into the still night, and cool her throbbing pulses in the breath of the pines. Throwing a dark cloak about her, she parted the curtains, and discovered Hassan on guard.

He was awake and alert in an instant; and she told him what she wanted to do.

"Wait," he said quickly. Then slipping to the outer entrance, he made a cautious survey. "All is quiet," he whispered. "The people are at the feast. Go, my Beautiful One."

Persea passed out. Hassan, waiting until she was within the shadow of the trees followed, with his hand on the hilt of the knife in his bosom.

Drawn by some impulse she could not analyze, Persea stole on along the edge of the forest until she came opposite to the dom-ring. How quiet, how peaceful, it looked now in the moonlight! There was no trace of the whirlwind of human passion that had so lately swept over it. The great rocks stood guarding nature's shrine for nature's God, little heeding what the name of that God might be. How beautiful the night was! though cold winds blew from the Fjord. The sky was so clear, the stars so countless, the air so pure! It was strange to be alone in this weird place. Alone? No! What was that in the shadow of the sacred stone? A man was kneeling there!

Her first impulse was to fly; but it was conquered by the sense of security in her perfect concealment. Then she crept nearer, until through the intervening space came the sounds of prayer. And the voice was Harald's; and he was praying to her Christ.

With beating heart, and great eyes brilliant even in the deep shadow, Persea listened to that prayer.

"Christ God, I love and worship thee, wherever thou

art, whoever thou art. Long has thy truth been knocking
at the door of my heart; and to-day, when I did open to thee,
such wonderful peace and gladness filled my soul that life itself
was naught but a glittering bauble compared with the joyful
consciousness of being thy follower. I have seen thy spirit
conquer the power of Odin. I have known the strength
thou givest to thy people; and I have come here to pray for
more of thy spirit, more of thy love. Receive me, O Christ.
Teach me thy ways. Help me to lift my people from their
unbelief. Help me to show them thy infinite love, that they
too, may love and follow thee."

The prayer ended, Harald bowed his head in his hands.
The hour, the place, the prayer, were so solemn and so fraught
with mighty thoughts that material things receded from his
mind. Peace entered his soul; and the spirits of the upper
world unrolled the scroll of the future before him. Surely the
Sun of Love was rising upon his native land; and who had
given them the first glimpse of the coming dawn? Persea.

At her name, the hunger in his heart forced him back to
earth and reality. Through his brain surged the word,
Persea! Persea! Persea! until it seemed to him that all
nature must hear the mighty tumult in his heart, and echo it
out past where the stars were drifting. He sprang to his feet
with a passionate cry of love and longing; and lo! Persea
stood before him.

She had stolen from her place of concealment to add her
prayers to his; but she shrank timidly back when she saw the
immense flame of earthly love burning in his eyes.

His mind questioned not the reason of her sudden appearance, — God had sent her to him, — and holding out his arms
towards her with yearning tenderness, he said in a voice that
quivered with unfathomable love:

"Persea, Angel of the Dawn, thou knowest how I love
thee. Come."

She trembled, swayed a moment. Then the long cloak was
cast aside; and she sprang to love's first embrace — so long, so
close, so warm with pent-up feeling. Harald covered her face,
her neck, her arms, with kisses; and drank in the fragrance of
her being until he was intoxicated with ecstasy. He called
her by every term of endearment he knew; he held her off at
arm's length and gazed upon her exquisite beauty with a

lover's delight; only to draw her into a closer, warmer clasp than before, until Persea whispered:

"Nay, nay, my Harald. Thou hast had my lips enough for this night. Hast thy love made thee mad?"

"Yea, and so will I ever remain. Since the night when I first saw thee upon the shores of Italy I have been mad because of thee, mad for love of thee. My lips were starving for the touch of thine; my arms were aching with longing to hold thee; my soul was consumed with the flame of desire for thee; and behold! I cried out through the night unto thee, and thou didst answer and come to me, — even as deep answereth to deep."

A long silence, love's silence, during which the very trees seemed to sway towards them with whispered blessings. Hassan, crouching behind the bushes, murmured to himself: "My Moon of the Desert has given her heart to him of the bright armour. The King will not be pleased. Hassan must watch, and remember always the great secret of the skali. The hour may come when he, too, can save life, — even the life of his Beautiful One."

Harald, releasing Persea for a moment, lifted her cloak and wrapped it about her, saying:

"The joy of caring for thee is mine at last. When I knew thee only as a captive to the King, I looked with jealous eyes on the very thralls who served in the skemma. Now, all privileges belong to me."

"But I am still a captive," Persea said fearfully. "Art thou certain the King will give me to thee in marriage?"

"Give thee to me? No! But I shall take thee. Listen. To-day, after thou didst leave us, I asked him for thee. He laughed, and taunted me; and I challenged him to weapon-crossing or ordeal. Nay, my sweet one, tremble not. It was the only thing left for a true Norseman to do. My cause is just and right; and with Christ as my God, all shall go well. Fear not. I shall win. Then, Persea, Angel of the Dawn, thou shalt be mine in truth. Mine for life, mine for eternity. Mine, mine alone!"

Out from the deep sapphire blue of the northern sky shone two stars. As Persea lifted her beautiful face towards Harald, one flashed strong and white, — one faded and flickered, as if a whirlwind from the borderland of eternity had passed over it.

CHAPTER XVII

THE WISE WOMAN'S CAVE

OVERHEAD stretched the same sapphire sky, lit with stars and the round white moon. Deep shadows lingered on rocks, and crags, and dark forest; into the gloom the moon was sending arrow-shafts of light vainly trying to touch the figure of a man who was striding on amid the shifting, silvery darts.

Higher and higher up the steep slope he climbed, until he reached a towering wall of grey rock overgrown with underbrush and tangled masses of leafless vines. Up this he scrambled with the skill and agility of a cat, suddenly disappearing, as if the frowning wall had engulfed him.

Heid, bending over her simmering kettle of herbs and crooning low to herself, heard the footsteps in the outer cave. She turned, and the Temple Priest stood before her.

"Welcome, Temple Godi of Thrandheim, to the hole of the Wise Woman. Drink."

She handed him a golden-tipped horn filled with mead from a bowl beside her. He drained it.

"Skal! Mother."

His eyes were dull and heavy. An overpowering weariness settled upon his huge frame as he sat down on a pile of skins, and dropped his head in his hands. He had left the Vetrar-blót, and come to clear his brain and gather his scattered plans together in the Volva's cave.

Without paying any further attention to her guest, the old woman continued her low crooning; but it gradually became a chant of woe.

"Thy sacrifice was offered not. On the altar of the gods the bowl still stands unfilled. Thor received not the blood; and a maiden, beautiful and strange, turned all hearts from thee and thy altars!"

Iron Beard sprang up.

"Yea, and how I hate her! Hate her because she is a Christian. Hate her because she is so beautiful that men bowed before her as the tree bends before the storm. Hate her because she has, by her dark tricks, won the heart and mind of our noblest leader in Norge. Hate her because she stopped the sacrifice which would have made the gods smile upon us once more. Hate her because she told of the White Christ in a way that my people have never heard before. Hate her because young and old cease not to speak of her. Hate her because she will do more harm to Odin and Thor than a hundred Olafs. Hate her because even my Sigrid, the Light of my Life, was won to her side. But she shall not live! By the sacred altar ring, I vow to offer her to the Asar, to break her white bones upon the rock, pour out her blood upon the altars, and give her dainty body to the Well of Sacrifices! So help me, Odin, and Thor, and Frey!"

He sank down, exhausted by his passion. Heid hobbled to his side, and waving her hands over his head, chanted a low, weird song. Gradually the purple left his face, the distorted features straightened, and under the influence of her piercing eyes and waving hands his lids slowly closed, his muscles relaxed, and he lay motionless. Still backward and forward over his head moved Heid's hands, while she murmured in soothing pity:

"Go! wild, grand spirit of the Northland. Go! roam amid the upper world, and forget the doom that is sweeping down upon thee and me, even as the dark storm-cloud sweeps down upon the sea-king's home and crushes the steed of the breeze."

Hardly had she returned to the fireside when she was startled by the faint, far-off echo of footsteps. She stooped and put her ear to the ground. Then she rose, and swiftly covering Iron Beard's form with a large skin, crept to one side and pulled back a curtain that hung before what seemed to be an extension of the cave. Clearer came the footfalls now. A light tread, yet echoing well within the hollow recesses of the underground caverns.

"'T is a stranger's step," muttered Heid. "Some one has discovered the pathway from the Fjord. 'T is a woman, a proud, cold woman. Ah! Heid is wise, very wise."

Quickly she stole back to her task, and did not even turn when a closely wrapped figure flung the curtain aside and entered the cave.

"Mother."

The voice was haughty, imperative. The old woman kept
on stirring the contents of her bowl, as she answered in slow,
solemn tones :

"And why does the sister of the Christian King visit the
Volva's cave? She must have treachery in her heart, either
towards the Wise Woman or the White Christ. Thou canst
not serve two gods."

Astrid cast aside her cloak with no trace of surprise at the
discovery of her identity.

"Prate not to me of any gods. I serve only myself; and
I have come to thee because I believe that thou canst help me
serve myself. Have no fear, only do that which I ask."

The old woman eyed her steadily, curiously.

"And what can Heid do for the most beautiful woman in
Norge?"

Astrid turned and said feverishly :

"Tell me first, do the people truly call me the most beautiful woman in Norge?   Do they call me that *now?*"

"And why should they not call thee that?   Is it not so?"

"Yea, but——" then she suddenly changed her tone and
manner. "Mother, dost thou not think that I am beautiful
enough to win any man's love?   Look upon me, and say if
there could be on this earth even one man who could see and
not love Astrid the Peerless?"

A clearer light played in the little eyes of the Wise Woman
as she replied :

"So, thou hast come to the Volva for a love potion."

"Nay," and the tones were fierce and cruel. "I have
come for a death potion!   Give me that which will put her
to sleep, and I will fill thy lap with gold."

The old woman moved to Astrid's side. Her fingers opened
and closed convulsively as she looked up into her face with a
keen, piercing gaze that seemed to read the secrets of her
mind.

"The sister of Olaf comes to Heid for a death potion!   I
can give it thee; but not for gold, not for gold!   The death
powder goes only to those who will receive the Sign.   Will
Astrid the Peerless pay the price?"

Quick came the reply.

"The Sign?   The price?   What meanest thou?   Speak;
and yet, before thou speakest, I will tell thee that so thou

leavest me my beauty and my life, I will receive thy Sign: I will pay thy price."

Heid chuckled exultantly to herself. Then she hobbled over to an old carved chest, and took from it a small iron charm. This she placed in Astrid's hand, saying:

" See! The Sign of Heid! It must be burned upon the flesh over thy heart."

Astrid started, and drew back; but almost instantly she recovered from her surprise, and receiving the piece of metal in her open palm, she closely examined it.

" 'T is covered with strange runes that I cannot read. What mean they, Mother?"

The old woman laughed, and muttered a few words under her breath.

" Runes like these are only for the Wise Ones to read. Thou beholdest the language of the Volvas, given to them at the beginning. The meaning is not for thee to know. 'T is Heid's Sign, and thou must receive it, or go thence empty-handed. Thou hast asked for a cruel gift; thou must pay a cruel price. Speak with thyself, and know surely whether thou art willing to pay. As for me, I have ended. The words of the Wise Woman are all spoken."

The crooked form turned again to its place by the fireside, leaving the King's sister alone in the centre of the cave.

Beautiful was she as she stood there. Beautiful, wonderfully beautiful with her perfect form and queenly head, with her long, fair hair that glinted in the firelight like spun gold, with her dark, rich robes and shimmering jewels that covered neck and arms, and gleamed from golden chains that fell almost to her feet. The gloomy cave was only a weird, uncanny setting for so fair a gem. Every deep shadow, every overhanging rock only lent their fantastic mystery to make more beautiful the one who stood in their midst. She was so still, so motionless, that it would seem as if the evil ones of the cave had bound her with invisible chains.

The winds were moaning through the far-off windings of the caverns. Faintly the echo of their wailings reached the abode of the Wise Woman. Were they chanting the requiem of the soul that was dying, the soul that was being swept into outer darkness by the fierce onslaughts of jealousy and hatred?

For, within Astrid's mind, a mighty tumult was raging, — the last great conflict between good and evil.   Her strong will and passions swept her from the heights to the depths in great waves of feeling; until her breath came in short, quick gasps, and her white forehead was damp with cold perspiration. Persea's face rose before her with all its loving sweetness; and its dark, tear-dimmed eyes pleaded for the joy of life and love. Life?   Yea, she might be willing to give her that — but love?

Out of the pealing thunder of the internal storm came a bolt of lightning.   It flashed across her vision with a white brilliancy, blinding her.   It passed, and behold! lying in its pathway were the scorched and blasted remnants of all that was good and pure in the soul of Astrid the Peerless.

Far off in the heart of the mountain, the moaning requiem died in an agonizing shriek.

The sister of the King glided to the fireside.   Heid, looking up from her simmering kettle, saw a white breast bared to the red light, and heard one word:

" Burn ! "

*   *   *   *   *   *

The old woman stood at the curtained opening, and listened while the echo of retreating footsteps grew less and less. Finally they ceased.   A wild exultation possessed her, making her tremble like an aspen leaf.   Dropping the curtain, she raised her hands and gave a sharp, wolfish scream of triumph that called Iron Beard back from the Spirit Land.   He threw off the heavy skin and sprang to his feet.

But Heid saw him not.   Rushing to the old chest, she took out a small package and threw it upon the fire.   At once the cave was lit with a ghastly greenish glare; and in this weird light, the old woman began to dance with strange, fantastic measures.   Round and round the fire she went, swaying her bent body and tossing her withered arms to the rhythm of the wild chant she was singing.

Iron Beard drew back into a far recess, hardly daring to breathe in the uncanny atmosphere which seemed to be peopled with forms and voices from the world of darkness.   Wilder and wilder grew the dance, louder and more triumphant grew the chant.

" The curse has gone forth,
   Forth into the house of Olaf Tryggvveson.
   False has he been to the Gods of Norge,
   And the Spirits of luck and victory will be false to him.
   He came to his kingdom,
   He ruled in might,
   He would cast down the image of Thor.
   But he was cursed !
   Cursed by the last of the Volvas ;
   And the curse has gone forth.
   It is burned upon the flesh !
   Burned over the heart of Astrid the Peerless
   There lies the curse of Heid.
   It will fall upon her,
   It will fall upon the King.
   Evil will come to Astrid,
   Evil and sorrow to Olaf Tryggvveson.
   Treacherous has he been,
   By treachery shall he die ! "

Then the shrill tones sank lower, and the dance grew slow
and solemn.

" The eye of jealousy is cruel.
   It looked upon the foreign maiden.
   Behold she was beautiful !
   Behold she was loved !
   And Astrid the Peerless was passed by !
   Then to the Volva came the jealous one.
   She asked for death.
   But 't is not for her to give the death-drink.
   The Christ Maiden belongs to Odin,
   Upon the stone must she be broken.
   The oath of the Temple Priest shall be kept.
   The powder is white,
   The powder is strong :
   But the Christ Maiden shall not drink.
   The Christ Maiden shall live :
   Live till the time of the Gods be fulfilled.
   'T is Astrid shall die !
   'T is Olaf shall die !
   Then Heid's work is done.
   She will follow Snotra :
   Across the Bridge of Asar will she go
   Into the world of Spirits."

The old woman sank into a heap on the floor. The light
died away, and the cave grew suddenly, profoundly still.

Iron Beard felt his way out of the inky blackness into the
starlit night. And the hills tell no tales.

CHAPTER XVIII

"I LOVE SIGRID"

THE northern sky was one broad flush of violet, shading off into pink lilac overhead. There it met the bands of crimson, yellow, and fiery orange which heralded the setting of the autumn sun. Tellus and Harald stood together on the top of the hill back of their home, watching the gorgeous banners that were thrown across the sky.

Tellus filled his lungs with the invigorating freshness of the evening breeze, saying:

"What a wonderful part nature plays in thy strange climate! In the Southland we have the beautiful tints in the flowers and the sweeping foliage; but here thou hast them all in a grand burst of glory across the sky. And what a subtile power lurks in thy very air! As it blows against my face, it fills me with all strength and joy of life. It awakens, too, a spirit of resistance; and no matter how it might sweep around me, I believe the human would rise to meet its force with equal energy."

Harald smiled.

"Wait, my brother, until thou hast spent an hour on our wild fjelds in a winter's storm. If thy spirit canst meet its strength, then thou art more than human. Thou hast yet to know Norge when the sun rises, only to sink back appalled at the desolation of snow and ice which stretches northward under the rule of the Storm King. See! It rises further south every day; and soon the long winter nights will be upon us. Then, only for six hours will the sun peep above the southern horizon. The ice-rivers creep slowly downward; those lofty mountain peaks lengthen their white robes until their grey sides are visible no longer; the wild winds roar and shout as they rush through the pines and swoop down upon our homes as if jealous of our shelter. The children of the Northland have gathered into their natures much of its weirdness, strength, and beauty. Think you not so, my brother?"

"Yea, the spirit of thy people, — thy men and thy women, — makes me to look and wonder and love."

There was something that thrilled in the tone of the last word, something which made Harald turn quickly towards Tellus with a question in his eyes. Tellus saw the look, and laying his hand upon his friend's shoulder, said :

" 'T is a fitting time, amid the beauty of the long twilight, to tell thee of the melody that is in my soul. Harald, one of thy strange, wonderful spirits has captured the heart of thy Standard-bearer."

Harald seized his hand in a grasp that threatened to crush the bone.

" My brother ! Who ? "

A pause, then the low, quiet reply :

" Sigrid, the daughter of the Temple Priest of Thrandheim."

There was a startled exclamation from Harald, followed by a long, impressive silence. Finally the Norseman spoke :

" I was glad when thou didst first speak; but thou hast dared much, and I know not what to say to thee. Sigrid ! It is astounding ! Tell me, is thy love returned ? "

" That I know not for a certainty ; though my heart is full of hope. Thou knowest how many times we have drawn rein in front of Iron Beard's skali ; and while ye wert talking of law matters and the King, my heart has found its resting place. Never has the opportunity come to me to speak openly of love to her; for she trembles like a flower before a tempest when I do but approach the subject. I love her too well not to know why she trembles. I believe that she loves me ; but in secret and in fear; for I am a Christian. Thou knowest her father; therefore thou knowest why her love is as still as death. The future looks dark ; but God is good. I believe that he will some day open the gates of love ; and I shall enter and be infinitely satisfied."

The two stood silently side by side, looking far off to the northern horizon ; each thinking his own thoughts, but feeling instinctively the sympathetic chord which bound him to the friend beside him. Tellus was the first to speak.

" But I did not bring thee out here to tell thee my secret. I want to speak of Persea. What if thou dost lose in thy trial with the King ? My sister will not, shall not be forced into an alliance against her will."

Harald struck his brow with his hand and said hoarsely :

"Say it not! Spare me even the hearing of those words. But I have planned all long ago. Behind the bend of the Fjord lies my fleetest steed of the breeze. It is ready for a long voyage; and during the King's feast days, it will be manned by my bravest warriors. If aught should happen to me, they have been told to obey thee. A small boat waits under the lee of the rocks. Dost thou need to know more?"

"Nay, I understand. Thou hast done well. I will take her and fly."

There was a sadness in his voice that Harald recognized and understood. He answered immediately:

"As for thy Sigrid, thou hadst better soon discover whether she loves thee; and if so, tell her all. If thou art forced to leave this land, take her with thee; for thou canst never return. Thou wouldst be killed the moment thou didst set foot on the shores of Norge. By the King, because thou didst carry off his prize; or by my father, because according to Norge's laws, thou hadst stained the honour of his name."

Tellus hesitated a moment. Then he said:

"'T is the only thing to do. If thou dost lose, may God guide us safely through the darkness that shall fall upon us. To him only can we look for help."

There was a solemn silence between them for many moments. Afterwards Harald spoke:

"Our lives are indeed without present joy; but to Christ all things are possible. Yea, the darker the night, the brighter is the light we carry. How wonderful it is! This love and dependence upon Christ. Never would I have believed that a God could make his presence so surely known to the human heart. Be calm and hopeful, even as I am; for God will give us those we love, if we only believe and trust him."

Tellus' face kindled with joy as he replied:

"And art thou sure, Harald, that thou art repaid for having announced thy acceptance of Christianity? Is it worth thy mother's tears, thy father's haughty anger, and the fierce condemnation of Iron Beard? Thou hast paid no poor price for thy conscience's sake."

Harald answered in that quiet, eternally satisfied tone that only the Christian uses, — the Christian who knows he has chosen the better part.

"I have suffered and endured much; but I am not sorry.

As for my mother, she has shed tears more because of the estrangement between my father and myself, than because of my acceptance of Christianity. Thou knowest that our beautiful story of Christ's love for humanity appeals directly to a woman's heart; and my mother has already felt its subtile influence. The day is not far hence when she will believe. My father and Iron Beard will fight to the bitter end. But they have not realized that they cannot wipe out the thoughts in the hearts of the people, even though they drive Olaf Tryggvveson from our shores. The spirit of Christ has spread its wings over the fjelds and fjords of Norge; and the King may come or go, but Christ will stay.

"Already have I seen evidence of change in the thoughts of the people. Many point the finger of scorn at Harald Rognvaldson and say, 'He has forsaken his country's gods,' but they are those who were ever jealous of my following, wealth, and success in vikings. Others have come to ask questions about this new God; and they have listened attentively, earnestly to what I spake to them. The Thrandheim is torn with conflicting emotions. Feeling is running high among the people; and the outcome is momentous.

"Iron Beard and his following can never be won to accept Christianity. They will resist until the life-blood flows out. The King has some adherents who believe him to be rich and powerful enough to win his way, and who wish to be on the winning side. But, scattered here and there, are those who would fain believe the story which Persea told at the Autumn Sacrifice.

"Hitherto the people have met the religion of Christ with a maddened resistance which left them no time to know the purity and beauty which lay underneath the false exterior that they hated and opposed. Of a surety 't will be a long time ere the bonder worship Christ in spirit and truth; for none there are to teach them the way save Persea and thee and me. But I do believe that the time of the downfall of the ancient gods is at hand; and that the people will eventually accept the Christianity Olaf offers. Then, if God spares us, 't will be our duty to teach them what they have done, to hold up Christ's banner before them until they recognize their God by something more than rites and ceremonies and a new name. I have not lost my Norse spirit of conquering; but now 't is the hearts of my people that I wish to capture. The Christianity that my Persea has taught me has not unnerved my arm nor weakened my strength. This will I show the men of Thrandheim when I meet the King ; and after I have conquered him they will believe more than ever in me, and consequently more than ever in Christ.

"Olaf was filled with an evil cruelty when he did place this meeting upon the last feast day, making it a spectacle for the amusement of the people. Of a certainty he expects to win ; and his hatred of me has led him to do all that he can to add to his triumph and my humiliation. Then, too, he is afraid of my influence among the bonder, and he would harm me there as well. Seest thou not the many reasons he has for putting off the meeting so long, and giving it such an air of mystery by refusing to say in what way he will measure strength with me ? I would have ended the matter at once ; but as he was the challenged one, to him came the choice of place and time and manner of test. But if to him the victory will be so far-reaching in its effects, will it not also be so to me ? Of that the King thinks not."

"And why does he not, at least, consider defeat ? " said Tellus. "Who is this man that he judges himself so invincible ? I have seen thee with a sword, and it is more than a plaything in thy hands, — neither do men care to meet thee in any combat of strength or skill. How then, does this Olaf dare to boast so surely of victory ? Is he a god among Norsemen ? "

"I wonder not at thy words ; but know that even among our agile and skilled warriors, the name of Olaf Tryggvveson stands supreme. Master of every kind of idróttir the Norseman knows, hero of deeds of strength, endurance, and agility that stand unequalled even in the old Sagas, he has won for himself a reputation that is unsurpassed. I will tell thee of one thing that he has done.

"Thou hast seen the towering Smalsarhorn which stands at the entrance to the Fjord below ? One day, his ship lay off its shore, and his men were laying wagers as to who could climb its steep, impassable sides. One tried and failed. Another went half way up, and there crouched, afraid to go on or return. Olaf then started up, reached the top, where he fastened his shield, and on his return carried down the hirdman who could not come by himself. So much for his

marvellous control of his body; and it is this which makes
him a wonder among men."

"Well," said Tellus, "if this man is so skillful a warrior
perhaps thou hast some real cause to fear defeat. Tell me, is
there no doubt in thy mind? Art thou confident that thy arm
will not lose its cunning and fail thee at the critical moment
of thy life? Thou hast spoken lightly of his plans for
triumph over thee. Hast thou never trembled lest all should
happen as the King expects?"

Harald straightened his broad shoulders and rested his hand
easily on the handle of his tolle-kniv. With quiet confidence
he answered:

"I have no fear. Thou hast said that I am not the
meanest of Norge's warriors; and besides, I go to this conflict with the strength of soul and arm that Christ can give.
Thou knowest what strength that is. I am sure I am right;
and I know God looks down and blesses my love for Persea.
He whispers to me, 'Fear not, I shall be with thee.' I have
prayed for strength and skill to conquer. Already do I feel
something strong within me which is not of earth, not of
this body; and it thrills me with the certainty of success. I
have provided against failure, not because I feared it, but because of Persea and thee. Now there is something else I wish
to do. See, here is a gold ring with runes which I have
broken in half. Take thou one piece whilst I keep the other.
Let it be an outward pledge of love between thee and me, —
a token to carry with us always, to comfort and sustain should
aught divide us."

With heart that felt oppressed by the sense of coming
danger, Tellus received the piece of gold. As he placed it
carefully away he said:

"Let it be even as thou hast said, for thy thought breathes
wisdom and comfort. In this uncertain life, there are moments when the tide of woe would seize us in its mighty rush
and hurl us high upon the rocks to die, but for the human love
outstretched to save."

The sun had disappeared, and the golden-warm tints
gradually faded from the mountain-tops. The young men
lingered upon the hillside, watching the changing beauty of
sky and earth; but as the stars began to appear, they silently
rose and descended the narrow path into the valley.

CHAPTER XIX

"THE END IS UNKNOWN"

FROM far and near, over fjeld and fjord, came the people to the King's feast. Long graceful boats glided under the lee of the cliffs; while all the roads were crowded with horsemen and horsewomen dressed in their costliest apparel, wearing heavy gold and silver chains about their arms, and with jewels flashing from fibula and belt. The horses were hardly less richly bedecked than their riders; and they tossed their heads in feverish excitement at the loud bursts of laughter, the notes of the lur, and the clanking of spurs and heavy trappings.

All was gaiety and gladness. Friend shouted to friend as newcomers joined the various groups; yet upon every face was written a subtle anticipation of something indefinite and unknown, as if there might be either pleasure or pain awaiting them, — which, they knew not.

"My name is not Ivar, if we see not some stirring idróttir in the next three days," said one of the young men to his companion.

"Yea. Eindridi and Harald and the rest of our skilled warriors will have no mean rival if the King enters the games," replied the man addressed.

"So say I. If Olaf can overcome Eindridi in the water, Christian or no Christian, I shall say that he is in league with Ran; for no man can do more water idróttir than Eindridi, unless Ran comes to his aid."

"'T is so," answered the other.

Just then a shout went up from the crowd, now numbering several hundred. They had reached a bend of the road; and as they turned, lo! Iron Beard, Sigrid, and fifty stalwart Norsemen were waiting to join them. Cheer after cheer told in what high esteem the people held the mighty Temple Godi. He waved his hand towards them in friendly greeting. Then, followed by his escort, he wheeled his horse into the road in front of the approaching crowd, and led down towards the valley.

But his presence reacted upon the people. That indefinite feeling of something unknown, something unsettled, made itself more plainly felt. The groups drew away from each other, voices were lowered, and conversation grew more confidential. Here and there were heard the words, " sacrifice, King, Christ Maiden, Sigrid, Harald Rognvaldson."

Two men were holding very close converse. Glancing ahead at the towering horseman in grey, one said:

" Why rides the Temple Godi with so few followers ? One would think he would wish all his men with him when he appears before the King."

" Hist ! " said the listener. " Dost thou not know, Thorleif, that Iron Beard fears treachery in the King ? He has heard that Olaf has destroyed every Norse temple on his journey northward ; and Iron Beard thinks of our beautiful house at Lladir. 'T is the costliest temple in all Norge, as thou knowest ; and he has placed a guard around it while the people are at the King's feast. 'T would be a good opportunity for Olaf to harm it, if perchance he should wish to do so."

" But, Erlend, Olaf has not forbidden worship of Odin. Thou rememberest the Thing ? And at the sacrifice, he stood by while his hirdman offered the boy whom we gave to the Christ Maiden."

" Bah ! " and the speaker's tone was filled with disgust. " Seest thou not that Olaf is but playing with the gods ? Little cares he for anything save his own will and wishes. Had he been in truth a Christian, he would have left the Thrandheim long since, or been burnt because he would not yield to our demands. He is a Christian only because it gives him more power, more friends ; and here, when it suited him, he bowed to Odin for the same reason. If that girl, who talked so strangely at the Vetrarblót, was asked to choose Odin or die, she would die ! I know it. I saw it in her face that day of wonders ; and her belief is as different from Olaf's as night is from day.

" I tell thee, Thorleif, there is something in this story of a perfect man who gave his life for the sins of the world ; something in this story of living and ruling by love, not by might. Thou knowest how my thralls fear me ; thou knowest that I have the name of a cruel, hard master. Nay, hold not up thy hand, for I know it. I thought it was the only way to make the brutes work. When I was accounted harsh, I laughed, and pointing to my well-kept buildings, my fat cattle, and my harvests gathered faster and better than any of my fellow bonder, I said: ' Behold! the result.'

" But when this maiden spoke of ruling by love, a strange pain came into my brain as if I had dealt unfairly with men; and thou knowest I am a Norseman, and would not wrong even an enemy. I went to my skali and pondered over the matter many hours.

" Meanwhile, Ulf, the thrall who keeps the cattle, a most unruly fellow, came to me in fear and trembling, and told me that a wolf had stolen one of the sheep. I questioned him, and found that he had neglected his duty. Before time, he would have received cruel punishment; but now I hesitated. Here was a chance to prove this new law. I said to my thrall: 'Through thy carelessness thy master has lost a sheep. If I forgive thee, and send thee back to thy post, wilt thou do thy duty hereafter?'

" 'The poor brute could not understand; and I repeated what I had said. Suddenly a light came into his blurred eyes, and falling at my feet, he called me by every kind name he knew, while he cried like a child. I myself was not a little affected. Afterwards he went out, and never have I had a better, more useful thrall than he has been. He tracked the wolves to their den and killed them, bringing me their skins in payment for the sheep I lost. He follows me about like a dog; and what used to be my commands are now done before I have a chance to speak. Something has happened. Something has changed in me; something has changed in the thrall; yet I know not what it is. I only know it was born of kindness and love; and that it can never die."

Thorleif looked sharply at his companion, as he asked:

" Hast thou then, become a Christian, even as Harald Rognvaldson?"

" Nay, Odin forbid!" the other answered hastily. " ' T would be no light tale that could take me from the faith of Norge; but still I feel that there is some strange truth in this Christianity,—some new truth that is so far above the human mind that it must have come from a God. Dost thou not have this feeling? Hast thou not felt that there was something fresh and strong in the maiden's story of Christ ? "

Thorleif answered with an indifferent shrug of the shoulders :

" I have thought of but little ; unless, indeed, it was the rare beauty of the Christ Maiden," and he laughed suggestively. " Methinks it is really that which has turned the people's heads. It was thought that Harald would wed with Iron Beard's daughter ; but now it is plain that he hopes to possess the Christ Maiden. She is beautiful enough to make any man forget his gods. I would renounce Odin myself if she would lie in my bosom," and he laughed again.

Erlend's face clouded ; and he moved uneasily in his saddle as he said, almost fiercely :

" Thou art mistaken. The maiden may be wondrously beautiful ; but 't is not her beauty that has so stirred the Thrandheim. What made her dare to face the people and stop their worship ? What power was it that held our strong passions in check, so that we stood quietly by and listened as she spoke to us ? There was something that came out from her, — some influence and strength that made us listen, and almost — believe ! "

Again Thorleif gave Erlend that sharp, questioning look as if to read his inmost thought ; but he replied indifferently :

" Well, if there was, mayhap this girl is a witch, and has cast a spell upon us. Who knows ? "

He pressed his spurs to his horse's sides, and rode ahead until he reached the white horse upon which Sigrid sat. He drew rein beside her with a pleasant greeting :

" How fares the dainty Sigrid as she rides to the feast ? Art thinking, no doubt, of the many hearts that shall beat faster at thy approach."

Sigrid looked up with a slight blush as she answered :

" Nay, I cannot boast of such power over any Norseman," and her blue eyes sparkled with a mischievous light.

" Tuts, tuts," replied Thorleif. " ' T is time Var heard thy betrothal vows. Art thou going to be like thy mother, who yielded not until thy headstrong father carried her off by force ? "

A half-frightened look came into the blue eyes. She said softly, in a voice that trembled :

"I know not; but when love calls, 't will be hard not to answer and go."

There was a brief silence, during which the small golden head drooped slightly to hide the unshed tears in the bright eyes. But quickly she gained control of herself, and said teasingly :

"Wherefore didst thou leave the gay ones behind? Methinks I saw Thora there. Hast been unkind to her?"

Thorleif smiled.

"So, thou wouldst cross swords with me and give thrust for thrust. Save thy tongue-strength; for Thora is even now at the King's skali. I came to thee because I was weary of hearing of this new Christianity and Persea, the Christ Maiden. All Thrandheim has gone mad over her; and verily I believe many would turn Christians if they dared. I knew that the daughter of the Temple Godi would have no place in her thoughts for this new faith."

Then the fearless spirit of the Norsewoman spoke :

"Thou art mistaken. I, too, have thought and wondered and questioned. Seest thou that great stone balancing on the top of yonder ledge of rock? Every time it feels the breath of Egir's Brother, every time it is bathed in the tears of the clouds, it inclines more to the Fjord or more to the valley. Some day it will break from its long resting place and go to a new home; but who can tell where? Will it sink into the Fjord to dwell with Egir's Daughters; or rest in the valley neath the dark pines?

"So is the heart of Sigrid rocked by the winds of doubt, and bathed with tears of unrest. There cometh a time when it, too, must leave its present abode; — but the path is all unknown, the end is all unknown. Ask me no more."

Thorleif said nothing; but in his face was mingled astonishment and regret.

Then Sigrid reined her horse very close to his side.

"Thorleif, thou art one whom I have ever trusted, else I would not have spoken as I did; and now I have a precious request to make of thee. When the change comes, if it takes me from my father who loves me to distraction, wilt thou give this package to him? It will help and comfort him."

She took from her bosom a small skin bag. Thorleif reached out his hand for it, saying :

" I will do it for thy sake; but what I have heard to-day makes me to grieve much. However, the end is not yet. I believe, as does Iron Beard, that the people have been bewitched; and that if only the ' Two ' could be sacrificed, Odin would reign as powerfully as ever before."

He rode on, leaving Sigrid repeating to herself, " If only the ' Two ' could be sacrificed ! Which two can he mean ? "

CHAPTER XX

KING AND CAPTIVE

ALMOST was the time for feasting at hand when King Olaf left the skali, and crossing the court-yard, mounted the staircase to the upper floor of the skemma. He passed through the outer entrance, on beyond to Persea's apartment.

The low, carved door stood open; and he lifted the heavy curtains and stepped inside, unannounced. When the folds of the velvet fell into place behind him, he unconsciously put his hands over his eyes, as though the picture he saw was too exquisite or too painful for him to look upon.

The room was low-ceiled and small, almost square, with heavy rafters overhead, and walls hung with dark red velvet. The floor was strewn with freshly gathered fir twigs, which filled the air with a faint aroma, whispering of the woods and the winds and the wildness on the mountain. A high bed with carved posts was built into one corner; and between the golden-fringed hangings he could catch a glimpse of fine linen and the coverlet of silk and eider-down. In the centre of the room stood a quaint, oaken table, carved and inlaid, upon which rested a roll of parchment and a boat-shaped lamp. There was also a couch, heaped high with cushions which bore the imprint of a form, telling that some one had just arisen from their silken softness.

On one side was a small, wide-silled window covered with transparent membrane; and in front of the window stood a chest which was ornamented with intricate designs of iron work. The lid was thrown back, and Olaf could see a shimmer of white silk and a mother-of-pearl jewel box.

Upon the fir-strewn floor before this chest Persea half knelt, half sat. She was dressed in her accustomed white, with a pointed girdle of plain leather. She had removed her kerchief, and her beautiful neck looked like the purest marble in the faint, soft light that came from the primitive window. Her hair was not fastened in its golden bands, but hung loose, almost covering her with its long, dark waves.

She was occupied with the contents of the chest, and heard not the King. Now she opened the jewel-box, and gave a little gasp of astonishment. On the soft lining lay a diadem of gold, surmounted by a diamond star of whitest, purest lustre. Beside the diadem was an exquisite girdle of gold filigree, ending with golden cords and tassels which would reach almost to the hem of her robe. She kissed the jewels, and then picked up a small stick that lay upon the floor beside her, and read again the message that Harald had carved upon it.

"To Persea, my beloved, greeting and love untold. The King's feast is at hand, and thou wilt be asked to take part in its pleasure with the people of Norge. Thou art mine; and I cannot see thee in coarse garb, neither would I have thee wear any gifts of the King. Therefore I have sent thee raiment suitable to thy beauty; and yet it is the white thou lovest. I want thee to be different from the Norsewomen; so I have put thy jewels all in one, — the great star which shall shine above thy head and make thee as the Queen of Heaven amidst the poor splendour of those about thee. Wear my small gifts, my beloved. Make thy wondrous beauty more wondrous yet for thy Harald's sake, — he who trembles at the sound of thy name, and lives only to love thee. May God's peace be with thee; and his hand keep danger from thee whilst thou art in the King's skemma. Carved by the hand of thine own Harald in Gornnanud."

Persea was so beautiful, as she leaned against the chest with a soft flush tinting her face and throat, that Olaf felt a sharp pain through his heart. Well he knew that that smile, that soft glow was for another. He had quickly guessed the meaning of the scene before him. His gifts and jewels had ever been returned. These would be accepted. Such a great sadness came into his soul that when he spoke, his voice trembled with the burden of it.

"Persea."

The stick dropped from her hand; and she sprang to her feet with a stifled scream. When she saw who was with her, she slowly drew back until she reached the opposite wall. There she stood, her dark hair falling about her like a cloak, her hands clutching the curtains behind her, the warm flush all gone from her white face, and her eyes dilating with surprise and alarm. Against the blood-red hangings, every detail of her beauty was brought into sudden prominence. If Olaf trembled before, he was overpowered now. Without moving towards her, he dropped on one knee and held out his hands imploringly.

"Nay! Nay! draw not from me as from a venomous serpent. Mercy! Mercy at thy hands; for I am consumed by the fire of love within me. Is my presence so hateful that thou canst not even smile? I will not harm thee: I came not here to harm thee. Only do I desire to plead with thee, to win from thee a smile, a look that would not be cruel."

She moved not; she smiled not. He gazed at her for a moment. Then he dropped his hands to his sides, and bowed his head in an anguish and humility of soul that sent the frightened look out of Persea's face, and replaced it with one almost of pity. She answered him quietly, but firmly:

"Thou art doing me harm by coming here, King Olaf. Even if my heart was free to love, thinkst thou that thou shouldst seek me in mine own apartment in the women's house? Where is thy Christianity? Where is thy conscience, that thou canst thus pursue me? I have told thee that I cannot love thee. Leave me, and feed the fire within thee with some love that is more satisfying than my constant refusal must be."

Olaf rose to his feet with a quick gesture of dissent, and began to pace rapidly back and forth across the room. Suddenly he stopped, and motioning Persea to the cushioned couch, he said:

"Sit there; for I have much to tell thee. I want thee to know Olaf Tryggvveson, to know his life, what it has been. Then thou wilt know what he must be now, — what such a life must have made him."

Persea took the seat he indicated. The King continued walking to and fro with arms folded upon his chest and head bowed. He talked rapidly and yet thoughtfully, almost as though he was relating a dream. He told about his father, his peril-surrounded birth, his slavery, his youth, his rise in the Russian court, his battles, his wide travels, his wealth, his following, his fame. Persea listened with growing interest to the unusual story; and by the time he reached the telling of

"DRAW NOT FROM ME AS FROM A VENOMOUS SERPENT!"
EXCLAIMED KING OLAF.—*Page 150.*

his world-wide renown, she was leaning eagerly forward, forgetting herself and the first part of their interview in the absorbing romance of the tale she was hearing.

Next he spoke of his religion; told how, in so many lands, and amid so many gods, he had hardly known what he believed. He had met his priest, Thangbrand of Bremen, while in Germany, and had become interested in him because he, was tall, strong, skillful of speech, a good clerk and warrior; one who, once angered, would yield to no man in words or deeds. He had seen the shield which Thangbrand carried, on which was embossed, in gold, the figure of Christ on the cross. He had asked the meaning of it, had accepted the shield as a gift from Thangbrand, and then invited him to enter his service. Later came the strange meeting with a priest in Ireland, who foretold so exactly what did happen to him, that he concluded to take this God as his God. Thereafter he had served him in the best way he knew.

"And so have I done," he continued, "for I knew of no other service than to make others believe in him, by force, if necessary. Thy picture of Christ as One who ruled by love, who wished no blood spilt in his name, was as new to me at the Autumn Sacrifice as it was to the worshippers of Odin. I know not from whence thou didst get this picture of a religion which should conquer by tenderness, and long-suffering, and humility; for I have been in the very heart of Christendom, — have been at Rome, — and seen the Christians there punish unbelievers with cruel torture, thinking that by so doing they were serving Christ. The laws of Christian countries are not those that thou dost hold to; and the priests of the Church do not live as thou hast said a Christian should live.

"I tell thee of this that is in my heart, for thine eyes reproach me for my Christianity; because they flashed scorn in my face when I attempted to please the people by attending the Sacrifice; because thou dost seem to think that I should be different since I profess to be a Christian. I do not know how to be different. I am a warrior, and love the smell of battle and the clash of arms. I cannot serve Christ, save by the might of my sword; and I know of no man who serves his God in any other or better way. Thou mayest be right; but thy creed cannot live while the blood of warriors flows in men's veins; and when will it not so flow? If we forgave our enemies, they would trample us under their feet. If we were kind to all men, we would soon be beggars and wanderers upon the earth.''

Persea stopped him.

"Nay. Thy love would win more friends than thy sword; and kindness more gain than compulsion. Suppose thine enemies could be brought to believe in Christ as I do? Suppose all men, all nations ruled by love? That is what the true Christian would strive to bring to pass."

Olaf shook his head.

" Thou art a woman, and canst not know the violence of men. That which thou hast said is impossible. Never could such conditions come upon the earth. Yet, if all were like thee, what a wonderful world this would be ! "

He stood still, and gazed thoughtfully out of the tiny window. He was trying to picture the world as Persea would teach men to make it; and in spite of his doubt, he could see colour-tints of truth that his soul told him would never fade. As he stood thus, Persea answered him :

" What I have said is not impossible. That which the Sacred Word tells us to do, we can do. I have known and tried the Truth; and I have found that wonderful trust and love and strength does abide with me. Know, King Olaf, that to be the Christian that Christ wants, 't is not needful to look to the priests. Find out what the Truth is for thyself ; and then thou wilt feel its power and wilt desire to follow it. Lastly will come a great love for the God of Truth which shall purify thy soul, and make thee wish to be like Christ. Yea, thou wilt learn to love thy fellow men, and to labour for them as Christ loved and laboured ; and thou shalt find thyself even ready to die for his Name's sake ! "

Olaf listened ; and though he could not grasp the full meaning of her speech, there was one thought, like a bright thread of gold in an intricate pattern, which his mind followed and believed. Therefore he answered :

" I know that thou hast done strange things since thou hast been one of my household. I know Ingiborg says thou art an angel in thy thoughts and deeds. I know the thralls love thee to madness because thou art kind to them; but 't is thy nature to be kind. A wolf from the wild fjelds would love thee if thou didst but let thine eyes rest on him. Yea, thou canst rule by love. Thou canst speak to the strongest arm that ever wielded sword, and make it as weak as a reed before thee. Rule me, O Christ Maiden, by thy love! Then I will lie at thy feet and do whatsoever thou shalt command, — even to sheathing my sword. Only love me, and let me love thee!"

He knelt again, this time close to her; and bent his head to kiss her white hand upon the arm of the couch; but she drew it quickly away.

Olaf looked sadly into her face.

"Not even a touch of thy hand? Why dost thou deny me this, — a drop of water to a soul that is dying of thirst for thee."

Persea trembled. This tenderness was harder to endure than his arrogance.

"I see that thou hast never known the Christ-love; and I understand thy Christianity better than before; but I do not understand thy love. Hast thou forgotten my words just a brief time since? Thy words of love to me are of no avail. When thou knowest that I am not free to love, thou art only blackening thy honour and thy soul by thy persistence. Leave me. Find some one who is free to listen to thee."

Olaf leaned one arm upon his upright knee, and bending forward, looked at her with eyes that burned with passion.

"Hush! Speak not again of any other; lest I forget and do some rash act. There is a part of my life I have not yet told thee. Listen.

"During the years I have roamed over the earth, I have felt many a maiden's arms about my neck. Why not? Am I not one whom women would love? I have received the burning kiss from maidens of the north and maidens of the south; and it was little I cared whether I held Yanusia of Russia, or La Torra of the City on the Sea. I wedded once, in Vendland, one whom I might have loved well; but she soon died. Never did I know real love until I saw thee. Never did I feel my blood rush through my veins like scalding torrents, or desire seize me with so mighty a power, until I saw thy soul that day of days when thou didst first step on our shores. From that moment all peace left me. I loved, loved with all the strength of my soul and my manhood; loved with a love that knew no bounds, knew no height, nor depth, nor breadth.

"When I saw thou wert drawn to another, such anguish smote me that I could neither eat nor sleep. But I have hoped always; for thy future was in my hands. Thou thinkest of this Harald because he was with thee at first; but he cannot love as I love. He cannot give thee what I can give thee. Nay! draw not away from me. Look not so upon me. Speak to me. Breathe thy breath upon me. Grant me but the saying of words of love to thee. Persea! Persea! Stay near me! Draw not away!"

He put out his hand to detain her; but she slipped from his grasp and stood in the centre of the room, trembling with excitement and anger. With flashing eyes she answered him:

"Hadst thou stopped before thou didst mention Harald Rognvaldson's name, I might have felt some pity for thee. But thou hast made me crush pity under my feet when thou asketh me to be false to my heart and my word. Thou didst speak of love that had no bounds. Dost thou think that thou art the only one who can feel such love? Even so do I love Harald Rognvaldson; and so I will love him to the end."

Olaf rose slowly from his kneeling posture, and said in a low, sullen tone:

"Dost thou know what that end shalt be?"

Persea's breath was coming and going in short quick gasps as she replied:

"I know, — the challenge. But I believe in Christ's power to help the right; and my Harald shall win!"

Olaf laughed sardonically.

"I believe in the power of the strongest arm, the quickest eye, the most expert idróttir. Know, O Persea, that while I do not wish to speak boastfully of myself, there is yet to be found a man who can stand against Olaf Tryggvveson. I decry not the skill or strength of Harald; but 't is no dishonour for a man to lose in trial with Olaf. Ask whom thou wilt, whether friend or foe. Thou shalt see them shake their heads, and tell thee that thy Harald shall fail."

Persea seemed to grow taller. With great trust and faith she answered:

"Still I say unto thee that he shall not fail. He prays also; and our prayers shall be stronger than thy strength, and more effective than thy skill."

Olaf laughed again.

" Pray on. But what wilt thou do when Harald lies de-feated, perhaps dead, at thy feet? Tell me that. What wilt thou say to me then?"

Persea shivered. Her lips were white; but they did not move. Then Olaf grew wild with love, and flung himself upon the floor at her feet, burying his face in her long kirtle and passionately kissing its rough border. In vain she tried to break from him. He implored, begged for some sign of hope, however slight.

" Persea! Dost thou not understand what a love this must be which would make Olaf Tryggvveson grovel at thy feet? Dost thou see how my heart has humbled itself before thee? Let me try to make thee love me. Speak to me. Look at me with those wonderful eyes and tell me that I am not hate-ful to thee! Tell me but that!"

He seized her hands, and strove to look upward into her face; but she turned her head, struggling desperately to free herself. He held her hands as though in a vise, while he commanded in a changed, hoarse voice:

" Answer!"

Then she ceased struggling, and stood erect, firm, with white face and lips. It was force fighting to compel love; a conflict which can have but one ending.

" Olaf Tryggvveson, till death and after death, I belong to another. I cannot give thee something which I have not, — something which I never will have for thee. This is the end. If thou hast aught of compassion in thy heart, release me and leave me; for thy presence, thy words, thy touch, are like poison in my soul."

For one brief instant Olaf held her, his handsome features distorted with passion and anger. Then he flung her hands from him with a suddenness and force that sent her staggering back against the wall.

" Fool! That is the answer thou dost dare to give one who has bowed to thee as he never bowed before, and never will again! My time will come soon. I would humble thee now, but for staining my honour in the sight of men. After I have met Harald Rognvaldson, my hands and honour will be free. Then I will not plead with thee. I will command, and thou shalt obey!"

Without another glance, he strode to the doorway, and lifting the heavy curtains, disappeared.

Persea watched the swaying drapery until it fell into its regular folds.   Then she clasped her hands, and knelt before the couch.

CHAPTER XXI

THE KING'S FEAST

The King's skali stood not far from the edge of the Fjord. Scarcity of time had made rough building a necessity; but great length and breadth made up for what was lacking in finish. It was long, low, immense; and under its rough roof a thousand people could be entertained.

The interior was especially adorned for the feast. The walls were covered with silk and velvet hangings, woven in the looms of the East, and embroidered in gold. Upon this gorgeous background the glittering shields looked like golden suns, and the brilliant weapons like shafts of blue lightning. The benches and high seats were covered with soft cushions. The long tables which stood between the benches and the fire were loaded with gold and silver tankards, huge bowls, and gold-mounted drinking horns of rare value. The floor was freshly strewn with fir, the great fires were lit; and the thralls were busy preparing the feast.

The people had assembled, the men coming in one door, the women in another. All were clothed in costly apparel of brilliant colours, reds, blues, purples; and glittered with golden torques, chains, and bracelets studded with gems.

The roof of the feast hall trembled with shouts from a thousand throats as King Olaf entered.

" Hail and health to the Viking ! "

Louder and louder rose the plaudits as he passed slowly down the hall to his high-seat; for the people of the Northland knew and loved beauty of person and apparel; and their King was kingly.

He wore a short tunic of scarlet silk edged with a border of gold embroidery, gold-coloured silk braekr and hosur, and high shoes of soft, yellow leather. Over his shoulder hung a cloak of scarlet velvet, lined with white fur, and fastened with a golden fibula. Around his head was a heavy band of gold.

When he reached the high-seat, he stood before it until the shouts died away. Then he spoke:

"Men and women of Thrandheim, happy is the day upon which Olaf Tryggvveson can welcome ye to his skali. Your horses have been placed in my stables; your boats are drawn upon the beach; the tables are spread; the fires are lit; the players have entered with harps and gigjar; the great Sagas are upon the lips of the Skalds; and it only remains for us to enjoy these pleasures after our manner. The maidens are fair; the warriors are brave; and the gods forbid that they should drink apart. Let the married ones sit together; but the young men shall draw lots, and each one sit beside the maiden whose favour he takes. I, too, will choose a mate; for I cannot drink without the smile of woman."

Cries of approval greeted the King's words. The young men pushed eagerly forward. Anxiously the maidens waited for the result; for the pride of the Norsewoman was great. No mean warrior, no one without strength and courage and a reputation for great deeds was wanted at their sides.

Thorkel Nefja held the cloth in which the lots were cast, and gave forth the results.

"Fridthjof has drawn Hervör of Bödvar."

A laugh rang through the whole hall; for it was well known that Hervör had nothing but hatred for Fridthjof.

"Truth, and they will have a merry time of it," said one, with a wag of his head.

"Who knows but her heart may melt with the ale," said another.

Thorkel called out again:

"Thorwald sits with Helga."

A tall slender fellow stepped towards a girl hardly into womanhood; but whose eyes flashed disdain as she drew back and said proudly:

> "I sit with no lad
> Who knows not the feel of the blade,
> Who has never seen the Valkyrias,
> Or sent the quick one of the shaft
> Into the path of the spears."

"Ha! has she not the spirit of the Norsewoman?" said an old warrior. "Thorwald will have to answer well to sit with her."

But the young man took her hand with quiet imperiousness, answering her doubts :

> " I am no lad.
> The wolves scream, the raven flies,
> On the ground is warm flesh.
> I have broken the wall of battle,
> I have pierced the Shirt of Gunnar.
> Many men fall down
> When Thorwald swings
> The torch of the blood."

Cheers greeted him as he took the maiden away.

The drawing continued amid much merriment and good-natured jesting. Tellus was fortunate enough to draw Sigrid's name. When he approached her, the colour came and went in her fair cheeks ; but she placed her hand in his and he led her to her place, trembling himself with the thought of the joy that would be his that evening.

Gradually the places at the tables were being filled. The King's attendants seated the people in the order of their rank ; while Hallfred Vandroedaskald, Olaf's greatest Skald, occupied the high seat on the south side. The drawing was almost over when Thorkel announced :

" Harald Rognvaldson has taken the favour of Astrid the Peerless."

Harald started in surprise. Who had put his name in the cloth ? But Persea had not yet entered the women's door ; though the King's household were all present. It must be she was not going to appear. He was perplexed, annoyed ; but honour compelled him to come forward to claim Astrid.

Resplendent in his gorgeous attire of cloth of gold, he was so handsome, so noble in his bearing that all looked and murmured ; and in the heart of Olaf the fierce jealousy and hatred grew fiercer.

Astrid stood waiting. Never was she more proudly beautiful than when she held out her hand graciously towards Harald. For one evening she knew he was to belong to her. She had staked a life and her honour on the issue.

She wore a low-necked, sleeveless kirtle of light blue brocade that swept the ground and trailed behind her in stiff folds. It was edged with embroidery of seed pearls, and a

pearl-strung girdle held its folds around her waist.   Her long
hair fell in two golden braids, almost to her feet, and there
was the soft lustre of priceless pearls amidst their sheeny
meshes.   Pearls glistened everywhere, making still whiter and
softer her alabaster neck and arms.

Truly she was a vision to make any man tremble; and
when Harald took her hand he felt again that mysterious
flutter, that powerful magnetism that had once before stirred
his manhood to its depths.   And this time he shivered, and
could not break the spell.

She drew him to the seat beside her, and began to talk softly
and brilliantly; while he, whose thoughts had been all of Persea, looked at the white bosom rising and falling beneath the
white pearls and listened, in spite of himself, to the voice that
was weaving a web about him.

All were now provided with companions save the King;
and the people were wondering what maiden of Norge would
occupy the seat beside him.   It was a place of great honour;
and yet one in which there lurked a great danger.   The King
could command.   What maiden would dare disobey?   The
chosen one might become the Queen of Norge; or he might
take all and give but little if he asked for the night-drink
from her hands.

Divining the people's thoughts, Olaf spoke:

"Ye are all mated.   I alone am left; but behold the one
who sits by King Olaf.   Is she not worthy to be called the
Queen of Norge?"

He motioned to the lower end of the hall, where the heavy
curtains fell across the women's entrance.   As the people
watched, Persea stepped forth.   A wave of excitement swept
through the skali at her appearance.   She was evidently confused, and knew not what to do; or why all eyes were turned
upon her.   Before she could know what was happening, the
King had taken her hand and was leading her to the seat beside his.

Among the fair ones of the North, her dark beauty was as
the red rose among the white.   She wore Harald's gifts, the
soft, pure silk whose clinging folds gave rich suggestion of her
perfect womanhood.   The graceful girdle encircled her waist
and hung low in front, weighted with its golden chains and
tassels.   On her head was the diadem; and its magnificent

star of diamonds shone above her dark eyes with an intense and radiating brilliancy.

To the people she seemed as something unknown, — a dream, a spirit who had strayed from the path of the stars and appeared in their midst. Absolute silence, — the silence of astonishment, — reigned in the hall. Few there were who were not transfixed by her beauty and spirituality, that mysterious soul-light which thrilled them, they knew not why.

But Iron Beard was without the magic circle of her influence. When he saw her, with that star gleaming above her forehead, he gasped for breath. Great cords stood out on his brow; and underneath the table his huge fist sought the handle of his tolle-kniv and closed upon it until it cracked. How he hated her! A mad, ungovernable fury seized him to see, bright above her head, the symbol that represented to him the power he so dreaded, feared, and yet defied, — that Unknown Light in the northern sky that was putting out the glory of Valhalla. Scarcely could he smother his wrath; but he did so by whispering to himself, " Not yet! Not yet! The net is not made fast. But soon, soon! "

Harald was mightily moved. He had concluded that she cared not to take part in the feast; but lo! she enters and sits in the Queen's seat. Does she, can she know what she is doing? He saw not the wonder and surprise in her face; he was only filled with misgivings and doubts that tore at his heart like maddened wolves. The room swam before him. Then he heard Astrid's musical voice:

" Ah! thou lookest at the Christ Maiden? Is she not a match for the King's fair manhood? At first she would not attend the feast; but the King talked with her and offered her the Queen's place. Womanlike, when she found she could have the greatest honour she was willing to appear."

There was that in her soft laugh that made the fangs sink deeper into Harald's heart. But no! it could not be! She was too good, too true, too pure. Then he asked:

" What ails the noble Ingiborg, that she appears not? "

Astrid answered indifferently:

" Methinks it came as the result of a quarrel between her and the King. Jealousy can be a real sickness, can it not, O Blest of the Nornir? "

The subtle hint made Harald's heart writhe; but his face was unmoved as he answered:

"Yea, but a man's cure is his sword. It is swift and sure."

There was a covert knowledge in Astrid's voice as she asked:

"And what then, dost thou think a woman's cure might be? The sword may not be used by us."

"That is for each woman to discover for herself; for no cure would suit all cases. For some, smiles; for some, tears; for some, strange deeds that a man's mind could not fathom. Women are as the wind-floating clouds. They drift with every breath, and smile or storm without warning or reason."

Astrid laughed her light laugh; but Harald did not hear her. He was thinking that he was here beside this woman; while just beyond sat his love, his life, his promised one, with the King. What ill wind had crossed their path?

Persea had not seen him yet; though her eyes were passing quickly over the long rows of guests, on to the farthest limit of the great hall. Finally she saw him. First gladness, then amazement and blanched cheeks as she saw by whom he sat. There was a swift interchange of looks, — questions, doubts, answers, all flashing together in a silent struggle to pierce the veil between them; but in vain.

The feasting commenced. The thralls rushed hither and thither with tankards and bowls of food. The fires roared and blazed. Ever and anon some huge log burned apart with a great splutter of sparks and loosened brands that made those near shout and laugh as they brushed from their clothes the burning fragments. Louder and more boisterous grew the gaiety and jesting. The strong ale sent the blood rushing swiftly through men's brains. Many a maiden heard words of love that made the colour mount into neck and cheek; many a whispered confidence was exchanged amid the gay tumult, the ring of silver tankards and the swinging of the drinking horns. The air was filled with an odour of mead and burning fir. It penetrated men's brains, and made them throw off their Norse reserve and be boisterous, boastful, or passionate, according as fancy or desire led them.

Olaf spoke warm love words to the white-robed form at his side, but she was as marble, white and silent. She felt the treachery lurking in the air. She knew that she had been deceived; that Harald had been deceived. She was not afraid of violence, either for herself or Harald until after the meeting with the King; but they must not doubt each other; not a shadow must fall between them. Hassan was waiting upon her. She whispered to him:

"Go. Fill Harald Rognvaldson's cup with love from me."

He raised his eyes with a glance that told her he understood. Then he waited for a chance to obey.

Persea's silence acted only as a maddening goad to Olaf's love. Finally, unable to endure longer his burning words and looks, she besought, commanded him to cease. But no word she could say, no command she could utter was heeded by the headstrong man.

"Nay, Persea, command me to do anything but this and I will obey thee as a slave; but love thee I must; tell thee so I must; and win thee, I shall!"

His hot breath came against her cheek, heavy with the odour of strong ale; and she shrank and trembled as from a devouring flame.

"How can I love thee when my heart is given to another? Thy words are but insults. Thou art cruel, and honour abides not with thee."

Olaf's face twitched convulsively at her scathing rebuke; but he kept on:

"Say to me what thou wilt. I no longer care. I only want thee, must have thee, shall have thee! Though Christ himself should plead for thee I would not give thee up. Though the wolves of the sea should bear thee to the farthest cavern on the other side of the world, I would follow thee. Though the winds should gather thee in their arms and carry thee out beyond the stars, I would find thee. Though the heavens opened and received thee, I would force the gates and enter! Now, dost thou, canst thou, feel the strength of the love that is pursuing thee? Yield thyself, for there is no escape. Were it not for the challenge, I would have thee to-night!"

A violent fear numbed Persea's heart; and her small hands were clasped so tightly that the nails grew blue. The awful blasphemy in his words, the absolute relentlessness of his will, and the scorching heat of his love overpowered her. When he ceased, and leaned towards her with the steely glitter of the

conqueror in his eyes, she swayed, and but for his arms would
have fallen.   He caught her and held her tightly to him for
one brief second, while he whispered :

" The first embrace, but not the last !   This was too cold.
The next will be warmer and closer ! "

He released her ere her strength to resist came back.   She
sank among the cushions, too frightened, too weak to move
or speak.   If only she could cry out !   If only she could fly
from this man !   Why had Harald not come forward to her ?
Why did he sit below with Astrid and let her be where the
King could so torture her ?

Meanwhile the King laughed purposely loud and long, as
though something had occurred to please him greatly.   Many
looked and whispered and glanced down where the Blest of
the Nornir drank with Astrid.   Could it be that he loved the
Angel of the Dawn as they thought ?

Harald had noted all; had seen the King's all-absorbed attention, the statue-like unresponsiveness of Persea.   Then
came a moment when Olaf seemed to be eating into her soul;
the next, — she fell into his arms !   Harald was not near
enough to see her pallor and alarm; and the sight froze the
blood in his veins.   He placed upon the table, untouched, the
horn he was about to lift to his lips.

Astrid, from beneath downcast eyes, saw his face, — and
smiled.

CHAPTER XXII

THE WANDERING SKALD

THE people began to clamour for more amusement.

"The Sagas! The Sagas! Let Hallfred sing to the King and his guests."

Olaf motioned to the Skald, and he rose and stood before his harp. It was a large instrument, higher than the man, with a heavy frame carved with scenes from the old Sagas and strung with silver strings. The Norsemen shouted with great acclaim:

"Hail and health to the one who has taken of Dvergar's mead!"

Hallfred bowed low. Then he swept the strings with a ringing prelude which silenced every tongue in the hall.

First he sang the Saga of Ragnar Lodbrók, the mighty viking who made the King of England to tremble, though he had but two ships; sang of his battles, his bravery, his victories, his booty; sang of his final conflict, when all his men were slain; sang of his enemies who could not harm him because of his magic armour; sang of the cruel death they gave him when they stripped him of his protection and threw him into a snake pit; sang his last song, slowly, while through the music and words sounded the note of agony; even though the dying one fain would jest.

> "I have fought battles
> Fifty and one
> Which were famous;
> I have wounded many men.
> I little thought that snakes
> Would cause my death;
> Often that happens
> Which one least expects.
> The pigs would grunt
> If they knew the hog's suffering;
> The gnawing hurts me;
> The snakes thrust in their snouts
> And stick to me cruelly;
> They have sucked me;
> Soon shall I be a corpse;
> I will die among them."

The Skald's voice died away with the minor notes. Forth broke the applause :

"Hail to him who has Odin's Gift! Hail to Hallfred the Skald! Sing on. More of the mighty deeds of the Norsemen."

And he sang on; sang Gunnar's song, and Hjalmar's, and Ovar Odd's, until he lost himself in the stirring scenes of the past, and seemed not to see the great host, the dark, smoke-covered rafters, or the blazing fire; sang until men's hearts grew bold with the wish to do great deeds, or tender with looking love into eyes that looked again. Finally he ceased with a ringing burst of music that swept through the immense hall like the noise of a far-off battle, bringing the feasters to their feet in a wild tumult of applause. Shouts rang out, cheers and cries of delight. Horns were drunk to the health of Hallfred the Skald. Costly gifts, chains, bracelets, and rings were thrown at his feet. He sat down, and drawing his harp to him, rested his head against it as if exhausted with his long recital.

Olaf, leaning towards Persea, whispered :

"Some day I will bring him to thee. He will sing thee a love-song that will melt thy heart and make thee love."

And she replied, with white lips :

"I need no love-song to make me love. I love already ; but I love not thee."

There was a baleful gleam in Olaf's eyes as he answered slowly :

"Lovest thou another? Yet see that other. Does he think of thee? Who loves thee better now, Harald Rognvaldson or Olaf?"

She looked, and saw Astrid kiss the rim of a drinking horn and hand it to Harald. He smiled, and raising it to his lips, drained it to the last drop.

"See how he drinks to the health of another, and forgets the health of Persea. But not so does the King. Instead of one, thou shalt see a thousand vessels lifted in thy honour."

He rose to his feet with foam-dripping horn.

"The King! The King! Quiet while the King speaks."

The noise quickly died down and Olaf spoke.

"We have eaten our fill of meat and bread. Now doth come the time for toasts; and the King has a name for ye to honour. But first hear why.

"A maiden is beloved by two warriors. To one she belongs by right of gift-token. He will not yield her; therefore he has been challenged to trial of strength and skill. The two will meet before all Thrandheim on the third day of the feast; and the victorious one shall have his wedding feast with the maiden on the last night. The warriors are Harald Rognvaldson and Olaf Tryggvveson; and they will strive for the possession of Persea, the Christ Maiden.

"So fair a bride should have her betrothal feast. To-morrow night she drinks with Harald Rognvaldson; but to-night I betroth her to myself. I offer her name for the first honour. Lift your brimming horns and drink. Drink to the health of Persea, the Christ Maiden, for whose favour even Kings will enter the lists."

Greatly astonished were the people; but they loved romance, and fighting, and the glory of victory, and this meeting would be an unusual occurrence. When Olaf raised his horn high above his head and shouted: "Hail and health to Persea!" they answered with "Skal! Skal!" and tossed off the contents of their horns amid the wildest excitement.

But Iron Beard and Jarl Rognvald raised not their horns during that health-drinking. Iron Beard muttered under his breath, "Let them fight it out. Mayhap there will be need for only one to be sacrificed. 'T will be easier for Rognvald. He knows not that I hate his son as I hate the Christ Maiden."

Rognvald let his eyes rest on Harald with pitiful longing and love. He listened with anguish in his heart to the coarse jests upon the coming duel, and the bets as to whether Harald could stand against Olaf. The father had aged greatly during the past weeks, and was no longer the stalwart lawgiver. He had lost his reason for living when Harald became a Christian; and the trouble had bowed his shoulders and brought deep lines of sorrow in his face. When he heard that his idolized son was to meet Olaf, and for the possession of the girl he blamed for all his trouble, the last blow had come. He rose and left the feast hall.

Meanwhile, amid the confusion and talk that followed the toast to Persea, Harald held out his horn to be filled and felt a light touch on his hand. Hassan was bending over it. He whispered:

"The Moon of the Desert told me to fill thy horn with love. I know her heart is sad to-night."

Astrid wondered why her influence over Harald waned so suddenly. Why could she not keep his eyes upon her? Was she not beautiful enough for him? Had she not charms enough to stir his blood? She would see!

Toast followed toast in quick succession. Men drank to their sweethearts, their wives, their friends. Some made vows, and pledged themselves with the Bragi Toast. Said Hafner Rovarsson:

"I vow before all men to slay Ivar Oremsson, who sent my foster-father to Odin."

Up sprang Ivar's brother, a large, rough man with bushy beard and coarse features red with ale and anger.

"And I vow to send Hafner over the Bridge of Asar if his shooting-serpent falls not wide of its mark."

A howl arose from Hafner's friends; and but for interference, a fierce fight would have taken place.

Then Thorwald stood up with love-light in his eyes.

"Behold, I vow to wed Helga of Heimer within a year!"

His vow was greeted with plaudits long and loud. The proud little Helga drooped her head and blushed rosy red in the fire-light.

When the confusion and laughter had somewhat abated, Harald Rognvaldson slowly rose. Every one leaned forward in great expectancy. What would he vow?

He had risen with horn in his uplifted hand, and a face on which there was no trace of passion or ale-wrought brain. Cool, calm, deliberate, — the people gazed at him and wondered at his quiet countenance.

"Many vows have been made here to-night, — vows of blood, vows of battle, vows of love. I have a vow to make which has never been heard at any of the feasts of Norge. One which will sound strange in your ears until ye do understand and believe in Christ as I do."

From a few, half-drunken feasters there arose howls of disapproval; but they were soon silenced. Even the enemies of Christianity wanted to hear this unusual vow.

Lowering his horn to the table, Harald continued:

"But first I have a tale that the people of Thrandheim should hear. They will listen; for the story is as true as it is strange."

He told of his meeting with Tellus and Persea; told of the

journey north and his promise to obtain Persea's release; told
of his father's speech to King Olaf, and its result—spoke it all
to the end.

The people listened in wonder and delight.   By such happenings did they know their great warriors.   No ordinary man
could have the Nornir to so guide his life into strange paths.

Harald ended by saying:

"And therefore did I challenge the King to such weapon-
crossing or ordeal as he might choose.   I know that Christ
does not love strife; but I know also that he would not have
me false to my word and honour.   Since only by challenge
can I give freedom to the Angel of the Dawn, I believe my
God does not forbid, and that he will give me the victory.
Hear! men and women of Thrandheim, this is my vow," and
he raised the horn.

"I vow that when Olaf Tryggvveson meets defeat at my
hand, I will give all the glory and honour of the victory unto
the White Christ.   'T will not be my strength, though my
arm is strong and sure, but the strength of my God that shall
conquer.   Ye shall all see and know that I have told ye the
truth," and he drained the horn.

A murmur of wondering comment swept through the hall.
Iron Beard's voice broke roughly into the growing excitement;
for it pleased him not.   He would take the people's thoughts
from this ever-present Christianity.

"Enough of toasts and vows.   Guess my riddle, men and
women of Thrandheim.   Whoever guesses correctly shall
have this," and he flung upon the table a spiral bracelet of
gold.

All attention was quickly centred on him; for the Norsemen were quick of wit, and loved to war with tongue and
brain, as well as with sword and spear.   Loudly Iron Beard
spoke:

> "Who are the play sisters
> That pass over lands
> And play at will?
> They wear a white shield
> In winter,
> But a dark one
> In summer."

A hum and buzz followed the telling.   Iron Beard waited
impatiently for a minute, and then called out:

" Ye are all ale-burdened and cannot think. 'T is but a child's thought.   Hear the answer.

> " Ptarmigans call
> The sons of men
> Feather-wearing birds ;
> Their feathers become black
> In summer-time,
> But white during the bear's night.

" Bah ! let me sharpen your wits with more gold.   See ! This also with the next answer," and he threw down a neck ring beside the bracelet.   " Take the wool out of your ears and listen.

> " Two bondwomen,
> Light-haired maidens,
> Carried ale
> To the skemma ;
> Horn was not touched with hand
> Nor with hammer shaped ;
> The wave-breasting one who made it
> Was outside the island."

Again the murmur, which was soon broken by Thora of Altheimar.

> " I know thy riddle.
> White-feathered skin
> Have the swans
> Which by islands
> Breast the waves ;
> Nests they build
> Had no hands
> But with other swans
> Eggs begat,
> Which women gathered
> And carried ale
> In the egg-shells."

Iron Beard tossed the jewelry to her, amid shouts of approval.

At this moment, the door of the hall opened.   A traveling Skald entered, wrapped in his great cloak, with bearskin cap on his head, and carrying his harp in its skin bag.   He was instantly given a warm welcome.   Mayhap he could tell them strange stories they had never heard.   Olaf commanded that he should be fed and warmed. Afterwards the King asked :

" Hast thou any new tale thou canst tell the guests of the King of Norge ? If it is a good one, I will reward thee with many gold rings."

Quickly the man replied :

" Yea, I have a wonderful tale. One which will fill thy sea-kings with fire, and make them long to sail out upon the Necklace of the Earth until they reach the jewel at the other end."

" What meanest thou ? " said Olaf. " Sing thy Saga. We are ready to listen."

The blazing fires were dying down. There was only a long pile of fitfully burning embers which cast a dull, red glow over the rich hangings and the brilliantly arrayed company. In this red glow, the stranger Skald stood and told his story.

" It is no Saga, O King, but a tale of the sunset which I bring to your ears. Hear me, O Vikings ! When your steeds of the breeze sail out of the Fjord, point their prows towards the West and sail on. Sail on for days and nights more than ye have ever before sailed from land ; sail on past the rocks of England, past Iceland and Greenland. If ye do continue, if your hearts do not grow faint, ye shall find a new and fair country. There the trees grow in plenty ; there the sun stays long above the horizon ; there the air is sweet and the waters pure ; a wonderful country which lies waiting for some one to gather its wealth ! "

Great was the interest the vikings took in this new tale ; though some doubted and said it could not be.

" Nay, doubt not," continued the Skald, earnestly. " For many years the winds have brought me whispers of this far-off land. I have seen its shores in my dreams, and drifted in spirit over its hills and vales. If ye are brave men, sail out over the Western Sea and find the fair land which is waiting for the grating of the Norseman's keel on her shores. For long years have I sung my song to ears which have heard not. Men laugh, and say, ' He is mad,' but I make oath upon the Hammer of Thor that my lips have spoken the truth," and he held above his head the charm that hung around his neck.

The sea-kings continued to question the Skald. With great vehemence he vouched for the truth of his story ; but the Norse-

men were incredulous, and most of them openly ridiculed the
idea of land beyond where the sky touched the rim of Ran's
world.   After they had talked some time, the King asked the
Skald if he could sing them a stirring song.   He said that he
could, and taking his harp, struck it several times.   The notes
were of a singular clearness, sounding like the tinkle of silver
bells afar off.

> " In Odin's hall an empty place
>   Stands for a King of Yngve's race ;
>   ' Go, my Valkyriars,' Odin said,
>   ' Go forth, my Angels of the Dead,
>   Gondul and Shŏgul, to the plain
>   Drenched with the battle's bloody rain,
>   And to the dying Hakon tell
>   Here in Valhalla he shall dwell.' "

Iron Beard and his following gave mighty shouts of approval
and joy.   This was a true song of Old Norway, and it suited
them well.   Horns were raised in honour of the Skald.   He
bowed, and continued :

> " At Stord, so late a lonely shore,
>   Was heard the battle's wild uproar ;
>   The lightning of the flashing sword
>   Burned fiercely at the shore of Stord.
>   From levelled halberd and spear-head
>   Life-blood was dripping, fast and red ;
>   And the keen arrow's biting sleet
>   Upon the shore at Stord fast beat.

> " Then up spake Gondul, standing near,
>   Resting upon her long ash spear, —
>   ' Hakon ! the gods' cause prospers well,
>   And thou in Odin's hall shalt dwell ! '
>   The King beside the shore of Stord
>   The speech of the Valkyriar heard,
>   Who sat there on her coal-black steed,
>   With shield on arm and helm on head."

Scarcely could the Skald be heard, so great was the delight
of the Norsemen.   Again he paused, waiting for the shouts
and cries and rattle of drinking horns to subside.   At the first
lull he struck once more the silver toned chords, and the air
seemed filled with faint echoes from the mystical feast-hall of
the dead.

> " Then Shōgul said, ' My coal-black steed,
> Home to the gods I now must speed,
> To their green home, to tell the tiding
> That Hakon's self is hither riding.'
> To Hermod and to Braga then
> Said Odin, ' Here, the first of men,
> Brave Hakon comes, the Norsemen's King, —
> Go forth, my welcome to him bring.'

> " Well was it seen that Hakon still
> Had saved the temples from all ill ;
> For the whole council of the gods
> Welcomed the King to their abodes.
> Happy the day when men are born
> Like Hakon, who all base things scorn, —
> Win from the brave an honoured name,
> And die amidst an endless fame."

He ended.   The enthusiasm of the Norsemen rose to madness.   He had struck the one great universal chord of feeling and passion which rang preëminently triumphant through all phases of a Norseman's life ; and he had struck it at a peculiar time.   It would seem as if the applause would never cease.   It thundered through the immense hall — lulled — thundered again, — lulled — thundered again, until the rafters and sides of the building vibrated with the immense sound.

At the Skald's feet the gift-heap grew higher and higher, — jewels and gold rings of value to make him free from want for the rest of life.   Finally Iron Beard arose and flung upon his shoulders the cloak he himself had worn.   'T was of magnificent grey fur, lined with red velvet embroidered with silver, — a fortune in itself.   It was the greatest gift-honour a Norseman could confer.   Almost did men trample upon each other in the tumult and noise that followed.

At last, from sheer exhaustion, the people grew more quiet. The young men began to remember the games on the morrow ; and knowing that they wished to awaken with vigour unimpaired by too much ale, Olaf declared the first night's feast over.

With one last " Skal to King Olaf ! " the guests drained their horns and withdrew to the booths and apartments.

Then spoke Astrid to Harald :

" Thou hast sat with me at feast in my brother's skali ; therefore will I come to thee ere sleep closes thine eyes, and bring thee a horn of southern drink to make thee dream sweet dreams to-night."

To omit this courtesy would have been a breach of Norse hospitality; yet an involuntary tremor of fear passed through Harald.

CHAPTER XXIII

THE TEMPTATION

HARALD was conducted to one of the sleeping rooms that opened out of the main hall. It was furnished with Norse luxury; but the young man noticed not his surroundings. He removed his cloak and flung it upon the back of a chair, into which he sank as if exhausted.

Though Hassan's message from Persea had brought him much relief, he was of unquiet mind and restless. During long hours he had been fighting Astrid's power and presence. He had seen the more than friendship in her eyes and actions; he understood now that this brilliant woman was madly in love with him. What a distorted pattern the web of life was weaving for him! He smiled grimly as he realized the whole situation. There was the King, loving and holding Persea from him, while the King's own sister had openly preferred him. He understood something of the game that they had played at the feast that night.

He dreaded the entrance of Astrid with the night-drink. Something evil seemed circling about him, drawing nearer and nearer. He tried to pray, but could not. Christ seemed not to hear, and mocking voices laughed at him.

At last he flung himself upon the couch, face downward. The burning wick in the open vessel on the table flickered and fluttered in the draughts, barely dispelling the darkness that was to him blacker, heavier than the darkness of other nights.

"Drink, Blest of the Nornir, and lie down to pleasant dreams!"

Harald started, and lifted himself upon his elbow. He trembled when he saw Astrid.

She had laid aside her stiff brocade, and was wrapped in a filmy gauze that enveloped her like a cloud. Except the pearls in her long braids, every ornament was gone. She stood attired in only the beauty of her womanhood, which the cloud of gauzy white about her made more dangerously intoxicating. Across the room she glided and offered the tiny Venetian cup to Harald. He took it from her; but ere he lifted it to his lips he said:

"I understand not this white garb thou wearest. Is not white the colour of slavery? Astrid the Peerless wrongs herself by so appearing."

She smiled one of her seductive smiles, saying:

"Drink, and I will tell thee."

He drained the cup. Then she sat upon the couch beside him and said:

"I wear the colour of a slave because I feel to-night that I am a slave. Yea, Blest of the Nornir, I am thy slave!"

Harald answered her gently:

"Nay, noble lady, say not such words to me. 'T is but an honour to receive the night-drink from thee, and I could not count thee as my slave. I do not want thee to say such words to me."

"Whether thou dost wish it or not, I have become thy slave to-night. Wilt thou not claim ownership?"

She leaned slightly towards him. It seemed to Harald that stars were shooting through his brain. He had a confused idea of Persea, duty, and honour; but mingled with all was a great temptation. He felt the conflict of good and evil. Which would be the stronger? He gazed with blurred vision at the cloud-wrapped form so near him. Compelled by her subtle influence, he placed his hand on her head.

"Astrid, dost thou know thou art very beautiful to-night? Surely the Nornir were kind to thee when they gave thee all of which a Norsewoman could ever boast."

A soft delight spread itself over her face and neck. She suddenly leaned heavily upon his breast and wound her white arms about him. He trembled violently, and made a feeble effort to disengage himself from her embrace; but the warm body only nestled closer, the soft arms only clung tighter as she whispered:

"Nay! Nay! let me lie upon thy breast. Am I beautiful in thy sight, and still thou knowest not that my beauty is for thee? The heart of Astrid the Peerless flew to thee on the day thou didst return from thy viking; and it has ever hovered about thee, though unseen to thy unseeing eyes. Fold thine arms about me and taste of my lips. Even as I lifted the cup of wine unto thee, so do I give thee the cup of my love. Drink, my Harald, for the draught is thine, and thine only!"

The atmosphere of the room was so stifling to Harald that he could scarcely get his breath. He struggled against the force that was dragging him down. He set his teeth. He stiffened his arms at his sides to keep from folding them about Astrid, as he replied :

" Thou art beside thyself to-night to say such words to me. Knowest thou not that in only one night removed I enter combat with thy brother for the sake of my love for another ? Tempt me not to stain my heart and my honour ! Think of thyself. Let it not be said that Astrid could forget that she was the King's sister, — could forget her worth and her blood and her fair honour ! "

Once again he essayed to remove her arms from about him. She resisted, almost fiercely.

" I tell thee I love but thee ! I know thy words are wise ; but this is a night of madness and love for me ! I came to thee to tell thee I loved thee ; and I will not go hence until thy lips have touched mine. Look upon them. Are they not lips made for kissing ? Come ! "

She gently drew his head down to hers. Harald saw the curved lips, so warm, so red, even in the faint glow of the flickering light. They conquered. He flung his arms about her. He leaned over her, every nerve in his body tingling with suppressed passion. Another second of this, and he would be lost to love and honour. This he knew ; this he felt ; but the current was too swift, too strong. He was sinking !

But his nobler nature, in its struggle against the wild waves of passion, sent one last mighty prayer for Christ's help. It came. Quicker than the lightning darts across the sky, mightier than any human mind could conceive, came that strength for which he prayed.

With an abrupt, powerful movement he put Astrid at arm's length from him, and then sprang to the centre of the room with face white, but stern, determined, unconquerable.

The woman was stunned, amazed. Confident of victory at last, she had closed her eyes as she felt his arms wind passionately about her. She was waiting for the touch of his lips that would bring him into her power; but instead of that touch came this rough tearing away, — this cold, stern face!

Then she, too, grew cold, — bitterly cold. She arose, and said:

"And is this thy kiss? Is this roughness thy embrace? What dost thou mean? Are my lips so distasteful to thee? Would my bosom be too hard a pillow for thy head that thou dost put me from thee in this manner?"

Harald trembled no more at her words. His voice was free from passion as he replied:

"Thy embrace and thy lips are not for me. Never will I take them from thee. Thou hast been a mighty temptation to me this night; but not again will thy beauty allure me, even for a moment, from the path of right and honour. What has happened here will remain locked within my lips. 'T is best that thou shouldst leave me now, lest others think that thou art indeed following all of the ancient custom. Thy fair name should be kept from such injury."

He stepped to the entrance and lifted the heavy curtains to allow her to pass out; but she did not move. In her face there was not only the bitterness of a love rejected, but a strange wonder. She saw by his actions and words that she had absolutely lost hold upon him, all control over him. She said:

"Dost thou know that when a woman's love has been spurned it becomes a hatred? Dost thou realize how I hate thee?"

Harald bowed low.

"It is best that thou dost hate me. I would rather have thy hatred than thy love; for it cannot bring such harm unto me."

An evil curve was on Astrid's lips as she answered:

"Dost thou think it cannot harm thee so much? Thou dost forget that with hatred like mine, there comes also revenge. And my revenge shall be more persistent than my love. To-night, thou thyself didst say that a woman's cure might be dark deeds that a man's mind could not even fathom. I cannot use the sword; but beware of my sting! I know full well where the poison will kill."

She laughed a low, cruel laugh.

But Harald would not allow her taunts and bitterness to

move him. He answered not a word, and still held the curtain aside for her. Then she stamped violently upon the floor in a furious rage.

"Thou man of all men! Thou man of iron will and heart of steel! tell me this. Whence comes that strength, that power in thee that has withstood me to-night?"

A brightness, a sudden joy illumined Harald's face as he answered:

"The strength, the power came from my Christ!"

Astrid shrank back. For an instant, fear came into her face. Then she made an impatient gesture, as if his words could not be true.

"Nay! There are some things in the hearts of men that I have never yet seen controlled by any god. I knew thou didst love another. I saw at the feast to-night that I could not hope to win thy love; but I loved thee, yea, I loved thee to madness, as thou dost know. I determined to have thee first. That would satisfy my jealousy and my revenge; for afterwards I could taunt her until she hated thee for thy falseness. I came unto thee, never dreaming thou couldst put me from thee. I knew thou didst believe in this Christianity that Persea believes in; but what of that? Before thou wast a Christian, thou wast a man! And I know that thou hast warm blood in thy veins; and I know that I almost won. I ask thee again, Whence this power to resist that which never fails to sweeps men out upon the boundless ocean of desire?"

Harald loathed this woman now. Yet he pitied her enough to keep the contempt from his voice as he answered, with great earnestness:

"Still I say unto thee that my help came from Christ. I felt my will giving way, and I prayed unto him. He answered by sending me such strength, such a change of mind that I put thee from me, and am no longer moved by thee."

Astrid shivered and trembled, and glanced fearfully upward as if she saw an unseen power in the air above her. When she spoke again, her voice was changed and low: her words had lost their boldness and bravado.

"Is it so? Is there a God who can do such a thing? Can Christ send such a mighty power unto those who believe and call on him? Then will I say this unto thee. I fear thy Christ! The God who can help a man to conquer as thou hast conquered must be the One True God; for the man who can conquer himself can conquer the universe!"

She caught her breath, and stood rigid, motionless, with arm and hand upraised in the gesture with which she had emphasized her last words. But suddenly she dropped her arm, and all the fierce jealousy and hatred came back into her voice as she continued:

"Yet never will I bow to man or God. I will be fair in my judgment of what has happened here to-night. We have fought a duel, — thou and I, — and thou hast won! I go; but remember that from this night, this moment of time, I live but for revenge. I shall not rest until I have made thee suffer even as I have suffered. Thy Christ cannot take the bitterness from thy heart, nor the agony from thy soul. Remember my last words to thee. Though it brings me death, I will be revenged!"

She was gone. Harald let fall the curtain. The room, the air, the flickering light seemed evil and poisonous.

He laid himself upon the couch; but sleep forsook him. Feverishly he watched through the tiny window for the first tint of red in the southern sky. All night he watched and prayed, hearing no longer the mocking voices. Peace entered his soul; and fervently he thanked God for the strength which had kept his lips pure for Persea's touch, his honour unstained.

CHAPTER XXIV

THE WISE WOMAN'S WARNING

High above the valley, sheltered alike from observation and the cold wind, Iron Beard and Heid looked down on the bonder of the Thrandheim as they went on with the games. From that height, the people were like moving spots of colour upon the brown and grey of the rocks and plain.

Heid was squatting upon the ground, with knees drawn up to her chin and thin arms clasping them. Her cloak hung about her, and a wolf-skin cap was drawn over her head and ears, making her look like some creature of the wilderness. Iron Beard stood erect. For some moments there had been silence between them. Then Heid spoke:

"Thou dost truly think that the King will seek to destroy the temple to-night?"

"Yea," said Iron Beard, "I do believe that such is his plan. Else why have so many of his men slipped off towards Lladir, one by one, and under different pretexts? Every warrior fully armed, also! None of the bonder have noticed; for 't was cleverly done; but Iron Beard has been watching for such tricks. Too old a wolf is he to be led into a snare, no matter how well concealed."

Grimly he smiled as his gaze wandered over the valley.

"Art thou sure that thy men can save the house of the gods?"

"Why so fearful, Mother? Are they not warriors? Olaf knows not that they are hidden within the temple; and I shall lead them myself. Scarcely will they miss me at the feast to-night. 'Twill be the second night, and the King's ale is strong. Men's brains will not be sharp."

"'Tis well," said the old woman. "The gods will need thee more than the King."

"So did I think; and 't will be a mad decree of Skuld if I save not our beautiful temple to-night."

There was another long silence. Iron Beard broke it by saying:

" I had all but forgotten to tell thee something more of importance. King Olaf has been challenged by Harald Rognvaldson to weapon-crossing or ordeal for the possession of the Christ Maiden. They meet to-morrow."

Heid tossed back her head and sent forth an exultant, cackling laugh.

" The curse !   The curse !   Did I not curse Olaf Tryggvveson from this very rock ?   Said I not that this new God would send him such a sorrow as would eat into his vitals ?   Said I not that he would pay for every shriek from the Skerry of Shrieks in the agony of his soul ?   He loves the Christ Maiden as only a man like him can love ; but he shall never know love of hers !   Agony untold shall he endure because of her. Sorrow upon sorrow shall come upon him through her. The curse of Heid has gone forth. Ha, ha ! Ha, ha ! "

She rocked back and forth in an ungovernable delirium of delight. The cliffs repeated her wild laughter until it seemed as if a thousand Nixies in the rocks were answering her.

Iron Beard asked, somewhat anxiously :

" Dost thou mean that Olaf will not win in this conflict ? There are none but count the Christ Maiden as his already. Thou knowest that no man has ever stood against him."

Angry was Heid as she replied :

" Said I not that he would never get the maiden ?   Harald Rognvaldson will overcome him."

Iron Beard frowned.

" Mother, I am not pleased that this should be ; for Harald did vow a vow last night to give all the glory of his victory to the White Christ. In my eyes, the cause of Odin would be more favoured should Olaf win. We can take the maiden from him, if he does."

Heid listened to his words with growing displeasure. She answered him abruptly :

" Olaf will fail ! "

The Temple Godi was disturbed. In his face was trouble as he asked :

" But, Mother, canst thou not change this one matter ? Seest thou not that if Harald wins, 't will be also a victory for the Christ we hate ?   'T would be so unlooked-for an ending that the people would believe that Harald won because of his

vow. Can we let such a thing come to pass ? What matters
it if Olaf wins ? The girl is given to the Well of Sacrifices,
and he cannot enjoy her long. The curse will descend ; but
't will be longer in the coming."

Heid arose, and there was a sullen despair mingled with the
anger in her voice.

" I cannot change my words. Thou hast told me that
which strikes a cold chill through my heart ; but what I have
said must come to pass. I have something more to say to
thee.

" This Christ Maiden is one upon whom my spells are as
the breath of summer. In vain have I brewed the witch's
broth, and called for her spirit that I might chain it to our use.
She comes not. When I think of her the fire burns out, and
the messengers of Odin depart. I fear her !

" Know that no mortal could resist my witchcraft save one
who is absolutely pure in word and deed ; one who has never
knowingly committed a wrong. Not before have I found
such an one ; though I have called upon those whom the less-
knowing considered pure and good. All have had their secret
sins, their hidden evil ; and I could do with them as I wished.

" But this maiden is beyond my power to harm. Seest thou
not that this very curse upon Olaf will be a blessing, a joy to
her ? I cannot tangle her in my web ; for her purity touches
the unseen threads, and they fall apart ! I cannot injure her
through another ; for though the King's sister asked for a death
potion for her, it will not harm her, it cannot harm her.
Neither canst thou harm her. Despair seizes me when I
think of her ; for if we conquer not her pure spirit, if we cannot fasten some sin upon her, — know that the cause of Odin
is lost ! "

She wrapped her cloak tightly about her trembling form.
But Iron Beard trembled not. Her words, her despair infuriated him.

" What ! Dost thou mean that we shall bow to this frail
maiden ? Dost thou mean that because of a woman, all
Thrandheim shall forsake Odin and Thor and Frey ? Dost
thou mean that I, Iron Beard, shall fail in my service to the
gods because a woman stands in my path ? I know thy wisdom. I would not offend thee ; but it seems to me that thou
hast spoken amiss. Such a thing cannot, shall not be ! This

very night shall she die! I desired to break her upon the stone in sacrifice; but if she troubles thee so much, I will send her out of thy way ere the sun reddens again the southern sky."

Heid raised her withered arms above her head in a horror of despair.

"Nay, nay! Lift not thy hand against her! Offend not those Spirits of the Pure which protect her! Thou canst not harm her, — I vow unto thee, — thou canst not touch a hair of her head with steel, or water, or fire, or earth. Thou dost not know what thou hast said. Thou canst not hear the spirit language within thee as I can. Thou canst not see the Invisible Ones which hover about this pure being, and make all arrows of evil to rebound and pierce the heart of the one who bends the bow. I have warned thee!

"Touch her not: make no effort to bring harm upon her head while she is sinless. If thou dost, thou shalt be visited with terrible sorrow. That which thou most lovest, that which is dearest and best of life shall be torn from thee; and thou shalt never know joy again!"

She buried her head in her hands, and rocked back and forth, moaning in an agony of fear and woe.

Iron Beard watched her with anger, fear, and indecision in his countenance. Twice he essayed to speak; twice his tongue refused to obey his will. All the time, the crouching figure at his feet continued to sway backward and forward, still wailing in terror. At last, he stood over her and said:

"Thou hast warned me. If harm comes, 't will not be laid at thy door. But more than ever do I desire this Christ Maiden's death; more than ever do I believe she must not live to influence thee and the people of the Thrandheim. She shall die! I cannot believe that this maiden can so harm me. I believe that she has bewitched thee somewhat, as verily she has bewitched many more. Thou art getting old, and age has made thee over-fearful. Iron Beard stops not because of a beautiful woman. When next I see thee, I hope to laugh at thy fears, and make thee give me thanks and praise for taking from the earth one who has so angered our gods. Farewell!"

He turned, and passed down the steep path. Heid ceased moaning, and sat motionless until the echo of his footsteps and the rattle of loosened stones was but faintly heard. Then she slowly rose, and pointed a long, skinny finger in the direction of the retreating sounds.

"So, O Blind One, thou dost think the Wise Woman's wisdom is tinged with the fear of old age! But for that, I might have told thee what would come to thee if thou didst lift thy hand against the Christ Maiden. I mourn for thee; but thou art headstrong and willful, and hast laughed at the Wise Woman. Wouldst thou not have stayed thy hand if I had told thee that thou wert raising it against thy Sigrid? Wouldst thou have persisted in this defiance of the Spirits of the Pure if I had told thee they would visit thy deed upon the head of thy precious one, the one thou dost call the Light of thy old age? Woe unto thee, O Temple Godi, for thy light shall go out, — go out forever, — and leave thee to moan in eternal darkness! Too late shalt thou know that the Wise Woman has yet a wisdom far beyond thine."

She dropped her arm. Wrapping her cloak closely about her, she disappeared among the rocks and stunted firs above the ledge.

*   *   *   *   *   *

In the King's málstofa sat Olaf and Thangbrand. The King was saying:

"To-morrow night will be the time to strike this blow at the heathen gods. The people will be awed by my victory over Harald Rognvaldson, his influence in the Thrandheim will be waning, and Iron Beard and his following will be ale-heavy. 'T is a dangerous undertaking; but I believe it will be a cure for their stubbornness. When the people wake to find their temple gone, their god destroyed, they will let thee baptize them. See thou that all happens as I have planned. In one night I shall have my desire with maiden and men!"

Thangbrand gave solemn promise to obey the King's commands, and then went forth from his presence.

But once beyond sight and hearing, his coarse features twitched with evil passion. Under his hood he muttered, "Not all things shall come to thee, Olaf Tryggvveson. The maiden would have suited me. Thangbrand will play thy game as he sees fit; and if thou dost lose, remember the blood-eagle!"

CHAPTER XXV

On the water, the splendour of earth, air, and sky, all mingled as the white-capped waves tossed and rolled in ceaseless motion, catching ever the splendour of towering mountain, wind-rocked fir, and rose-tinted sky, — holding them all, tossing them all, shouting gaily to them all.

With the splendour of nature came the poorer splendour of man. Upon the Fjord rode King Olaf's fleet of vessels. Long, graceful ships were they, built for speed and strength. Not the least conspicuous among these deer of the surf was Astrid's own vessel. It was large and elegantly built. Every timber was of the best, every ornament of the richest, and thirty-four pairs of oars sent it through the water as the bird skims the air. Many a time had it swept up and down the Fjord with its beautiful mistress in command; until the eagle-prowed sea-steed, with its golden banner, was known by every dweller near the Fjord.

There was much activity upon the King's vessels on this second morning of the feast; and if the people on the shore could have seen beyond the bend of the Fjord, they would have beheld Harald Rognvaldson's dragon-ship also covered with men who were stowing everything needed for a long voyage, and making a final examination of ropes, anchors, and sails.

The games were ended; and it was nearly time for the second night's feasting. Men were talking of the fine idróttir they had witnessed, — the long jumping, backward and forward, of men wearing armour and carrying war weapons; the wrestling, the ball playing, the swimming, and the marvellous tricks which King Olaf could perform; for he had out-classed all Thrandheim.

At the conclusion of the games, Olaf had gone into one of his long boats and ordered the men to row. As soon as the oars were in motion, he took three tolle-knives, and stepping upon the moving oars, walked up and down upon them; all the time tossing the three knives in air, and keeping them constantly in motion. Great applause had been given him when he came to land. The people spoke among themselves, and were astonished at the King's agility.

*　　*　　*　　*　　*　　*

Hassan was standing on guard before Persea's door as usual. A thrall-woman approached with a silver tray, upon which stood a tiny Venetian cup filled with wine. She said to him :

"The noble Astrid sends greeting to thy mistress, and asks that she take this draught of rare wine to renew her strength and make her beauty shine like the sun at the feast to-night."

Hassan took the cup, and answered :

"The Moon of the Desert has not yet come to her bower; but the gift of Astrid the Peerless will be placed on her table."

The thrall-woman went away; and Hassan stepped inside the curtained doorway. Holding up the glass, he examined it carefully. Then he muttered to himself, "The wine an enemy sends is not for a health-drink! My Beautiful One will be beautiful enough without thy strange draught, O Jealous One!"

He peered out of the doorway. Finding the court-yard empty, he threw the cup and its contents far over the boer. Then he returned to his post.

Soon Persea entered the skemma. After arraying herself for the feast, she reclined upon her couch until Harald should appear. To-night she was in truth to be with him. The King could not prevent their having had speech with each other that day; and all was well between them. Harald had vowed unto Olaf that Persea should sit beside him on the second night. The King had sneered and answered :

"Said I not so last night? I will give thee one more taste of the wine of her presence. 'T will only make my victory to-morrow bring a greater sting unto ye both. Look into her eyes and think that to-morrow night she shall be mine!"

An angry flush had risen in Harald's face.

"Thy words are but boasts. To-morrow, when the silver boat sails across the upper world, remember what thou hast just spoken; and see if thou didst not lie!"

Persea was thinking of all this, and how close was drawing the time of the great meeting. Hassan broke in upon her thoughts with the message that Harald waited without. Swiftly she rose, and throwing her cloak about her, went out to him.

The outer room was empty, and Harald sprang to meet her. Closely, hungrily, his arms folded about her. He had thought that his love could be no deeper; but to-night he was almost beside himself with the intensity of his passion. The memory of his victory over temptation illumined his happiness until he was blinded by the mighty force that had taken possession of him. He would not have given the sacred purity of that touch upon Persea's lips for all that the world had to offer of pleasure or gold. Half-frightened at his passionate embrace, Persea broke from him and stood at the entrance to her room, saying in trembling voice:

"Harald! Thy kisses to-night make me quiver with a strange fright. Thy love is a whirlwind which takes my breath from me."

Harald took her gently, tenderly back to his heart.

"Poor, frightened little bird! Beautiful Rosebud of the South, whose heart is so tender, so sensitive that the breath of thy lover makes thee to tremble. Fear not, my Angel of the Dawn, only know that Harald loves thee as never man loved before; only know that he loves thee better than life, or death, or himself; only know that he would choose hell with thee, rather than Paradise without!"

Persea stopped him with an imploring gesture.

"My Harald! Say not such words. They are mad and wicked, and become not one who is a Christian. Thou hast forgotten, in the rashness of thy Norse spirit, that love for Christ must come first, must come before thy love for me. Hush! I know all thou wouldst say; but listen, and I will show thee how thy words were not wise, nor good, nor pleasing to Christ or me.

"Thou knowest that I will never ask thee to follow me to hell. That is an easy path along which any wicked one could lead thee. I want thee to climb with me towards Christ and eternal happiness. The way upward is steep. The path is strewn with countless dangers, countless sorrows, countless battles that must be fought. Thou hast heard me speak of the *Voices* that called to me out of the world. I heard them clearly at the Autumn Sacrifice; and from thenceforth I knew that God had brought me here to do my small part in soothing this great nation-soul which knows not his love.

"This is my life. I must climb on if I would fulfill my destiny. Now I ask thee, wilt thou help me to live before this people as a Christian should live? Wilt thou, if need be, smother thy desires, so unaccustomed to control, and love Christ and me enough to climb with me to the Gates of Paradise, so that we may enter, hand in hand? This is the supreme test of thy love, — not to follow me to hell; but to rise with me to Paradise!"

She pointed out and upward through the open door to the starlit skies. In the faint light, with the great star scintillating above her head, she was more of heaven than earth. Her beauty, her purity, were supernal.

Harald, rebuked and humbled, knelt at her feet. As he lifted her hand to his lips, he felt the madness in his veins give place to a new, all-powerful love which penetrated to the depths of his soul and purged it of all that was selfish, all that was tainted with the blind rashness of desire. His love was still human. He still longed for her; but with his longing came that sacred love for her soul, which was so surely a spark from the Divine Fire. He realized how much there was yet for him to learn: how much of earth to stifle, of heaven to win. But the end, — was it not worth all the sacrifice? He said softly, reverently:

"My Angel of the Dawn, forgive. Yea, my love is strong enough to climb to any heights. We will go through life, hand in hand, helping each other, helping this people to mount higher and higher towards Christ. Some day we will reach the Gates of Paradise and enter, — still hand in hand! O my Love, my Love! Never did I know how I loved thee until now!"

Many moments Harald knelt, with lips pressed to Persea's hand. After a time, the maiden spoke:

"We must go to the feast hall. Our absence will be noted. Come."

Harald rose and led her down the staircase, and across the court-yard into the skali.

Their absence had been noted. Astrid, with gay laughter and brilliant wit, was holding converse with Erlend; but ever and anon her eyes scanned the assembled guests with anxious gaze. She began to watch the main doorway with feverish anticipation. She thought to herself: "She comes not. He comes not. The draught did its work. Astrid is revenged."

But even at that moment, the door was flung open and Harald entered, leading Persea by the hand. Astrid drew back into the shadow of the hangings with white, set face. When the two came opposite to her, she glared into Persea's eyes with a fierceness that made the Roman girl shiver as though a cold wind had struck through her heavy mantle. It was well that she could not know the thoughts that followed her.

Astrid whispered to herself, " She still lives. She lives and walks with him! The cup was deadly, I know; for the little beast, to whom I gave the drops, kicked and died. Yet she is here. What has taken my triumph from me? Perhaps 't was that God whom they serve; but I will not give up. The Norsewoman shall yet have her revenge, though she follow them both to the ends of the earth. I will snatch the cup of happiness from their lips, even as they have snatched it from mine."

Places of honour for Persea and Harald were awaiting them; but the girl shrank back and whispered :

" Not there. Let us not sit so near the King. I cannot endure his gaze upon me."

So they withdrew towards the western end of the hall where Tellus sat with Sigrid. Murmurs followed them as they sat down. Harald knew that men counted it strange that he should be in so low a place; but he cared not. Soon after, Hassan appeared among the thralls. When he saw his mistress, a curious smile flitted across his face, and he murmured: "If all Hassan has heard to-night is true, Allah is watching over the Moon of the Desert."

Olaf had placed Astrid beside him; for he had no desire to play the lover with any of the maidens of the Thrandheim. Persea, and Persea alone filled his brain. When he saw she was not in the place he had prepared for her, he was more than ever enraged at her, more than ever mad to subdue.

The feast went on with wilder excesses than the night before. The ale was strong, and men drank heavily. 'T was not long before it began to rise into their brains. The feast

hall rang with boisterous laughter and rude jests. Persea beheld the rough company with anxiety in her face. Harald
saw, and said :

" Our rude feasting seems coarse in thine eyes; but thou
must remember the land upon which we live, and the wildness
about us. Our lives and our pleasures are bold and fierce because they must be so; just as thy southern friends are languid
and voluptuous in their sunny, balmy land. But be not
alarmed, my Sweet One. The Norsemen do not easily lose
their brains. The ale is but making them merry. We count '
not that man great who takes so much that he loses knowledge
of himself. Besides, why shouldst thou shrink and tremble
when I am by thy side ? "

He leaned towards her, and laid his hand upon hers. Persea blushed and smiled. Harald felt her fingers tremble in his
close, warm grasp. How that slight movement thrilled him !
He forgot the future, so fraught with peril. He lost himself
in the wild delight of the present. As he whispered words
that only she could hear, Persea also forgot the world about
her, and began to realize that she was just upon the threshold
of love. If God gave her to this man, the years beyond were
filled with a possibility of happiness which her maiden heart
could scarcely comprehend. Their love was indestructible,
through all life and eternity. Something of this Harald saw
in her face; and he fain would have fallen at her feet in the
rapture of knowing that his thirsting heart was drinking from
a fountain which would flow eternally for him.

Meanwhile, Tellus and Sigrid were talking earnestly together. The girl's face was troubled. There was pain in
her blue eyes as she listened to her companion ; for her heart
was being torn apart by conflicting emotions.

" Ask me not to do this thing. How can I leave my
father ? How can I, who have always been his most precious
treasure, forsake him in his old age ? Even now, for the first
time in my life, I am not pleasing him ; for he urged me not
to come to the feast to-night. But he did not return ; and I
wanted one more hour with thee. Thou must not ask me for
more. Nay, nay, I will not ! If the King wins, take thy
sister and fly. That is thy duty; but though I crush my
heart, I will not go with thee. Christ would not have me go.
I know he would not ! "

Tellus bowed his head sadly.

"I would not have thee do ought that thy conscience says is not right.   We will leave our love in Christ's hands ; but know that thy Tellus will ever be true to thee.   If I go hence with Persea, be not downcast.   I will return.   Wait for me through a thousand nights.   Then know that if I have not come for thee, I am waiting thy coming in the world beyond. There we will be together, soul to soul, even though thou art denied to me on earth.   O my Sigrid !   I love thee !   I love thee ! "

Scarcely had the words left his lips when the great door of the skali burst open, and Iron Beard, blackened and bloody, sprang into the midst of the feasters.   His drawn sword was dripping red, his helmet was gone, his eyes were wild with terrible anger, and his gigantic frame trembled with rage. Raising his bloody sword, he shouted hoarsely :

"The temple of the gods has been destroyed !   Thor has been cast down from his chariot !   To your feet, men of Thrandheim, and avenge the deed !   Kill the King who has done this evil thing !   Avenge the gods ! "

Yells of fury broke from hundreds of throats.   In a twinkling, the feast hall was a battle ground.   Olaf's warriors sprang to his side, the followers of Iron Beard fell upon them ; and a hand-to-hand conflict began.   Tables and benches were overturned.   The screams and cries of the women mingled with the hoarse shouts of the men and the clash of arms.   Terrible to see were the blows that were given and returned, as the King's men fought their way towards the door.   Swords descending, crashed through helmet and skull, sunk deep into shoulders, or ran through bodies to the hilt. There was no mercy given or expected.   Above the ringing of steel, the crashing of mighty blows, the groans and shrieks, rose Iron Beard's cry :

"Avenge the gods !   Death to the Christian King ! "

At the first instant of alarm, Harald and Tellus had placed the maidens behind them, next to the hanging, and stood with drawn swords to defend them.   The other women were crouching and shrieking behind the overturned tables; but Persea and Sigrid clasped their arms about each other, and stood, pale and trembling, yet silent.

The great centre of the fight was towards the other end of

the hall, where Olaf's men were trying to reach the door; but Olaf himself, with a small body-guard, had deliberately faced about, and was fighting his way inward towards Persea. Evidently the King would rather lose a thousand kingdoms than that woman he loved. Tellus and Harald saw and understood, and the Roman said:

"Is the King mad, that he attempts to capture Persea before he flies? Even if he succeeds in seizing her, he cannot fight his way back through yonder warriors who have the berserk-rage upon them."

Harald looked at Tellus in grim despair as he answered:

"'Tis true; but we are all caught like beasts in a trap. There is no possibility of escape, no possibility of life. We are but two. Olaf's twenty will soon lay us low. If the sword kills not, then death in a worse form. See! The scattered firebrands are already setting fire to the skali! Thou mayest escape with Sigrid; for the King is indifferent to thee, and the warriors of the Thrandheim will not touch the Godi's daughter. But at the last moment, I shall send Persea to Christ, and then follow."

Tellus could not answer. The two men set their teeth, gripped their sword-handles, and awaited the onslaught of the King's guard.

While they waited, Iron Beard saw them, saw the star-crowned figure behind them; and his thunderous voice rang out another battle-cry:

"Death to the Christ Maiden and Harald Rognvaldson, the Christian!"

And he, too, started for the little group, his heavy sword cutting its bloody path before him. Sigrid gave one shriek of agony, and sank upon the floor, pulling Persea with her. Scarcely had they touched the ground when the hangings were slightly raised; and they were dragged under, beyond, into a damp darkness that smelt of earth. Hassan's voice sounded in Persea's ears:

"Quick, Moon of the Desert, rise and fly down the passage. I opened the secret door in the wall. Go!"

"But Harald? Tellus?" gasped Persea.

"I will bring them. Go ye on; for the King is trying to get ye. The way is dark, but smooth. 'Twill lead out on the shore by the low firs. Go, ere 'tis too late."

Persea staggered to her feet, assisted by Sigrid who had risen with a strength that belied her slight form. Together they felt their way down the dark path. Hassan lay on the floor and raised the hangings slightly. There was a clear, wise coolness in his actions. He knew the time was short; but he knew also that to show any one else the secret opening was to betray all. As he peered cautiously out, he saw that Iron Beard was three-quarters down the hall. Still was he sending forth that cruel cry :

" Death to the Christ Maiden and Harald the Christian ! "

But he was coming alone to do the deed. The warriors of the Thrandheim would not take the life of the Blest of the Nornir, neither cared they to shed the blood of that maiden, even at Iron Beard's command. Besides, all were fighting madly with Olaf's warriors. Straight on came the infuriated Norseman, more beast that human, hewing down men like blocks of wood, coming faster than the King.

Harald and Tellus waited for him with stern faces. This enemy was worse than a dozen Olafs. They must meet, not an ordinary man, but a giant with superhuman strength who was maddened with hatred and religious frenzy. Harald gripped h's sword with new strength as he said :

" When he comes, parry his first blow, and I will strike under his arm."

As he spoke, a warrior leaped from the side of the hall and barred Iron Beard's further progress with uplifted sword. The mighty Priest hesitated a moment, then closed with him. A cry of horror rang from the throats of the Norsemen as they saw the Temple Godi and Jarl Rognvald crossing weapons in the death battle. A dozen rushed forward to separate them, — and this was Hassan's chance.

" Hist ! "

The men glanced behind. Lo! The maidens were gone, the hangings trembled, Hassan's face appeared !

" Crawl under the hangings. Quick. The Moon of the Desert has escaped already."

The men knew the boy's shrewdness and wit. Tellus obeyed. Harald gave one glance up the hall. His father was well championed. Through the smoke which was rapidly filling the skali, he saw the impassioned features of Olaf as he fell fiercely upon the last group of men who stood between him and the spot where he supposed he would find Persea. Harald understood his daring now. Of course, Olaf knew of the secret opening, and was counting upon making his escape that way. Harald dropped to the ground and followed Tellus into the darkness.

Hassan replaced the heavy log, and then with one word, "Haste," he sped down the passage. The men groped their way as rapidly as possible, Harald leading. He said in a whisper:

"We will escape to the boat. Neither the King nor Iron Beard can touch Persea there."

They came out into the cold night air; and found the maidens crouching beside a low bush. "Follow the shore up to the small boat," said Harald, lifting Persea in his arms. Even in their peril, with the sound of conflict ringing in their ears, and the remembrance of the hatred and jealousy that were pursuing them, Harald thrilled at the touch of the burden he was carrying. He strained Persea to his heart as he pushed rapidly on through the scrubby pines and underbrush. Suddenly he stopped, and gave a low whistle.

A man sprang up just beyond them and shoved a small boat out from the rushes, saying:

"'T is thou, my master? I had begun to fear for thee. What has happened?"

"No time for words. Quick, Tellus, place Sigrid in the bow."

Sigrid moaned.

"My father, O my father! I cannot leave thee!"

She struggled from her lover's arms and fled back towards the skali. Hardly had she gone a dozen paces when she stumbled and fell. Tellus, bounding after her, lifted her from the ground. She answered not his passionate calling of her name. Something warm and sticky trickled over his hand. He bore her back to the boat.

"There is no help for it. She must go. She has struck her head and knows nothing. Christ has decided for her, — and me."

The boat pushed off. Soon it had rounded the cliff. There upon the dark water rode the noble dragon-ship. Few were the explanations or questions. The rowers took their seats, the warriors gathered their weapons, and the boat swept out and down the Fjord. Just as they reached the bend which would shut out the view of the peninsula, a bright flame shot into the air. In the light they could see the King's warriors running to the shore and putting off to the vessels in the harbour.

"Bend to your work, men!" cried Harald, "for the King is driven out; and I would not have his vessels sight us. I am no coward; but one against his fleet would be fearful odds."

The rowers replied with long deep strokes that sent the ship shooting swiftly over the waves. Ere the night was spent, they had passed out of the Fjord, beyond the rocky fringe of islands; and with all sails set, were bounding over the white-capped waves of the North Sea.

*   *   *   *   *   *

In the bitter chill of the early morning, Heid was shivering over her small fire. The curtain to her cave was suddenly torn aside. A man, wild-eyed and bloody, with broken sword and dented shield rushed in and fell upon the ground at her feet, writhing in agony.

"Mother! Mother! They have taken my Sigrid! They have stolen the Light of my Old Age! Madness is coming upon me! O my Sigrid! my Starlight, my Moonlight, my Sunlight! Gone, gone, gone!"

He swooned away. Pityingly Heid removed his armour, bound up his wounds, and washed the blood from his face and matted beard. Then she made a soft bed of skins and dragged him upon it. Many months he stayed in the cave with her while his wounds healed.

But throughout all the Thrandheim the people mourned him as dead.

CHAPTER XXVI

"THINK OF ME!"

OLAF TRYGGVVESON stood on the high deck of his dragon-ship, and looked back towards the Thrandheim — driven out of the finest district in Noregs-veldi; driven out without having established Christianity; driven out without the woman he loved! What mattered that it was all owing to a blunder made by his warriors in destroying the temple on the second, instead of the third night? With Olaf there remained only the sharp sting of defeat when victory had seemed assured.

But Thangbrand laughed under his breath when the King raved.

And Persea? Where was she now? He scanned the horizon anxiously; but no sign of sail. Three nights since, he had emerged from the secret passage just in time to see the faint image of the ship that bore her away from him, ere it vanished in the darkness. But he had not seen it again; although his rowers had strained every muscle and hoisted every sail in the endeavour to win the extraordinary reward he offered for the capture of Harald Rognvaldson's vessel. While he thought his bitter thoughts, Astrid drew near and spoke:

"Several days have passed, and yet no sign of the dragon-ship thou art pursuing. Thinkst thou not that this is strange?"

Olaf ground his teeth as he replied:

"Yea, 't is more than strange. But Olaf will yet conquer all things. He lives but for three purposes, — to bring his army of the south into the Thrandheim; to let the light of day into Harald Rognvaldson's throat; and to possess the maiden who has scorned his honourable love."

Astrid turned slightly from him; and he did not see, in her face, the dawn of a daring determination as she answered him:

"Hast thou considered why we have not sighted the ship thou seekest? See! We have sailed southward, — the way any ordinary sea-steed would point as the winter winds toss the waves with a madness that even the Norseman dreads. But the man thou pursuest is no ordinary man; and he has given thee the slip. Yea, even now his dragon is leaping in the teeth of the north wind. He has gone towards the Shifting Lights, most likely towards Iceland. Every stroke of thine oarsmen sends thee farther from him."

Olaf raged in fury. Not towards Astrid, for he recognized that her woman's wit had discovered the truth; but at his own failure to see, long since, what was so self-evident now. Astrid waited until his anger had begun to subside; and then she spoke again:

"What has been done, has been done. Why consider thy ill luck? Rather look to the future. Two courses lie before thee, — to sail southward after thine army and come back to force the Thrandheim to accept Christ and thee; or to turn thy fleet, and search the north for thy rival and thy slave. Thou canst not do both. Is there not grave reason to believe that thy entire kingdom may be lost if thou dost not speedily subdue the Thrandheim? Is this not of more consequence to thee than thy personal enmities and loves?

"Now I have a plan to unfold. Yonder sails my strong-winged bird of the waves, manned by warriors who are renowned for their skill in shipcraft and fighting. Is it not a match for Harald Rognvaldson's dragon ship? I will go aboard; and at my command, the eagle-prow shall be turned northward. I will bring unto thee thy enemy and thy slave. Ask me not why; but know that Astrid the Peerless has reason to hate. She will do this deed better than thou couldst, for she hateth more! Let me go."

Olaf looked keenly into her face. What he saw there was all-sufficient. He answered:

"Go!"

In an hour Olaf, still on deck, saw the last of Astrid's vessel as it was sharply outlined against the weird lightning that played in the northern sky. He watched it disappear, laden with his hopes and fears, and thought that the days would indeed be long until he saw it again. But Astrid would find them, though they had taken refuge in the palace of the Storm King himself. When Persea was again within his grasp, he would wait no longer.

She had cost him dearly. Because of her, he had lost the support of the most influential man of the Thrandheim; because of her, he had not gained the good-will of the Norsemen at the Autumn Sacrifice ; because of her, he had left a matter of grave importance to another who had brought disaster and defeat; because of her, he had lost half his kingdom. She should pay the price, since her beauty had been such a curse to him.

Was it only his troubled mind, or did the wind bring sounds of mocking laughter to his ears ? But he put aside the uncanny thoughts and revelled in sweeter ones of revenge.

As he pictured Persea lying on his breast, her dark eyes haunted him. He knew how they would look when he held her against her will. He could see the flashing scorn give place to a dumb terror that affected him strangely; even though it was but the picture of a thought. He was suddenly conscious of the fact that he was pitying her.

But what if she was already a wife ? At this thought he was possessed with jealous passion. The veins upon his forehead stood out like cords. If this thing was true, she was happy with it. She was looking into Harald's eyes with other looks than were haunting him. She was gladly giving all that wonderful beauty to the one she loved. But she would curse that beauty ere he had done with her. Yea, curse it, and mayhap even the God who gave it. As his imagination ran riot with pictures of passion and hate, a vision seemed to appear before him. There, at the outer edge of the deck, stood Persea.

He saw her with outstretched, imploring hands. His heart clearly heard her sweet, pleading voice float to him out of the darkness of the night :

"What have I done, O King Olaf, that thou shouldst make my beauty such an evil thing to me ? Is it my fault that thou dost love me ? Will Christ bless the doing of the vile deed that is in thy mind ? Rule thy actions with the Christ-love, not with passion, and cruelty, and revenge. Pursue me not with thy violence. Let thy love give me my life and my happiness. Think of *me*, of *me* ! "

The voice drifted away among the sounds of the night : the vision slowly vanished; but Olaf stared after it with dumb, bewildered countenance. When it had faded into space, when there was nothing left but the rhythmic rush of the waves, and the weird sound of the wind among the rigging, he

sank, trembling with new feeling, upon a pile of sail. Burying
his face in his hands, he tried to understand this message that
had been sent into his soul out of the black infinitude of
space.

That new, new thought, — to think of *her*. Could he put
aside his own desires, his own happiness, to think only of
hers ? He knew that to do this would be something better,
purer than any of the great deeds of his life for which men
had sung his praises in song and story. This would be something divine ! Yea, he understood the Christ-love at last, —
even as Persea herself understood it. But was he strong
enough for this supreme test ? He thought of the words Persea had spoken from the sacrificial rock on that memorable
day of the Autumn Sacrifice. " The man who bears pain, or
goes forth to battle, knows not the strength of the man who
follows in the footsteps of Christ." It was so. Could he,
should he reach out for this strength which all his bravery and
prowess had not given him ? Should he strive to conquer
himself, for Persea's sake ? Should he put aside his happiness
to bring happiness to her ? Could he change his passionate
desire to this pure love ? He thrilled with the new life that
had awakened in his soul. He prayed to the Christ.

What that prayer was, only God knew ; but when it was
over, the King's brow was less crossed with lines of passion.
There was the first light of dawning truth in his eyes.

But Olaf could not easily conquer that self which had so
victoriously ruled his life since boyhood. He paced rapidly
up and down the deck for some moments, gazing into the
north with a mingled expression of longing and sorrow. If
Astrid was permitted to continue her quest, pain and loss
might come to Persea ere he could prevent. Should he give
command to his fastest ship to bring Astrid back to his fleet ?

He half-turned to do so. His lips framed the words that
should declare his purpose ; but suddenly a cloud swept across
his face, the deep passion-lines returned, and he whispered
fiercely to himself : " Fool that I am ! Why should I ?
Lives there a Norseman who would not drink the draught to
the last drop ? "

The order was unspoken. The ship that had left the fleet
on a cruel errand, sped on its way, unhindered.

But through the long days and nights following, Olaf could

not rest, could not find relief from his aroused and torturing conscience. Ever the winds brought to his ears a wailing cry, — a cry that smote upon his heart and made it tremble with fear, and longing, and bitterest anguish, — " *Think of me, of me, of me !* "

CHAPTER XXVII

A VIKING QUEEN

MEANWHILE Astrid, standing beside the great gilded eagle-prow looked not backward but forward. The sails above her head roared and cracked, and bounded in their strong harness like frightened horses. The wind was rising; the waves were getting higher. The icy spray stung her face and clung to her long hair; but she only drew her fur cloak more closely about her and laughed at the fury of winds and waves. She shrank not; though she knew she was sailing into a corner of the world where death lurked in a thousand forms. High and wide and deep are laid the invisible snares. Cliffs, reefs, and banks, ice, currents, mist, and winds, — all reaching out cruel hands towards the human soul who dared to defy their strength and mystery.

For many nights and days the gilded eagle flew towards the home of the North Wind. It began to meet the advance-guard of the ice-world, and was forced to change its course to the southwest. To starboard, the ice-pack stretched off towards the horizon in vast fields of snowy white, — a boundless pavement, — broken by pathways of dark water. It rose and fell with the motion of the waves, sending forth incessantly a mysterious, faintly-ringing dirge.

On the edge of the floe, two icebergs kept watch over the wild waste of water, and whiteness and sky. Great glaciers were they, which had slipped into the sea and become restless, wandering islands, beautiful but death-dealing. Mist was their cloak by day, and darkness by night. Though the Norsemen strain every ear to listen for their coming, their footsteps are unheard upon the mighty waters.

It was sunset of the second day beside the ice-floe. Still the *Eagle* kept on without sight of any vessel upon its wide horizon. The west was rioting in colour; and as the ship came near to the great islands of ice, the sunset was reflected upon them. Their lofty spires seemed to be shooting flames: the whiteness was tinted with pink and rose; and in the dark blue caverns strange metallic tints gleamed, — copper, bronze, and gold.

The sun set; the long night passed, and in the southeast came the faint glimmer of another short, cold day. Still the Norsemen saw nothing but the vast fields of ice and the great bergs. Then Astrid commanded to change the course still more to the southwest. No boat would be reckless enough to get entangled in that relentless, crushing whiteness. They left the wide ice-fields; but still were they haunted by the bergs which surrounded them on every side, dipping, turning, gliding forward with resistless march that made the Norsemen keep a sharp lookout.

As the ship slipped farther towards the south, the great white mountains became less numerous, and so less dreaded. The *Eagle* sometimes swept close by them rather than change her course. Then even the rude, rough Norsemen wondered at the marvellous beauty of these crystal mountains, suspended in the vast transparent green of the dark waters. Every curve, every prominence, every depression was filled with delicate colouring of white, grey, pale greens and blues; while the surf rang in the caverns and sounded upon the crystal shores with muffled roar.

But powerful forces were working invisibly upon the cold, fixed death; and they would inevitably conquer. So it was, that as the golden *Eagle* flew across the waves with snowy wake, a shout arose from the lookout. The Norsemen rushed upon deck. There, far over the water towards the south, they saw one of the white, wandering palaces. Walls and towers were falling apart and plunging with seeming silence into the green ocean which leaped, and tossed, and rolled with tremendous commotion. Billows of foam sprang high, and burst in air. Enormous green waves, burdened with white wreaths, rolled away in widening circles, racing among and over the fragments of ice which were reappearing from the depths on all sides.

Then the sound-waves broke upon the Norsemen's ears, — tremendous, awful — a thousand peals of thunder bellowing over the vast expanse of water, telling of the destruction of a crystal world. On they swept towards the north, bearing the news of the death-struggle to the land that had given form to the perished one. After the passage of the sound-waves, there upon the bosom of the ocean lay only a mass of white ruins, with one tall tower left standing in the midst, rocking slowly to and fro.

The Norsemen gazed at each other and read the thought that leaped to the minds of all. To see the destruction of the Ice King's Palace was an evil omen. No Norseman could witness such a catastrophe and ever hope to come safely into harbour.

As if to confirm their fears, out of the sunset sky came a fierce, whistling wind. Dark storm-clouds rose swiftly above the horizon. The Norsemen saw their inky blackness, and shook their heads ominously as they hastened to furl their great sail and prepare their sea-bird for the coming struggle.

The sea rose high, and the greenish-blue water was striped with froth like veins in marble. The staunch ship dashed, breast-deep, through the white banks that rolled up towards it, bursting them all, and sending foam and liquid fire far out into the night. The wind grew to a hurricane. A terrifying darkness spread over the whole sky and sea. The ship was riding upon the bosom of the storm and the blackness.

All alone, far out upon an unknown waste, far from quiet harbour or helping beacon-fire, in the midst of unseen horrors, the Norsemen fought the mighty Storm King. He unlashed his terrible wolves of the sea, and they leaped towards the eagle prow with maddened roar and cruel fangs. They sprang upon it with frightful force, one after another, pounding, tearing, crunching. The brave ship shivered and trembled; then rose grandly from among them, shaking their frothy brine from her golden head, and leaping forward to meet the next attack.

Hour after hour rolled by; but still the mighty battle raged. The ship began to suffer from the incessant onslaught. One immense wave broke upon her deck. There was a crash, shrieks drowned by the voice of the tempest; and the mast went overboard, carrying a dozen brave men with it. Relieved of this strain, she rose again to the conflict; and for a while struggled on bravely.

But the men were becoming exhausted. Those who gripped the steering car, and for hours had kept the vessel from swamping in the trough of the waves, were beginning to feel the terrible strain. At last there came a tearing, twisting wave that wrenched the cumbrous oar from its place, and now the vessel was but the plaything of the storm. Man after man was swept overboard; until barely half of the crew remained. At Astrid's command, they took refuge in the small cabin.

There, trying to keep from freezing, tossed about by the furious waves which seemed to be holding off their doom for the purpose of quenching their fiery spirit and subduing their courage, they yet were brave and fearless. Not even the woman quailed at the terror above and about them. Rather did she encourage them all by her wise words and assurances that all would yet be well. But one enormous wave fell full upon the ship. It shivered, trembled, cracked,—and then was heard the final, desperate cry:

"The ship is leaking!"

All except Astrid prepared for death. She held aloof and watched the various ones as they offered prayers to Christ, or Odin, or Egir; and she wondered which would be heard. Which God was the real God? Where would their spirits fly? She would pray to no God. She never prayed during her lifetime; therefore why offer a poor petition now? No; she would enter the Unknown as she had lived; and she would go willingly if only she had been revenged!

However, even while the men prayed, the sea seemed to subside. The ship leaned no more towards the water; but slowly righted herself, and the waves were not strong enough to throw her again. The wind was blowing less fiercely; and when one of the men ventured on deck, lo! the storm was retreating sullenly towards the east. The white-capped waves snarled under the curving prow, but leapt no longer at its throat. The *Eagle* had out-weathered the storm.

Yet the victory had been dearly bought. Water was creeping in through many places between the weakened, strained timbers; so that the men could not cease baling to man the oars. Every inch of plank and rope was covered with ice. With mast and steering oar gone, even the unconquerable Norsemen saw little hope as they rallied to one last desperate effort to keep their vessel afloat till dawn. The quieting waters only delayed their doom. Ere another night, the green waves would open to receive them; and the icebergs would be their bautastones.

Finally, the long night of bitter cold and suspense came to an end. They saw in the southeast the first, faint tinge of red, the widening circle of light, the red-gold sun,—and there, not a quarter-league away, the dragon-ship of Harald Rognvaldson !

Astrid, wet, frozen, exhausted, with only a leaking ship between herself and death, yet ground her teeth in rage as she saw the vessel that held those she hated, knowing that she was powerless to wreak her vengeance upon them. What could she do, when yonder ship was all unhurt by the storm ? Its masts were standing, its sails were spread, and all was well on board. For the first time, hopelessness dulled her spirit of defiance.

The other vessel had sighted them, and was changing its course, doubtless to offer assistance, since it could see it was sadly needed. Then the fire came back into Astrid's eyes. Take aid from Harald Rognvaldson ? Owe him her life ? Never ! She would throw herself into the sea first.

But while the dragon-head was drawing closer, other thoughts came into her mind. After all, the future was still hers. There were more ways than one for a woman to take revenge. Had he not said so ? She would accept the situation, and bide her time. It would come ; it must come.

She turned to her men and said briefly :

" Ye do know that we came in pursuit of this ship that is approaching us. Our own vessel is no longer safe. Our warriors have perished. We can neither fight nor return to Norge. When yonder ship comes alongside, we will say we were driven out of our course by the storm ; and they will doubtless take us on board. Tell nothing of the purpose of our voyage. King Olaf's command may yet be obeyed. Meanwhile, obey mine."

The warriors pledged their word to do her will in the future as in the past. There were none who did not idolize her, who would not go to any lengths to win approval from her proud lips. She was their pride, their delight. By her daring, her courage, and her endurance, she had won the right to rule them. Their Viking Queen could do no wrong.

On board Harald's vessel, many conjectures were being made about the ship they were approaching. Harald and Tellus strained their eyes to catch the first glimpse of anything that would give them definite knowledge.

Said Tellus :

" The vessel is certainly Norse-built. See, the mast is

gone ; but there is the carved prow. Besides, I know the lines of thy wonderful ships. The men are assembling on deck, and they are Norsemen."

Harald gripped his comrade's arm.

" Yea, Norsemen, and enemies, too. Yonder is the ship of Astrid the Peerless. She herself stands in the midst of the men. Dost thou not see her tall form and long hair ? "

Tellus looked and saw. He said :

" Their ship must be leaking badly. See how low it lies in the water. We will have to take them on board."

From behind the two men came a voice that was filled with evil foreboding :

" Then the viper will be nourished in the very nest of the dove. Have a care what thou doest, O Master of the Golden Armour."

Harald turned to see Hassan gazing at the disabled vessel with a stony indifference that belied the warning he had just uttered. The man knew well what this boy of few words meant. An undefinable fear came into his mind ; but he put it aside and replied quietly to Tellus :

" We will certainly rescue them from their perilous position. We would not leave our bitterest enemy to perish thus. Still, we must be cautious until we know their minds towards us ; for Harald does believe that Astrid the Peerless is more to be feared than all of King Olaf's fleet."

CHAPTER XXVIII

"WHITHER SAILEST THOU?"

IT was the fortieth day of Astrid's presence on Harald Rognvaldson's vessel. Her men had mingled with the warriors upon the ship, and had long since ceased to consider their misfortunes. Norsemen grieved not over the turn of the tide. Astrid held herself proudly aloof from all except her own. Persea and Sigrid would have been kind to her; but she repulsed all their efforts at companionship with sneers, and even taunts which sent the colour into their cheeks. After one of her cruel speeches, Sigrid sought Persea weeping bitterly:

"Why did not Tellus leave me to die upon the shore? Then, at least, no evil could have been said about me. Who will ever believe my coming was not of my own will? Who will ever believe my Tellus has been only my protector, my brother, even as he is to thee?"

"Weep not. We did what was best; and since God must have guided us, we should not grieve. No matter what that cruel woman may say, we are pure, and will so remain. Christ will watch over us always. No evil shall come to us."

Sigrid only trembled more violently.

"I know not how to tell thee of the fear that is in my heart to-night. When Astrid spoke to me there was an evil gleam in her eyes that filled me with terror; yet thou knowest that I am not easily frightened. Something cold reached out from her and took hold of my heart, making the blood freeze in my veins. There is evil lurking in the air about me. I shrink from the future. Talk to me of Christ. It is all thou canst do for me. If I love him, I shall go to him when the blow falls."

While Persea spoke to the troubled girl of the Christ she loved, Astrid searched the boundless expanse of water with restless eyes. Where was this daring Harald taking his ship? With all her keen discernment she had not discovered what she most wanted to know; for even Harald's men were ignorant of their destination.

Though already so far from home, the dragon-head still pointed southwest. The wind was not so fierce and cold; the light lasted longer. Yet the boat sped on, seeming to be but a fixture in the centre of a great circle of water and sky. It was growing wearisome to Astrid. Always hastening forward, yet never getting farther from the line behind, never getting closer to the line before. Above her arched the sky with its rose-tinted border. She longed to lift the far-off edge and see beyond into the unknown.

The day was sinking beneath that crimsoning border; and the night, with all it might bring to her, was coming up out of the east, casting its shadow across sea and sky. The ship was sailing through the twilight, that weird, lonesome meeting-place of gloom and splendour that ever thrills the human heart with a mysterious power. This influence Astrid felt; and it took the strength of endurance from her, it made this doubt unbearable.

She turned quickly to descend to her tiny, curtained recess in the cabin, and saw Harald Rognvaldson behind her. She stopped, and addressed him imperiously:

"Tell me whither this sea-snake is speeding. Many long, unhappy days have I been beholden to thee for food and shelter. Still no sign of land, no course but one on which a Norseman has never sailed. What means it? When shall I be able to leave this ship which thou must know is worse than Nifl-hel to me?"

Harald's face grew grave at her violent words; but he replied without anger:

"I am sorry that thou dost feel thus. I hold no malice towards thee. I would gladly do aught that would make thee more content with thy lot. Canst thou not forget the past and ——"

She stopped him with a quick gesture.

"No, I will not forget. Say not the word to me. There is nothing I wish to forget, not even my last words to thee. When I saw thee coming to rescue me, I would fain have jumped into the sea rather than owe thee aught. But I did not because I had not yet had my revenge. Dost thou hear? Throw me into Egir's arms if thou wilt; but ask me not to forget."

Harald felt a thrill of admiration for her marvellous courage as she thus hurled defiance in his face upon the deck of his own vessel; but he said nothing. She continued :

" Thou hast said thou wouldst do aught that would make me more content with my lot. Tell me then the secret of thy destination ; for this waiting is driving me mad."

Harald walked to the edge of the deck and pointed to the west.

" Dost thou remember the story of the Skald who came to thy brother's feast ? Dost thou remember his instructions to point the prow westward and sail on, farther than ever man sailed before ? Dost thou remember what he said the daring one would find ? "

Astrid stared at him with astonishment.

" I remember. This new land is in thy mind."

Harald smiled.

" I knew that no one would follow us into the unknown. It is my thought to explore this land, if so be we come there-upon. When the spring warmth has opened the Northern Sea I will sail to Iceland. There I have kinsmen who will shelter me until I can hear from the Thrandheim and know whether I can safely return with my bride; for when we reach Iceland I shall drink the wedding cup with Persea, according to the laws of the land. Now I have told thee all, more than even my brave warriors know. I feared they would grow faint-hearted at so long a voyage."

Astrid was bewildered at the man's daring.

" Art thou not afraid that evil will befall thee ? Thou hast risked much upon the tongue of a wandering skald."

Harald put his hand under his cloak and drew out a strange object — a carved, bowl-shaped piece of wood, with one end of a long, hollow reed fitted into it. He held it up before Astrid.

" See what was found floating upon the water to-day. I know not what it is ; but only the hand of man could fashion such a thing. It tells us we are nearing land and land that is strange."

She examined the unknown object. Its uncouthness made her remember how far she was from home, how long she would have to wait for her revenge. She said with her old bitterness :

" It matters little to me. The coming days will be long to

Astrid the Peerless. When thou reachest Iceland, wilt thou let me journey on to the south of Norge?"

Harald shook his head.

"Nay, lady. 'Twould not be wise for Harald to send word to Olaf Tryggvveson where Persea is sheltered."

"So, thou wouldst hide? ' Hast thou forgotten that thou didst challenge him for possession of the maiden? Thou hast not kept thy appointment. Thou hast taken the prize without winning it. Thou hast no honour."

Harald's face grew stern and white. He turned upon Astrid and spoke as one who would brook no further insult, even from a woman.

"I have taken only as circumstances compelled me. Had I not escaped with her, Iron Beard would have killed her ; or, with twenty men at his back, Olaf would have snatched her from me. But never shall human soul say that Harald Rognvaldson has no honour. Yea, I will send thee to thy brother. Tell him that Harald Rognvaldson will return to meet King Olaf at whatsoever place and time he may name. Much as I love Persea, I love my honour more. I shall not take her to wife until I have settled this matter, and made even thee who hatest me say that Harald Rognvaldson's honour is as pure and unstained as the white tears that fall from the clouds."

He turned abruptly and descended to the cabin. Astrid watched until his winged helmet disappeared below the deck. Then the evil flamed out in her face, more cunningly wise than ever. "Dost thou love thy honour so well?" she whispered. "'Twill give Astrid more time to poison thy happiness. Perhaps thou wilt wish thou hadst never reached land with Astrid the Peerless. But I warned thee, I showed thee my teeth. If I win, why I win. If I lose, death will be sweeter than to see her in thine arms."

She wrapped her cloak around her, and walked to the forward limit of the deck, where she sat down on a huge coil of rope, close by the gilded dragon-head. There she stayed for many hours, thinking thoughts that seemed to make the ship leap and tremble with fright as it sped along.

The wind was gathering strength, tuning every cord and straining every sail. Far and near the waves were all hastening in the same direction, rolling, tossing, crumbling into foam, leaping madly in their play and passion, and scattering green fire far out into the night.

All things were moving forward with one will and one step, — winds, clouds and billows, Norsemen, sails and golden dragon, — keeping time to the mighty music of the winds and waves, while the great evening star, as it stooped towards the horizon, beckoned them on into the vast unknown.

CHAPTER XXIX

CHRIST'S LAND

OUT of the sea rose the sun, dripping with the brine of centuries. It brought the dawn of the day on which the first wave of destiny should break upon the shores of the New World.

The sleeping continent, clothed in its primeval grandeur, lay just over the rim of the western horizon. All unconscious, the hills slumbered on. The red man went forth to his hunting-ground with no knowledge of the tiny speck that was rounding the great earth-curve, drawing nearer, nearer, as the sun climbed the sky.

The dragon-ship was leaping forward under pressure of sail and oar, its decks crowded with men who shaded their eyes and peered anxiously towards the long line of the western horizon. They knew now that the destination of their staunch vessel was the strange land of the west. Their hearts beat fast with the thought that their bold leader had led them into such untrodden paths. They had observed many signs of the near approach to land. Birds had appeared, twigs and branches of trees had floated by, and far above them a majestic fishing eagle dipped and glided.

Grandly the brave ship approached the New World. The high, curved prow was shining with fire from the rising sun, the bright-coloured sails were filled stiff with a boisterous wind, the long lines of oars were moving in perfect unison, the sides were covered with burnished shields. The stalwart men upon the high deck were well worthy of the honour that was coming out of the west to greet them.

A dark streak on the horizon.

"Land! Land! Land!"

The shouts echoed far and wide over the waters, spreading out in widening circles of sound until they struck upon the shores of that mighty ocean, — the first message of the white man to the Western World.

Flocks of sea birds flew about the ship, uttering mournful

cries. They dipped their great wings into the foam and then
swept swiftly over the golden-headed dragon, scattering glittering drops upon prow and mail-clad warriors, as if to prepare
them by a sacred baptism for their landing upon the virgin
soil.

Nearer and nearer came the long, black streak. The shore
towards which they were steering was low and fringed with a
sandy beach. Beyond were stretches of forest land, out of
which the bare branches of tall trees outlined themselves
sharply against the sky. Westward the land rolled away in
undulating hills clothed in the brown and evergreen of winter
garb, with here and there a space which gave a glimpse of
white snow, or opened a vista into the interior where the hills
rolled farther and farther inland, until they were lost in the
blues and purples on the distant horizon.

The sails had been furled, and only half of the oarsmen were
propelling the boat; for Harald was too wise a viking to risk
a rush upon an unknown beach.

Gradually the cries and shouts gave place to silence. The
Norsemen saw this fair, bright land with a peculiar bounding
of the heart. Accustomed to the wild grandeur of their towering mountains and deep, dark fjords, those quiet hills seemed
like a fairy garden; and the wind that blew against their faces
was but a summer breeze beside the Northland's winter
tempest.

Yet the glamour of the landscape did not deceive them.
Beautiful as it was, they watched it silently now. No more
boisterous expressions of delight, no more shouts of bravado or
surety of conquest. They looked and wondered what was
behind those purple and blue hills? What lurked under the
shadow of those mighty forests? What dangers awaited them
on that still, unknown shore? What countless eyes were
watching them, even now, from a thousand hiding places?

To all appearances, they were sweeping bravely to their
conquest; but there was something in that still landscape,
something in the rolling hills and mighty forests, that whispered of a power which was only sleeping. The Norsemen
knew not what it might be; but they believed, and believing,
gave unconscious homage.

While this subtle knowledge was creeping into the warriors'
hearts, Persea had appeared among them. Harald stepped

quickly to her side, and pointing to the shore, now distinct and near at hand, he said :

" Christ has been kind. Behold the land of which the Skald told at Olaf's feast ! "

Persea gazed at the shore with wonderment. Then God's spirit spoke to her spirit. Her bosom rose and fell with deep breaths ; her eyes dilated as though they saw marvellous visions ; her body inclined forward as though she listened to some voice from the New World. Still seeing the unseen, still listening to the unheard, she raised her hand, and pointing towards the sleeping continent, said :

" Men of Norge, Christ has given us this joy, this first knowledge of land that is all unknown to the inhabitants of the world behind us. It is fair to see. It is virgin, pure, unstained by the sins and wickedness of that world we have just left.

" Behind us, the nations of the earth groan under a bondage of sin and woe. There is no place for the human soul to worship God in spirit and in truth. But Christ's truth cannot die. The time will come when it shall make men so strong that they will burst all bonds of tyranny, and come forth to build a new nation beyond the Western Sea, which shall recognize truth. Christ has vouchsafed to us the first landing upon the shore he has sanctified. Let us take possession of it in Christ's Name, and for his use. Let the land be called Christ's Land ; for Christ shall rule over it as long as the sun shall endure.

" Upon this shore, countless blessings shall descend of which humanity, as yet, knows nothing. Even as we have fled from the wrath and destruction that menaced us in the world of men, so shall the coming centuries find the burdened, the seeker of truth, the sorrowing, the persecuted, flying from the error and finding here the peace of Christ. It is Christ's Land ! Let us keep it sacred to his Name in every word and deed ! "

She had spoken as one who sees beyond the limit of human vision ; and when she finished, sea, earth, and sky seemed to quiver with the mightiness of her words.

Though her thoughts were all but unintelligible to the Norsemen, they scoffed not ; for, even the roughest reverenced her for what she was, and therefore reverenced her words.

Harald and Tellus could alone comprehend something of the greatness of her thoughts. The leader of the Norsemen spoke to his men in grave command :

" Ye have heard the words from the lips of the Christ Maiden. What she has spoken shall be sacred to us. I name this land ' Christ's Land ' in honour of the Christ who has led us hither through many perils. By this name shall we know and speak of it ever hereafter."

The men placed their hands upon their swords and said solemnly :

" It is Christ's Land. All hail to Christ the White ! "

So was the New World given to Christ by rough, passionate men who knew not what their eyes had seen, nor what their ears had heard ; but who stood upon the viking ship and honoured the name of Christ, led by one whom God had chosen and to whom he had given the power of his spirit.

CHAPTER XXX

THE GATE OF UNREST

HARALD commanded to cast anchor and lower the small boats. The solemn naming of the land was soon forgotten in the excitement of treading upon that unknown shore. The strong limbs and courageous hearts of the Norsemen were tired of the enforced inaction of the viking ship. They rejoiced at thought of new adventures which probably awaited them.

Lots were cast to determine who should be among the first landing party. It was Harald's thought to keep the ship in constant readiness to sail, while two bodies of warriors were landed, — one to explore the shore, the other to penetrate inland a short distance. It was decided that such an arrangement would be safest, and give immediate and sufficient knowledge for a suitable building site.

The verdict of the lot drawing was not received without some grumbling from those who had been unfortunate enough to be left behind; but finally, amid much noise and shouts for success and good luck, the boats pushed off. Harald commanded one force, while one of his keenest, wisest men, Hjalmar Ovarson, directed the other. Tellus was left in charge of the boat; for Harald wished to be assured of the safety of the women while he was away.

The latter were upon the deck, Persea and Sigrid leaning against each other. Astrid stood apart; but all were watching the boats as they beached their human freight. They saw the warriors as they swiftly touched coat of mail and sword-belt to be certain they were secure, grasped their shields and long spears tightly, and started upon their momentous journey. One party plunged into the forest; the other passed swiftly down the shore, just under the shadow of the nearer trees.

The sun was yet high in the heavens. Four or five hours must elapse before they could hope to see their friends return. Sigrid trembled and sighed; for to her, there was no peace, no joy, no blessing in the new land. Though she had witnessed Persea's faith and trust, and believing in Christ, had tried to believe with all her heart — yet she could not be comforted.

Ever was she thinking of her father, — the dear one she had left in the midst of danger, — and she sorrowed and believed he had perished. This land which had drawn her away from him seemed not hallowed, but accursed to her. She dared not tell her thoughts to Persea lest she be misunderstood; but the shore looked cruel, the dark shadow of the forest whispered of evil, and she trembled at the thought of what the darkness might be hiding from them. Christ grant that their friends return unhurt! Christ grant that they all leave this land safely and reach their own rocky shores once more! What would she not give for a glimpse of the low red sun behind the mountains? What would she not give for a sight of the great hall, the bright fire, a massive high seat, and that dear figure with long grey beard? Her heart was beating fast with feeling and fear; but she struggled against her sadness as she silently watched the shore.

Tellus crossed to her side and looked brightly, tenderly upon her small figure. She smiled at him; but behind the smile he did not see the grief that would not be stifled, the sorrow that would not go by, the fear that even love could not quell.

To Astrid, the scene appealed with all the glamour of adventure and excitement. She chafed at restraint, and inwardly wished that she was with those on shore, exploring and treading where Norsemen had never tread before. Truly this Harald Rognvaldson was a man who was absolutely fearless, and would stop at no danger nor tremble at any peril — except the loss of Persea.

He had braved this long journey, this unknown path which took him far beyond the knowledge of men, simply to find a spot where he could place her in safety. Yet he would not possess her now. He would have to wait many days. Astrid laughed within herself. She could scarcely understand his self-control, except when she thought of that night he had withstood temptation; and even then she shrugged her shoulders contemptuously. What did Harald and the Christ Maiden know of love? 'T was but a luke-warm draught they were drinking. She alone of all the world, knew how to love; yet love was denied her.

She grew dizzy with the tempest in her soul, and left the deck.

CHAPTER XXXI

THE EXPLORATIONS

THE sun was dipping far towards the west. The watchers on the boat were growing anxious as they shaded their eyes from the sunset glare and closely scanned the darkening purple of the shore. 'T was time the exploring parties returned. The guard on board the vessel stood in groups and pairs, talking seriously. Said one :

" I begin to fear lest some evil has befallen our friends. Surely they should be on the sea-snake ere the darkness comes upon us."

" Yea indeed," answered another, " they lack not mind wisdom enough to know that. Perhaps they have met some unknown beasts or some giant savages who have wiped them from the earth. 'T is no easy task for a Norseman to keep his sword sheathed when he trembles for the safety of his friends. The moments are hours, and the steed of the breeze is a Nifl-hel."

The calm voice of Tellus answered the unrest :

" If the sun goes down behind yonder tall cedar and still they come not, then must we follow after. But they agreed to blow the lur if danger threatened, and the voice of the horn can be heard an hour's journey. Certainly the call for assistance has not come to us. Besides, they went forth under the sign of the White Christ; therefore I believe they will all return unharmed. See ! The lower edge of the sun touches the sharp point of the cedar. Watch the shore; for ere the dark spear pierces the upper rim we shall see somewhat of our brethren."

He spoke with confidence; and the truth-ring in his voice lifted a little of the gloom from some of the faces. But one of Astrid's men scowled and said :

" Yea, they have the lur; but many things might have happened to prevent them from using it. Perhaps even now Fridthjof, who carried it, has been sent to Odin. To my mind, yonder sunset sky is coloured with blood. Mayhap we have reached the end of the world where Nidhöggu dwells in Helga Pool, and the warriors have breathed its foul breath!"

His words brought back the fear of uncanny things into the Norsemen's eyes. They looked towards the red sun, now almost cut in two by the dark outline of the cedar. Their kindled imagination beheld the blood, and saw in the far depths of the black forest the horrible monster that their ancient religion had placed in the Nifl-hel, which received those whom Odin spurned from Valhalla.

But Tellus appeared not to hear. He was watching the shore with all intentness. Suddenly he cried out:

"Look between the tall trees below the rocks. Is that not the glimmer of steel? The men return; and the sun is yet above the tree-tops. Those who trust in Christ the White need fear no Nidhöggu."

The Norsemen saw, and their far-reaching cry, "Haoi-a-o-haoi!" swept across the waves towards the shore. Back to their ears came the answer, "Haoi-aoi-haoi!" Harald's men were leaving the shadow of the forest and coming up the sandy beach, waving their shields towards the viking ship.

Glad was the welcome that came to the exploring party when the boat returned. The warriors were beset with questions, which they answered with wild enthusiasm. It was a beautiful land they had walked upon. Such trees! Such streams! Such an abundance of wild life! Such richness of soil! They had found nothing evil, nothing more dangerous than a few bear tracks. There were a hundred suitable sites for their winter home within close reach of the shore, where fresh water would be at hand; and where they would be sheltered from storms or cold winds from the ocean.

The men who had not shared in these experiences listened with jealous wonder; but all cheered again for Harald Rognvaldson whose daring had brought them such unusual possibility of adventure and gain. Loudly and gaily they talked and boasted.

When the first excitement of return had subsided, Tellus asked Harald:

"Didst thou see aught of Hjalmar?"

"Has he not yet returned? That is bad news, truly. See how dark it is getting. These twilights are not long like the twilights upon the mountains of Norge. Scarcely does the

sky redden ere it changes to purple and the darkness descends.
I fear our friends have forgotten this strangeness of light and
have ventured farther than they should. Hark! Was that
not the lur? Silence on the boat! Listen!"

The men stood motionless, rigid, alert, anxious to catch any
sound from the black forest. Eric muttered under his breath:
"The White Christ has not conquered Nidhöggu, no matter
what the Christians may say. The blood days are not yet
ended."

Out from the wooded depths of the forest came again a faint,
far-distant sound. Its origin was certain.

In an instant the boat was filled with anxious warriors.
The long oars cut the water with deep, powerful strokes
wielded by arms with muscles of steel, and governed by brave
hearts that trembled for the safety of their brothers. As the
boat was beached, they heard the lur again, this time much
nearer. The men sprang upon the shore, and grasping shields
and naked swords, rushed into the gloomy wood.

On board the vessel, all things were placed in readiness for
weighing the anchor and departing should necessity compel.
Another boat was sent to the shore so that all who reached the
beach could return at once.

Then followed a period of the most intense anxiety. The
watchers on the deck beheld the deepening shadows on the
shore, and trembled for the safety of those who were enveloped therein.

Persea grasped the railing of the deck, leaning far out in the
vain endeavour to see further into the increasing gloom. What
evil had befallen them upon this land she so loved, and which
had seemed so teeming with blessings to her? Surely Christ
would be kind. Surely he would guide and guard for his
Name's sake.

Astrid, for once, put aside her reserve and questioned seriously
as she scanned the shore. Many of her own men were in the
second party; and she was really alarmed that danger had
crossed their path.

The shadows had lengthened now so that the white line of
the beach was the only visible sign of the shore. From that
white line came the heavy wash of the waves as they broke,
and it seemed to the troubled ones that the wind brought other
faint, indescribable sounds to their ears. Were they groans

and cries, or only the moaning of the surf in some hollow among the low rocks?

Deeper grew the darkness. More alarmed grew the watchers upon the boat. Sigrid stole to a corner aside. There Tellus found her sobbing grievously. With all tenderness he gathered her in his arms and tried to kiss away the hot tears.

"Sigrid! My Little One! Be not so frightened. The men are well able to take care of themselves. We shall soon hear their shouts upon the shore. Be thine own brave self, my Little One. Nestle close to my heart and put thine arms about my neck. Thy wound and thy weakness have made thy tears flow. Fear not; no harm shall come to thee. Dost thou not trust thy Tellus?"

Gradually the sobs grew less violent. Then she said:

"Thou knowest that I trust thee; but my fears are not for myself. I fear for us all. In spite of what Persea has said, this whole land and sea and sky are evil to me. I cannot rest, even though I have thy love to comfort me. The sunset stares at me under dull eyebrows, and I see naught but blood in the gaze. The long roll and roar of the leaden tide haunts me with its monotonous moaning. The wind brings whispers of unknown horrors from those black forests, whose skeleton trees are like the uncanny claws of evil things that are reaching out to seize me and drag me into some dreadful snare. And now the danger has come. Some of our brave warriors have met, in truth, those things which have been in my mind. Even the darkness is different from the darkness of Norge. I can almost hear the swish of evil wings as they sweep around us in the night!"

Tellus soothed her as best he might, endeavouring to calm her troubled brain, and to prove to her that her fancies were unreal and without truth or foundation. Ere he had succeeded, they heard the shout from the beach:

"Haoi-a-o-haoi!"

The men rushed to the side of the boat and gave answering calls. They could soon discern the boats approaching. Tellus commanded torches to be brought. Before the boats reached the viking ship the anxious question rang out over the water:

"Are ye all there?"

"Yea, and scarcely a skin broken," answered the gruff

voice of Hjalmar. The boats pulled alongside, and he continued :

"But we had a close run for it ; and by Odin, the rascals were no mean men. They have powerful muscles ; and they know well the use of the bow. But we escaped their clutches, though we nearly did for one of them. We have brought him with us ; so stand aside, and ye will all see the manner of man we have found in Christ's land."

Amid the rattling of oar-locks, the confusion of many voices, and the clanking of armour, the Norsemen leaped on their ship ; and then a dark, limp form was lifted on the deck. Wild with curiosity, the men crowded about the prostrate form, holding aloft flaming torches. The red glare fell upon a man of copper-coloured skin, well formed and sinewy, with high cheek bones and straight, black hair. His clothing was the dressed skins of animals, decorated with coloured shells and quills.

One of the Norsemen held his weapons, which he passed around for inspection. They were a stone-headed hatchet and a bow, with arrows tipped with flint points. Much were the warriors astonished at the strength and excellence of the wild man's arms.

"It seems to me," said one, "that this Skroelingi is no weak foe. The Christ's land has no dearth of defenders if there are many like him."

"There are not a few of them hiding in the woods," said Hjalmar, "and they might have done for us had we gone a few paces farther."

While they questioned and looked and wondered, the blood from the deep gash in the man's head trickled down, unheeded. He was certainly unconscious. One of the Norsemen stirred him roughly with his foot, saying :

"Halfred's arm is no mean weight when it falls. The man is most dead. Best give him over to Ran's keeping. He will sleep sound enough in her green-walled palace."

"Yea," said another, "he will never lift his stone ax again. The water is the best place for him."

Harald's voice, from without the circle, asked the men to step aside and allow the women to see the strange man. They obeyed, and Persea was the first to reach the wild man's side. With a low cry, she sank upon the deck.

" What have ye done? Why did ye stain Christ's land with a deed of violence ? "

The warriors felt the wailing sorrow in her voice. It touched their rough hearts. Hjalmar answered her :

" It was not by our choice, Christ Maiden, that the strange one came to death. He attacked Halfred, and some one had to fall. Thou seest who it was."

Persea laid her hand upon the wounded man's heart.

" He lives ! "

At her touch and voice, two black eyes opened to consciousness. The first instant they flashed around a quick, penetrating glance that seemed to pierce the outward shape of men and things and search for treachery or descending violence. Then he saw the woman bending over him. Henceforth he saw nothing else.

He lay quiet under the touch of her hand ; motionless while she called for water and bandages, and dressed the ugly gash in his head. Then she ordered him to be carried below, where the wind was less chilling. He was laid upon a soft couch and covered with a warm robe. Laying a cool, tender hand upon his head, she bade him rest, in Christ's Name.

At the sound of her voice, unmistakable in its gentleness and kindliness of meaning, the wild man's eyes flashed with a sudden, occult light. Afterwards they followed all her movements, until she left the cabin. Then they stared about the small apartment with great interest and curiosity. Finally, exhausted nature claimed its dues, and the Skroelingi slept.

On the deck, the warriors wrapped in their long cloaks, were recounting the adventures of the day. Said Hjalmar :

" When we struck into the forest, we plunged on for some time amid snow-drifts and tangled underbrush, and finally came out upon the banks of a large stream. This we wished to cross ; but as the middle of the current was swift and had not frozen, we had to wander up the bank a considerable distance ere we found a fording place. At last, we came to a narrow portion strewn with rocks, which we easily crossed. Hardly had we reached the other side when Rodbrok discovered the tracks of a hoofed beast in the snow. As they pointed in the way we were going, we followed them.

" A short distance beyond, we came upon a broad, flat track which bespoke the human foot, though encased in some soft covering. Of course we were much attracted to these foot-prints. We followed them closely, but very carefully; for I was of no mind to make hasty acquaintances in this unknown land. Still it was unlikely that hurt could come to twenty stalwart Norsemen from any one human, be it wild as the wolves of Noregs-veldi. We were getting deeper and deeper into the forest, and had gone a great distance, ere we were aware, in our excitement of mind, that we had travelled farther than we should. I called the warriors to a halt.

" We were about to turn back when our ears were assailed by the most dreadful yells. They came from the forest in front; and immediately a shower of arrows fell upon us. The men held up their shields, facing about; but not a wild man could be seen. Again the unearthly screams filled the air, and another cloud of arrows came against us. Now we saw that the savages were hiding behind trees, and shooting therefrom. The men were for falling upon them; but I remembered Harald Rognvaldson's parting command to shed no blood of man or beast upon this first journey through Christ's land. As we had certainly done no deed to call forth their violence, I judged it wisest and best to retreat towards the boat. The men obeyed, though not without some murmurs; for it was truly hard for a Norseman to show his heels to a pack of wild men. But I was thinking beyond the moment, and I knew it was better thus.

" As soon as the Skroelingjar saw us depart, they followed at a distance, uttering still those fierce yells that were enough to make a coward yield his spirit to Odin in despair and terror. They also continued to drop their arrows among us; but our brynjas stood us in good need. Save for a few scratches, we reached the edge of the stream all unhurt.

" As we neared the bank, one of the wild men who was swifter of foot than his comrades came close to us and fell upon Halfred with his stone ax. Swift and cunning as he was, he was no match for a Norseman. Ere his weapon descended, Halfred laid his head open with his sword, sending him flat to the ground. Cries came from the woods behind us when he fell. Halfred lifted the fellow to his shoulders and we gathered close to him, hastening our steps.

" Now the Skroelingjar came closer than ever before. I saw, in the dim shadow of the woods, that they were many more than we, and that they were about to fall upon us. Therefore I gave command to blow the lur. Even if we fought our way safely to the boat, it was wise to let our companions know that something unusual was happening. The wild men must have considered that the horn was some signal ; for they did not follow beyond the stream. Soon the woods behind us were as silent as when we first trod therein. The deepening shadow of the night fell upon us without bringing any further peril. The stranger foe disappeared as suddenly as they had come.

" I would have commanded Halfred to leave the wounded Skroelingi under the trees ; but he said that it would be well to keep him. The other warriors would be glad to know the manner of man we had encountered. In good time we heard the shouts of those who were coming to answer the call of the lur. We shouted back, and both parties met in the forest. Our friends were glad indeed, to find us all alive and sound of limb. The rest ye know.

" The land is fair and peaceful enough. One would wish no better place in which to spend the days till the warmth opens the northern seas ; but these wild men must be considered. 'T is likely they far outnumber us. If we are not wise and cautious, the spring may find our bones bleaching in the forest, and the dragon-ship wrecked upon the beach."

A thoughtful silence fell on the hardy vikings while they considered the danger that had arisen out of the forest, to contend with them for the possession of Christ's land. They were not fearful ; but they all wished to live to carry the great news back to their own world.

The flickering torches cast unsteady rays of yellow light upon their stalwart figures and fair Norse features as they reclined in various easy postures, and discussed their situation. One proposed one thing, another something else ; but no one brought forth what was plausible and possible. Behind every plan, behind every purpose lurked that unknown evil, — the wild men, — and the very mystery of their appearance, numbers, and existence made the danger more threatening.

At last the night-watch took their place upon the deck, the torches were extinguished, and the men stretched themselves for sleep. Soon the silence of slumber was upon the vessel.

Then, sailing out of the midnight skies, came the fairy

dreamship, bringing wonderful visions to the unconscious Norsemen, visions of mighty lands all their own, of renown, of adventures such as no hero of song or saga had ever enjoyed before; visions of strange men and beasts, of fierce struggles which made them gasp and groan in their sleep.

And to more than one came visions of the Angel of the Dawn, as she had looked and spoken that day when the new land rose out of the west.

CHAPTER XXXII

THE WHITE LILY

BUT while the Norsemen slept and dreamed strange dreams, far back in the forest the Skroelingjar gathered around their fire and held solemn council about the ones who had come to their shores, invaded their hunting grounds, and tracked their hunters almost to the village.

The scouts had returned from following the trail. They told of a marvellous sea-serpent that rode upon the waves of the Great Water, and of many more of the white-faced, light-haired strangers.

The old men shook their heads, and gravely said that they should watch and wait, lest the newcomers were from the Spirit Land. What else could come out of the sunrise?

But one young brave rose to his feet, and called for blood to avenge the death of Silver Eagle.

"Was he not his brother? Was he not fleet of foot and strong of arm? Had he not been killed and carried off by these of strange mien, — doubtless to be eaten by their serpent? Let the warriors dress in their war-paint and go forth to avenge their brother."

Murmurs of approval broke from the lips of the younger braves; but their old chief rose in his place and said:

"Does the bird fly into the mouth of the snake because his mate has been devoured? Will the deer leap towards the fangs of the wolf that has mangled its young? Why then has the red man less wisdom than the wild ones of the forest? The braves must know the strength of their enemies, lest they be consumed, and the camp-fires of the Wampanoags no longer burn in the forest.

"Did the arrows of the warriors harm these strange ones? Did not the darts glance from their bright bodies? Who but spirit men could so turn aside the sharp points? And when Silver Eagle, in his rashness, would have buried his tomahawk in a glittering head, did not the eyes of Red Fox see the bolt of lightning with which he was struck down? If the Red Fox can war with those whose skin no arrows can pierce, and whose

darts are drawn from the Thunder God's quiver, let him go
forth on the war-path. Manatocsin has spoken. May the
young braves learn from his wisdom."

He resumed his seat upon the ground. The older warriors
looked stolid approval. Most of the young men seemed
ashamed, and cast sidewise, anxious glances towards the dark,
impenetrable gloom that encircled their camp-fire, as if they
feared some foe was hiding there.

But Red Fox was not subdued. He had had few chances
to win the feathers for his head-dress. His heart was burning
to accomplish some marvellous feat that would give him a great
name. The wise chief's cool words could not quell his desires.

The silence of the wood was unbroken save by the crackling of the fire, and the far-off howl of the wolf. The Skroelingjar smoked their long pipes, looking steadfastly before them.
No one answered the words their chief had spoken.

'T was a wondrously striking scene, — that dark forest with
mighty trees whose lofty tops seemed almost to touch the
stars, the white snow-drifts at their feet, and the wind sweeping through their branches bearing messages that no man could
understand, — and in the midst of the wild solitude a circle of
red-skinned warriors around a small fire, whose light scarcely
reached to the tops of the great trees.

North, south, and west, the land stretched away under the
starlit skies in vast expanse. Rugged mountains and wide
prairies, broad rivers and rushing water-falls, wondrous lakes
and virgin forest, — all bursting with the mightiness of God's
gifts; but knowing no tread save the moccasined foot and the
furry paw. For untold centuries the stars had shone upon
this vast, beautiful continent. They had watched it, night
after night, through countless eons of time. They had seen
the tiny yellow glow from thousands of the red man's fires;
but to-night, one of those twinkling flames trembled with the
red man's destiny.

There, out upon the waves, rocked the spirit that was to
conquer this wondrous land, and gather its wealth for the
blessing of all mankind. Though the generation that gathered
around that tiny fire would fall, though their children and their
children's children through four centuries of time would still
dwell in peace upon the land of their birth, — yet the golden

viking ship had brought the first whisper from the east, the first breath that was destined to sweep away the red children of the forest. The sun by day, and the moon and stars by night, watched and guarded until God's final mandate went forth, and the New World opened its arms and took suffering humanity to its great heart.

And while the stars stooped and listened, and the trees swayed and quivered under the touch of the North wind, the red men kept unbroken the solemn silence. For many moments the braves sat thus. Finally a tall man put aside his pipe and arose.

"Why do my brothers sit longer in council? The voice of Manatocsin has been heard. Who so wise as he? Let us follow the trail of the strange beings, but lift no hand against them till we know their strength. Then we will strike suddenly, and they shall track us across our land no more."

Grunts of approval greeted his words. Slowly the warriors arose; but ere they had dispersed a man emerged swiftly from the forest and glided into their midst.

His deerskin clothes were wet and frozen, his head was wrapped in a white cloth stained with blood, his moccasins were torn to shreds, and his naked feet left red tracks upon the snow. But he stood among them tall and straight and strong, with never a shiver of pain or a deep-drawn breath to tell of his exhausting flight through the wilderness. The warriors said in solemn amazement:

"It is the Silver Eagle!"

The man made no reply; but motioned to the warriors to resume their seats. They did so. When the stillness was complete, he spoke:

"The braves of Manatocsin's tribe have been sitting in council. They have been speaking of the men we found in the forest to-day. And ye did all think that Silver Eagle had crossed to the Happy Hunting Ground; but he was speeding through the forest, bearing a great message to his brothers. The Silver Eagle knew that the warriors would gather round the fire to-night. He wished the ears of the braves to hear what had happened to him, and know what sights he had seen."

Many pairs of flashing eyes quickened at his words. He continued:

" The Silver Eagle knew nothing until the evening stars
shone out. Then he found himself being borne along through
the forest. He was cunning, and feigned death; but his ears
could hear and his eyes could see. Just beyond the wolf's
den, many more of the same kind came rushing through the
forest. The woods rang with their loud noises. After much
strange language, all went on towards the shore of the Great
Water. There they stepped into canoes, still carrying Silver
Eagle, and went out to the golden serpent which lay upon the
waves. Lo! this is only a wonderful canoe, made of trees;
Silver Eagle felt the wood when they laid him down."

A whisper of surprise went around the council fire. One
great mystery was a mystery no longer. But Silver Eagle had
more to relate.

" The ones in glittering blankets crowded about Silver Eagle
as he lay, still feigning death, upon the top of the canoe.
They brought firebrands, and looked into his face, touched
his skin coverings, and passed his tomahawk from hand to
hand. One of them put an arrow to the string and drew it
back with a strength that sent it whizzing far out over the
water. Then I knew that these were some far-off tribe of
men who had wandered to our shores. They are unlike men
we have ever seen; and they have weapons and blankets that
are unknown to us; but they are not spirits; for I saw one
as he wiped the red blood from an arrow wound in his cheek."

Another louder and more delighted murmur arose. Red
Fox gripped the handle of his tomahawk with more strength
than ever.

" The white-faces grew tired of looking; and one struck
with his foot. Then was Silver Eagle ready to spring at their
throats. He felt another touch upon his breast; but when he
opened his eyes, very marvellous was the one he saw. She
was as beautiful as the lily that lies upon the water. Her
voice was as the soft note of the dove; her eyes rested on Silver Eagle, and he no longer wished to kill.

" When she spoke, the warriors drew back and left her
alone by Silver Eagle. She washed his wound and bound this
bandage upon it. Her touch was as gentle as the summer
wind, her breath was like the breath of the wild honeysuckle.
When her hand rested upon Silver Eagle, he was held by
its power; yet he feared it not.

" She spoke again. The men lifted Silver Eagle and carried him to the inside of the great canoe. He was strong, and could have leaped from their arms; but the spell of the White Lily was upon him and he had no wish to go. He hid his strength, and they thought his wound had made him weak. The inside of the canoe was filled with things which his eyes had never seen before. He was laid upon skins and covered with a wonderful covering. He knew that whatever these braves might have done unto him, there was no danger now; for the White Lily had taken him under her protection.

" She came again to his side, and he thought he heard the south wind calling to the flowers, so gentle were the sounds that came from her lips. He closed his eyes and she left him. He waited until the braves were all asleep. Then he crept out of the canoe and sank into the water. He is now in the camp of his brothers. They have heard his voice."

He sat down near the fire. Red Fox sprang up and shook his tomahawk over the red men's heads.

" What says the great Manatocsin now ? Does the wolf fear his kind ? Does the wildcat slink from the wildcat ? Let the war-dance go on. These strange ones are men, not spirits from the sunrise; men like ourselves with blood in their veins ! What if they have wonderful weapons ? Are the hearts of the warriors so weak that they trust not their own strength ? Let the sunrise see the braves of Manatocsin's tribe upon the serpent canoe. We will try the strength of these warriors from the other side of the world. It is the time for deeds that our children shall tell to their children. Let us kill the men who followed upon the track of our hunters. Let us take their weapons from them. Let us put on our bodies the glittering skins that no arrow can pierce. Who then shall dispute our hunting grounds with us ? Not even the powerful Narragansetts will dare haunt the land of the Wampanoags ! "

More than half of the braves leaped to their feet, brandishing their weapons and shouting for the death of the strangers. The eyes of Silver Eagle grew small, and shot queer glances towards those who clamoured for the shedding of blood. When they had given vent to their feelings, he rose again. This time his voice was stern, and cut the frosty air like keen arrows.

" When the Wampanoags go upon the war-path against these strangers, the feet of Silver Eagle shall leave their camp-fire forever. If ye bind up the wounds of a wolf, will he not lick the hand that has eased his pain ? Why should the heart of the red man be less kind than a beast's ?

" Who first raised the bow, ye or the white-skinned ones ? Would the flesh be open upon my head if I had not fallen upon the one who gave me the blow ? Let the strangers alone. 'T is more than likely that they will soon point their serpent canoe westward, and depart as they came. The heart of Silver Eagle remembers the voice of the White Lily. It will ring in his memory forever ; and for kindness he will not give death. If his brothers have wisdom, they will talk of friendship with these men from the sunrise. Lay the toma-hawk aside and offer the peace pipe ! "

Quickly after him spoke the old chief :

" Silver Eagle has spoken in the language of the Great Spirit. He is no coward. His arm is as eager for the deeds of warriors as the arm of Red Fox ; but beside his wisdom, the wisdom of Red Fox is only child's talk. More shall come to us through friendship than through fighting.

" To-morrow shall Silver Eagle return to them with a belt of wampum from Manatocsin to their chief, and the peace pipe shall be lit. Let the fiery blood of the young braves cool in their veins ; for all fire is not warming, all courage is not bravery, all bloodshed is not to be praised. Go back to your wigwams. Wisdom shall rule the councils of the Wampa-noags ! "

His words gave the final decision. The red men rose and disappeared within the folds of their tents. Silence soon reigned in the forest.

But Red Fox chafed under the rebukes of the evening ; and his heart burned with the unsatisfied lust for blood and war-honour.

*   *   *   *   *   *

Persea slept sweetly through the long night, and rose to greet the dawn which smiled upon her with marvellous radi-ance. She smiled back, not knowing that, but for her, it would have been a dawn of horror and death.

Ere the sun was well above the horizon the Norsemen discovered that the wild man had escaped. None had seen him, none had heard him. Only a blood-stain upon the side of the vessel showed where he had slipped into the water. The men shook their heads, and said that there was something to be feared from those who could boast such strength and endurance.

"Yea," said Hjalmar, eyeing critically the distance to the shore. "'T was no small thing for a man to swim thus far with a broken head. The touch of Ran is chilling to the muscles of the hardiest warrior. The heart must be strong and filled with warm blood to fight with her white-breasted daughters while the north wind blows."

"'T is so," replied Harald, "and the men upon Christ's Land are not only strong and brave, but cunning. Let no Norseman leave the dragon-ship to-day; for we know not what the flight of the wounded one may mean to us."

The Norsemen lounged about the deck while the sun mounted in the heavens. Just as it reached the zenith a single file of Skroelingjar, led by one with a white bandage about his head, left the woods and stood on the shore, waving aloft branches of green.

Harald answered the peace signal, and then rowed to the beach. There he exchanged gifts with the men of Christ's Land. He signed to them his desire to abide for a time on the shore, and they signified their willingness that he should do so. Long and solemn council was carried on by means of sign language and guttural grunts of approval, ending by the passing from mouth to mouth of one of the queer-shaped bowls filled with a burning, pungent herb.

Afterwards, Silver Eagle brought a delicate necklace of shells, and pointing to the vessel and his head, gave mute testimony of his gratitude to the White Lily.

Ere a fortnight had gone by, the Norsemen had erected their shelters upon the shore, and were revelling in the delights of the wilderness and the mild climate.

CHAPTER XXXIII

THE SWEEP OF THE TIDE

AFTER the men of the Thrandheim, in their berserk fury, had driven out the King who had dealt treacherously with them, they returned to their homes in boastful triumph. Had they not, once again, earned the right to be called the strongest, most loyal of all the sons of the Northland? Let the men in the southern districts cringe and bow to this King, and be sprinkled with water by his thick-necked priest. The Thrandheim warriors would still be Norsemen. They forgot not their old glory, nor their Norse gods; and the king who ruled them must not forget.

But though they boasted and rejoiced, peace and contentment came not back to dwell among them. Into the hamlets and boers scattered over the fjelds and mountains there crept unrest, and secret misgivings, and gloomy forebodings. For, when the people's fury had abated, they looked about them and behold! the old ties of the past were rent asunder. They could not go back to the life of former days.

They had no king, nor even a leader. Their lawman, Jarl Rognvald, could not help them by his wise counsel; for he had been carried from the burning skali sorely wounded, and now lay upon his bed waiting for the call to Odin's feast.

Their great-souled, majestic priest they mourned as having already crossed the Bridge of Asar. He had plunged into the fire and flame at the further end of the skali; and they had seen him no more. None doubted that he lay buried beneath the smoking embers of the great building. He had gone to Odin on the flame steed; and it was a fit entry into Valhalla for him. Already were they gathering the huge stones for his mound, which they purposed to make as grand and great as was his memory in the hearts of his people.

Yet the loss of their leaders was not their greatest sorrow. Their magnificent temple was in ashes. Its brilliancy and wealth had vanished in smoke wreaths; and woe of woes! their beloved Thor, their god, was but a headless, charred thing, repulsive in its very likeness to a man.   They saw it lying there, helpless, hideous, — and their hearts were numbed with an indefinite fear.

What reward had been granted them for all their loyalty? Thor had not prevented the destruction of everything that belonged to him.   Had he then no power?   Even the stirring memories of the past, when confronted by the destruction of their priest, their temple, and their god, could not bring from their chilled hearts the old flame of trust and belief.   After all their desperate battling with word and sword, their joy of victory was turned to bitterness and fear.

As the days passed on, they became more and more harassed by disquieting thoughts.   The future was dark and hopeless. Their best men were gone.   Their god had fallen even while they shed their noblest blood in his behalf.   These calamities had shaken to its depths their belief in his power; yet to whom should they bow?   There was no god to take his place. None?

Erlend stood at the gateway of his boer and spoke earnestly to Thorleif:

"Thou sayest we have no god?   Shall I read unto thee the signs of the times?   Listen.   When the earth lies under the spell of the white death, still there is life in the darkness beneath.   Even when the throbbing life is pushing its way through countless millions of roots and fibres, still there is no outward sign, no note of triumph.   The winter has gone; yet nature seems unchanged.

"Then some day, lo! suddenly the whole earth is tinged with a faint, indescribable green.   Man sees that indefinite greenness and bends down a branch to find its source; but the hundreds of brown tips seem absolutely dead.   His unseeing eyes do not discover the *one* bud which has burst its sheath, and with the scattered millions of its companions, is giving the delicate life tint to the far-reaching valley and mountainside. And there is an exquisite melody in the air, which holds his spirit spellbound, but which ever eludes and melts into space when he tries to follow the sound to the singer.   His unhearing ears do not catch the silver dropping of the tiny beck at his feet, though it is one clear note in the vast harmony that is sweeping over the awakening world.

"Thorleif, hast thou not noticed that the people of the

Thrandheim are beginning to speak the names of their old gods with coldness and indifference? The darkness and ignorance of the past still hold them in partial captivity; but down, far down in the hearts of the people, new thoughts are slowly rising — thoughts of the Christ Maiden's words, and of the life they have seen in her and Harald Rognvaldson.

"They are awakening to the fact that the events of the past few weeks have left a deep impression upon them; they begin to realize that the dwelling of the Christ Maiden among them was more than an episode in their life. About this point their interest settles; to it their minds return again and again. There is no outward expression of this, but the wisest see that only to Harald Rognvaldson and the Christ Maiden came the real joy of victory.

"Some of the warriors who were fighting upon the shore recognized Harald's ship as it glided out of the cove, and saw the white-robed figure upon its high deck. The Blest of the Nornir had escaped the vengeance of the Temple Godi and the King. He had sailed away, taking his love with him. They alone had conquered fate. And they were Christians! The people marvel that they escaped from the burning skali; but tongues are quick with strange tales. Certain of the men vow that they saw the ground open and swallow them. Others say that a cross shadowed them and hid them from sight.

"These tales only strengthen interest in the White Christ; for the God-empty minds of the Thrandheim are reaching out pitifully for some hope, some promise of a strength greater than their own. Perhaps this Christ of the Christ Maiden was a real God after all. Certainly he had helped his own when Odin and Thor had not intervened to save their temple or their priest.

"And the people can easily account for the King's ill luck. If this God was a God of love as the Christ Maiden and Harald had witnessed, then the King had not pleased him. Somehow they know beyond all doubting, know surely, that Harald Rognvaldson would never have betrayed their temple so treacherously; nor would he ever have shed a drop of Thrandheim blood in the name of his God."

"Yea," answered Thorleif, "we do believe that the King's misfortune is only the result of his violence and passion. If the White Christ is a real God he has lost the Thrandheim and his bride because he did not rule as his God would have him rule."

"And if ye think thus," said Erlend, "what will come next? Ever and anon the thoughts of the Thrandheim will swing back to that one great thought which the events of the past have sown broadcast in their hearts, — *the White Christ has been stronger than their ancient Norse gods!* He has protected his own and saved them from the violence of the King and the Temple Godi. He must be a God worthy of the name! Dost thou understand these signs?

"The new life is pushing its way upward through their souls. The faint, indescribable beauty and tenderness is breaking forth, tinging the whole thought of the Thrandheim with hope, though they know it not. The women, bending over the wide wounds of their husbands and sons, cry out, in their hearts, for the God of Love who would sheathe all swords. The men, thinking of the cruelty and ill-faith of their past kings, long for a ruler who would rule faithfully and with honour, little matter whom he worshipped.

"In the whirl of their outgoing tide of hatred, the men of the Thrandheim have seemed to be stronger, fiercer, more determined than ever before. But no matter how the waves rush out, how sharp the rocks they leave uncovered, or how far-reaching the beach they leave barren, in God's own time the waves creep back. In God's own time the last rock is covered, the white beach is washed to the furthest limit of its white sands.

"Remember my words, Thorleif, son of Eric. I declare unto thee that the rush and turmoil of centuries has all but spent itself. Now the tide is turning, bearing high upon its white crest the new life, — the life of love, the life of Christ the White!

"I know, because over me has swept that love, that life. I do not understand it; but can the shore resist the sweep of the tide?"

CHAPTER XXXIV

THE CALL OF THE LOON

On the shore of Christ's Land the Norsemen built three rough houses. The largest was used by most of Harald's men. Near it stood a smaller dwelling, built like the first of rough logs, but carefully plastered with mud to keep out the cold. This was the home of Persea and Sigrid. Here also, Harald, Tellus, Hassan and a few others stayed to protect them. The walls and floor were covered with thick furs, and the room was furnished with as much comfort as the viking ship could provide. A curtain of deerskin hung across the farther end of the room. Behind this the maidens slept.

From the first moment of landing Astrid had gathered her men about her. Thenceforth, no communication was held with the other Norsemen. In silence and apart they built their own house. Though Harald offered Astrid a shelter with Persea and Sigrid, she haughtily refused, saying:

"Have I not been long enough beholden to thee for care and shelter? Thinkst thou I would choose to be under the same roof with thee, — and her? Nay, Astrid will abide with her own. She asks for no protection from Harald when the earth is under her feet and the stars over her head. Leave me."

Proudly she pointed to his companions; and just as proudly Harald turned and left her. They spoke no more together for long days and nights.

The Norsemen understood, only too well, that the safety and quiet of their life during the winter would depend upon keeping an unbroken peace with the Skroelingjar. They welcomed the savages to the camp, and gave them presents of glittering ornaments, but no knives or shields. Too wise were they to add to their advantage of numbers an equality of weapons. Manatocsin often came to visit the strangers with whom he had made peace. Harald was careful to give him the warmest place by the fire, and the choicest piece from the venison haunch.

The old chief was satisfied that the Norsemen meant no harm.   When he understood their intention of leaving in the spring, he solemnly laid upon his warriors the vow of a peace that was to be kept to the end.   Before the council-fire he spoke of the gifts they had received, and the meat they had eaten at the camp-fire of the strangers.

"To the white warriors," he said, "the Wampanoags would be friends, so that when they returned to their own land they would say the men of the West knew how to give friendship for friendship."

The Skroelingjar listened and said, "It is well."   After that they mingled more than ever with the white men, guiding them through the wilderness, showing them the haunts of the wild game, teaching them the silent language of the forest, and astonishing them by their keenness of sense, and savage knowledge of the ways of bird and beast.

To the Norsemen, the passing of the winter was as the reading of strange runes.   The moment they were housed, and were assured of the friendship of the red-skinned Skroelingjar, they turned with burning hearts towards the land that stretched far away to the north, and south, and west.

From their savage friends they learned that there was little knowledge of what lay beyond that dark line of blue and purple that melted into the sunset sky with mysterious silence. To the south, they were told that the shore curved in a great hook washed by the sea; but to the west and north lay boundless lands which were owned by tribes of other Skroelingjar. There were rumours of rivers and wondrous lakes, of lofty mountains and deep, dark valleys, of forests, so thick that the sunlight scarcely reached the ground, and of great waters that thundered unceasingly.

Filled with desire to see beyond the distant horizon the Norsemen travelled far inland.   They found forest-covered hills and wide rivers, still and frozen now; but to the land there was no end, no limit.   For leagues they travelled, striving perchance to climb to some distant hill or mountain peak that promised a far-reaching view into the strangeness beyond. But when they gained the coveted point, their eager eyes looked out only to see the same dark blues and purples lying on the horizon, with the same mysterious silence brooding over them.

After several such journeys they became wonder-stricken at the vastness and beauty of the land they had found across the great sea. They ceased to think they could find its boundaries, and said: "It has no end. Christ's Land must some day become the home of a great nation, even as the Angel of the Dawn did foretell."

They gathered around their huge fires, feasted and told tales, and sang the old Sagas. But they sang most of all the praises of their leader, Harald, the Blest of the Nornir, who had led them to where they could see what no man of the east had ever seen before.

New and amazing to the Skroelingjar were all things belonging to the Norsemen, from their mailed armour to the viking ship, which rode safely in a quiet harbour where a river emptied widely into the sea. But nothing took their attention as much as the three women.

The story which Silver Eagle told of the White Lily whose voice was as the summer wind, and whose touch had been so kind, made them haunt the shore until she appeared. From afar they stared at Persea, Sigrid and Astrid with bright, wonder-filled eyes. Sigrid soon ceased to interest them; for she dwelt timidly within the house, and they seldom caught a glimpse of her small form. But Persea moved fearlessly about with her pure, quiet eyes, and the smile of peace upon her lips. With quick instinct they saw the reverence paid her by the Norsemen. They brought presents of furs and decorated skins, and laid them at her feet. She returned their kindness with gifts from the viking ship; and her beauty and gentleness went far towards keeping the minds of the young braves from thoughts of warfare.

The presence of Astrid's crew, with their haughty mistress, was continually a menace and trouble to Harald. He knew that these men who loved him not were no glad addition to his fighting force. He thought of the long months of waiting on the shore, and the long months of sailing on the sea. His mind was troubled to think that during all this time he must dwell with those who hated him for what he was and for what he had done. The landing upon the shore of a new world had only widened the gulf between him and these men. Now, intense jealousy of his success helped on their hatred. They would have none of his favours. They would not even hunt

nor search the wilderness with his men.   He knew that Astrid
was his mortal enemy.   But he knew not how to meet her
unswerving cruelty of purpose.   Could he know how and
when a woman would choose to strike?   Sometimes he was
sorely tempted, if only for Persea's sake, to order that all in
the third house be made prisoners; but his best men were opposed to this.

They pointed out that they were four times as numerous as
the little remnant of Astrid's crew, and that therefore there
was nothing to fear.   It was also most certain that imprison-
ment would make them more bitter, more daring, and would
render it a difficult matter to manage them on board the ship.
So finally Harald let them do as they pleased; and they
pleased to live apart, isolated from the ones to whom they
owed their lives.

Astrid breathed into their hearts and minds her grim determination never to forget the reason for their journey northward; until, instead of gratitude for their deliverance from the
wrath of the sea, they blamed Harald for being the real cause
of all their misfortunes.   They had sailed into the region of
danger in pursuit of him.   They thought of the ship lying
fathoms deep in the icy water of the north, and cursed the
man who had lured them into such a mad chase.   Astrid would
listen to their curses with flashing eyes of approval.   When
they had spent their man's wrath, she would add her woman's
subtle poison with the words:

" 'T is surely true that because of Harald Rognvaldson we
have lost friends and ship; but blame him not without pity.
He has been bewitched by the foreign woman.   She loved
him, and by her evil arts she did turn the storms from his
path and lead him to this unknown land and people.   Who
knows what the end will be?   Those who clasp hands with
evil spirits must come to evil.   Much have the followers of
Astrid suffered; but lay the weight of your anger upon the
woman who has lured one of the bravest of Norsemen to
deeds that will be his undoing."

Guided by her thoughts, and dominated by her will, the
name of Persea came to be almost as odious, as maddening in
their ears as it was in hers.   They, too, hated the foreign
woman.

The Skroelingjar had been quick to notice that there was

something different about those who lived in the hut apart.
They were not welcomed about that camp-fire ; nor did those
white men make any attempt to be friendly with them.   Harald's order to preserve peace was obeyed only to the letter of
the law.   The savages were treated as the wild creatures of
the forest — neither noticed nor feared.   Great was the con-
trast to the Skroelingjar between Persea's gentle sweetness and
Astrid's haughtiness.

Astrid's fair beauty had excited wonder.   She could never
move from her hut that she was not subjected to the searching
scrutiny of savage eyes ; and sometimes even she grew restless under their silent, piercing stare.   But if the Skroelingjar
wondered at her rose-tinted skin and long, fair hair, they were
not less astonished when they saw her come forth dressed in
her suit of armour and go with her men into the forest to
hunt.   Some followed her trail and told that she could kill,
too, when the deer leaped from its covert.

Yet none of the Skroelingjar dared lay gifts at her feet ;
though much they gazed and secretly worshipped.   Of all who
fell under the spell of her beauty and strength, Red Fox was
most completely enthralled, though he hated those around her
with savage, jealous hatred.

Since the night when Manatocsin had rebuked him before
the council fire, and struck aside his hand that was raised
against the strangers, he had known no rest.   His eyes were
never still.   Always they were glancing here, there, everywhere, like those of a wounded beast brought to bay.   Towards his own people he grew sullen and morose.   When he
followed the deer tracks through the snow he asked for no
company.

Like the others of his tribe he visited the white strangers'
camping ground; but no gift passed from his hand to theirs.
Never did he sit by their fires or help them in hunting.
Silently he moved among them, with closely wrapped blanket ;
seemingly seeing nothing, but in reality with every sense alert
to learn all things concerning the dwellers upon the shore.
He knew their strength and their habits.   He watched them
from hidden places with his keen, bead-like eyes.   More than
once he clutched his bow and arrows when they crossed his
path in the forest.   Down in his wild heart the desire to match
his strength against the strength of these men grew stronger

and stronger. Day by day his step grew more stealthy and his weapons were clasped more closely in his hand. He knew not how nor when he could satisfy his lone thirst for blood ; but at any moment the chance might come.

There was only one thing he wished to consider in striking the blow — Astrid. She held his arrows in his quiver. He feared to strike lest he might have to lose sight of her. He constantly haunted the vicinity of her dwelling, crouching like a panther behind the rocks, satisfied if after many hours he caught one glimpse of her face. Like a panther he crept upon her track when she walked alone in the forest, as she often dared to do.

During these solitary walks she sometimes felt disturbed and uneasy, and looked about her carefully for a lurking forest danger; but even her eyes could not detect the still form among the tangled undergrowth, nor catch the glitter of snake-like eyes that watched her from tree or covert.

On one of these occasions Red Fox thought she had discovered him. A savage resolve leaped into his mind. If she made a movement to fly, he would seize her and carry her off to his old enemies, the Narragansetts. Upon promise of much booty they would keep her in their wigwams while the braves came back with him to destroy the white strangers.

But Astrid had not discovered him; and when she turned away he did not molest her.

So passed the winter. Spring began to cast its warmth over the forest; but still Red Fox haunted the footsteps of Astrid without her knowledge. His untutored heart was beginning to be dissatisfied with the meagre sight of her face. His constant nearness to her had begun to make him reckless and less awed by her silent haughtiness. Then too, he had heard rumours of the departure of the Norsemen. He was alarmed at the thought of losing sight of her for all time.

One day Astrid came out of her shelter with her bow and arrows, just as a white-breasted loon flew over her head. She shot at it ; but the arrow fell short. With a scream of fright the bird wheeled and made for the forest. The next moment it fell at her feet, pierced by a bright-feathered Skroelingi arrow.

In great wonder Astrid looked to right and left ; but she could not see the archer who had brought down the bird.

She waited, expecting one of the dark-skinned men to come from the forest to claim his shot. No one appeared.

Then she picked up the bird, still wondering and unsatisfied. As she did so, from the woods came the cry of the loon, clear and near by. She was startled. A swift fear smote her; for the cry of the great diver was held by all Norse people to be an omen of evil. She stood still, half-frightened, half-amazed until the weird call rang again from the forest. This time she instinctively heard the note of insistence, of longing, of appeal. She knew not from whom it came nor what it might mean; but impelled by some inward voice she raised her head and gave back to the forest an answering cry.

Then a tall, dark figure appeared for a moment at the edge of the woods. She saw no face, only a blanket-wrapped form that waved a hand to her and then quickly turned and disappeared amid the shadows of the trees.

With a woman's quick wit she read the story of a savage heart in the dead bird and the form she had seen beckoning to her from the forest. Though such a lover was but dirt under her feet, she was not displeased. All during her life men had bowed to her. Her vanity and selfishness had lived upon their homage until it was a part of her existence. Now she had met an unusual wooer, a savage who lived in the woods and dressed in the skins of beasts! She laughed to herself as she went back to her rough house. Here was much food for amusement in this cursed land.

She threw herself upon her couch and was thinking lightly of the whole incident, when a new thought entered her mind. She sprang to her feet with wide-opened, startled eyes, and hand pressed to her heart as if to hush its sudden throbbing. Was it in this manner she might gain her coveted revenge? Would it be possible?

For a space of several moments she stood silent, immovable. Then she lifted her cloak from the couch and went out.

A number of the Skroelingjar lounged around the fire or squatted before it. She eyed them all, swiftly, carefully; yet she saw no figure that was like the one which had beckoned from the edge of the forest.

The Norsemen were sitting about, polishing their armour

and weapons, and laughing gaily. The spring was advancing rapidly, and the ship was nearly ready for the long voyage homeward.

As Astrid scanned the motley crowd, she noticed a tall Skroelingi who stood apart from the others, half-hidden among the tree trunks. Something in his attitude aroused her interest. She quietly retraced her steps and stole around to a clump of bushes from which she could watch without being watched. As she looked, she saw hatred of the Norsemen in his face, and the gleam of covetous desire in his eyes when they rested upon the bright shields or the keen-edged weapons. This discovery made her tremble with excitement. If her surmise that this was her savage lover was correct, then he was doubly the tool to her hand. While she watched him she saw the tense straightening of his arm as if he would bring it heavily down upon the head of the man nearest him, and the hand that grasped the edge of his deerskin robe was tightly clenched.

She could not be certain that he was the Skroelingi who had shot the bird except by one final test. Even her fearless nature shrank from applying that. She drew back into the bushes, her blood leaping through her veins, making her turn red and white by turns. Would she be able to stand unharmed before the terrible danger that she was about to face alone ? Could she be sure she could use her power over this magnificent savage, and not be crushed by her own hand ?

Thrills of fear, such as were utterly new to her, shook her purpose to its very foundations. She dared not, she dared not go forward in this path. The danger was too great, the punishment too fearful if perchance she should fail. If perchance she should fail ! If she failed, what mattered it if her flesh was food for wolves and her bones bleached in the forest ? What mattered it if she did lose honour and life, if she could not wreak her vengeance ? This was her only chance. She must stake all upon it, and gain or lose as the Fates decreed.

She became Astrid again, with flashing cruel eyes and will that knew no thwarting, hatred that was insatiable.

With unfaltering steps she entered the forest alone. After she had gone some distance, she stopped, and turning towards the camp, gave the long call of the loon. It vibrated through the half-awakened foliage with tremulous wildness, leaping on, on, until it reached the ears of Red Fox.

He started, listened with savage joy in his bead-like eyes. His nostrils became distended as though to inhale some rare perfume. His form quivered with intense eagerness. From far back in the woods came the call the second time.

He turned quickly and entered the forest with great strides that soon changed to swift running. On he sped with un-erring instinct, answering the call with long drawn cries that sounded to Astrid's beating heart like the panting breath from some evil spirit that was approaching to devour her. But she did not shrink nor tremble when the bushes were pulled violently apart, and Red Fox leaped to her side.

Instead, she held out her hand to him and smiled.

CHAPTER XXXV

A FOREST TRAGEDY

As the earth, turning, in its course, brought brighter sunlight to the shores of Christ's Land, the Norsemen watched with keen pleasure the lengthening days, the bursting of leaf and bud, and the new gentleness of the west wind. The time of long waiting was nearing an end. Though their present residence was on a fair land, yet to them there was a fairer, — the land they called home.

Now that their curiosity had been satisfied about the country which they had discovered; now that they had travelled through its forests and followed its rivers into the distant hills; now that they had learned the life and ways of the dark-skinned Skroelingjar, their interest in the present began to wane. Faces were turned eagerly towards the sunrise. They were anxious to reach their own home and tell the remarkable story of Christ's Land.

Some distance down the shore, away from the sight and hearing of others, Persea and Harald sat side by side and talked of many things. Harald stretched himself at full length upon the sand. Clasping his hands back of his head, he said thoughtfully:

"No matter what may await us on the shore of Norge, I shall rejoice when the sea-snake is gliding towards the sunrise; and my joy is not for us alone. Greatly does my heart ache for the Temple Godi's daughter. Didst thou ever see such a hopeless despair as she carries in her heart? Nothing has the power to bring the smiles to her lips, or chase the regret from her eyes. She was not ready to give up her father for Christ and her lover. She is like a flower which has been uprooted and planted in a foreign soil from which it can draw no nourishment. Sometimes I have even wished that Christ had not decreed that she should have fled with us. Her sadness saddens me; yet I know not how to comfort her."

Persea's eyes filled with tears at Sigrid's name. She answered with troubled voice:

"Thy man's heart cannot truly understand the depth of her woman's grief and fear. She struggles with her unhappiness and strives to put it from her; but the very effort is pitiful to me. She knows no peace of mind by day or night. In vain have I tried to make her happy once more. She has lost all of her daring and courage. She clings to me in mortal fear if she does but hear the sound of the wind among the trees.

"Just an hour ago she sobbed in Tellus' arms because he was going on a short hunt in the forest alone. Yet she knows her fear is unreasonable; for when he would have put aside his spear for her sake, she would not have it so. She smiled through her tears and gave him luck in his hunting. It grieves Tellus sorely to see her so unhappy."

"Yea," answered Harald, "it must lie heavy upon his heart to see the tears in the eyes of his love. I know it must; for how should I feel if thou wert grieving that thou hadst left the North Land with me? My Persea! I could not live without thy love!"

He lifted himself upon his elbow and buried his face in her lap, breathing heavily. She laid her hand caressingly upon his head, twining loving fingers in his thick, fair hair. He raised himself quickly and caught her in his arms.

"Thou art so pure, so perfect, my Angel of the Dawn! Thou hast pointed me to the Christ. I know that to follow him is great joy to the inner spirit, that part of us that belongs not to earth; but still I am earthly. I love thee with the soul-love, and shall love thee so as long as the soul lives; but withal I am a man and human. I love thee also as a man loves. Thou art so high above me that thou canst not understand this human yearning for the human. There are times, yea, and now is one of them, when my heart is weeping drops of blood for love of thee; when my whole being cries out for thee. Yet I may not take thee to myself because of an evil woman's taunts. Pray to the White Christ for me that I may be patient and abide his time to enter into the fullness of my joy."

Persea had hidden her face in the thick folds of his cloak. He felt her tremble in his arms and tenderly he held her to him.

"Forgive me. I have frightened thee once more by my mad loving; but thou canst trust me. Though I must e'en yet wait to win thee from King Olaf, and though each moment of waiting is pain, yet thou canst trust me. If at times I seem to love thee too madly, be not angry with me. There are moments when the heart must speak. Then I must tell thee how I need thee in my life."

Persea lifted her face, warm with blushes.

"Dost thou think that I am not human enough to know how thou dost need me? I, too, feel the emptiness of life without thee; but in Christ's time all joy shall come to us. Great will be the happiness that others have held from us so long."

Back behind the rocks Astrid stood listening. She smiled one of her hard, cruel smiles when she heard Persea's last words. Then she turned, and keeping carefully out of sight of those on the beach, entered the forest.

She walked on for some time until she came to a huge, fallen tree. She stopped and gave utterance to the cry of the loon. Instantly it was answered, low and near by. Red Fox stepped from some tall underbrush and approached her.

The Skroelingi's eyes were not less restless than they had been the night of the council, many moons ago. From the day he had sent an arrow into the breast of the loon he had met the Gray Bird many times by the fallen tree. At first, words were not intelligible, but signs were. It did not take long for Red Fox to understand that Astrid's hatred of the white men was singularly akin to his.

Slave to her magnetic beauty, never doubting in his savage mind that he could win the prize that lured him on, he had made great sacrifices, from the Skroelingi's point of honour, to do her will.

Everything had melted to the purpose of Astrid the Peerless. Now, her chief anxiety was to hold this wild nature in check until the time she wished it to break forth. The savage blood was hot and reckless, and was growing ungovernable in its desire to gratify its hates and loves. To-day Astrid had hard matter to bring him under her will.

Ever and again, as she signed and spoke in one-worded sentences he interrupted with impatient gestures, and pointing to the sinking sun, touched his stone hatchet significantly, turning in anger when she would not give assent. It was only after she had used all the strength of her woman's arts, and even let him throw his blanket around her and draw her close to his side that she won him to anything like obedience.

Finally he was conquered. With one deep breath that seemed to draw all her being into his, he bent over her in farewell. Then he turned and departed as silently as the passing of a shadow.

After he left her, Astrid sat down upon the fallen tree. She leaned her head upon her hands, — her beautiful head with its fair face, — but the face was clouded with anxiety now. This man of the woods was as hard to control as any untamed beast. If he failed her at the last moment there was nothing left but to die quickly. Not for many more days could she keep down his desire to shed blood; but she would not despair of success. She must have her will, her revenge. For Harald, a choice of life with her or death. For Persea, — well he had said himself that a woman's revenge was ever cruel, — let her wait and see. Woman against woman it would be.

During the space of an hour she sat and thought. Sometimes a shiver shook her frame. The vast forest echoed no sound but the low soughing of the spring wind, or the stealthy rustle of last year's leaves as some timid wild thing stole through the pathless tangle. The Norse maiden gave no heed to aught around her. Even the far-distant howl of a wolf only made her look to her belt where a long, slim knife hung ready for her hand. At last she drew herself together with a sign of real weariness. Rising, she turned slowly back towards the camp.

So deep in thought was she that she heard not the oft-repeated howl of the wolf coming nearer and nearer. Neither did she know that it had been answered from the woods to the right of her path. She did not realize her danger until she saw two shadowy forms skulking through the trees. With a sudden thrill of horror she looked about for some point of apvantage, something that offered a fighting chance for life ; but there was nothing save the tall, branchless trunks of trees that shot up into the air with unvarying straightness.

One look behind. Then she cast off her cloak and flew through the forest on nimble feet. She knew she could expect to keep out of their reach only for a moment ; but that

moment would bring her nearer to the camp. Perhaps some
one would come to save !

The beasts stopped to snarl and quarrel over her cloak.   In
a few seconds that was torn in shreds.   Then they leaped full
speed after the flying woman.   She heard the patter of their
feet upon the dead leaves ; she heard the sound of their panting breaths ; and knowing her last moment of flight had
come she sprang aside, braced her back against an enormous
oak trunk, and drawing her knife waited for the first attack.

Surprised by her sudden stop, the wolves hesitated.   In that
moment of respite she sent the cry of the loon into the darkening forest, — once, twice, again, — with all the terror of her
perilous position in its far-reaching signal.

One of the wolves sprang at her.   She struck at him ; but
she missed his throat and only cut deeply into his side.   With
a howl of pain he dropped back.   The other, much larger and
stronger, leaped forward at the same instant.   Catching her
left arm, he sank his teeth to the bone in the effort to drag
her down.   Another moment's struggle and his jaws would
have met in her throat, — but through the woods came Tellus, fast on the track of the wolves which he was hunting.

Shouting encouragement, he sprang to the rescue.   A short,
fierce battle ; and the two beasts lay dead at his feet.

He turned to Astrid.   He had lifted her from the ground
and was helping her to stand.   His knife, red with blood was
still in his right hand when Red Fox burst upon them.

The Skroelingi had heard the loon's call from far back in the
forest.   He had recognized the note of terror in it.   Now he
saw Astrid in the embrace of one of the white men she
hated.   Her arm was covered with blood, and a knife dripping
the same dark hue was held over her.   In his frenzy he did
not notice the wolves upon the ground.   With a wild yell of
jealousy and hate he sprang upon Tellus and buried his stone
hatchet in his head.

The Roman sank to the ground without a sound.   To
Astrid, all things grew black.

When she came to herself she was lying on the couch in
her own hut.   Sigrid sat by her, bathing her head.   About
her stood her men with anxious faces.

"There, thou art better now.   Sleep, and forget the danger thou wert in."

But Sigrid's voice brought back all the horror of the forest tragedy. Astrid stared wildly at her. With white lips she said :

" Tellus, thy lover ? Where is he ? "

" Thou must not talk," answered Sigrid, " or thou wilt bring on the weakness again. The Skroelingi who brought thee home said that thou wert attacked by wolves and he had saved thee. Why dost thou speak of Tellus ? He went into the forest some hours ago to hunt. I am expecting him to return even now. Dost thou wish to see him when he comes ? "

With a pang of real agony for the sorrow coming so soon to this girl towards whom she bore no malice, Astrid motioned her away. She beckoned to one of her own men.

" To Harald Rognvaldson ! " she whispered. " Quick ! Tell him to search the forest for the Roman. I know not whether he be dead or alive ; but he saved my life only to be struck down by the Skroelingi. Thou dost understand. Fly ere thou art too late. Let not the evil tidings come to the ears of the girl. Too soon must she know the worst, if worst it be."

The man bowed and went quickly out of the hut. Astrid turned to Sigrid again. She put aside the inquiry that was in her face by saying :

" Thou wert gracious to come to the assistance of a woman who has treated thee with the indifference and even contempt that Astrid has."

Sigrid replied quietly :

" It was not for me to judge thee ; nor was it for me to re-member thy words against thee when thy messenger did come to our hut and beg for a woman's hand and help to restore thy life. I am a follower of Christ. Through him is given me the wish to show kindness even to those who reproach and think evil of me falsely."

" Thou didst well not to let the foreign woman come to me. I would rather have the hot tongue of the wolf on my flesh than her hand. I am grateful, truly grateful to thee, not only for thy kindness, but because thou didst spare me the pain of waking and finding her by my side."

Again the wounded woman thought of the tragedy in the woods. She groaned aloud in anguish of mind. Why had that man saved her life, only to lose his? Had Red Fox murdered under other circumstances she would not have felt so troubled; for the brother of Persea had been of little consequence to her. But to owe him her escape from a cruel death, and then see him pay the price of his life! This brought the bloody deed before her in a new light. She felt that there had been some strange twisting of her plans. Furthermore, to have this girl tending her wounds so carefully brought more regret for the Roman's death. She moaned again.

Sigrid, thinking her wound gave her great pain, said tenderly:

"Does the wound so torture thee? I would that I could give thee some ease; but I know not what more I can do."

Astrid turned her head towards her and said quickly:

"There is something more thou canst do that will greatly ease my pain. I am sorry for the cruel words I have spoken to thee in the past. I know thy lover was a brave man. 'T was no dishonour to cling to him on such a night of horror as was that last night upon the Thrandheim shore. I have no ill will towards thee. Wilt thou forgive me and let me be thy friend? Thou wilt find that Astrid the Peerless knows how to be a friend as well as a foe. I would be thy friend through my life. Wilt thou accept my friendship? That will ease my pain as nothing else."

Surprised beyond measure at the pleading sorrow in Astrid's voice, yet glad indeed to hear such words from this woman of wrath, Sigrid leaned over the couch with tear-wet lids.

"Accept thy friendship? Art thou not a Norsewoman like myself? Could I possibly refuse to forgive thee, even if I desired to do so? But more than I am a Norsewoman I am a Christian; and as such there is no joy so great as the joy of being a friend to one who was mine enemy. Gladly will I be thy friend. Here is the sign of peace between us for all time."

She bent and kissed the lips of the wounded woman. With feverish eagerness Astrid kissed her back and said:

"I will be true and kind to thee. Thy happiness shall be my first thought. I shall strive to make up to thee what thou hast lost through me. O Sigrid! Sigrid! I am so grieved, so tortured for thee!"

" Nay, be not so aroused, my sister. Why should the past so trouble thee ? Sleep. Forget all except that thou hast found a friend."

But Astrid could not be comforted. Sigrid tried to soothe her, thinking her troubled sayings were only the result of her wound and the memory of her encounter with the wolves.

While she spoke, there came to their ears the sound of unusual happenings. Loud cries, mournful and apprehensive of danger, came from the woods. Sigrid turned to Astrid with the old timid look in her eyes, and started to her feet.

The Norsewoman raised herself from her couch and said :

" My wound is as nothing to thine ! In a few days I shall be healed ; but thou shalt carry the hurt to thy grave. I can keep it from thee no longer. Go out and learn what they are bringing from the forest to thee. If thy Christ be a God, pray to him for strength. Thy lover saved me, while I, all unknowingly, brought death to him."

With lips dumb in nameless terror, Sigrid burst from the hut and flew to meet the company of men that were emerging from the forest. They saw her coming, and reverently laid the rough bier upon the ground.

When they lifted it again they carried two forms ; for across the dead body of Tellus Sigrid had fallen unconscious.

CHAPTER XXXVI

ONE RAY OF LOVE

As soon as Harald had examined the body of Tellus, he called his men together to consider this unlooked-for act on the part of the Skroelingjar. While they were still talking, Manatocsin came out of the woods and stood in their midst. He was alone. The Norsemen could find nothing but real grief in his face and mien as he said in his imperfect speech:

"Manatocsin has heard. Where is the tomahawk that was buried in the white brother's head? Let the eyes of the chief of the Wampanoags rest upon the weapon, that he may know who has broken the sacred peace and brought shame into the hearts of his people."

In silence the stone ax was handed to him. He gave it one searching glance. Throwing it upon the ground, he said bitterly:

"'T is as Manatocsin thought. Red Fox has done the evil deed. Let the ears of the white brothers be opened to the words of the chief. They will know how this came to pass. They will not cast the dishonour of a broken peace upon the Wampanoags."

With many tragic signs and gestures the old man related the story of the events of that first night when the viking ship lay at anchor in the bay. He told them of the wrath of the Skroelingjar and their thirst for blood; told of the fiery speeches of Red Fox, and his determination to match his strength against the men from over the Great Water. He spoke of the sudden appearance of Silver Eagle.

Here the Norsemen bent forward, listening with intense interest. They looked at each other in amazement when they learned all that the man had seen and heard while they thought him limp and unconscious. There came a quick thrill through their hearts when he told of the sensations which Silver Eagle felt when Persea appeared, and the effect of her gentle ministry upon his mind.

At the close he told them how the words of Silver Eagle

had decreed that the strangers should sleep in peace. The
Norsemen were silent from the great fullness in their hearts, —
the fullness of blessing upon the head of the woman whose
small hand had held back the untamed bloodthirst of hundreds
of savages.

On that first night they had been boldly confident in their
warrior's strength and skill to keep them from harm. They
knew now that they were bold through great ignorance of
their danger; and that it was Persea, and Persea alone, who
had woven the thread which had moored their bark to the
New World in happiness and peace. They knew now with
what skill and power the Skroelingjar could have attacked the
boat that night. They knew the silent, stealthy approach, so
different from their mode of warfare. They knew what the
end would have been. A terrible foe leaping suddenly out of
the blackness of the night; a battle fierce and bloody but
quickly over, — and a viking ship rotting on the sands.

When Manatocsin had finished, Harald replied kindly. He
said that the chief's words had been wise; for now the Norsemen knew that there was only one foe in the land. They had
lost a dear brother. Their hearts were sore with pain; but
they would no longer blame the Wampanoags for the evil
deed. All they asked was that Red Fox should be punished
for his treachery.

" This will Manatocsin do with his own hand," said the
chief, " if the snake in the grass can be found. But he has
not returned to his wigwam. The wind has brought further
disgrace to his name by whispering that he has joined the
Narragansetts, the enemies of his people. If this be true, he
is beyond the reach of Manatocsin unless the Wampanoags go
upon the warpath; but if the white chief desires, the war
dance shall begin."

Harald, whose vessel was already tugging at its anchor-
ropes, would not leave his quarrel to be fought out in blood
between the inhabitants of Christ's Land. He thanked the
chief for his words; but said that in a few days the white men
would leave his land. He would not ask his friends, the
Wampanoags, to shed the blood of many for one. That
could not call back the spirit of the one who was gone; and it
would only bring a great loss to Manatocsin.

The chief went back to the forest. The men laid Tellus

under the ground in his suit of armour. Then the preparations for departure were rushed forward. The sooner they set sail the better now.

Sigrid grew quiet and calm after the body of her lover had been put out of her sight forever. It was her turn now to comfort Persea, whose heart was bleeding sorely at the loss of the brother love and companionship that had been hers from infancy. As she mourned bitterly for him she said:

"The cruel suddenness of it all! To see him go out in the strength of his manhood, only to be brought back to us cold in death! It seems to me that all I love are marked for violence. My heart is breaking with grief."

Sigrid gave an unexpected reply.

"To me, this sorrow is not sudden. Did I not shiver when first I saw this land? Have I not lived with the fear of an unknown evil floating o'er me? That is why I am calm now. I feel, at least, as if that lurking horror was gone. It is easier to face a trouble that is known, no matter how great it may be, than something that hovers over us unseen, only present to the spirit that deals not with material things, but which hears sounds not heard by the ears, and sees sights not seen by the eye. It may be strange to hear me speak these words, but I tell thee that I shall sleep better to-night than for many nights past. When I lie upon my couch I shall say to myself, 'It has come.' After that I shall forget myself and all the world. The feverish light in my brain will go out. I shall sleep with Christ and the stars watching overhead. Peace and oblivion shall come to me. Perhaps while I sleep, Christ will be merciful and call me. There would be no greater joy than to follow Tellus, leaving my body to lie beside his on the shores of Christ's Land."

"Christ forbid!" said Persea with throbbing heart. "Is not the loss of my brother enough, that thou shouldst wish to leave me alone with none of womankind except the one yonder who hates me?"

Into Sigrid's mind came the memory of the unusual actions and words of Astrid, which she had forgotten in the sorrow for the dead. She repeated the conversation to Persea, ending with:

"Was it not singular that she should be so softened by my small act of kindness? But I must see her and find out what she meant by blaming herself for the death of Tellus. How could she have aught to do with it ? "

" I know not; but I do know that she is evil enough to do things of which thou couldst not dream. Hassan has warned me many times. But yesterday he told me how she sent me a poison drink the last feast night. Now I know whence came that look of bitterness and evil which I saw in her face when I entered the skali with Harald.

" Go and hear what she might say to thee of Tellus; but keep thine eyes open for treachery. Christ knows I have no anger in my heart towards her; but I trust her not. If she offered thee her friendship, it may be that God has touched her heart; but until thou art sure of her sincerity, take care lest she send harm upon thee."

Sigrid clung to Persea's neck.

" Oh, why is there so much sorrow in the world ? Why does man hate man with such fierceness when love is so much sweeter and brings so much happiness ? "

" It is because the world knows not Christ. 'T is his teaching that shall bring peace to the world. In his time he will send forth great and noble men, and they shall carry the pure word of truth to all nations. They shall be like torches in the darkness, filling the world with light. If those who carry them are struck down by hands that love not the light upon their dark deeds, the flame shall not perish. Some one else will snatch the precious brand and hold it aloft to the gaze of the suffering world. The world shall bless the light though the torch-bearer be trampled under cruel feet."

" Thy words are marvellous," said Sigrid. " When thou speakest thus, I seem to hear a beautiful melody in the air, as if radiant spirits were singing some heavenly refrain. Dost thou not hear it ? Perhaps it is clearer to thy soul than mine. Perhaps thou canst understand its meaning as my poor soul cannot."

Persea's face shone with a light that was beautiful beyond thought. She kissed Sigrid tenderly, saying:

" Now I know thou dost love and understand me. *The Voices !* Thou, too, hast heard them. Give thy soul to listening. Mayhap they have a message for thee."

" A message for me ? " said Sigrid wonderingly. " Nay, I am not worthy ; but thou shalt be one of the torch-bearers of whom thou didst speak. Already thy light has warmed many chilled hearts; and the end is not yet. I am too weak, too bowed with the weight of much sorrow to lift my spirit to the under-standing of such melodies. Yet because thou hast bidden me listen, I shall listen. Kiss me once more, and let me go to Astrid."

Persea kissed her with a silent prayer and sent her forth. When she had departed, there came upon the Roman maiden a chill of horror that was so great a reaction from the thoughts and feelings of the past few moments that she knew something evil had suddenly spread out black wings between herself and Christ. The terror and unknown fear that had so haunted Sigrid settled on her heart and brain. She went swiftly to the side of her couch and knelt in prayer. Only Christ could bring peace and comfort in her sorrow and heart-fear.

Sigrid found Astrid moving about with no visible sign of weakness or wound. She received the girl with a tender sweetness so new in Astrid the Peerless that Sigrid could not think ill of her. Tears came into the eyes that hitherto had been glassy with anguish. When Astrid saw the wet lids, she took Sigrid's hand in hers and said earnestly:

"Weep out thy anguish. It is well when the tears come; for then the heart is not utterly dead."

She gave a dry, choked sob, which smote so pitifully upon Sigrid's ears that she wept still more violently. Astrid held her close and continued:

"Thou seest I have suffered until tears come no longer. Dost thou understand that there can be a sorrow as much greater than thine as the fury of the winter tempest is greater than the soft stirring of the summer wind? Weep on. But with thy tears of sadness weep tears of joy that thou canst still weep."

When her grief had spent its bitterness, Sigrid remembered why she had come, and said:

"Tell me what thou knowest of the death of Tellus. Thou didst speak to me in riddles; yet I see now that thou must have known what was to be found in the forest. If thou art indeed my friend, tell me all."

Astrid's face grew white. She put the girl from her, saying half to herself:

"I had hoped that that speech of mine would not have been

remembered.   Forget it, Sigrid, for what can we do to change the past ?   I did not wish nor will thy lover's death.   Let that suffice thee."

But Sigrid would not forget.

" Nay, how can I be satisfied when I know there is some mystery thou couldst reveal to me ?   If thou didst mean all the strong words of friendship thou didst speak to me; if thou wouldst do aught to ease my aching heart, tell me what thou knowest.   I cannot believe in thee if thou dost hold so great a secret from me."

Then Astrid's mind was filled with alarm.   She did not wish to tell.   Many times had she regretted that she had let slip her knowledge of the death of Tellus.   She feared that her dark secrets would be dragged into the light.   Now, confronted by Sigrid's appeal, she knew not what course to pursue.   She found herself yearning over this girl, longing for her love as she had deemed it impossible to long for anything like human love again.   If she refused to say anything, then she realized that she could not expect the girl to believe in her offers of friendship.   Her past had been too stormy, too violent in Sigrid's eyes for her to trust in a friendship that would deny the thing she had asked.   Astrid saw she must risk the danger or lose this companionship for which she felt so great a hunger, and she chose the former course.

Briefly she spoke of her walk alone, the approach of the wolves, and the coming of Tellus to her rescue.   She said nothing of the cry of the loon; but told how a savage had sprung suddenly from the thicket and struck Tellus down.   She had known no more until she found herself in her own hut.

" But I do not see," said Sigrid, " why thou shouldst blame thyself for the madness of one of the Skroelingjar.   Why he should strike, I know not, unless he too, was following the wolf track and was angered that Tellus had killed his quarry.   Thinkst thou not that this jealousy must have been his motive for the bloody deed ? "

Thankful to find so easy a way to satisfy Sigrid's curiosity, and thinking within herself as she answered that her words were only too grimly true, she said :

" Yea, the savage was undoubtedly jealous.   These Skroelingjar know no control except the desire of the moment."

She did not say who had urged him to hate and roused him to kill. In her soul she knew the blood of Tellus was upon her hand; and it had come so suddenly, so unwished for after her own deliverance, that she shrank from the stain of it.

While this shadow fell upon her she remembered what she had planned for the future. She had no thought of foregoing her revenge; but there was Sigrid, now. Could she not be spared the seeing of it all? Astrid had some intangible feeling that through kindness to this girl she might atone for some of her violations of law and conscience. Void as she was of regret, and facing the future with a cool courage that was ready to pay any price for her revenge; yet there lurked deep down in the inner recesses of her being that sure knowledge of the shock and recoil of the blow she would strike. When it came, it would perhaps be easier to withstand if she could know that to this girl, at least, she had made some measure of atonement. Therefore she spoke:

"Dost thou wonder that after what has happened to me I am no longer content with the company of my men or my own thoughts? For several days I have known the presence of woman, and thy nearness fills me with delight. Wilt thou not stay with me? When we go upon the ship I shall see thee much and be always near thee; but Astrid has a great love for thee awakening in her heart. She would have thee with her."

But Sigrid remembered Persea's words of warning. Fearful of some hidden evil, she would not consent to remain. Astrid pleaded and besought; but to no purpose. The more urgent grew her appeal, the more firmly did Sigrid refuse. When finally she rose to depart, Astrid said:

"I wish that thou couldst be persuaded to stay. I believe that thou dost not trust me. I am not sure that I can blame thee; yet I need thee sorely, — more than thou dost dream. But if thou wilt not stay, go thy way till next we meet. Remember at that next meeting that withal I love thee, and would not harm one hair of thy head."

With uneasiness in her mind, Sigrid left the hut. But the stalwart forms of the Norsemen, with their sense of protection, soon quieted her fears. When night came she slept, by Persea's side, the sleep of the weary in body, brain and heart.

As she sank deeper and deeper into the oblivion of slumber,

marvellous visions floated before her. Tellus appeared and beckoned to her. Beautiful melodies sounded in her ears. At first they came as faint, sad minor strains; but they grew and changed as they increased in volume, until through her dream rolled a magnificent harmony of sound like a grand triumphal chorus, filling her soul with a sublime courage.

She woke to hear in reality the hideous war cry of screaming savages, mingled with the tramp and jar of many feet outside their shelter.

CHAPTER XXXVII

THE WRATH OF MAN AND GOD

AFTER the departure of Sigrid, Astrid stayed at the door and watched the sun set. It went down in blood tints that evening; and against the vivid sky the forest-covered hills looked inky black. The brilliant light paled to gold, then to purples and grays, until they were lost in the darkness of the night. Now the stars came out, and a silver-rimmed moon drooped towards the horizon.

Still Astrid stood at the door, looking at sky and land, and hearing the sounds of the forest, — yet heeding them not. Her brain was busy with thoughts that shut her eyes to all sights and closed her ears to all sounds.

"It is as true as death," she said to herself, "that I love this girl with a sudden and great love. It is the pure love of woman for woman; the love of the bereft for the bereft; the love of the injurer for the innocent injured. Had she stayed with me, — but no, she would not stay! She went from me to her arms. Now the old desires rise within me. I rejoice that I have planned so well, so well. The weakness has gone. In three hours the great star will reach the horizon. Then the will of Astrid shall triumph over those who put her to scorn.

"Sleep, Harald Rognvaldson! Sleep well to-night; for thou shalt wake to a strange changing of the pattern of thy life. Thou didst turn the golden web of my happiness to black. Now into thy future let the same dark threads be woven! There is one moment of my life for which thou shalt pay a price thou little dreamest. Thou hast grown over-confident in thy pride. Thou hast snapped thy fingers at defeat and death. Thou hast called new worlds out of the sea to shelter thee from thy enemies. But then it was a man who threatened thee. Now a woman is planning thy downfall; and a woman plans well.

"The star is sinking fast. Soon I, the scorned, shall be the scorner, or else — but why think of that? Let the end come. Let it bring triumph or the torment of all the hells of all the gods, — still let it come! There is always one open door; and if I pass through it I shall not go alone!"

About her the night wind blew inland laden with the dank sting of the salt spray, bringing messages from the spirits of the ocean to the spirits of the land. Out in deep water the viking ship lay rocking upon the waves. Already her prow was pointed eastward and met the inrush of white-capped waves with proud lifting of her golden head. Soon she would not only receive their attack, but leap to meet them as she cut her trackless path back towards her far-off home.

Astrid turned from the dark wall of forest to face the salt-laden wind. She saw by the dim starlight that graceful form rising and falling on the swell of the waves, keeping perfect time to the sound of their break upon the beach. She watched its outline for a moment, then with the whispered words, " It is a goodly sea-snake; it will sail the seas well, no matter who stands at the prow," she turned and entered the hut.

Her men were lounging about the fire. They wore their swords and tolle-knives; and spears and shields lay within reach. Upon their faces was a look of expectancy. They started at every sound. When Astrid entered, they half rose, reaching for their weapons; but she motioned them back.

" Not yet," said she. " 'T is some time ere we go forth. Rest, even sleep, if sleep ye can; for there is that before us to-night which shall need all strength of arm and all courage of heart. But ye have both, my sea kings, and ye will not fail me! Give me once again the sacred pledge, that I may feed my soul with the surety of success."

One by one the great bronzed men knelt before her and swore their Norse oath to serve her with sword and knife while life lasted; to own her leadership and to obey, — let her command what she would.

And they meant their oath, these men with muscles like iron and hearts that knew not fear. She had led them until they knew she could lead. She had taught them to wish as she wished and to plan as she planned, until, in perfect accord with her desires, they moved together towards one common end. But there were some things which Astrid had not told, had not dared to tell. Therefore she asked for the oath once more; lest in the coming hours her will might be disputed, her plans thwarted, even by these.

After all had spoken the solemn words, a silence deep with meaning, fell on the little group. Words were not near to lips that might grow stiff in death ere the sunrise. Astrid disappeared behind the curtains that screened her couch, and left the men to their thoughts.

Into the fire they gazed with eyes that, though stern and set in cruel purpose, yet held a light from other days. Old memories arose, — the memories of friends and places far away; memories of pleasures long gone by; of touch of sword and kiss of woman; of low, wide-eaved dwellings; of cool, dark fjords. Such visions of the past come to men who, walled in by fire, are facing the consequences of a leap through the flames.

Slowly the great star sank towards the horizon. In ten minutes more it would rest for an instant, then drop out of sight into the infinitude of space. Now Astrid came silently forth, wearing her hunting garb of short tunic and small fur cap. In her belt hung her long, keen knife. She fingered its handle nervously as she looked at the warriors who had risen as she entered, and had lifted spear and shield ready for use. She gave to each a long, searching glance. No fool was Astrid to be sure that treachery could not find a place in her following; but she was satisfied with what she saw in face and stalwart form. Then she spoke:

"The time has come for us to accomplish that for which we left King Olaf's fleet, many months ago. With Eric and Ovar I go to the forest; but ye shall creep along the edge of the wood until ye reach the smaller hut beyond. There wait, as still as the stones, for me. When I come, ye know well what to do. See to it that he escapes not, neither lifts sword against himself; and Sigrid, handle with gentleness and pity. I grieve that she must be witness to the deeds of this night. For the rest, our time will be short if we would pay no dear price for our joy of vengeance. I have said enough. The forest calls us. Come."

Followed by the Norsemen, Astrid left the hut and struck boldly into the forest. Soon she stopped and gave the cry of the loon. The tall form of Red Fox appeared beside her like a spectre among the dim, uncertain shadows. She spoke to him and he gave the low, "Woof! woof!" of the bear. At the sound, myriads of spectre forms slipped silently from covert or tree trunk, and stood with him. Then Astrid knew the wild savage had kept his word; for these were the great braves of the terrible Narragansetts, and they were awaiting her will.

One night, long ago, a woman's hand had stayed the wild man's wrath and made the darkness a canopy of peace and security under which the Norsemen slept unharmed. To-night, a woman's hand was lashing the savage wildness to serve her evil purpose, and the darkness was but a canopy of despair and death which was slowly descending upon them.

Carefully and cautiously Astrid and the two Norsemen led the stealthy-footed Skroelingjar towards the camp. Not a twig cracked under their light tread; not a branch swung as they passed. Scantily clothed, and holding stone axes in their hands, they crept, half crouching, through the forest. In long, dark lines they twisted in and out among the tree trunks,— lines like the sinewy folds of some huge serpent.

When they reached the edge of the clearing, the lines parted. The great snake crept around the sleeping Norsemen until its black folds encircled it many times. Tighter and tighter grew the coils, almost touching the walls of the camp; yet still their presence was undetected. Behind strong logs and barred door the Norsemen slept. There was nothing in the sounds of the night to tell the lone watchman within that a thousand weapons were raised to strike.

While the Skroelingjar closed about the larger camp, Astrid and her warriors surrounded the smaller one. Red Fox would have stayed by her side; but she pointed to the other building and whispered:

" Go! Bathe thy tomahawk in the white man's blood. The death wounds given here must be given by the hands of my brothers. After thou hast done thy part there, the Gray Bird will go with thee. Dost thou understand ? "

Red Fox understood and obeyed.

Then passed a moment of tense silence. It was the silence that comes before the bursting of a mighty flood; the silence that grips air, earth and sky ere the tempest tears the heavens apart : the silence of the moment when men listen for the hoarse cry of surprised resistance, and the scream that follows the knife-thrust in the dark.

A tiny tongue of flame crept up a pile of brushwood in the

clearing. At the same instant the blood-curdling war cry of the Narragansetts rang through the air. The Skroelingjar leaped towards the large hut, bearing a great log which they hurled against the stout door.

Within, the Norsemen had sprung from deep sleep, dazed and not easily comprehending what had come upon them. The air was filled with wild sounds; their shelter was shaking with the force that was breaking upon it; and as the men grasped sword and shield and stood ready to battle, they asked each other, " What has come to us ? "

Ere any could answer the door gave way, and into the hut, lit only by the dying embers of the night's fire, burst the painted savages. Those who remembered the old tales now shouted :

" 'T is Nidhöggu and the Fenris wolves ! "

Every man's heart beat against his ribs with swift terror. They truly thought that foes not earthly leaped towards them as they saw in the dim light the naked, painted bodies, hideous in ghastly colours, and caught the glint of eyes that burned with savage love of killing.

But the spirit of the Norseman prevailed. Whether the foe was human or devil, they saw some one to fight and they fought, meeting the shrieking war cry with their brave " Haoi-aoi-haoi ! " and giving blow of sword for blow of savage axe.

They fought for life and limb; for comrade and friend; for liberty; for Harald and the Angel of the Dawn whom they loved; for home, which they saw as the drowning see; for the fruits of their perilous voyage; for fame and fortune; but they fought a losing battle.

The fire was soon trampled down. Then the fierce struggle went on with only a fitful, flickering light from the burning brush outside. The Norsemen grasped shield and sword with giant strength and struck at gliding, crouching forms; but out of the darkness came crafty blow aud treacherous grip too quick for parry or counter move. Where one sword thrust went home, two swung in empty air. Yet all the while descended the great stone axes and knotty war clubs. Armour was battered and broken, shields were splintered, swords were snapped like straws, heads were crushed, arms swung useless, limbs gave way, men sunk to the ground, swept down under savage blows which overwhelmed them as the avalanche overwhelms. The end was near.

When the attack began, Astrid rushed to the door of the smaller hut, and beating violently upon it, cried out in a voice that treacherously feigned terror:

"'T is Astrid! Open! The Skroelingjar are upon us!"

Harald, in that first moment of alarm, had no thought of treachery from her. He knew surely that the savages were attacking them. Thinking not of an enemy, but of a woman needing protection, he sprang to the door and pushed back the bar. Instantly it swung swiftly open, pushed inward by a dozen hands. Astrid stood in the room, her men behind her with boldly drawn weapons.

Then Harald knew what evil had come upon him; for not in fear did this woman enter his abode. She was glorying in her triumph ere she spoke a word. She knew that the man before her understood without words that her moment had come. She only looked at him, — a look that scorched him with a vast mingling of love and hate, cruel enough to kill. With one swift glance towards Persea's curtain, Harald grasped the handle of his tolle-kniv. The half-dozen men behind him did likewise. They understood vaguely that Astrid hated their leader; but they did not understand how great that hatred was.

When Harald's hand went to his knife, Astrid's men sprang towards him. She waved them back imperiously.

"Fools! Would ye spoil my task so well begun?"

She turned to Harald.

"Rememberest thou? Ah! thou dost remember. This is the hour when thou shalt pay. Hearest thou those sounds? Thy men are being killed like sheep in a pen. Savages from the woods are tearing their hair from their heads; and they are doing this at my command. Yield to me, thou and thine; for Astrid the Peerless conquers last, though the victory comes late!"

Even while she said the words, she felt a sickening sense of failure. She could never conquer that man who looked at her with calm, quiet eyes while she told of death and treachery. He had not flinched nor quivered an eyelid. He was thinking, not of himself, but of Persea. He had no time to care for Astrid's taunts and boasts.

This she felt. Nay, more than that; because as she waited for him to speak, she caught the echo of her words. The depths of evil and treachery that lay bared at their saying struck chill on her own spirit. She had triumphed in her way; but that was not triumph over him if she could not move him more. What difference did the butchery yonder make to her if he knew it and would not tremble? What difference did her stinging words make to her if he heard them and let no shade of anger or disappointment cross his face? What difference did anything make if all she had done, all she could do, would not touch this man's power of self-control? For in truth, Harald Rognvaldson looked at that moment as though the majestic calm of the fathomless ocean depths could be more easily disturbed than he.

But, as if a lightning flash had revealed it, Harald was seeing the terrible struggle in the next camp. He knew what was happening there, else his brave men would have swarmed to his rescue. He saw his following gone, all his plans thwarted, his ship in the hands of savages or enemies of his own colour, himself a prisoner, reserved for a fate unknown, but not less surely cruel. For his dying friends he sent up a swift petition to Christ.

The seconds he had been silent had seemed hours; yet he could not speak. For himself he cared not. He could lose fame, fortune, life itself without a fear or tremour, — but Persea! And Christ forgive his selfishness — Sigrid! What would become of them? His words, his actions must all be planned for them alone.

Astrid's rage was increasing under his calm silence, with the contempt it told. Was there nothing that she could do that would take from him this indifference to her love and hate?

The curtain parted. Persea stepped forward with Sigrid clinging to her side. Their faces were white with fear. They had come forth, trembling at the noise of entrance into their shelter, and the fact that Harald had not come to them.

In Persea's presence, Astrid saw Harald's calmness broken with acute anguish. Here was some one through whom she could make him tremble! All the maddening experiences of the past months struck deeply into her soul. In one heartbeat, she knew herself scorned, despised, cheated even of the fullness of revenge, — except in her!

With sudden, swift movement she snatched the knife from her belt and leaped towards Persea. Harald himself could not have stayed the uplifted hand; it fell. But there was another movement as swift as hers, a woman's cry — almost of joy — and the descending knife sank to the hilt in Sigrid's breast.

She had come out with the strains of the dream music ringing in her ears; the music that had given her such wonderful strength that she knew there was some need for it, some crisis to meet. She saw Astrid's face, dark with evil passion, turned towards Persea; she saw the sudden leap of hand to knife, — and she knew what was given her to do. With great joy she answered the beckoning of Tellus, and followed him into the glory of the life beyond.

So like a tigress's spring had been Astrid's movement, and so unexpected the result, that men lost their power of motion and were as stone; while to Persea came the blessing of unconsciousness.

Astrid, with her eyes staring in horror, half staggered, half shrunk from the falling form which sinking, covered her with the spurt of its heart's blood. Then she shrieked, — a shriek of despair and hopelessness, ringing above the terrible sounds of that night with a soul-cry which all who heard remembered while they lived. It was the cry of the mortal who had dared to defy the Omnipotent, and across whose face the lightning bolt of his wrath had been drawn.

But the cry roused men to action. Harald and his few followers sprang to the protection of Persea. Astrid's men grappled with them; but as it was happening with the unequal odds in the farther camp, so it happened here. The battle was swiftly over. Harald and the few who remained to him were bound hand and foot. There was no power left in Astrid to do Persea harm; for the still form on the floor with the blood-stain upon its breast had paralyzed her hatred. Persea, yet unconscious, was bound with the rest.

Astrid then gave command to place the body of Sigrid upon the couch of furs. She gazed at the beautiful features, radiant even in death with the great joy of the vision beyond, and she shivered. This one whom she had sent to death had brought into her life a brief knowledge of pure love. It was as though some heavenly spirit had plucked a rose from the garden of infinite love, and in passing had wafted to her one deep breath of its sacred perfume.   She had known something very precious; but so swift and fleeting that it seemed only a dream. Now it was turned to a dull pain and a fearful memory.   She remembered vaguely that she had planned to be kind to this still form; that she had promised it gentleness and devotion, even great sacrifices of self-pleasure, if she could help bear its burden of sorrow.

And now!   There lay that one she had loved, with red on her breast that she herself had drawn from her heart, when she would have given kiss.   The Norsewoman bent over the cold forehead, hesitated, then drew back.   No!   She could not touch that whiteness.   It mocked her with its purity; it cursed her with its stillness.   Something dark passed before her eyes.   Back to its old abiding place crept the sullen evil and the hate.

With cold command she had the body of the murdered girl covered from sight.   Then she sent half of her men to the ship to prepare for departure.

By this time the struggle was nearly over, within and without.   The brush-wood fire showed the blood-covered Skroelingjar ravaging the grounds, and possessing themselves of all the Norsemen's weapons, armour, and clothing, — Red Fox greatest among them.   Astrid looked coolly out; then turned to Harald and said:

"I have played a difficult game for a woman to play.   I must not tarry at my work; for at any moment these Skroelingjar who have done my killing may turn against me.   Thou art in my power.   The tide goes out and my ship goes with it. If thou wilt give thy word to take me for thy wife when we reach the home land, I will put thee on board ship.   If thou wilt not, thou shalt stay here with thy handful of men. Judging by yonder sights, thy shrift shall be short.   Choose quickly — to go with me, thy promised bride, or to stay with these."

Harald shuddered at her words, more at the thought of a life with her than the thought of death from savage men. There was no question of his choice; but his soul was agonized for the fate of Persea.

With closed eyes and pallid face she lay upon the floor.   As his burning gaze rested on her, his heart was wrung with anguish, despair, and love.   He turned to Astrid.

"Thou hast not told me of her. What is in thy mind? Do as ye will with me. I would rather take death in a thousand embraces than thee; but when thou leavest me here what shalt thou do to her?"

His voice thickened, trembled, broke. Astrid looked and laughed.

"At last have I made thee feel, thou man of iron. So I swore to myself, — to make thee feel, to tremble at my voice. If not in love for me then in fear: if not in fear for thyself, then in fear for her. Thy alarm is not without cause. I leave thee here, since death is so welcome; but I take her hence with me."

"And wherefore?" asked Harald fiercely. "What shalt thou do unto her? Dost thou take her to King Olaf? Is it death at thy hand? Speak! Almost I feel as if the strength of a God would come to me that I could burst these bonds and send thee to a judgment beyond the grave."

He groaned and writhed in his agony. Astrid watched him, her brow drawn with hate.

"I will answer thy question, that thou mayest have food for thought in the time that is left thee. When I finish my speech to thee, thou wilt wish that I had said that I would deliver her to the King. That would be too slight a vengeance for Astrid to take; for King Olaf is no mean man. He so loves thy Persea that he would be happier in the dirt at her feet than upon his throne. If I gave her to him, all kindness, all care would be hers. Because she was in his power and thou wast gone, he would not be cruel or insistent. He is noble, and he would win her love, not force it. Soon thou wouldst be only a faint memory to her. Thinkest thou I could be satisfied with so poor a revenge? Nay, more than that have I in my mind, though perchance the King may embrace her in his passion ere the end comes. That will be as he wishes. I cannot again raise my hand against her," and she shuddered as she said the words. "Already have I sent death to her twice; yet she has escaped me.

"But I am not the only enemy she has. Dost thou remember the wrath of Iron Beard against the Christ Maiden? Think how the Temple Godi must hate now, when his daughter has been taken from him. Think how he will hate when I carry this maiden back to him and say, 'She killed thy Sigrid!'"

With a hoarse cry, Harald fought and strained at his bonds. He was almost losing his reason under the exquisitely cruel torture Astrid's words caused him. Panting with the vain struggle, he said with set teeth :

" Wouldst thou lay thy blood deed upon yonder innocent one ? Wouldst thou tell this black lie ? "

" I would even do that," answered Astrid. " If it had not been for her I would not have lifted the hand that pierced the heart of one I — but that is gone. Yea, I shall go back to the Thrandheim and give over Persea to the judgment of the Temple Godi. Thou knowest the laws. Tell me, what death shall she die ? "

" Nay, nay ! It cannot be ! Christ would not permit it. He would not sit on his throne and see this terrible thing. Taunt me no more with thy evil words. Christ is stronger than thou. Thou shalt not, shalt not ! "

" But I tell thee I will. So have I planned. So will I execute. So will I be revenged. Thou shalt be left here to rot, a thousand leagues from her. She, for whom thou didst spurn my love, shall lose life and honour. I can say what I will. Who will be there to dispute my word ? I shall say that which will make the woman thou lovest go out as black to men's eyes as thy scorn has made me. Thinkst thou not that I know how evil I am ? Knowest thou not that I blame thee alone for all that I am ? So hast thou built my life, and if thy building seem not good, — if perchance it has become the dwelling place of fiends incarnate, — then blame not the building, but the hands which shaped and peopled it ! "

Now did Harald know the manner of woman Astrid was. The vastness of her evil purpose, the fierceness of her hatred, the strength of her will, all were bared now. He gave up every hope. He watched Persea's white face as one watches a vanishing spirit. Already she was dead to him. He forgot Astrid, forgot the world. He saw each curve of her features, the exhausted droop of her long lashes, the delicate nostrils, pinched and narrow with mental anguish, the lips he had kissed so passionately, the perfect outlines of her beautiful form ; but he saw as a man sees the face of the dead. All was over now. He would stay here to die ; she would go yonder to meet the same cruel fate. He had only one wish, one thought. He wanted to see her eyes once more. Then let them take her away to her death. The sooner the parting here, the sooner the meeting there. Christ would unite them.

Astrid, watching the man's face intently, saw the mortal anguish leave it just when she thought she had given him the most cruel blow. She saw him turn to Persea; she saw the infinite love and tenderness in his face; she heard him speak his loved one's name softly, gently, as though regretful at awakening her from some pleasant dream:

"Persea."

The girl moaned. Her return to consciousness seemed to give intense pain; but the long lashes lifted from the white cheek and her dark eyes gazed into his. She shivered and murmured:

"What is it, Harald? Why dost thou not come to me? What is the horror that is in my brain?"

And Harald answered in a low, quiet voice as one would soothe a frightened child:

"I cannot come to thee. See, I am bound hand and foot. Thou art going from my sight, and we meet no more until our spirits rush together beyond the grave. Earthly happiness was not for us, my Angel of the Dawn. But let peace enter thy soul. Pray that the time may be short, the journey swift; for the meeting is sure. There is peace and perfect faith in our Christ, my Persea. Through him we shall join our souls beyond the grave. Grieve not, tremble not; but endure to the end. We shall conquer, we shall be happy in ——"

"It is enough!" cried Astrid hoarsely. "Carry her out!"

The men seized Persea roughly. She shrank from their touch; but as they lifted her and bore her past Harald her eyes gave him the look his soul longed for, — love and perfect faith. Her lips sent him swiftly her last message:

"'T is the will of Christ. Beyond the Eternal Gates watch and wait. I shall come!"

CHAPTER XXXVIII

THE LAST LOON CALL

RAPIDLY did Astrid and those with her make for the beach. About the camp the Skroelingjar were yet wild with the smell of blood and the lust of spoil. Even Red Fox, in his eager greed for the weapons he had so coveted, had forgotten for the instant his crazed love for the Gray Bird.

Meanwhile, all unnoticed, she had entered the small boat and was gliding out to the viking ship which, with oar-blades poised in strong hands, was but waiting the arrival of Astrid to push rapidly out upon the darkness of the deep.

Suddenly Red Fox realized that he had not yet reaped all of that night's promised joys. With great bounds he crossed to the smaller hut. He looked in, and saw nothing but men lying upon the floor as if dead. With burning desire in his heart he turned from the hut and peered into the forest. All was still. Perhaps she was in there, in among those dim shadows, waiting for him! He raised his head and gave the cry of the loon.

Astrid trembled as she heard the weird call ring out on the night, laden with the savage passion that was seeking to claim her promise. She cried low to her men:

"Pull! Pull! Strain the oars till they crack! If we reach the ship one moment too late I shall be crushed by yonder savage. I gave my promise. Yea, and if we escape not I will keep it. I promised to stay with him in the woods if he gave me the help he brought to-night; and to let ye return to your land. Yea! So I promised.

"There is the call again! Be quick! Pull hard! Save me! But there is the ship just beyond the bar. Another stretch, one more leaping over the waves!

"The cry again! It is nearing the shore! He has followed our track! Thinkst thou he can pierce the darkness so far? Faster, faster, men of Norge, if ye value the life and honour of your sea queen. Ah! The ship! Leap up quickly, all of ye. Nay, I will not go first, I will be last. Obey! Do ye remember your oaths? There, that is well.

" The cry of the loon! He is on the shore. He has discovered our flight. Quick, a hand. Pull in the boat. Bend down the great oars, up with the sails. We are off! We are off! Listen to the shrieks on the beach and the madness of the loon cry now! The shore we leave is not as quiet as the shore we found. We have won, and we are on the ocean once more, with a stanch vessel under us and the King's command obeyed. Point the prow straight into the east and sail towards the home land.

" We have conquered through storm and peril, through death and destruction, through endless days and dark nights, through long waiting and patient endurance, through dangerous paths and against fearful odds. Who shall say ye are not Norsemen? Who shall say that a woman cannot lead to victory ? "

Far out now in deep water, the men gave vent to their feelings long pent-up. They yelled and shouted and leaped about, mad with joy. Then, kneeling, they kissed the edge of Astrid's tunic and swore that never men nor ship had such a leader.

They had heard, in the boat, that she had risked for their sakes something worse than death. Had their plans failed, had they been defeated or cut off from escape, she would have given her honour to save their lives. Could they do aught but worship her for what she had been, what she was to them ?

CHAPTER XXXIX

THE VOYAGE HOMEWARD

In full possession of a well-fitted vessel, Astrid's men found the summer sea far more pleasant than had been their westward sailing. For many days they lifted sail and oar without hindrance from any contrary wind. All day, all night, a strong western breeze pushed them on. They forgot the cold and terror of the north, and the envy and hate that was theirs in the west.

They had triumphed over their enemies, the enemies of their King and their Viking Queen. The foreign woman who had wrought all the evil was being borne back to a punishment. Now they thought of the boasting of great deeds on feast nights, the telling of marvellous tales, and the receiving of great honour and reward from King Olaf. Small wonder that they laughed and sang and looked eastward with hungry eyes.

But, cruel and hardened to human suffering as they were, they smiled not when they remembered Harald Rognvaldson and his handful of men left to the savage rage which they had escaped. Yet, there was no thought of regret. If the fortunes of war had been unusually severe to Harald, was not his offence great? He was dead now, at any event; for even the Skroelingjar's torture could not last through sixty risings of the sun. It was done. All had travelled the path life had paved for them. So had the spirits decreed, whether Nornir or Christian God.

Astrid was the living spirit of victory. Her jealous hate satisfied, she was bright and joyous, and laughed back at sunny sky and fair winds with a face that was as guileless as a child's. She delighted her men with great praises of their courage and prowess. She helped their imagination to picture the triumphant home-coming; for by this time, surely, King Olaf had returned to the Thrandheim with a victorious army.

As she spoke in this manner, truly she was as a beautiful flower whose exquisite form and delicate colouring filled the soul of mortal with delight; but whose touch was torture, whose perfume was death.

So thought Persea, as after days of tossing upon her couch, burning with fever, moaning with pain, crying out the torture of mind and heart in unconscious ravings, she came back to reality and found her bitterest enemy watching over her, giving her all the care one woman could give another.

Such indeed had Astrid given; but with a fine sense of cruelty that wished to save her victim for the fullness of revenge. She had leaned over Persea's pillow and listened to her cries for her lover with cold, immovable features. Whose fault was it that he had been left behind? Why had not this woman been content with the love of one great man, and left Harald Rognvaldson for Astrid the Peerless, who had waited so long for her heart's mate? No right had any woman to the love of the man whom Astrid loved. Yet this one had not yielded the right, and now she should suffer. Let her moan and rave in her sickness!

Had not Astrid spent wide-eyed nights of worse torture, conscious of every pang, every heart-throb? Had not Astrid lost lover and friend? Ah, that friend! How Sigrid had smiled when she died! But the memory of that blow; of the knife sinking into soft flesh! If it had not been for her, lying here, the hand would never have been lifted. Should Astrid forget? No. Coax back the wandering mind and fight away the sickness, so that she should pay pang for pang and life for life!

And Christ permitted that it should be so. Slowly, but surely Persea was drawn away from the edge of the spirit land.

On the day when her eyes had first opened to consciousness, she had turned her head weakly and looked about her with puzzled expression. Where was she? What had happened? She soon realized that she was in the tiny cabin of the viking ship. But why was she thus alone?

The curtain before her couch was lifted and Astrid stood by her. Back to Persea's mind rushed the full knowledge of the past. Her eyes closed in weakness and pain, and her white lips moved with the prayer, "Christ above, send me strength to accept thy will."

From that time on, Astrid stayed not long at the bedside of

her captive. She brought food and such comfort as she could; but no words passed between them. With greater strength came no flashing joy of life into Persea's eyes. But peace was there and a wistful yearning. Her soul was looking beyond this world into the veiled hereafter, seeing there the goal of happiness and satisfied soul-longings.

If the quietness, the patience, the calm endurance of the Christ Maiden awoke any interest in Astrid's mind, she veiled it well. Sometimes Persea caught a deep, piercing glance that wished to probe into her wounds, to see their depth, to know their pain; but her dark eyes met the unfeeling inquiry without shrinking. Where Astrid desired to find bitterness and woe she only saw that unfathomable depth of strength and peace which defied all her hatred to disturb. The calmer, the more fearlessly Persea met her gaze, the greater became Astrid's desire to crush that power which had so towered above her will, first in the man, now in the woman.

One bright day when, by Astrid's command, Persea had been carried upon the forward deck to breathe the fresh, balmy air, she looked up into the face of the Norsewoman and asked quietly:

"Why dost thou show this kindness, when hitherto thou hast not hesitated to crush all of life that was dear to me? Wherefore didst thou not leave me to die with him I loved? Wherefore art thou bearing me back to thy Norseland?"

A spasm of hate crossed Astrid's face; her throat was choked with its sudden up-springing. When she spoke, her voice was strained and cold.

"Harold Rognvaldson asked me that question while thou wert unconscious on the floor of the hut in Christ's Land. I had tried to move him, to make him love me, or fear me,— and I failed. Then I struck at thee, and I saw him tremble and shiver with fear. So I told him I would carry thee back to Norge; first as a captive to be returned to the King; next and sweetest to me, as the one who had buried a knife in the heart of Sigrid. Thou shalt be delivered to the mercy of the Temple Priest and the law of the land.

"I have not changed my purpose. I have coaxed thee back to life that I might have full vengeance. How I hate thee! Thou didst keep love from me, and didst make me slay one against whom I would not have raised my hand. Thou shalt pay with thy life. Upon thee shall I put the evil of treachery and broken faith, yea, and the shedding of blood. Those about me hate thee as I hate thee. They think it well that thou shouldst suffer the law. Is thy question answered ? " As Astrid closed with a sneer upon her lips, Persea grew white, and trembled in her weakness. The effect of her words was as wine to Astrid. At last she had made these strange ones tremble before her will. So she spoke again :

" I am rejoicing that the end of the journey is near. Have I not done the deed I promised ? Have I not conquered ? Those who brought me shame have tasted the same cup. Those who dared to stand in my way are returning to death. Why should not my heart rejoice, if I have seen my desire upon all who oppose the happiness of Olaf and Astrid ? We are of a breed which brooks no interference. As we will, we do. Let those who laugh count the cost of laughter."

Christ's strength had come to Persea meanwhile. Like Harald, she recognized no hope of mercy from this woman's hatred. There was left nothing but waiting and enduring. If Christ willed this ending to her life, she would die as he would have her die, trusting his love to the end. Calmly she replied now to Astrid's last words :

" I am in thy hands. Thou canst do unto my body as thou wilt ; but blame us not for thy sorrow and loss of love ; neither say that we laughed at thee. We did but love, long ere our eyes rested on thee. Why hast thou pursued us with thy hatred ? Hast thou no thought for another's heart ? Is it my fault that Harald Rognvaldson stormed the village on the shores of the inland sea and took me captive ? Is it my fault that he reached out for my heart ? Is it my fault that I could not say him nay ? Why didst thou not put aside thy love that was so unwisely given ? Had I not the same right to life and love as thou hadst ? Is there no thought in thy soul that thou hast done cruel wrong ; that thou hast, with no gain to thyself, given treachery for truth, death for life ?

" When thy vengeance is completed, wilt thou be made happier thereby ? Think of all thy life to come, when thou shalt have the memory of thy deeds crouched like evil beasts at the door of thy heart. There is no anger in my heart towards thee ; only a sorrow that thy soul is so black. Thou canst not destroy our happiness ; Christ gives us that. But is there no inner voice that tells thee thou art destroying thine own soul? Does not something within tell thee that God shall call thee to account? Does not something plead with thee to show mercy to others, lest there come a fatal moment when from thee shall be taken all hope, all mercy ——"

Astrid stopped her with an imperative gesture. She held her head proudly erect, and in her countenance was unconquerable will, as she replied:

"Prate not to me of gods. I was not created to bow to unseen spirits. If there are gods, Christ must be the true God, for in his name have I seen deeds which the human could not do. I have done those things which men would say are worthy of death, and of unknown torture beyond. Yea, I have tried to lure the unloving one to the shores of sin; I have stirred the poison cup, and sunk deep the knife; I have tracked, and betrayed, and deserted. But I have not finished. I shall give thee over to dishonour and death, with a tale that is false in every word.

"Thou askest if no inner voice has told me I am evil? Yea, many times did it speak. One night long since, in a cave on the Fjord, it tore through my soul with its note of warning, and went out into the darkness, leaving only the wound of its going, which will never heal.

"I loved. To me love meant all that life had to give, all that the spirit world could promise. Without love I am dead forever, body and soul. I care only that those who caused me to suffer may suffer also. I have endured already the torment of a thousand hells, and I fear nothing. I know there will come a day when I shall pay a full price for the sweetness of my vengeance. Let it come! Astrid the Peerless shall know how to meet it! From somewhere out of the sky a bolt shall fall on me. I shall sink down through bottomless space until I reach that hell reserved for me; but still I feel no regret for deeds done, no desire to pause ere my vengeance is completed. Is it enough? Then speak no more to me of Christ and mercy! I obey not the one, and I ask not for the other!"

*   *   *   *   *   *

The summer days shortened. The waves began to leap more roughly; yet still the horizon lay straight and sharp against the eastern sky. The ship's crew grew anxious.

They did not know that they had been caught in the great
sweep of the ocean's strength, and were being carried to the
south of their home land over the curve of the world.

They had now sailed eastward more days than Harald
Rognvaldson had sailed westward, and the sailing was no
longer pleasant. Storm after storm broke over their heads.
The ship was tossed about by day and night. When at last
the sky cleared and the stars shone out, they saw new and
strange constellations above their heads. Yet still no land.
Then more storms, more darkness, more terror of sailing an
unknown sea. But when the storms swept by, lo, a harbour
just beyond !

They went ashore to find they were far south of Norge in
the land of the Franks. They sailed up a river and visited
one of the towns. Here they rested and prepared for their
further battle with winds and waves. They heard rumours that
Olaf Tryggvveson had been accepted as King throughout all
Norge. This faint echo from the home land made new life
course through their veins.

Just another stretch of water to conquer, another beating
against the storms brewed in their own wild sea, another harbour to make, — then home, to rest and feast, and to hear
their names upon all men's lips.

They pushed boldly out upon the breast of the waters and
sailed northward. At the beginning of spring, nearly a year
from the time they had left Christ's Land, they cast anchor in
the Thrandheim Fjord, and heard men shouting to them from
the shore.

Persea, though knowing well that her hour of trial was at
hand, felt no fear, no shrinking. Since they had entered the
Fjord she had almost lived in the spirit land. Never before
had she so surely heard the *Voices* as she heard them now.
Her soul was lifted above mortal things, and saw bright,
glorious forms beckoning it to follow them upward along a
path of light leading straight to Heaven's Gates. She was
conscious that all her sorrow, all her joy, all her remarkable
changing of life and home, all her meetings with lover and foe
had only been a preparation for this supreme moment of test.
For this she had been created. Her spirit, in its Christ
strength, leaped far above the weakness of the flesh and prayed
only that God might be glorified ; that she might so meet this

hour that men should know beyond all doubt that the power of the White Christ was the power of a God.

In faith and peace she would go to meet her life's climax; her hand in Christ's, her footsteps following his, — even though they led down to the dark Garden of Gethsemane.

CHAPTER XL

THE POWER OF DREAMS

WHILE the pulse of the Thrandheim was beating with doubt and uncertainty towards the old gods; while the thrilling thoughts of the White Christ and the Christ Maiden were pushing their way up through the darkness of ignorance, — all through those long days the Temple Godi lay upon the rude couch in the witch's cavern, and crept slowly back to life and strength. Heid ministered to his wants with skill and wisdom, brewing strong drinks from her herbs, which made the wounded flesh heal and the fever-filled brain grow cool and quiet.

As strength returned, the Temple Priest was given to spells of deep thought, during which Heid's eyes watched him under her thick brows; but her lips spoke no words. Sometimes his forehead was drawn in anger; sometimes he bowed his head upon his hands and groaned aloud; sometimes he looked towards the outer world with wistful yearning. But it was not until many days had passed that he gave voice to those inner feelings. Then, one night, he spoke to the Wise Woman:

" Thou hast dealt kindly with me, good Mother. When I think of my empty nest on yonder mountainside, I fain would hide with thee among the rocks until Odin calls me. Great disaster has come upon the Thrandheim and upon me. My mind is as the restless wind, hurrying hither and thither over the world, but having no destination, knowing no rule of life. The loss that has come to me came because I listened not to thy words of warning. I have suffered the price of that instant's doubt of thy wisdom. I must carry that pain till I cross the Bridge of Asar. This I know and understand; but my mind is troubled with other thoughts.

" Thou tellest me that the men of the Thrandheim are in a stupour since the night of the great fight. Their temple is gone; and though the King is no longer here to burden them with strange gods or rule them with strange rules, yet they

have not met at the Thing Plain nor chosen them a leader.
Neither have they kept the sacrifices. Wherefore this inaction ?   Have the men grown cold ?   Have they lost spirit and
love of their native fjords and fjelds ?

" Something tells me that my people need me sorely ; but
there is that within which lays cold and dead upon my heart, —
an unknown fear.   It is this that holds me with thee when
my manhood tells me I should show myself to the people.
Help me, Mother, with thy great wisdom.   Tell me what and
why I fear.   When I know this hidden thing, I shall be
strong again."

Heid lifted her face from her knees, where she squatted before the fire, and answered slowly :

" Thou fearest that which thou couldst not conquer.   The
Christ Maiden left the Thrandheim shore as pure and strong
as the mountains which lift themselves to the sky.   Thy
anger towards her was as the useless raging of the tempest
against those distant peaks.   Knowing that, thou dost fear to
go forth, to gather together the Thrandheim, lest, just as thou
hast bent all men to thy will, she appear again upon our
shores, and by one lifting of her white hand, crush thee and
thy hopes.   This is what thou fearest.   Thou dost believe
that she will return.   Thou dost tremble at the thought ; for
thou knowest that if ye meet again, 't will be to thy peril and
downfall.   Look into thy mind.   Is this not true ?   Has not
Heid shown thee the hidden thing that lies cold against thy
heart ? "

Iron Beard dropped his head upon his breast.

" Yea.   Thy wisdom has shown it clearly.   It is the Christ
Maiden I fear ; yet such a fear of woman makes my man's
blood grow hot with shame.   Why should I let her sap my
strength and purpose of life ?   Why should I let her make
me weak for Odin, and hopeless for the cause of the old
gods ?   Tell me, must I ever live thus ?   Is the sickly fear
of a woman to chain my life to a narrow path, to forbid the
doing of great deeds, to cripple the hand that would battle for
Odin and Thor and Frey ?   If thou dost love me, Mother,
break these invisible chains that bind me.   Call thy spirits
from the heights and depths, and brew me new strength of
heart, new purpose, new courage ! "

His head was erect now.   His hand came down on the

oaken chest by the couch with the strength of old, making the cavern sound hollow with the tremour of the blow.

Heid seemed not to have heard. She did not even turn towards him; but the light that shone from the fire into her little eyes only made greater a brightness that was already acute, penetrating, and burning with strong thoughts. Suddenly she rose from her crouching position by the fireside and turned towards the Temple Godi. Her bent figure leaned, trembling, upon her staff; but the deep, sharp lines of wisdom and age in her face grew deeper and sharper in the red glow. She fixed her piercing gaze upon him and said:

" So thou dost wish that the invisible chains be broken? Thou dost ask Heid to call forth those who obey her, and have them fill thee with new courage? It shall be unto thee even as thou dost wish, great soul of Norge. Listen! Something has happened to break the spell of the Christ Maiden. Something has happened to give our enemy into our hands.

" Heid has had unwonted visions in the long watches of the night when she sat by thy side. The messengers of Odin have flown thick about the witch's cave. They have screamed in triumph and soared aloft with swift, sure wings. Dost thou remember the night when I sang the spirits' song before the fire? Dost thou remember how I sang that thou wouldst break the white form of the Christ Maiden on the rock of sacrifice? Thou didst fail because thou didst not heed my warning, but reached out thy hand too soon to grasp thy prize.

" I told thee we could not harm her till she had sinned. Now the spirits bring me word that she has fallen, fallen, fallen! I know not how nor when; but somewhere, it may be leagues upon leagues away, a fierce conflict has been raging.

" Thou dost wish to break the fetters of fear which bind thy soul. Then go forth, spirit of the Temple Godi! Go forth into the greatness of the invisible world and follow thy enemy over sea and land. See and know and believe that she has sinned; for with her sinning shall come the glory of Odin. Go forth! Leave thy body! Search and find, and tell what thou findest!"

Her small, piercing eyes looked straight into Iron Beard's with fierce, uncanny burning; her voice, strong and ringing with command, vibrated through him like a trumpet-call to battle. His spirit leaped to obey. She crept slowly towards him, never for one instant taking away the piercing fire of her gaze. She moved her hands before his face. A stony stare came upon it; he grew rigid. Again she commanded:

"Spirit of Odin's priest, go forth!"

He fell stiffly back upon the couch, with wide open eyes in which there was no mortal consciousness.

Quickly Heid hobbled to his side and leaned close to his lips, trembling like an aspen leaf as she asked:

"What seest thou, spirit that roamest over the earth?"

In measured, expressionless tones, Iron Beard began to speak.

"Something afar beckons me over the sea; but the sea is so wide, so wide, so deep, so strange! Never viking sailed this way before. Never ship dared cut these great, green waves. Still I float on, on, on. I see strange lands, strange people, savages killing and burning. There is a hut where Norsemen lie as dead. There is a small form on a fur-covered couch. It has long, golden hair and round, white arms twined with silver bracelets. There is a red stain over the heart. The red drips down. The form is white and still. I know it! Sigrid! Sigrid! Light of my old age! Done to death! Thy body a gift to the burning! Where are the rest? Where wanders she, the hated one?

"Ah! The sea beckons me again. A single viking ship fares eastward. A woman guides it; a tall, fair woman with the King's likeness in her face. It is Astrid the Peerless! Beside her stands the one for whom my spirit has searched all earth and sky. She trembles! The King's sister points towards her! The sky grows black. The sea rises. I see no more. Voices call to me! I am coming, coming, coming!"

His voice, strong at first, died away into unintelligible whispers. Heid smoothed his brow and laid her hands over his staring eyes, all the time talking gently, soothingly to him:

"There. It is enough. Return to thy abode, spirit that wanders over the earth. Return with great courage, great purpose, great knowledge. That is well. Sleep now. Rest from thy going forth. Rest, and dream not."

Iron Beard's features softened; his eyes slowly closed; his limbs relaxed; he sank into a deep slumber, with breathing as calm and regular as an infant's. Heid watched beside him, her mind busy with thoughts of the words he had spoken. " 'T is a strange decree of the Nornir that the King's sister should stand beside the Christ Maiden. Astrid bears the curse of Heid over her heart; and by that curse she can do naught but evil. Why then fares she towards the shores of Norge with the fallen one ? The future is not clear to Heid. There is some mad mixing of the spells she has cast. Her wisdom cannot pierce the cloud that hangs so thickly over the fate of the gods of Norge. Once more shall Heid brew the witch's broth and sing seid. Mayhap the vision of the Temple Godi will be made plain to her eyes."

She hobbled to the fire, hung over it the blackened kettle; and with many uncanny words and signs, she put therein sundry packages which she took from the old chest. When the steam started to rise, she began the witch's dance about the fire, evermore keeping time to her grotesque movements with a weird, wild song, unintelligible to any human ear.

But no great ecstasy came upon her as aforetime. In vain she said her strongest spells. They brought her no surety of comfort. Finally, when the fire had burned out and the broth ceased to bubble, she sank to the earth with pitiful wailing :

" The spirits do but play with me. They mock me with gladness, yet hold darkness over that which is life and breath to me. They whisper of the sin of the Christ Maiden, yet they give me no surety of her fate. They promise me that Astrid lives under the curse, that she has done but evil; yet why did the Temple Priest see the Christ Maiden in her power ? Thicker hang the clouds over Heid's mind. Troubled is her heart. May the gods of Gamle Norge forsake not the Thrandheim ! "

All through the long night she watched by Iron Beard's side; watched and wailed out into the darkness the burden of her heart in weird, minor chants that made even the gaunt wolf outside the cave slink away in shivering fear.

When morning broke, she rose and touched the priest's forehead. He awoke with a start, springing to his feet in bewilderment. He saw the sloping sides of the cavern, the fire sputtering in the centre, and Heid's bent form before him. He passed his hand across his eyes.

"So I am here, with thee in the cave? I thought, I thought —— Mother! I have dreamed strange dreams this night!"

"Yea, know I not those dreams? But tell me what they have done for thee. I promised thee new courage, new strength and surety of success. Dost thou fear aught upon land or sea?"

"Nay, I fear nothing. I do but burn with desire to rend and crush. Mother! I saw the Light of my Old Age lying white and still with a dark wound over her heart. I knew the Christ Maiden as the one who had done the deed! Let her come back to Norge. Let all the winds push her towards my outstretched hand. Let every wave swing her nearer, nearer, till they drop her at my feet. We shall crush her, and with her crush the god who would put out Valhalla's light in the sky. I go forth unto my people. I send out the Thing-bod. The men of the Thrandheim shall gather in their might and live as aforetime, — for fighting, for feasting, and for the gods of Gamle Norge!"

His huge frame towered aloft in its old strength; his face was lit with the old fanatical fire; his mind held once more the old, grand thoughts, — to keep alive the worship of the gods, to keep bright that far-off light in the sky.

He went forth. The Thing-bod, with the mark of Odin's priest, flew swiftly from boer to boer. Men cried out in greatness of astonishment when they saw it, — a summons from the dead. But good news travels fast; and hot upon the tracks of the Thing-bod came the surety of the Temple Godi's presence. "He lives! He was but wounded; and the Wise Woman has kept and healed him."

All Thrandheim leaped to horse and rode furiously to the Thing Plain. Now might law and order arise out of the chaos of the past year!

Yet, whilst riding, there were not a few who wondered whether they could follow their old time priest in all things. They knew he would call upon them to rebuild the temple, to take up once more the worship of the gods. Could they do it? Could they lift again that black "Thing" which still lay where it had fallen, and give it offerings as aforetime? Or could they carve out a new god and believe that it was more to them than the dead, unfeeling wood?

They were glad that they had once more a leader who was tried and true; but they went not to the Thing Plain with hearts burning for Odin. They thought their hearts were dead. They were bitter towards their gods, and they faced Iron Beard with that bitterness written openly upon their faces.

They needed no urging to range themselves under his leadership, to plan against attack, to consult for the future. Rumours had already reached them of the coming of King Olaf with a large army from the south. They must know how they should meet him.

Long the discussion lasted. Some spoke for war till death, rather than bow to this Olaf who had so tricked them in the past; some counselled outward obedience; but the greater weight of argument came from the careful, cautious minds which spoke for parley and consultation with the King, until they could know what would overtake them if they fought, or what would come to them if they yielded to his rule.

Through all the discussion of the Thing, no man mentioned the name of any god. They ignored the great issues of the past which had dealt so largely with this one theme. Was it by tacit consent? Or was it with a subtle fear that a thought so loosened might grow into a mighty avalanche, that should make desolate their homes and scatter them broadcast upon the earth — brothers no longer?

Iron Beard noted with darkening face this studied avoidance of that which was dearest to his heart. Blaming the losses of that fatal night on his own rash mind which rebelled against the Wise Woman's warning, he felt none of the unrest that pervaded the Thrandheim. Moreover he feared the White Christ no longer. Had not Heid promised him the Christ Maiden for a sacrifice to Odin? Had he not dreamed that she was coming to him, and coming with fear in her hell-deep eyes? He had feared only her; for the King, whom he had once opposed, could be opposed again. If he had yielded to the Thrandheim threat once, he would yield again. So, strong and masterful in that inner knowledge and confidence, Iron Beard finally turned to the assembled bonder and said sternly :

"Ye talk well of laws and ruling and possible submission; but in all your words why have ye not spoken of what gods

ye shall choose to worship?   When Olaf Tryggvveson landed
first on our shores, what was the message he brought to you?
Ye know full well.   He stood before you on the Thing Plain
and, holding up his dead Christ nailed upon a Cross, he bade
you worship it.   He bade you give up your grand and strong
belief in Odin and Thor and Frey.   He bade you turn from
feasting to listen to the mutterings of his evil priest; and after
death to choose Heaven rather than Valhalla.

"Do ye remember how ye replied to his words that day?
Do ye remember the sudden glittering of sun upon drawn
sword and shining knife?   If Olaf returns with an army
greater than ye can oppose, do ye think that he will not fling
his god again in your teeth?   Speak out your minds on this
matter.   Is your zeal grown cold?   Will ye cringe and bow
and give up your gods, like cowardly nithings who dare not lift
a hand?"

Cutting words were these.   The faces before the Temple
Godi reflected the dark anger in his own.   Erlend Olafson
arose, the same who had changed the harsh ruling of his household to the largeness of the Christ Maiden's teaching.   He
spoke out that haunting doubt which lay heavy upon the heart
of the Thrandheim.

"Use not the word 'Nithing' to thy brethren, O priest of
Odin, lest we forget our relationship to thee.   We have not
deserved those harsh words at thy hand.   Thou shouldst not
thunder cowardice and condemnation at those who have stood
for the old gods against fearful odds.

"Yea!   We threw the King's words in his teeth when he
commanded us to worship his White Christ.   We drew
weapons, and stood ready to battle to death rather than suffer
the gods we loved to be put out of our heart and homes.
We stayed the inrushing wave of Christianity, even as the
Thrandheim had stayed it thrice before.   We made the King
give fair words for his harsh command; and even then we slept
by our weapons, lest treachery should creep upon us unawares.
We were brave and burning with love for Odin and Valhalla.
When the moment of fighting came, didst thou find a man of
the Thrandheim who leaped not to do battle for his gods?
Tell me, priest of Odin, didst thou see cowards or nithings
amongst thy ranks of warriors that night when we rushed with
thee to defend the temple?   Nay!   Blood was afire.   Men

were ready to save their gods or yield life in the effort; yet when the morn broke, what gain had we?

"Of a surety the King had been driven out; but we killed him not. As his ships pushed off we heard his dire threatenings, — the promises of evil to come. We know he can keep his word; therefore our victory without his death was but the dashing aside of a blow, only to have it descend more swiftly and surely upon our heads. We fought for the gods of Gamle Norge; yet where was the image of Thor when the battle was over? There, where it lies still, — black, silent, a thing for vermin to dwell in! Where was the temple we rushed to save? There, in ashes, though not an arm in the Thrandheim drew back from its defense!

"We looked upon these things. We pondered what gain had come with our loyalty to our gods. We found none. An angry King gone forth only to return with greater wrath; a ruined temple; a fallen god, — what rewards were these for lives gone out, for swords wet with blood, for wounds deep and wide?

"Yea, and one more loss have we. Where is Harald Rognvaldson, who ever led to victory? Where is he whom the Nornir blessed, and who was the beloved of all the Thrandheim? He had turned from the ancient gods; not because a King commanded, but because one day a maiden spoke words so beautiful that even the mountains bent to listen. She spoke of the White Christ as none ever spoke before. She melted men's hearts to tenderness, and brought life where Thor would have commanded death.

"We knew not, on that day of days, what her words would come to mean to us; but now the Thrandheim thrills with their memory. Our gods gave us naught but defeat and destruction and loss of brave men. But this Christ Maiden and Harald Rognvaldson moved with charmed lives through such perils as never men met before. Think ye the men of the Thrandheim are such fools as not to see who won the victory that bitter night? What have our gods done for us? Why should we lift sword in defense of that which has already been laid low? We have no settled mind in this matter. We have lost trust in Thor; yet the Christ of King Olaf appeals not to us with its forms and ceremonies and strange worship.

"There is but one memory which is deep and lasting. It

is the memory of the Christ Maiden's story. It is the memory of Harald Rognvaldson's acceptance of Christ, — he, the best and bravest of Norse warriors, whose example no man has ever been ashamed to follow. If Olaf will let us worship the White Christ as that maiden did, we find no hatred in our hearts towards the once hated name; yet how can we know the truth, save faintly, when she has departed?

"We are as ships without rudders, drifting helplessly with the tide. We have no thought of where we shall land; but deep in our hearts we find new desires, new longings. Perchance from some far-off land the Christ Maiden shall hear us crying for light and shall return to tell us more of that God who knows how to protect his own. Then even the Thrandheim may prefer a God who is powerful to save, rather than one who falls upon its face and cannot rise!"

Iron Beard, inwardly raging, searched the faces of the men and saw little disapproval of the bold thoughts which had come from Erlend's lips. Yet the priest was not troubled in his anger; for he knew he held the balance of power. Cunningly would he use his knowledge. Feigning to understand their change of feeling, he answered Erlend's words:

"So, this is the voice of the Thrandheim in the matter of god-worship. It is not for the Temple Godi to command ye to do what is against your will; but know that he shares not your distrust of the ancient gods. He believes that they dwell above in the great courts of Valhalla, that the Valkyrias still ride forth, that Odin still gives luck and victory. Think as ye like about the Christ Maiden and her God. Perhaps some day she will return to your shores. Then ye may decide which god ye shall serve. If she return with Harald Rognvaldson as pure and perfect as when she went forth, mayhap even Iron Beard might listen to her!

"Nevertheless, ye know not what may come to pass. I ask but one thing in this matter. We will say no more about the gods of Norge until something is sent to direct our thoughts more surely; but if ever the Christ Maiden comes to the Thrandheim with a black sin upon her soul, with her purity and perfect life stained by that which strikes horror into your hearts, will ye give up this wandering from the worship of the gods who have guided the footsteps of all Norsemen since the world began? If ye find her weak and evil;

if ye see the strength that she boasted as coming from the White Christ turned to naught; will ye then return to the sacrifices and receive the sacred sprinkling of blood as aforetime?"

And the people, relieved and glad that their brave leader showed so little anger at their doubt and uncertainty, gave willing vow as Iron Beard had asked.

They came, one by one, laid hand upon the stalla ring, and spoke the binding words.

CHAPTER XLI

THE skali of the Temple Godi was adorned as for some festive event. The thralls had borne in logs so heavy that their strength barely sufficed to cast them upon the fire. The long tables were set with bowls and tankards of food and drink. Iron Beard, in his high seat, was attired in the costliest of apparel and loaded with chains and bracelets of his favourite silver. His face reflected the brightness and good cheer about him. Why not?

To-night the spell would be broken. Men's eyes would be opened and the grand gods of the Northland would once more reign in the hearts of the Thrandheim. He had fervently prayed to Odin and Thor to be patient with the people until he could bring them back to the neglected sacrifices and the old-time worship. This was his lone purpose of life. Every other tie that bound him to earth was severed. Let him once more scatter the blood of sacrifice upon the walls of a new temple and then Odin might summon him to Valhalla. His work on earth would be done.

One by one the guests arrived, and after greetings from their host, took seat according to rank. Food and drink were passed. Laughter, jesting and good cheer seemed to fill the hall; but behind the laugh was the look of inquiry; behind the mirth was hidden anxiety; behind the good cheer was the subtle sense of something that would happen ere they finished quaffing the horns lifted to their lips.

They knew not what Iron Beard would say to them. They only knew that, a few days before Harald Rognvaldson's vessel had entered the Fjord and anchored in its old place; and that it came back guided not by the man they loved, but by the King's sister. They had taken her prisoner and, wonder of wonders, had found upon her ship the Christ Maiden. Astrid had refused to say aught unto any one save the Temple Godi. Therefore they had brought her, and those with her, to Iron Beard.

The days had gone by. Then had come a summons to a

feast at the Temple Priest's skali; and they knew there was some great significance in this assembling. Some there were who viewed all happenings with indifference. Why this turmoil and disturbance about gods? Give them peace and a good king! Then could they ride forth on the vikings as beforetime.

Others could ill disguise the anxiety in their faces, especially Erlend, who drank his mead in long, deep draughts, as if to hasten this portion of the evening and arrive at that which was to come. The feasting at last grew wearisome. Conversation lagged as the men looked curiously or anxiously at their host, expecting each moment would disclose the reason for their assembling.

With a sudden striking of his great fist upon the table, Iron Beard stilled the noise in that long hall as the howl of the wolf stills all other sound in the forest. Then he spoke:

" Men of Thrandheim, ye know ye are summoned here for some greater purpose than to sit at feast. Hear now the reason ye meet with me to-night. Ye know who has come to our shores but lately. She thought to find Olaf Tryggvveson ruling here once more. She sailed boldly in, to find herself a captive. She has told me a tale that is not like most tales; and as the telling has determined some questions upon which we have not agreed, I have summoned ye here that from her lips ye might know the truth. Call hither Astrid, sister of Olaf Tryggvveson."

The door of the skali opened and Astrid entered, followed by those of her crew who had lived to return to the Thrandheim. Could Norsemen behold her and not glory in her superb Norse beauty? She was robed in dark blue velvet, embroidered in silver. Her hair hung in two long braids, twined with pearls. Bands of pearls crowned her head, and entwined her bare neck and arms.

Slowly, with downcast eyes, knowing well the part she was playing, toying with men's minds as a child toys with inanimate things, — placing them hither and thither at its pleasure, — she traversed the half length of the hall in feigned humility and fear. When she stood opposite Iron Beard she would have knelt before him; but he leaped to his feet and, taking her hand, led her to the seat of honour beside him.

Astrid's grace, humility, beauty, and queenly appearance

swept all men to her feet in silent adoration. She let fall upon them the latent brilliancy of her glance; and they forgot kings and gods in their human worship of a woman. Knowing well the impression she was making, Astrid sat quietly at ease, throwing over these men the magnetic power of her beauty. Her heart leaped joyously in the surety that every second of time brought her greater place and power in their minds; and place and power were what she wanted tonight.

When the excitement of her appearance had subsided, Iron Beard turned again to the doorkeeper and thundered out:

"Now bring forth the woman who has caused the wrath of the gods to descend upon the Thrandheim."

All men present knew whom he must mean. The ominous wording of his speech confirmed the evil foreboding in the minds of those who wished no harm unto the Christ Maiden. What were they about to hear? Whether anxious or indifferent, whether for Christ or Odin, every mind was deeply curious, every eye was riveted in breathless attention upon that doorway through which she must come. There was a tense silence in the hall. The curtain was lifted and Persea stepped forth.

Not as Astrid had come, came this woman. White and wasted and wan was she. That beauty, which would have appealed to these rough, material men, was all but gone. She was clothed as of old in white; but it was heavy vadmal and hung loosely about her. The brilliancy of Astrid's passing yet thrilled the Norsemen's hearts, and had made their men's blood leap with sense attraction.

But this woman, following so closely in her footsteps with guard on either side, struck all the gross feeling of the senses with a blow that numbed. They saw little womanly beauty to admire, but they missed it not in her; for from her eyes shone the same fire and spirit they had seen on the day of the Autumn Sacrifice. There was no fear in her pale face, though chains hung from her small wrists. Straight before her she looked, the soul-light in her eyes heightened by sorrow and utter dependence upon the Christ love. As one walks across a stage to take part in some unreality so Persea walked before these men. She knew what awaited her; she saw no ending save one. Yet she came not as the conquered, but as the conqueror. Something radiated from her which said, " I am greater, stronger, more powerful than ye."

Astrid's white fingers gripped the oaken arms of her chair. The impression she had made she saw swept away in an instant. But she would bring it back. She would rule all men this night!

As soon as Persea came before Iron Beard, he motioned her to one side, and turning to Astrid he said :

" Sister of Olaf Tryggvveson, the men of the Thrandheim wait to hear thy story. Speak, fearing not, except that thou shouldst not tell all thou knowest."

Thus commanded, Astrid arose, and in rising, changed from the humble woman to the imperious one. She stood with queenly grace, her gorgeous robes trailing about her feet, and began to speak as one who knows no word of greater weight than her own.

" As your prisoner I stand before you, men of Thrandheim, and I care little what ye do with me ; but with my life the lives of others have been sorely tangled. Perchance it would please ye to know somewhat of that which has happened to certain of your people who, commanded by Harald Rognvaldson, took ship and sailed away long nights since, when the shores ran with blood and the night was lit with burning. Harald Rognvaldson took with him on ship two women. One ye called the Christ Maiden ; the other was Sigrid the Pure, daughter of the Temple Priest."

Iron Beard groaned aloud and buried his face in his hands.

" Ye also know that the Christ Maiden was a gift-token to the King. He loved her and would have made her his wife. Ye know that Harald Rognvaldson loved her also, and had challenged the King because of her. When ye drove out Olaf I rode beside him in my golden bird of the sea. I found that his grief was divided between his loss of the Thrandheim and his loss of his love.

" We had seen Harald's vessel slip away from us in the night ; but though we sailed hard and fast we saw it no more. Foreseeing that Harald Rognvaldson had glided away to the north, I conceived the purpose of aiding the King by turning after his enemy, while he continued his journey to the south to bring his army back to conquer the Thrandheim. He bade me go. In the teeth of the winter storms I turned my *Golden*

Eagle and leaped with wide-spread wings after Harald Rogn-valdson's sea-snake."

A murmur of applause thrilled through the room. These men knew only too well what that meant, — that daring the northern sea when winter was coming on. It was not strange that Harald should have the courage to do so. He was a Norseman and would dare anything on land or sea, — but this woman! She was a Norse Sea Queen, in truth.

With brief but burning words, Astrid told of the days and nights they had skirted the creeping ice pack; of the days and nights they had fought the winds, the sea, and the bitter cold; of the final struggle, the approaching death; and then their rescue by him whom they had come to destroy.

All this time the men sat as still as if carved in stone, — hands resting on table or horn, forms leaning towards her, eyes fixed upon her face in breathless interest. Not a sound save her voice and the crackling of the fire broke the intense silence of the room. She continued her story with growing force in voice and mien.

" Yea, he rescued those of us who were left; and my ship sank to the bottom of the sea. But what think ye? Did I not have less hatred in my heart towards him now? I had come out to slay and take captive; but I was the one who was made prisoner. And never jailer more kind; never woman in misery more gently treated. Ye know Harald Rognvaldson. Ye know better than my poor words can tell how honourable would be his treatment of me and mine."

On the faces before her was universal approval of her words. She had well said that they knew Harald better than she. Many had sailed with him; and never leader so fierce in battle, so honourable to foe, so gentle to women. Another thought came also into their minds. Though she was his enemy, she could be just to foe.

With inward exultation, the King's sister saw these men following her leading as the bees would follow honey. She would let them drink deep. It was not likely that her tale would ever be re-told. Let them hear it now as she would have them hear it. Let them believe and do her will, think-ing it to be their own. After that she would rest.

Now, dropping out of her story any hint of the enmity be-tween Harald and herself, she began to tell of the wonderful ending of the voyage. Here she struck the great key-note of Norse love of adventure and discovery; and her words made the blood of the warriors rush through their veins in wild, exciting pulsations. A new land in the west! A land of forests, and streams, and fairness so great! A land so vast that vikings could not find its limit! The glory of it, the pride in the courage of that man who had leaped at one bound from shore to shore of that great, unknown sea, made them start to their feet with shouts of wildest joy. Horns were drained to the honour of Harald Rognvaldson, greater yet than any Norseman who had lived in song or story.

And Astrid smiled, — not at the plaudits for Harald, — but because the more men loved and worshipped him, the more would they hate the one on whom she would put his betrayal and death.

After the men had shouted themselves hoarse and the wonder had somewhat abated, Astrid spoke for the first time of the people they had found dwelling on that distant land. She spoke of their fierceness and prowess, and what care Harald took to be friends with them. Then she paused for a moment, as if to bridge by solemn silence a dark chasm between those last words and the ones she now spoke.

"To make ye see clearly the linking of the events of which I shall now speak, I shall ask some questions. I would that ye answer without restraint. Ere the Christ Maiden came to Norge, was not the name of Harald Rognvaldson spoken in the same breath with the name of Sigrid the Pure? Was it not supposed, throughout the Thrandheim, that some day the son of Jarl Rognvald would take to wife the daughter of the Temple Priest?"

The men glanced at each other and at Astrid. Nods and murmurs of assent answered her question without delay.

"Remembering this, who was it who drifted from that alliance, and why? Ye answer me in your hearts, 'Harald Rognvaldson, because he met the Christ Maiden and let her draw his heart from his Northland love.' On the night that Harald fled from the Thrandheim, can ye find no reason why Sigrid fled with him? Pure as she ever was, when he faced death and danger at her side and besought her to enter ship with him, — feeling even then a great pain in his heart because of her, — she listened and went with him. No sin did Sigrid the

Pure commit; and afterwards she mourned exceedingly that she had let her heart listen to his voice when it spoke at a season of mad alarm.

"Now, with her presence ever before him, Harald drifted from under the spell of the Christ Maiden. His heart went back to its real home; and then, men of Thrandheim, ye should have seen the gentleness and peace of this one ye thought so holy drop from her as the leaves drop from the trees in autumn. Then ye should have beheld her in her real nature, jealous, quarrelsome, brewing discontent, working all manner of evil spells on Sigrid until she grew so timid that she would do nothing but sit and weep.

"This led Harald Rognvaldson to openly prefer Sigrid the Pure, and try to make her happy with his love. He told me that it was his purpose to sail to Iceland in the spring and there drink the marriage cup with her. As for the woman who had tricked and deceived him with her witchery, he would give her over to the King; he desired her no longer."

The chains on Persea's wrists clinked faintly with the tremour that passed over her body; but still her soul gazed fearlessly into the bold, curious faces that were turned towards her. Every one expected her to speak, to deny, to defend herself, to do as any accused one would do; but they listened in vain. Her white lips were silent.

She had spoken before, in Iron Beard's presence. She knew how little any speech of hers would avail. Evil minds had planned well the destruction of her body. Let them do as they would. She cared not; for she lived in the soul-life. As she had hungered to show these strong, untamed hearts the love and tenderness of Christ, so now she hungered to show them the courage, the power, the fortitude which he could give. As she went down to death, she would go as Christ went, following his steps, blessing even her tormentors, silent when evil tongues spoke falsely.

After the brief interval of silence, Astrid, with a significant gesture towards Persea, continued:

"Knowing these plans of Harald, the Christ Maiden grew sullen and morose. Meanwhile the spring came on. The ship was made ready for departure. The peace with the Skroelingjar had been kept unbroken; and the Norsemen slept without fear, having little thought of danger from the forest.

"On the very last night they purposed to spend upon the shore, a horde of strange Skroelingjar stole out of the wilderness and fell upon the camp so suddenly that men all but struck the first blows in their sleep. With my warriors I rushed to Harald Rognvaldson, as the Skroelingjar were running towards his hut. Desiring to save Sigrid, he would have seized her and borne her off to the ship in safety; but yonder Christ Maiden guessed his purpose. Her fury and hatred broke forth. She leaped before him and struck a knife deep into the heart of Sigrid the Pure. Innocent, pure as the white mantle that lies upon the distant mountains, she fell, done to a cruel death by the hand of this woman. See! This has dripped with the life blood of the Temple Godi's daughter!"

She held high above her head the long, slim knife. Swayed by her words as the wind sways the trees of the forest, the men sprang again to their feet. Not in gladness as before; but with faces purple with rage, and hoarse voices that thundered curses against the Christ Maiden. But amid their terrible threatenings Persea stood quietly with clasped hands, and eyes that looked beyond their hate into God's face. Her calmness was only broken when a drinking-horn, thrown by some rude hand, struck her breast. Then she staggered, and would have fallen but for the rough support of one of the guards.

Astrid and Iron Beard had not stayed the Norsemen's wrath till now. The curses and bitter words were music to them both; but Iron Beard wished not violence to cheat him of his vengeance. He sprang in front of Persea and cried out:

"Enough! Would ye take rett? Is the forfeit not mine? Think as ye will; but lift not hand against one whom the gods have claimed!"

In his words was the prophecy of a punishment which would satisfy the most bloodthirsty. The cries ceased. A few there were who were not moved by the general spirit; but who watched the white-robed maiden with pained, questioning eyes, filled with doubt and sorrow and great alarm.

While some hated and some sorrowed, Astrid spoke again:

"Ye have not yet heard all my tale. Together we fought the Skroelingjar; but we were soon pushed to the shore. With us we carried the Christ Maiden; for my heart burned with vengeance. A fearful fight we fought. The forest was alive with wild men, and we were so few! Sad was the ending of that night for the Thrandheim. Leagues away, a hundred of your best warriors are rotting on the shore where Harald Rognvaldson's dead body lies cold across the form of Sigrid the Pure! Upon the head of this Christ Maiden rests his death and the death of his warriors; for it was she, who, in vile hatred, betrayed the camp to the wild men."

Groans, cries, bitter denunciations drowned Astrid's voice, and strong men wept. Harald dead! The Blest of the Nornir, — the one who had sailed farther than Norseman ever sailed and seen a world no Norseman had ever before seen, — he dead! Left as prey to beast far from his own, with no mound to cover his resting-place!

From under her sweeping lashes Astrid shot a glance of hate and triumph at Persea. For the second time, the chains on her wrists clinked with the trembling of her form. But the Norsewoman's heart beat with inhuman joy. "Strength measured with strength," she whispered, "and I have won! May the spirit of Harald Rognvaldson come and see the price Astrid asks for a love rejected!"

The Temple Godi arose. His stalwart form, towering above those about him, was shaking with violent passions, — sorrow, hatred, revenge. He stretched forth his arm, and swinging it slowly to and fro, began to speak with voice that was filled with the authority of his priesthood.

"Yea! Weep and mourn, men of the Thrandheim. Mourn for the brave lives gone out. Mourn for the loss of the Blest of the Nornir. Mourn with me for the death of my only one. O my daughter, the Light of my Old Age!"

His voice trembled, broke, and died away in long-drawn sobs. His anguish was answered from all parts of the room by wails and cries of sympathy. For a moment he stood with head bowed upon his breast. Then he shook off his sorrow and spoke again:

"Mourn as men and Norsemen for all these woes that have come upon us; but mourn most of all because ye have not been faithful, in the dark days, to the memory and worship of your mighty gods. Know ye that I am to blame for some of the evil which has come to the Thrandheim. I disobeyed the counsel of the Wise Woman and tried to do that which the gods had not yet willed to be done. What that was is not your need to know; but therefore has punishment come upon me. I bow before the Mighty Asar in contrition and humility.

"But ye, too, should bow in humility and contrition; for ye also did bring down the anger of the gods upon your heads. Remember ye the Autumn Sacrifice? When the sign came that the gods were not pleased, when that offering was to be made which should turn aside the threatened wrath, what did ye? In a moment of weakness ye listened to a tale of strange gods, and laid not the great sacrifice upon Thor's stone. Therefore did the King escape. Therefore does the house of Thor lie in ruins. Ye, in your blindness, have not seen the cause. Ye have deserted the gods. Ye have not built again the altar to Thor. Ye have whined and said the Mighty Asar had no power. Think upon your evil deeds. Is it strange that the wrath of Odin and Thor and Frey lies heavy upon the Thrandheim? Repent ye, ere the gods visit ye with more evil."

He paused. Across the faces of the men various expressions had been passing. The latent hope that had lingered in a few eyes died out. Following the lead of this masterful mind, which they had always followed in things spiritual, they mentally retraced their steps to that fated Autumn Sacrifice, and fear came upon them. This Iron Beard saw. Quickly he seized the moment to declare what was the greatest desire of his life. While they feared they would be obedient to the Temple Godi's will.

"To-night ye have heard that the one who led ye away from the great sacrifice has reddened her hands in innocent blood. She has lured your best warrior to sorrow and death. She has had little dealings with the truth and love she said were the teachings of the White Christ. She is the slayer of my Sigrid, and by the law of the land I claim rett for the life of my daughter. But who shall pay? This woman is a slave; she has no wealth; she has nothing to pay the debt. Therefore I claim her person as rett; she is mine.

"I summon the Thrandheim to the Spring Sacrifice, sixty nights hence. There will we regain the favour of the gods by offering the Christ Maiden upon the stone. This only will bring back to us the favour of Odin and Thor. Join with me in this sacrifice and I will promise ye all success, all joy. The maiden is evil, a murderess, a betrayer. She merits death.

Thor has been kind to send her back to us for punishment; and shall we reject this opportunity to regain his favour? Will ye dare arouse his greater wrath? Has she not, by the evidence of many tongues, been laden with the guilt of much crime? Remember your oath upon the stalla ring! Give her over to the gods. Join me in the Spring Sacrifice, and cry to Thor for mercy as I cast her upon the rock!"

There was scarcely a score of men in all that multitude who did not raise their voices in the shout with which Persea was given to death:

"A sacrifice! A sacrifice! Honour the Mighty Asar! To the rock with the Christ Maiden! To the rock! To the rock!"

And Astrid laughed aloud.

CHAPTER XLII

"I BELIEVE!"

WHITENESS everywhere; mountain, valley and Fjord stretching as far as eye could see, silent, beautiful, perfect in its unbroken purity. Up from the northern horizon shot rays of red, green, orange, and violet light. They played and crossed each other: they sent long streamers of colour high into the zenith: they drew back, clung together, swayed to and fro, and finally hung across the sky, — a vast, wonderful curtain of gorgeous light, trembling with the breath of the universe, even as a silken drapery stirs at the touch of the summer breeze.

In the midst of this whiteness, and under this marvellous sky, two men stood near the ruins of the King's skali and talked earnestly. Said Thorleif:

"I cannot find the bag, though I have searched as closely as I might. The snow hinders me. When this thick covering is all gone, doubtless I shall discover that for which thou so longest. I know it must be hereabout; for 't was in my bosom when we left the skali. Somewhere between there and the Fjord it lies, hiding its secret from us ——"

"Until it be too late," broke in Erlend; "and meanwhile the Spring Sacrifice comes on apace; meanwhile the Christ Maiden suffers and dies; meanwhile the spark of life and hope that was so sweet to my soul goes out, and leaves me in blacker darkness! Yet she bade me not despair. She has no fear. She goes to her death, not as one who faces the unknown, but as one who knows the way, — as one who steps from darkness into light. Would that thou couldst understand how strangely I was moved when I stood in the presence of this Christ Maiden."

Thorleif drew his cloak about him with a quick, decided movement, and said:

"Tell me all. There is unrest in my heart. Never have I been at ease since the night of Iron Beard's feast. Ready am I to avenge death, to sustain honour, to meet valiant foe;

but the ending of that night has ever seemed to me like the leaping of the wolf pack upon a stray lamb.

"That maiden, pale, weak, alone, enduring the taunts, the terrible accusations, the revilings, the final condemnation without a voice to speak for her, without a word from her own lips, — it savours not of things possible nor earthly. Had she been guilty, she would have shivered or shown fear; or else stormed violently at her accuser. Had she been innocent, she would have used such power as she has to sway men's hearts. Her silence was too amazing to understand.

"I speak not alone for myself. I know that many in the Thrandheim are sorely perplexed in this matter. We have given the girl over to the rock, according to our oath on the stalla ring, and she dies at the Spring Sacrifice. We know we must accept the testimony of many witnesses, — yet her silence! her silence! It moves us strangely; it troubles us sorely. Thou hast said that she has broken that silence to thee. Tell me, I pray thee, the words that she spoke."

Erlend answered solemnly:

"I will tell thee all. But to make thee understand I must say that which will place my life in thy hands. Yet I speak, for Christ's sake. Mayhap, by my words thou shalt believe that he is the true God."

"Am I a beast, that I should deal falsely with the friend of my life?"

"Know, then, my heart so yearned for the safety of this maiden that I had intent to save her, whether innocent or guilty; to carry her away by force or stealth and hide her from Iron Beard's wrath; to take her, in the end, back to her southern home.

"With this thought, I went to Iron Beard and gained his permission to see the Christ Maiden. I found her calm, fearless, seemingly thinking not of the fate reserved for her. At first she would give but scant reply to my questions. To all my inquiries she answered: 'What wouldst thou have me say? I am but one against many. Is there law in any land that would take the word of the one accused against the word of all witnesses who testified? None there are to speak for me, save Christ; and he speaks through me, giving me strength to endure all that shall come to me, for his Name's sake.'

" But I did plead with her for more fullness of knowledge. She listened earnestly, and saw that my soul was sadly moved for her. At last she said: ' I am not guilty. Is there any reason why I should have sent to death the woman and man I best loved ? ' Then did I answer:

" 'Yet has Astrid given the reason. Wast thou not rejected and jealous ? ' And the Christ Maiden's dark eyes filled with unshed tears, as she said to me : ' Jealous of one who would some day be my sister ? Know, Erlend, that Sigrid the Pure had given her heart to my brother. It was he who carried her, wounded and unconscious, upon Harald's ship.' "

" Didst thou believe this ? " said Thorleif excitedly.

" Yea," answered Erlend, " I believed ; and thou wouldst have believed also, couldst thou have been present. I wish that all the Thrandheim could be made to believe. Therefore is the bag of such value. As the Christ Maiden told me, Sigrid said that she had carved a message to her father, telling of her love and change of faith ; and she had given the message to thee, fearing that she would some day be torn from her father's side without word or sign. Seest thou not that this small thing holds power for the Christ Maiden ? If Sigrid loved Tellus, then there was no reason for jealousy, no reason for Harald's change of heart."

Light was breaking into Thorleif's mind. He remembered the mysterious words of Sigrid's speech that day so long ago, and understood them now. The Christ Maiden spoke the truth. He laid his hand on Erlend's arm and said :

" I believe ; but tell me more."

" Then I asked for the real fate of Harald and Sigrid. Long I pled for this knowledge from her lips. Only did I get it by promising to tell it to none save thee. Sigrid was murdered ; but Harald Rognvaldson was left alive in the full strength of his manhood ; left bound hand and foot ; left to the mercy of wild men and burning brands ! "

" Who did this, and wherefore ? Who murdered and bound ? Who left the Blest of the Nornir alone to die ? "

" That the Christ Maiden would not say. There must be some deep plot in which the King's sister is not lightly concerned. To all my entreaties, to all my questions she only answered : ' When Christ was upon earth, evil ones hated him, falsely accused him, and delivered him to torment and death. He endured all, that by his sufferings and death men might be cleansed from their sin. Because he loved men, he endured their mockings. To those who love him he gives his strength, that they may follow this law of love. I will not speak evil of any one. For some reason Christ has brought these dark days upon me. Why should I shrink from treading the path of his footsteps ? He has given me his peace and strength to bear all that may come. In patience I await his will. I leave the punishment of the guilty to him. I say, as he said when hanging upon the Cross, — Father, forgive them, they know not what they do.' "

" Never heard I such a creed," cried Thorleif. " What madness is this that thinks submission to evil tongues and falsehood can be following a God ? "

" Even so did I speak," answered Erlend, " and she replied that perchance, after her death, the people's eyes would be opened. They would discover her innocence. In sorrow at their ruthless destruction, they would be minded of that Christ who had given her strength to die. Moreover, when I told her I would lay plans for her escape, and pledge my sword and honour to preserve her from evil, she did gently decline my offer. With sweetness, and in tears, she did thank me for my faith in her and in Christ; but she would not go hence. Christ had spoken to her soul and told her to stay and endure. She would obey."

" And yet," said Thorleif, " though she may be innocent; though our minds tell us that she is ; though the very stones cry out in her defense; yet must we stand aside and see her hurled upon the rock. We can do nothing."

With a hopeless gesture, he flung his cloak apart and dropped his arms heavily to his side. Erlend lifted his face, and the weird light of the shifting, swaying glory that hung in the north fell upon it, showing a hope there, — pure, perfect, masterful. He touched Thorleif's shoulder.

" Despair not; Christ can save her. This she says; this she believes. When I sorrowed for her she comforted me with that thought. I have prayed, and into my heart has come a wondrous hope and assurance. She has told me that my faith must not waver; that I must pray and believe that she can be rescued even to the moment of her death; and that because of my faith, Christ shall save her for his cause and the Thrandheim. When thus she spoke to me, it was as if some one had touched my eyes. I saw what wonderful things could happen. I knew how peace could yet come upon our fjelds and fjords,— the peace of Christ. Dost thou remember the day I spoke to thee of the new life that was springing up in the Thrandheim? Hear me once more.

"Sometimes, just when the earth has sent forth the first tiny promises of spring, back from the Northland sweeps the wild winter, mad with the surety of defeat,— colder, more biting than ever before. The music of the trickling beck is stilled, and the first buds hang black and limp upon the deadened tips. Yet, can the cutting hail and the bitter wind kill the life that is thrilling through countless fibres far down in earth's warm bosom? Its first budding had been blackened, but other buds are waiting to open. The coming of life is delayed, but who doubts that life will surely come?"

The curtain of light swayed to and fro across the sky, as if unseen angel hands were waving it in triumph. It glowed, shifted, changed, melted into a crown of gold, sprang out behind that gold into myriads of arrows,— red, green, violet, orange,— making a halo of rainbow light, against which the golden crown glowed with intense brilliancy.

Erlend lifted outstretched hands to the magnificent sky, and said with quick-drawn breaths:

"See! A sign! A sign! Over the Thrandheim floats the omen of victory. It has spoken to my soul. Persea shall live, yea, live for Christ and the Thrandheim! I believe! I believe!"

CHAPTER XLIII

THE HAMMER OF THOR

In Sigrid's skemma, Astrid sat by the fire alone. She had thrown a velvet cloak carelessly about her. Its thick folds hung over the arms of the oaken chair and trailed upon the rush-strewn floor. Over those folds her hands moved restlessly; while her head leaned heavily back against the deep carving behind her, as though too weary to bear the burden of the long, yellow hair that fell across each shoulder in heavy braids.

The strength and will had died out of her face for a short period of time. She was thinking of Sigrid now, — Sigrid, in whose dwelling, by a strange twisting of fate, she would sojourn many days; Sigrid, whose life had been so briefly in touch with hers, but whose memory would never leave her, could never be effaced from her brain. Yonder was her distaff and loom. Beyond stood her embroidery frame, with its last unfinished tapestry still stretched across it. The needle was there, — the needle she had touched and moved swiftly to and fro. The whole room was saturated with memories of her. At every turn of the eye Astrid saw something so like her, so suggestive of her presence that she shivered and shrank even from that chair which must have often held her small form.

The fire burned low. Still Astrid sat and listened to the faint echoes that filled the air with Sigrid's name. She tried to stop her ears against their murmuring; she tried to close her eyes to the associations of her surroundings; she strove to forget, to forget; but she ever remembered, and remembered more clearly, more poignantly.

She brought reason and will to fight her feelings. Why should she let this thing, which she had turned to her own use, so trouble her? What could the girl be to her, more than any other woman? And other women had received scant sympathy or attention from Astrid the Peerless. She had had speech with Sigrid but for a fleeting hour. How could that sink into her life and dye it with its deep feeling and love, until her soul writhed under the burden of that blow which had struck so deep ?

She passed her hand rapidly backward and forward over the thick folds of her cloak. Little difference did reason and will make with the tortured pulse of that hand. If she could only rub away that terrible stain !

Sitting there in the shifting light of the log fire, half-conscious of another presence in the room, and of the low sweetness of another voice; thinking of love and hate and revenge; dreaming strange dreams; smiling or shivering by turns — Astrid the Peerless gazed with unseeing eyes into the flames and knew not that a visitor stood in the doorway, — a small, bowed figure wrapped in a great cloak, and leaning heavily upon an oaken staff.

Silently Heid stood, watching the face by the fireside, and studying the varying expressions that she saw; studying them quietly, cautiously, trying to steady the palsied shaking of the staff in her hand, lest it tell of a stranger at the door.

But her scrutiny gave no satisfaction. She took a step forward and brought her staff heavily down upon the floor.

" Has Astrid the Peerless so little welcome for the Wise Woman ? "

Astrid started from her chair with a shiver of fright, as quickly sinking back when she saw who had spoken. She answered coldly :

" Astrid denies not warmth and mead to one who knocks at her door."

Heid hobbled over to the fire and squatted before it in her usual attitude, — her long, skinny hands grasping her knees, and her head bent forward. She gave a shrill, cackling laugh, and said :

" Not so cold were the words of Astrid the Peerless when she visited the Wise Woman in her cave on the mountainside. Hast thou no further use for my wisdom that thou dost give me such scant welcome ? "

With mind filled with thoughts of Sigrid, who would have lived had the white powder done its work, Astrid answered bitterly :

" I went to the Wise Woman for aid. I gave my breast to be branded with her witch's sign; yet that which I bought with burning was of no avail. Why should I seek again that which has once failed me ? "

The old woman scowled angrily.

" And did I say the Christ Maiden would take thy draught ? The powder was strong. Had it passed her lips, thy wish would have come to pass. She touched not thy cup. Hadst thou asked me, I would have told thee that she would not."

Astrid leaned forward and answered the old woman's scowl of wrath with one of equal anger.

" Why, then, didst thou give me the drink ? Why didst thou burn thy mark upon my breast if thy powder was not to do its work ? "

Astrid did not see the triumphant gleam in Heid's eyes. She only heard the sternly spoken answer :

" Yet, if the powder did not thy will, hast thou never crushed thy enemies ? Where is Harald Rognvaldson who scorned thy love ? What fate hangs over the Christ Maiden ? Has not the mark of the Wise Woman led thee on to thy triumph over thy enemies ? Know that it has given thee a charmed life in the midst of many dangers ; it has given thee mind to plan daring deeds, and strength to carry out thy plans ; it has warmed thy hate and chilled thy love. Without those runes on thy breast, thou wouldst never have seen Norge again. Spurn not the Wise Woman's wisdom, nor count her touch as worthless. They have brought thee all fulfillment of thy desires."

Astrid looked at the crouching figure at her feet with new interest. Was this really the truth ? Had she gained her desires through that purple brand upon her breast ? She suddenly became exquisitely conscious of its presence. It burned and glowed with a new-felt warmth.

" Mother, forgive me. I felt the pulse of mighty purpose in my veins. My mind has been thronged with daring thoughts. My hands have been doing daring deeds. I have swept on to triumph over those whom I hated, and have been but dimly conscious of the fire within me which was feeding my hate and fulfilling my desire. I have thought that it was but the outbursting of my great will and the sounding of the depths of my hatred. Mayhap 't is true that thy burning has been the source of my wild daring and strength, yea, and of my

victory. Burn it deeper, Mother. Give me more of thy wisdom, more of thy uncanny strength."

Under her breath Heid muttered, " The curse ! The curse !
Yet I understand not its working. The future is clouded;
the way is not clear." Then aloud she said:

" Thou art daring indeed to ask for that power which is
given only to those who can hear Odin's message. Yet I
will brew thee more if thou wilt pay another price. Swear to
me now by the name of Sigrid that the tale thou hast told
to the Thrandheim is true : that the Christ Maiden did commit those dark deeds. Swear to me; for upon thy swearing
rests the fate of Norge.

" Thou knowest not how much thy tale means to the Wise
Woman. For long months since the Christ Maiden landed
on the shores of Norge, Heid has been waiting and watching
for her sinning. She has brewed the witch's broth and sung
seid and called forth the hidden spirits. But the Christ Maiden
came not within the charmed circle. Now thou dost bring
her to Iron Beard with a tale that has given her to the Well
of Sacrifices. Yet still my spirits will not come at my call to
join in the victory dance.   The green light burns low and the
smoke therefrom clouds my spirit vision. To thee is given
the power to make strong the charm and give clear vision to
the Wise Woman. Swear now. Swear by the heart of Sigrid
the Pure that the Christ Maiden has sinned ! "

At the first mention of Sigrid's name, Astrid had started
from her chair and stood erect before the bent figure of Heid.
Her face grew white, even in the ruddy glow of the fire. Her
eyes stared into the shadows beyond her as though she saw
there something that held her vision with unnatural sights.

" Swear by the heart of Sigrid the Pure ! "

The words rang in her ears with a terror hitherto unknown
to her. By any other token in heaven or earth she could have
sworn the smooth-sounding oath, — but upon the heart of
Sigrid the Pure, — here, in this place so filled with memories
of her ! Swear by that heart she had pierced ! Nay, for the
memory of that moment of pure love, she could not. She had
reached the limit of her crime.

Heid had been watching her with a tremour shaking her
aged form, — a tremour that made her crouch lower as if cow-
ering under a descending blow.

Astrid raised her arms with a gesture that let her heavy velvet cloak fall about her feet. Then, with eyes still staring into the blackness beyond the fire's light, she answered the Wise Woman's question:

" Why hast thou asked me for this oath ? Thou canst not now cheat me of my vengeance; and I know that thou, too, dost desire the death of the Christ Maiden. Therefore I fear not to tell thee the truth; and only the truth can I tell; for by that heart I will not falsely swear. Hear me, Woman of the Cave. Astrid the Peerless made the red stain on the breast of Sigrid. Not in anger towards her. Nay, nay! I loved her; but she sprang to take the knife I had lifted over the Christ Maiden's heart, — and the dark deed was done! Shrink not from me, Mother! Curse me not! The deed itself has cursed me until my veins burst with agony."

Heid had staggered up from her place before the fire, and stood leaning heavily upon her staff, her bent, wizened body still trembling with a tremour which was not all of age or weakness. There was madness in the gaze that fastened itself on Astrid's face. In a voice shrill with terror she spoke:

" Has the Christ Maiden done no wrong ? Besides the death, thou didst tell of a betrayal. Does she not merit some of the evil thou hast spoken against her ? Has she returned to Norge as pure as when she left ? Is there no stain, no spot upon her soul ? Speak, I command thee, speak ! "

And Astrid, raising her head with the old fearless pride, answered :

" The Christ Maiden loved Harald Rognvaldson. In my eyes that was sin enough. I have brought her to dishonour and death. Let the rest be. Astrid is not afraid to tell thee that because she was rejected, she betrayed Harald Rognvaldson and left him defenseless amid wild men and burning logs, — left him to die, since he chose not life with her ! "

Heid grasped her staff with both skinny hands to keep from falling. The spirits had played her false. Odin's birds had not spoken the truth in their messages. Her dreams had been but mocking visions. Her incantations had fooled her in their unfolding of fate. Once more she must hear the terrible truth. She cried out :

" Say it again. Swear by the heart of Sigrid the Pure that yonder Christ Maiden has not done those deeds for which the

Thrandheim has condemned her to the Well of Sacrifices. Swear by the heart of Sigrid the Pure and by this sacred sign!"

She reached under her cloak and held before Astrid a large, golden Hammer of Thor.

With a voice that had lost its feeling and was again but the expression of her will, Astrid gave her reply:

"The Christ Maiden shall die upon the stone because, for her, Harald Rognvaldson rejected the love of Astrid the Peerless. By the heart of Sigrid the Pure, and by yon Hammer of Thor, I swear that she has done no other sin!"

Heid bowed upon her staff in a gesture of despair. Then she lifted burning eyes to Astrid's face and said hoarsely:

"Go on in thy evil ways. 'T is but the working out of Heid's curse. Yea, the curse shall last, and shall eat into thy flesh until my vengeance be satisfied upon Olaf Tryggvveson. By treachery as great as thine shall he die! But there is a power stronger even than my curse. It shall conquer thee as it has conquered me. The Christ Maiden is still pure! Woe unto the Star of Valhalla! To the hills, to the hills, ere the Light goes out!"

She turned and hobbled quickly out of the skemma, muttering wildly to herself, and grasping tightly the Hammer of Thor.

*   *   *   *   *   *

As the day of the Spring Sacrifice approached, Iron Beard sought the cave of the Wise Woman. The fire was black upon the hearth; the fur couch was unpressed by human form; the magic kettle hung empty in its dark corner. The Temple Priest roamed through the windings of the mountain cavern, calling Heid's name, searching out every one of her hiding places; but he found her not. Finally, being of the mind that she had withdrawn herself for a time even from his chance intrusion, he descended to make ready for the great sacrifice.

He did not know that, far away on the mountainside in a lonely, barren spot seen only by the All-seeing Eye, the body of the Wise Woman lay face downward amid the rocks, her stiffened, outstretched hand still grasping tightly a fragment of a broken Hammer of Thor.

CHAPTER XLIV

"LO, THE MORNING COMETH!"

MANY leagues to the southeast of the land of Norge lies a broad, tropical sea. Its tides sweep coral-fringed shores; its surf thunders on beaches where palms wave their graceful branches; its waters glow and sparkle with millions of irridescent tints.

When the world was new, God looked down upon this turquoise sea flashing in the beauty of the eternal summer that hovered over it. He saw in its bosom a great passionate warmth that throbbed and beat with desire to be set free, to kiss other shores.

Away to the northward lay a land of fjelds and fjords and rocks sublime : a land where men could not live without touching the Hand of the Infinite, and breathing the breath of the skies. But on this wondrous land the Ice King had built his palaces. His white domes reared themselves upon the mountains : his cold highways filled the valleys : his wild armies rushed through the grey skies overhead, ever building higher his white domes, ever freezing thicker his icy highways, until the wonderful land lay lifeless under his bitter ruling.

Then God bent over the world, and touching the throbbing warmth of the turquoise sea, he led it out through the waters of the deep. Mingling not with the strange waves that rose beside it; lured not away by strange currents that crossed its path, the warmth of the turquoise sea followed the beckoning of the Infinite across the northern ocean until its pulse beat upon the land of fjelds and fjords and rocks sublime.

The highways of the Ice King trembled, quivered, and swept out to kiss again that kiss so warm and gentle. The palaces of the Ice King crumbled and fell until only the farthest peaks owned his sway. The wonderful Northland was freed from its white bondage, and given to man's habitation and pleasure.

At times the Ice King sweeps down in wrath and builds again his crystal palaces; but they cannot long endure.

Evermore does that warm kiss touch those winding shores, — the kiss that comes from the passionate lips of the far-off, turquoise sea.

In the skies of Norge the constellations circled and changed ; and the sun crept up the southern sky, helping the warmth of the turquoise sea to melt the white palaces and loosen the icebands that bound the streams and rivers.

Almost in a night came the fullness of spring. The lightgreen of the birch showed pale amid the dark needles of the pines; and the crevices of the rocks were hidden behind the unfolding of vine and shrub.

In the Thrandheim, its coming was not as the coming of other springs. Usually, at the first melting ice, the men hastened to clear away their viking ships and prepare for their long voyages southward. Arms were burnished; shields were strengthened; sails and oars were carefully put in order. When all was ready, there would come the summons to the Spring Sacrifice, where many offerings were made to the gods for luck and victory during the summer vikings.

But this spring brought no thought of summer viking to the warriors of the Thrandheim. Arms were burnished; shields were strengthened; ships were made ready for sailing ; but all these preparations were in reply to the rumours, every day growing stronger, that Olaf Tryggvveson was sailing northward with his army.

During the winter Iron Beard had laboured to quiet the unrest, to quell all fear of Olaf Tryggvveson, to put aside the doubts and wonderings. He tried to teach that ill-luck had come because of their unbelief. He pointed forward to the greatness of the Sigrblót that was drawing near, and bade his people get ready for the luck and victory which the gods would surely send when they had been honoured according to custom.

And because they knew not what else to do, men prepared to give such an offering of sacrifices as the temple ground and dom ring had never seen before. Yet were they the preparations of the desperate in heart and purpose. The unrest that Iron Beard had forced into silence still quivered in their hearts. They knew that ere the spring passed into summer the Thrandheim would meet and grapple with its fate. What that conflict would bring forth none could foretell.

But during the weeks that had elapsed between the Christ Maiden's condemnation and the Sigrblót, the Thrandheim had had time to think. The tale Astrid had told was vouched for by all her warriors; but passing strange it was that not one of Harald's valiant men had escaped death on that far-off shore.

Then, the Christ Maiden herself! Whether innocent or guilty, she showed no fear, no dread of her fate. She dwelt quietly a prisoner in Iron Beard's skali; and upon her face was a glory such as made men hush their speech and look with wonderment.

Still, their word had been given and the Sigrblót was at hand. If Christ the White was the True God, he would take care of his own. If Thor still thundered in the heavens, he could not refuse this offering. A battle of the gods was drawing near. The Thrandheim could only wait until power clashed with power.

The day of the Sigrblót crept slowly into existence with a silence so profound that it seemed to have descended from the soundless reaches of space. One by one the stars withdrew their light, as if God had called them back into his crown. The southeastern sky began to glow with pale light as though some hand was holding a dimly burning taper behind the veil of clouds. The light changed to rose-colour, and to red that deepened and glowed over mountain and Fjord.

From the door of his skali Iron Beard saw the dawning of this day, and muttered to himself: " Ere that light fades, the Christ Maiden shall lie with crushed, broken body at the bottom of the Well of Sacrifices. Then shall the Thrandheim give the old-time homage to the gods. Then shall Iron Beard see the Star of Valhalla flash grandly in the northern sky! ' Great All Father, thou who sittest in thy might at Valhalla's table, accept the sacrifice of the Thrandheim this day. Send the Valkyrias to lead us to victory over the King and the White Christ! ' "

He reached out his hands beseechingly towards the northern sky. The red glory of the morning fell over him; but upon his upturned palms the red seemed blood-stains, — deep and dark.

The people had gathered on the ancient temple plain of Lladir, to offer the great Sigrblót.

Above, an opal sky flecked with fleecy clouds. Below, the

opal of the sky reflected in the Fjord, which lay as a bright jewel among frowning cliffs. Above, fair winds laden with faint, undefined sweetness wafted from the far-off southland. Below the murmur of many voices, the hum and stir of many moving forms, the lowing of cattle, the bleating of frightened sheep, — and the final hush of expectancy as Iron Beard stepped in front of the rough-hewn shrine, and made ready knife, bowl and fire for the sacrifice ceremonies. Above, a mystic murmur that seemed to the waiting multitude a weird message from the dim, distant centuries, — a murmur of the mystical past when, out of the gaping void of Ginnungagap, Ymir had sprung from the melting rime; a wild murmur of tumult among the gods; of the eternal struggle between good and the evil; of the despair and darkness of Ragnarök; of the beating of the human soul against the bars of its mortality, as it strove to know the beginnings of time and humanity. Below, the tall, strong sons of the Thrandheim making their desperate stand before Thor's shrine. Their southern brothers had cast down the old altars and broken in twain the sacrificial stones; but here on Norge's fairest Fjord the human was still grappling fiercely with the supreme question.

Bruised and broken with that struggle, yet still reaching out with undaunted will for the truth, they had answered the call of Thor's priest. If above the mystic murmurs of the past there rose a clear, sweet melody that sang of hope and peace, — they heard it not. Even those who appeared before Thor with shattered faith, came with hope so deadened by the thought of the Christ Maiden's fate that they could not hear the faintest echo of that sweet refrain.

When the full rays of the sun struck the rough shrine which the people had erected on the site of the old temple, Iron Beard lifted his knife over the throat of the first victim. Midst dense smoke of burning wood and the feverish, excited murmurs of the multitude, he solemnly invoked the aid of the all-powerful gods to lead them to victory over Olaf Tryggvveson; so that they might live in the freedom of old, still worshipping the gods that had watched over Norge since its beginning. Impassioned was his prayer, weighted with the burden he was carrying on his heart, burning with the fire of a great heart's greatest desire. It stirred and lashed the multitude with its fervency until they groaned and cried aloud.

The impassioned prayer, the groans and cries, lifted themselves on the wings of the morning and drifted out over the Fjord, mingling with the mystical murmurs of the past.

During this prayer there was one man in that worshipping multitude who heard no word; who was stirred by no fanatical zeal. Instead, in a low tone, he spoke to the tall, fairhaired woman by his side:

"Pray harder, Drifa. Surely the dear Christ will not let this awful death come to his maiden!"

"Yea, I am praying," whispered the woman, chokingly. "But the sacrifices have begun and the bag is not yet found. If the search of months has not coaxed it from its hiding place, how then can the last hurried look of a moment? I am praying; but my heart is heavy with fear."

"Nay, nay!" answered Erlend. "I tell thee I had an omen of victory vouchsafed me the day I first opened my heart to the fullness of faith in Christ the White. Not for naught did the golden crown appear in the northern sky. I will not lose faith. Believe with me. Believe and pray; and our faith shall save the Christ Maiden. She herself has said that faith could conquer earth, and sky, and sea, and heathen gods, and cruel sacrifice. Waver not! Let us have faith so wonderful that, if all else fails, Christ himself shall descend to earth to grant our prayers! Believe, believe!"

The woman, catching the depth of his trust, looked up into the opal sky and prayed as only a woman can pray. But Erlend prayed with eyes wandering anxiously over the assembled crowd, searching for Thorleif's stalwart figure. He only would be the one to bring Sigrid's bag to Iron Beard. Surely there would be something in that bag which would tell the Temple Priest that not because of Harald did his daughter depart from him. If they could prove one of Astrid's assertions false, why might not great things happen? It was their last, their only chance. Christ would give it them.

The sacrifices went on. One by one the people led forth their offerings. One by one the fattened cattle fell before the shrine, pierced through the throat by Iron Beard's long knife. The smoke grew thicker; the air was heavy with the scent of blood and burning entrails; and ever and anon, above the thunderous tones of the priest rose the snorting and trampling of cattle crazed with the sickening odours of fire and blood.

The wild, colossal sacrifice excited priest and people until they cowered under the thick column of black smoke that rose over their heads, half-seeing in its fantastic shapes the outline of the Valkyrias, or the wide-spread wings of Hugin and Munin.

The sun rose to its highest point in the southern sky, seemed to pause, and then swung slowly downward. The last animal had fallen under Iron Beard's swift, keen stroke. The last life-blood was trickling slowly into the immense hlaut-bolli, now so brimming with gore that the red crept over its copper rim and filled the hollows of the strange symbols stamped deeply in its sides.

Drifa seized Erlend's arm. He felt her fingers sinking into his flesh as she whispered:

"'T is over! The Christ Maiden's hour is at hand; yet Thorleif appears not. Take me away. I cannot look upon that which is to happen. Take me away, quickly!"

The man's muscles swelled under the woman's grasp as he clenched his fists in answering agony. His lips moved convulsively; but without sound.

The last tremendous moment had come; that moment for which all Thrandheim had been breathlessly waiting; that moment which should witness the triumph of Thor over the White Christ. Every man and woman in that tense, anxious multitude trembled when, at the loud command of Iron Beard, two warriors lifted the skin at the entrance to his tent, and Persea stepped forth.

The quiet life during the long winter had brought back the Christ Maiden's marvellous beauty. She raised her eyes heavenward and her lips moved. The people knew she prayed. Could it be that she was deserving of the doom which awaited her? A wave of tremulous feeling seemed to pass through the crowd. A sound almost like a long-drawn sob arose. She was so beautiful! She looked so pure, so innocent! She had told them such wonderful things!

Then the thick, strong smoke of the sacrifice swept into their faces with the odour of past centuries of worship. They remembered that they were bowing before Thor. To him they were looking for luck and victory; and this maiden represented the power which would crush the old gods. The Thread of Fate was in the hands of the Nornir. Let them spin it out for weal or woe; for no mortal hand might mar that spinning now !

" Bring forward the Christ Maiden ! "

The Temple Priest's voice rang out the command in exultant tones. Was not this the moment of the victory of the gods ?

With calm, steady steps, Persea walked between the two warriors until she stood at Iron Beard's side. Even Astrid's burning stare could not make her tremble or grow pale. " She goes to the death I promised Harald to give her," thought the King's sister; " yet it is I, not she, who trembles and burns ! A moment more, and my vengeance shall be complete. Never did human plan or know such vengeance as is mine. Let come what may, — in this world, O Harald Rognvaldson, I have won ! "

The Temple Priest glanced rapidly over the sea of upturned faces. There was that in some of them which stirred a mighty anger in his heart. They thought not as he thought; they longed not for the sacrifice of the maiden. He would throw their unbelief in their teeth. Yea, they should condemn the second time.

" Hear ye, men of Thrandheim. Knows any man reason why this woman should not pay the price of her sin ? Stands any man before me who would dare snatch from Thor's altar the supreme gift for which the gods send favour ? Holds any man in his hand aught which would speak for this woman, whom many tongues have accused of base deceit and ——"

From the outskirts of the crowd a man's voice broke in upon his words :

" Hold ! Temple Priest of Thrandheim, I come to thee with a message from thy Sigrid. Lift not hand against the Christ Maiden until thou dost read her words ! "

Iron Beard caught his breath, stared from under his bushy brows, and then called out sternly :

" Why this outcry from my people ? Yonder man, is he not Thorleif, my friend ? Open a passage through, that I may know what this portends."

The crowd parted quickly ; and with great bounds Thorleif reached the priest's side. As he did so, Drifa caught Erlend's arm again and whispered :

" Speak when the moment comes. Speak for the Christ

Maiden's life, even though it bring thee death! I, — thy wife who loves thee, — tell thee to do this for Christ's sake. It is the least thou canst do."

Erlend answered calmly:

"Fear not. Within me is the strength that Christ gives. He holds the power in his hands. Pray and believe!"

Thorleif, holding out towards Iron Beard a shrunken, mildewed bag of skin, said:

"Knowest thou, O Temple Godi, this bag?"

Iron Beard took it in his hands. A tremour passed through his gigantic frame. He crushed the tiny thing to his heart, murmuring brokenly:

"'T is Sigrid's! O Light of my Old Age! I gave it her. She did wear it about her neck. How camest thou by it?"

Thorleif told what he knew. His words pierced the heavy, smoke-laden air with a distinctness that reached the ear of the farthermost worshipper on the outskirts of the crowd. He told of his conversation with Sigrid the day she rode to the feast. Iron Beard, startled, trembling, leaned forward, — hanging upon every word that dropped from his lips. Thorleif told how she had given the bag to his keeping; and how it had been lost. But he had found it at last, half-buried beneath the sands of the beach. In justice to the Christ Maiden, Iron Beard should open it and know what was therein; for Sigrid had not taken her departure from him without thought.

"Open therefore the bag, Priest of the Thrandheim, and know why thy Sigrid left thee."

Iron Beard's fingers shook as though palsied. Scarcely could he pull apart the rotten cord which drew it together. 'T was Sigrid's, and back upon him had come all the sorrow of his loss. Suddenly he paused. He turned to Astrid.

"Sister of Olaf Tryggvveson, ere I listen to this voice from the dead, swear to me that Sigrid left Norge because of her love for Harald Rognvaldson. Swear, by the sacred ring!"

Astrid felt the earth slipping from beneath her feet; but she rose and flung back defiant answer.

"What I have spoken I shall not alter. Open the bag. Astrid fears no voice, — even one from the dead!"

The string broke in Iron Beard's trembling grasp — the bag

opened, — but out upon his hand rolled only the rotten fragments of a rune stick. The message Sigrid had carved was
lost forever.

Astrid turned to Thorleif with a taunting laugh.

"So thou didst not believe the words of Astrid? Look
closer. Perchance thou canst read runes that are lost in air,
and tell Astrid the Peerless that she has lied."

Iron Beard crushed the soft wood in his hands and cast it
upon the burning altar, crying out:

"The silence of the message is but Thor's proof that the
Christ Maiden is marked for sacrifice. The Great One
waits! Room towards the sacred rock! To Almighty Thor
I give the soul and body and blood of this maiden!"

He laid rough hands on Persea. The crowd drew back.
Then arose a man's hoarse, despairing cry; and Erlend leaped
in front of Iron Beard.

"Spare her! Spare the Pure One, for she has not sinned!
Persea! Persea! I shall lose Christ if thou diest! Thou
didst say that if we did but believe and pray, Christ would
rescue thee. My prayers he has not heard; but O Persea!
Christ Maiden! pray thou! Christ will surely hear and answer thee, even now! Pray! Pray!"

He fell at her feet and clutched her robe. Persea looked
upon him with the light in her eyes growing into a flame of
faith that almost transfigured her, so great was its spiritual
radiance. She turned to Iron Beard.

"Wilt thou grant me one last moment to pray as this man
has asked?"

Though crazed with passion of sacrifice and hate, the
Temple Priest saw an extra triumph in this request, e'en
though it delayed the great offering. He laughed mockingly.

"Yea! Take time to pray to thy dead Christ. Men of
Thrandheim, the Christ Maiden prays for deliverance from
Thor's rock. Listen! If her God hears her not, then will
ye know that Thor rules all things, — even the White Christ!
Be still, lest her prayers be not heard!"

The people needed no command to be still. In that group
before them, — the gigantic, bronzed priest, blood-stained and
terrible in aspect, and the beautiful woman with dark eyes
turned heavenward, and hands resting tenderly upon the
bowed head of the man kneeling at her feet, — they saw

something that forced a stillness, tense and momentous. Instinctively the people drew closer. Their priest had cast a
bold challenge to the Christ Maiden's God. The decisive moment of conflict had come. Thor and Christ must measure
power with power.

Closer drew the breathless, agitated multitude. The air
became as still as the calm before the breaking of the tempest.
Persea's voice broke that stillness.

" O Christ, God of love, thou who didst die to bring
eternal life to those who believe in thee, reach out thy mighty
hand of power and save me from this death. Save me, not
for my life's sake, but for the sake of this tortured heart before me. He does believe in thee. He has shown wondrous
faith. Save me, that this tiny spark of love and faith which
has been kindled in this wild land be not lost. He has
prayed, believing that thou wouldst hear prayer. Now, even
when death is but a few steps from me, he cries out to thee
through me. Save me, that he may know thy power and
love. Save me, that all here assembled may believe that
thou alone art God. Save me, that thy name may be
mightily exalted above every name in this wonderful land
which knows thee not ! "

Her voice floated out over the heads of the silent multitude
and died away amidst the whispering of the winds and the
sounds of the forest. The kneeling man clutched still tighter
her white robe, and crouched closer to her feet.

The people stirred not. Even Iron Beard was bound to
silence by invisible bands. Some power thrilled the air; some
mighty force seemed to touch and hold people and priest
spellbound. They trembled, they knew not why; but ever
they looked, — yea, looked and listened.

Suddenly, from far down the rocky road there came the
faint beat of a horse's flying hoofs. A wave of tremulous
excitement rippled over those tense, anxious faces. Nearer
and nearer, louder and louder came that furious clatter.
There could be no mistaking it. Some one was riding madly
towards the Thing Plain. The people fastened wildly staring
eyes upon the opening in the woods.

The kneeling man heard; but only leaned closer to the
maiden, whispering, " I believe ! I believe ! "

Persea heard ; but took not her glorified gaze from heaven,

though her breath came quickly through her half-parted lips.

The sound grew clearer. The rider had turned the bend — he had mounted the last, steep slope — he was tearing along the last level stretch — he was in sight!

He waved a banner wildly to and fro, — a banner with a black raven embroidered upon it. But one man in all the Thrandheim could carry that symbol. From a thousand throats rose a hoarse, almost terror-stricken shout:

" Harald Rognvaldson! Harald Rognvaldson! "

The wild skies of Norge never arched over a wilder scene. Some shrieked and leaped in maddened frenzy; some stood with arms outstretched towards their beloved leader, while tears rushed like rain down their bronzed cheeks; some threw themselves on the ground, offering frightened prayers to Christ the White; some stood motionless, gazing heavenward in such ecstasy of joy and thankfulness that earthly sights and sounds were forgotten; some shivered and trembled, and hid their faces in their hands, afraid to look upon the one whom the Christ Maiden's prayer had called from the dead.

Iron Beard gave one choked, desperate cry and sprang towards Persea. He would yet break her on the rock and — but Erlend's hands were at his throat.

When that fierce struggle was over, and priest and warrior had been parted, Harald Rognvaldson had reached their midst and stood with Persea in his arms, — seeing nothing, knowing nothing but that he had come in time to save her; that he held her close to his heart! Only the God of Infinite Love could understand the perfectness of that meeting.

A moment thus; then Harald turned to face Iron Beard's crazed wrath and the hard, white countenance of Astrid the Peerless. He opened stern lips to speak; but Astrid stopped him with her old, proud gesture.

In a voice clear and strong with unconquerable will she addressed him:

" Nay, burden not mine ears with thy long woman's tale of woe! I will bring swift ending to the game we have been playing. A mighty game it has been, O Harald Rognvaldson! A game born amid passion and power; a game that has reached out over measureless expanses of water; and has called a new land from out of the seas to give a footing to its players; a game that has wrestled with all forces of earth and air and sky and sea.

" Now have we played the game to its end. I will be fair. We have matched mind to mind, strength to strength, daring to daring, yea, and God to God, — and thou, Harald Rognvaldson, for the second time, hast won! Enjoy thy triumph in thine own way; but pity not Astrid the Peerless. What she has done, she would do again, — yea, a hundred times over! She will prove to thee that she fears neither man nor God!"

With proud, flashing eyes and erect form, she turned from Harald to the infuriated priest who was glaring at them with bloody fists clenched in fearful passion.

" Temple Priest of the Thrandheim, thou hast been fooled and blinded by a woman's wit. Thy Sigrid did die on the foreign shore; and there also was Harald Rognvaldson betrayed to a death that passed him by. But the blow that pierced thy daughter's heart came not from the Christ Maiden's hand, neither betrayed she any man! Temple Priest of the Thrandheim, I gave Harald Rognvaldson to the wild men! I buried the knife in the heart of thy Sigrid!"

Iron Beard threw up his blood-stained hands and staggered back — then caught himself and bent forward in a half-crouching posture.

" Thou! Thou didst the deed? The Light of my Old Age done to death by thee?"

He crouched lower, breathed deeply; then his huge form quivered as a tiger quivers ere it springs, — and like a tiger he sprang upon Astrid the Peerless. Swiftly through the half-stunned, frightened crowd he bore her. High above his head he swung her, — once, twice, thrice, — and then with all his gigantic strength he hurled her upon the sharp, upturned point of the sacred rock. There was a dull sound of cracking bones, a woman's shriek of agony, — and all that was left of Astrid the Peerless rolled, a crushed and bleeding mass, to the foot of Thor's stone.

The heavy smoke of sacrifice spread over the heavens like a thick, black pall, and hid that shapeless mass from the light of God's sun.

CHAPTER XLV

CHRIST THE WHITE

A HUNDRED war vessels lay rocking on the waves of the Fjord; and on the shores of the River Nid a large army was camping; for Olaf Tryggvveson had returned to the Thrandheim, even as he said.

The King was sitting in his tent of pell. On a low cushion at his feet knelt Ingiborg. She had twined her arms about him and was resting her head upon his shoulder.

"Tell me more, Olaf. It is passing strange that thou shouldst find the Thrandheim so easily won for Christ, when aforetime they were ready to kill thee at the mention of his name."

Olaf leaned his head on his hands and said slowly :

"After I had promised them all forgiveness for the past, and wise ruling that would bring peace and happiness to their disturbed land if they did but give obedience thereto, then I paused for a moment.

"The warriors stirred uneasily. I knew that Iron Beard had not left his skali since the Sigrblót. People say that he has not lifted his face to the sight of men; neither will he speak nor take food. So I hoped to win them to the Christ without much trouble; but when first I spoke to them, I heard low murmurs and saw a few dark faces. Then was I angered at their hardness of heart; for after all that had happened, could it be that they still longed for the bloody sacrifices ? In wrath I spoke the second time. 'Tell me, do any hesitate yet as to whether they will serve Thor or Christ ? Have ye not grovelled enough at the feet of a god made by men's hands ? Have ye not prayed enough to a god who hears not ? Have ye not drunk your fill of bloody sacrifices that avail not ? If perchance any here should yet cling to the old gods, Olaf will not forbid sacrifice; but that sacrifice shall be such as Norge never witnessed before. If blood be what ye want, I shall redden your heathen altars with the richest blood of the Thrandheim. Behold! men who will yet worship Thor, I name for your sacrifice Orm Lyrgia of Medalhouse, Styvkar of Gimsar, Kaare of Gryting, Orin of Lyra, and Haldor of Skirding-stedia. These will Olaf offer upon Thor's rock!'

"At my command, my warriors seized and bound these men. When I looked again into the faces of those before me, I saw my trick had been well played. Men who, in stubbornness of heart, would still refuse the White Christ, were pale and sick with the thought of such blood-letting.

"Then a man rose from their midst. Wan and weak was he and leaning upon a staff for support; yet all grew quiet to listen to his words; for he was Jarl Rognvald, their wise law-man, called back to earth by the joy of seeing his son once more. He said: 'O King Olaf, thou hast come back to the Thrandheim with power and strength to lay waste our boers and scatter our warriors to the winds; yet thou hast offered us no violence. Thou hast dealt with us in gentleness and peace. The hearts of the Thrandheim warriors are not so hard as to be unmoved by thy kindness.

"'Great changes have taken place since the time when we rejected Christ the White, many months ago. Thou knowest that none were so bitter towards the new god as Jarl Rognvald. None believed more truly in Odin, and Thor, and Frey; none more willing to die rather than be false to the old belief. Yet to-day, Jarl Rognvald stands before thee and says he is ready to worship the White Christ as the only God of the universe; for the prayers to that God have saved his son from such perils as only a supreme power could save. Before all men I renounce the ancient gods. I swear to worship only the God who is the True God, — Christ the White!

"'Thus I speak for myself; and I make bold to say that all the Thrandheim will take oath with me. We have seen a power greater than Thor's. We have felt the touch of a God-love that thrills us far more than any of Odin's fierce, wild promises.

"'We ask but one thing of thee. Thou hast with thee a man whom thou sayest is a priest of Christ; but he teaches not as the Christ Maiden has taught. He tells us naught of Christ's truth. His ceremonies have no meaning in our eyes. Send him away. Give us such priests as will lead us in the

paths in which the Christ of Love would have us led.   Grant
us this.   Then, King Olaf, the Thrandheim will accept Christ
the White.' "

" And didst thou give them their wish, my brother ? " asked
Ingiborg, eagerly.

" Yea," answered Olaf.   " 'T was no task to send him
from me ; for even I was weary of his coarseness and cruelty.
He could talk of naught but torture and burning; and Olaf
has learned that kindness has made more converts than ever
the sword could make."

" So now, peace dwells by the Thrandheim Fjord, — and
Olaf Tryggvveson is King over Christian Norge ! "

Brother and sister were silent for a time.   Then Ingiborg
spoke with a sweet gentleness :

" Thou hast conquered thy kingdom.   Now wilt thou not
conquer thy passions ?   Surely thou didst not mean the words
thou didst speak yesterday ?   Surely thou wilt not raise hand
against Harald Rognvaldson for the possession of the Christ
Maiden ? "

Instantly the King's whole manner changed.   His face
grew hard and drawn, and Ingiborg felt him stiffen in her embrace.   But she clung closer to him and said :

" Be not cruel, my brother.   Hast thou forgotten the days
in the Southland when we did talk together of Christ's love ?
Hast thou forgotten thy thoughts of tenderness towards the
Christ Maiden ?   Wilt thou let the old evil passions rule thee
until thou dost crush all happiness from her life ?   O my
brother ! fail not in this critical moment.   Greater it is to rule
the spirit than to strive with swords.   Send word to Harald
Rognvaldson that thou wilt give over all claim to the Christ
Maiden.   Conquer thyself.   Send the message, and receive
the blessing of the White Christ."

But the veins on Olaf's brow only grew more purple ; and
his eyes stared out over Ingiborg's head with the old steely
cruelty in their blue depths.

" Thou art asking of Olaf more than the human can do.
Have I not met the Thrandheim with kindness and forgiveness ?   Have I not followed Christ's teaching, and remembered not against them the fire and sword with which they
drove me out ?   Did I seek any vengeance for Astrid's
death, — cruel and shameful as it was ?   I know she did sin

blackly; yet Kings do not often forgive such deeds against their own.

"I have struggled with my vengeance and my passion, and I have conquered much. But when I saw those two together on the cliff; when I came upon them unawares and beheld her in his arms and saw his lips touching her lips; when I knew that to-morrow night would be their bridal night, — I could endure no longer. He shall never know her as wife! Ere that moment comes I shall claim that form and those lips for my own! Did not Harald Rognvaldson challenge me for that possession? Unclasp thine arms from about my neck! Cease thy woman's cries and tears! Olaf has decided."

He thrust her from him with violence, and strode out of the tent.

CHAPTER XLVI

THE WEDDING FEAST

OVER the Thrandheim, like God's blue heaven, curved the promise of peace. It sang in the rushing, foaming streams that leaped from cliff or mountainside; it stirred in the rustle of the trees and the music of the wind; it burst from the tiny throats of the birds; it blushed in the flowers that clung in the crevices of the rocks; it rocked on the waves of the Fjord; it lay in purity upon the far-off mountain peaks.

Worn out by the storms of the past; exhausted in battling with doubts and fears, weary of quarrels and bloodshed, the men of Thrandheim rested on the swell of the tide and were content to let it float them gently into harbour.

Iron Beard's despair and silence removed the only mind strong and fierce enough to force them back into the storm and darkness of the past; and Olaf Tryggvveson's graciousness was a bright beacon light which beckoned them into the harbour of peace. They turned once more to the joys and cares of daily life; and first and greatest of all festivities came the bridal of Harald Rognvaldson and the Christ Maiden.

All the warriors and fair women of the Thrandheim had gathered in Jarl Rognvald's skali. Rare and costly fabrics hung on the walls: gold and silver vessels filled with mead and food loaded the long tables. Wealth, beauty, life, and love were everywhere.

In the centre of the cross-bench, at the end of the skali, Persea sat between her bridesmaids. White-folded was she, in rarest of silks shot with threads of gold and embroidered in seed pearls. Priceless jewels hung around her neck and clasped her white arms. Her bridal-fald was fastened to her dark hair by a diamond star, — the memory of that other feast night so long ago.

Harald was in his high seat clad in tunic of cloth of gold, — perfect in manhood, kingly in appearance, radiant with joy, burning with love. Scarcely could he take his mist-filled eyes from that star-crowned one at the end of the hall. To him had come at last the perfect day of existence. Every breath was heaven-sent: every moment brought him greater joy and ecstasy.

As men ate and drank, laughed and sang together, one called out:

"When shall we hear the singing of thy Saga, Blest of the Nornir? We wait with expectant hearts to know how thou didst come to the happiness that is thine to-night. Deny us no longer. Command Egil the Skald to stand forth and stir our viking blood with his songs of thee."

Approving shouts arose from all parts of the hall, growing more and more imperative until Harald waved his hand in assent. Out of the crowd of feasters stepped Egil, the silver-voiced. His tunic of purple silk did not cover his arms, about which wide, golden bracelets were bound; and his long, fair hair fell almost to the girdle at his waist.

He placed his harp upon the floor in front of him and touched its strings. Through the hall floated an ethereal melody, that made boisterous laughter and speech gradually cease. It was as though some one had laid a tender hand upon their merriment and hushed it to silence. Amid that silence, deep and throbbing with untold happiness, the Skald lifted his voice and sang his Saga of Harald Rognvaldson, Blest of the Nornir. He sang of his wonderful birth; of his strength, beauty and prowess; of his great vikings; of his victories on land and sea.

Then, in the sweetest of melodies, low and thrilling and deep, he sang of the love that had leaped into life under the warm skies of the far-off Southland. He extolled the beauty and priceless worth of her who was the beloved one. With words and music that melted men's hearts, he sang the sacredness and unfathomable depth of that pure and perfect love of soul for soul.

The love-song died away in faint, far-reaching notes of sweetness. Egil bowed his head, and paused for an instant. When he again touched the harp, the music had changed, and in mad, tempestuous strains came the recital of Olaf Tryggvveson's entrance into the viking's life. In rapid, heart-stirring tones he sang of the taking of Persea, the Autumn Sacrifice, the feast, the conflict, the flight.

Now his music seemed filled with the creaking of cordage,

the sting of the salt spray, the lash of the waves, and the whistling of the wind.   He was following Harald and his love out over the waters of the deep, — afar into the unknown. Into the music crept a weird whispering of the mysterious Pilot whose hand rested, unseen, upon the steering oar, and guided them to a land no man had ever seen before.

Then minor chords crept into the singing ; and Egil wailed of treachery, deceit and desertion.

Up to this time the guests had listened to a story which was not all new ; but now, with bated breath, they leaned forward. How had Harald Rognvaldson re-crossed that measureless, unknown sea without ship or oar ?   In what marvellous manner had the White Christ preserved his life and brought him into this moment of triumph and happiness ?

In a measure and music like unto the soul-stirring Kalevala of the far north, the Skald sang on :

> " At the coming of that black night,
> Scenting danger in the twilight,
> Off the Arab lad had stolen
> To the wigwams in the forest ;
> To those who in peace had taken
> Of the Norsemen's meat and bounty.
> Told them of his fears of evil,
> Told them of the deep dark secrets
> That the trees had whispered to him.

> " Without sound they listened to him,
> Listened without word or gesture ;
> But when he had ceased his speaking,
> Silently arose each warrior,
> Reached for bow and swiftest arrows,
> And in stealthy lines of shadows
> Crept back through the darkening forest.

> " While the night was red with burning,
> While the blood was flowing thickly,
> While the men lay bound and helpless,
> Bound and helpless and deserted,
> Came from out the depths of forest
> Friendly wild men to their rescue.

> " Fiercely fought the Narragansetts,
> Fiercer yet the Wampanoags ;
> And when, high in heaven above them
> Shone the eastern star of dawning,
> Vanquished were the evil wild men ;
> And the Norsemen, death delivered,
> Stood once more upon the seashore."

As the Skald paused, Harald looked upon his guests and
said :

" But what, think ye, were our thoughts as we stood alone
upon that shore ?   Can ye fathom all the anguish of that black
and bitter moment ?   Behind us, amidst the red embers of our
shelters lay the dead bodies of our comrades.   Before us,
leagues upon leagues of water rolled between us and our
home land.   Gone was our sea serpent, and with it every hope
a viking could have.   Are ye surprised when I say that in bitterness and violence we cursed our fate ? "

As if to answer his question, Egil struck his harp a ringing
chord and sang:

> " Then before them stood their leader,
> Harald, Blest of all the Nornir,
> And he bade them cease their cursing,
> Cease their mad and useless ravings.

> " Why this bitterness and anger ?
> Why this desperate despairing ?
> Do the gods snatch brands from burning
> Without reason, use, or purpose ?
> Has the Christ no aim nor meaning
> In his wondrous care and guidance ?

> " Threatening perils have rolled o'er us
> Like black storm-clouds, tempest laden ;
> But like storm-clouds that, dissolving,
> Break in gentle, soothing showers,
> So these dangers, dark and dreadful,
> Have not harmed us in their passing,
> Have but brought us wondrous knowledge,
> Wondrous knowledge, gain and pleasure.

> " Shall we now give only curses
> To that Power which has led us ?
> Is there naught within your man-souls
> Which, like bird that sings of morning
> While the dawning is yet fettered
> With the seal and sign of midnight, —
> Rises, thrills, and pulses through you
> With the surety of triumph ?

> " Look about you, men of Thrandheim ;
> See you not yon tall, straight cedars
> Lifting up their strength above us ?
> See ye not yon oaks and pine trees,
> Wood in plenty and perfection ?

> " Lo ! our arms are strong and mighty,
> And ere cold winds blow from Northland
> We shall launch a goodly vessel,
> That shall breast the treacherous billows,
> Brave the storms and skirt the ice-pack,
> Till we ride in peace and quiet
> On the blue Fjord of our home land
> In the harbour of the Thrandheim."

" Ah," said Erlend, as Egil's notes of hope pulsed joyously through the hall, " who but Harald, great in courage and faith in the White Christ, could so lift these men from the depths of sorrow ? "

" 'T was all I could do," replied Harald, " and at least it gave us something to do and a reason for living until it was done. So it was that long ere summer had departed we had built our vessel. Small, rude and rough was it, but yet 't was strong and heavy to withstand the winds and waves. Then we bade farewell to those strange men, who had given us such great and needed friendship, — such friendship as dwells only in the bosom of the soul that reaches upward towards the Perfect, — and with a prayer to Christ the White, we sailed out upon those mighty waters."

Harald's head sank upon his hands, and in Egil's song the joy and hope gradually changed to grief and despair as his deep, rich voice sang of the sorrows of that sailing.

> " Towards the north they turned their vessel,
> Towards the distant shores of Iceland.
> Many were the days they counted,
> Many were the storms they weathered,
> Great their suffering and sorrow,
> And their courage, strong and manly,
> Weaker grew, and left them, drifting
> Helplessly upon the salt waves.
>
> " Worn with hunger, mad with thirsting,
> Down they lay with covered faces ;
> Made no movement, sang no death-song ;
> But in silence and in suffering,
> One by one they died, and dying
> Prayed to Christ the White to take them
> From this world of pain and evil
> To the perfect peace of heaven.
>
> " Out upon the lonely ocean,
> Tossed by salt waves, windward driven,
> Only three men left within her,

Rode the tiny, rough-hewn vessel.
Parched with thirst and weak with hunger,
Harald, Hilmir, and Karlsefni
Left the boat to winds and currents,
While their blood-shot eyes looked wildly
Far across the waste of waters."

Harald had lifted his face from his hands and now stopped
Egil with a swift gesture.

"But the great joy of that moment, when from out the
north came a speck upon the ocean, growing larger and larger
until close beside us lay a staunch viking ship manned up by
strong Norsemen!

"It was Bjarni and his followers making their visit to his
father in Greenland, and Christ the White had sent wind, and
currents to drift him southward to our aid. Can ye realize,
my friends, what those kindly faces meant to us? Can ye
feel, as we felt, the life-giving grasp of those hands and the joy
of that haven of rest and safety?

"We journeyed on to Greenland, but though our welcome
was great and our new-found friends urged us to stay with
them, my soul stirred in warning tones within me. Not a
moment must I delay, lest upon the head of the Christ Maiden
a dark and terrible doom should fall."

"Yea," said Erlend, "and ye came! ye came!"

The guests reëchoed the words, "Ye came!" until Egil
silenced them with an uplifted hand and sang:

"Not to ye, O men of Thrandheim,
Need I sing of Harald's coming!
Well ye know the wondrous story
Of a faith that knew no weakness.
Well ye know the wondrous answer
Which descended out of heaven
When a maiden prayed to White Christ!

"Praise to Harald, greatest viking
Who has thrilled our hearts with wonder!
Praise to Harald, Blest of Nornir,
Who has brought us peace and quiet!
But the rarest, sweetest blessings
Rest upon the bride, white-folded!
She who brought into the Northland, —
Cold and dreary, and forsaken, —
All the warmth of Christ's great world-love.

> " Angel of the Dawn, most perfect,
> Thou hast banished fears and doubtings.
> Gone are all our thoughts of Odin,
> And supreme in heaven above us
> Reigns the White Christ, pure and holy,
> Christ of Light, and Love, and Wisdom ! "

A moment of golden silence followed Egil's singing. Then, from out that silence, even as the sunlight bursts from the sun, broke a flood of applause. The singing had made men thrill with the pride of life and love ; it had made them wonder at the power of the White Christ ; it had filled their hearts with the joy of living and doing. More than all, it had made them radiant with the peace that permeated every heart that day. Lifting high the golden horns they drank to the health of Harald, Blest of Nornir, and his beautiful bride, Persea, the Christ Maiden.

"Skal to Harald! Skal to the Christ Maiden! Skal! Skal ! "

The hall was filled with the sounds of joyous revelry, — the tinkling of gold and silver vessels, the sheen and rustle of silken clothing, the music of many happy voices. In the midst of this gladness the door of the skali was flung widely open, and the keeper thundered out :

" Room at the bridal feast of Harald Rognvaldson for Olaf, King of Norge ! "

Men paused with drinking horns half-raised to their lips. Speech and laughter were hushed in astonishment. Olaf stood in their midst, smiling graciously, arrayed in gorgeous apparel, and attended by a kingly guard.

Quickly rose Harald.

"Welcome to our feast, King Olaf. Greatly honoured would be any bridal to which thou comest as guest. Harald Rognvaldson's heart is warm with joy at thy presence. Brighter will sparkle the mead when thou dost quaff it. Greater will grow our joy when thou dost share it."

The King, still smiling graciously, replied :

" Olaf's greeting to thee and yonder beautiful bride ! If thou speakest truly, — if the King's presence makes whiter the mead-foam and greater the joy in your hearts, — can it not add also to the glory of the wedding-feast by providing such entertainment as never guests knew before ? "

Harald's eyes searched the King's smiling countenance. Behind that gracious manner he saw something lurking,— something cruel and cunning. The tiger in Olaf Tryggvveson was crouching and creeping. The bridegroom felt a mighty force grip his heart and almost stop its beating.

The King had not forgotten and forgiven as he had believed. From the moment of Olaf's landing, Harald had looked for the answer to his challenge of many months ago; but it had not come. The King had been kindly in his greeting, reverent towards Persea,— had said naught of the past. But now! Deep and dark had been the evil purposes in his heart. With his hatred of old, he had waited to strike until the striking would bring the greatest pain. Well, what matter? Was not a just God still ruling in heaven?

Faith touched that which had gripped his heart. His breath came back. He felt again the warm blood flowing in manly pulse through his veins. He spoke:

" Gladly will I welcome aught that would give pleasure to the King or my guests. Never Thrandheim wedding had more of joy in its feasting than this one here to-night. If thou wilt make it equally rich in entertainment, thou wilt have the thanks of Harald Rognvaldson. Let the King speak."

Still the smile on Olaf's countenance. Still the tiger in him crouched and crept.

" Hast thou forgotten, Harald Rognvaldson, to whom thy bride really belongs? Hast thou forgotten that thou didst challenge me to a settlement of my claim and thine by trial of sword or ordeal? If thou hast forgotten, Olaf has a clearer memory. What better time than now to decide the matter? What better sport for thy guests? What greater honour for so lovely a bride than that warriors should match skill with skill for the pleasure of being with her on her bridal night? "

While the King was speaking, the peace and joy of that wedding feast vanished as a flame blown out. Drinking horns were replaced, untouched, upon the tables. Startled, anxious faces scanned King and bridegroom. Only Harald seemed unmoved and fearless. Men marvelled when they heard the calmness of his voice as he answered Olaf:

" The King has spoken the truth. I have been waiting long for the answer to my challenge. Name the manner of conflict which most pleases thee. Harald keeps his word.

He is ready and willing to help thee give the guests at his wedding such stirring sport as is not usual, even in our stirring north."

Lightly answered the King, as if the whole matter was of little moment:

"We will shed no blood. 'T would mar the gladness of the bridal hour to know that it had been bought with red life. Let us have instead, a test of skill in weapon-throwing. Hang against the wall one of the golden bracelets that the bride wears on her white arms. Here are six tolle-knives,— sharp-pointed, balanced to the weight of a hair. Take which three thou wilt. It is but child's play to strike the centre of the golden ring at fifteen paces. Let us quickly know whose bride the Christ Maiden shall be to-night!"

Every man present knew that to Olaf Tryggvveson such idróttir was as breath-drawing. Faces grew dark as thunder-clouds. Though Harald was skillful in all Norse sports, little chance had any man against Olaf. He was but playing with the Blest of the Nornir! Men muttered under their breath.

King Olaf paid no heed to the dark faces nor muttered wrath. Norse law and honour gave him all right to the test and the result. They could not stay his hand; they could not thwart his purpose; they could not take from him the prize. He held out the knives.

Carefully Harald chose three, feeling their points and weighing their oaken handles. As he toyed with them, he said:

"Methinks, King Olaf, that fifteen paces is too easy a throw when so great a reward awaits the winner. Lengthen the distance,— mark off thirty paces. Let us have more than child's play since ye must needs lay claim to that which I have won by greater love, by greater strength, by greater daring, by greater peril than thou couldst ever know!"

The guests stared, open-mouthed, at Harald, not believing what their ears had heard. Was the Blest of the Nornir mad, that he so deliberately cast aside every chance of winning? Thirty paces was a distance that would make even the most skillful of weapon-throwers uncertain of aim.

But Harald waited for the King's answer as one would wait for a reply to a jest.

The tiger in Olaf Tryggvveson no longer crouched and

crept. In anger and passion he answered Harald, his voice choked and hoarse:

"Make the distance what thou wilt. Make it three times fifteen paces if it pleases thee! Olaf Tryggvveson shall yet silence thy boasting and possess thy bride!"

On the cross-bench, Persea trembled and grew pale as ivory.

At Harald's command, a space was cleared; and upon the door a golden bracelet was fastened. The bride had chosen it herself from those on her arm, and had whispered a prayer as she saw it hanging, a ring of fire, upon the weather-stained wood. Then the paces were marked off.

Olaf cast the first knife. It flew furiously through the air and struck the panel of the door two hand-breadths from the bracelet. The sarcastic murmur that followed its striking told how poor that throwing was for Olaf, renowned in idróttir.

Then Harald stood up and lifted his knife high above his head. His eyes fastened intent gaze upon that ring of gold. His arm straightened and shot out. The knife flew swift as arrow from a bow and struck in the door close beside Olaf's, — but nearer the bracelet.

The murmur which greeted his effort was tense with feeling. 'T was as uncommon a throw as Norsemen had ever known. Men saw that the game would be a desperate one. The faint applause that stirred the air died away quickly. Lips were trembling too much to give sound to the greatness of the inward feeling.

Again Olaf threw. This time with a steadier hand, a cooler nerve. The point sank deeply into the wood close to the outer rim of the bracelet. The King smiled grimly. The next time he could strike well into the centre of that golden ring.

Men watched Harald anxiously as he took his place again; but they saw no fear, nor trembling of hand nor arm. There was the same clear gaze, the same steady aim, the same sure flight. For the second time his knife struck close beside the King's; but farther from the bracelet.

The score was now even. The guests moved excitedly. King Olaf was proudly confident; and if Harald showed any sign of inward feeling, it was satisfaction with the result of his efforts.

For the third and last time the King stood forth. He

measured the distance with keen, careful eye. He poised the knife exactly. He threw it with perfect aim and sure strength. It struck the door full in the centre of the golden ring.

Women cried out. Men groaned, or bit their lips in furious, helpless rage. The Blest of the Nornir could not do better than that! His day of happiness would turn to blackest, bitterest night. Some bowed their heads in their hands, unwilling to even witness his last throw, — so useless now.

Olaf waved Harald to his place with merciless taunt:

"Surely, thou who hast done so much that Olaf has not, can now do better than the King. Throw well this time, Harald Rognvaldson, for there is present danger that thou shalt lose thy bride!"

Harald seemed not to be conscious of King nor anxious guests nor white-faced bride. He was living in another world. Those about him faded into misty distance. The murmur of voices sounded in his ears like the rush of far-off waters. He only knew that there was sure, solid ground beneath his feet; he only knew that he held his last knife in his hand; he only knew that to win Persea he must throw as never Norseman had thrown before. Some voice whispered to him, gave him definite purpose, directed his gaze, steadied his arm, endowed him with strength.

An instant he stood thus, leaning forward with upraised arm, motionless, rigid as if chiseled from marble. Then he put forth that mighty strength which had been given him.

There was a flash of steely blue, a fierce whistle of flying missive, a dull, dead sound — and the blade which Harald had thrown quivered and trembled in the handle of Olaf's knife.

Astonishment clutched at men's throats and let no sound come therefrom. They looked, — doubting their senses, not believing their own eyes. But their unbelief could not last long. In the oaken handle Harald's knife still quivered.

Then a tempest of maddened joy broke forth. It surged and rolled through the skali in peals of sound that shook the heavy oaken walls and roof, as the thunder-clap shakes earth and sky. It was immense, uncontrollable. It brought men to their feet in wild delirium. Some tossed their arms in air; some struck the heavy tables and benches with blows of joy that threatened to break bone and wood. Harald Rognvaldson's victory was their victory. His joy was their joy.

Through all the tumult Harald knelt at Persea's feet ; and with lips pressed to her hands, offered thanks to the White Christ. Olaf stood motionless, gripping his sword handle till his fingers were numb, hiding in his cold, white face a terrible rage and disappointment.

As the tempest spends its strength and drifts down the curve of the sky, so the tumult gradually grew less and less. Men ceased their shouting, and took again their places at the feast table. When there was once more a measure of quiet in the skali, Harald Rognvaldson arose and said :

" Many nights ago, at the King's feast on the shores of the Fjord, all men did hear a vow that Harald Rognvaldson made. Ye did murmur and wonder when ye heard it ; and some there were who called out in anger. Unwonted and wondrous changes have come to the Thrandheim since that night ; but my vow still stands. Now does Harald keep that sacred vow.

" I won in contest with Olaf Tryggvveson because the White Christ was with me. From the moment the King spoke, a Spirit of Light and strength stood by my side. It whispered to me to change the throwing distance. It directed my arm ; it put such faith and courage in my heart that I had no thought of fear. When the end came, — when all seemed lost, it told me what to do. It breathed into my soul ; it touched my arm ; it gave me strength. 'T was not skill of Harald's that won him the prize. To the White Christ, the God of Justice and Love, belongs all honour of victory. Lift high your horns of mead and drink to the glory and honour of Christ the White ! "

With hearts awed by the presence of that Unseen Power which was greater than the human, the guests lifted reverently the foaming horns :

" Skal to Christ the White ! Skal ! Skal ! "

While they drank, Olaf shivered and trembled. The terrible rage left his face. He bowed his head. Then, as if shrinking from the gaze of men, he turned, and with one last humbled look towards Persea, passed quickly out of the skali.

Until the early hours of the morning Ingiborg heard him praying in his tent, — praying the White Christ for forgiveness and faith ; praying that all happiness would come to Persea, bride of Harald Rognvaldson.

CHAPTER XLVII

THE FALLING OF THE STAR

THE guests still sat at feast table, drinking and talking o
the amazing events of that bridal night ; but Harald and Persea were no longer present.

Thrilled with happiness and love, Harald had whispered to
his bride. Together they had left the feast hall, followed by
glad shouts of joy and blessings untold. Once out into the
balmy night air, Persea clasped Harald's arm and said :

"Take me up on the hillside. Let us breathe God's pure
air and still our beating hearts in the silence and beauty of the
night. See how blue the heavens, and how bright the stars !"

So, in their bridal garb, they turned from the skemma and
sought the narrow path on the hillside. Half-way up was their
favourite resting place, — a tiny, grassy knoll which over-
looked the Fjord. To the right, far above them towered the
black face of the cliff. To the left lay the valley with its
winding river. Beneath them rippled the Fjord, whose waves
beat with musical rhythm on the rocks below.

Surpassingly beautiful were earth and sky and water on that
bridal night. Harald drew Persea into his arms. In joy and
hope they talked of the love and life that stretched away into
future years, — and beyond those years into eternity. Suddenly Persea tore herself from Harald's embrace and pointed
upward, whispering :

"What is that upon the top of the cliff ? Look ! Is it not
the outline of a man and horse ? How came they in that perilous place ?"

Harald followed Persea's pointing, and upon the extreme
edge of the precipice he beheld a horse and rider, — immense,
motionless, as if part of the rock on which they stood. He
breathed deeply, and answered :

"Knowest thou not who it is, my beloved ? There is but
one man in all Norge who could make that outline against the
sky. 'T is Iron Beard, Temple Godi of Thrandheim."

Then Persea trembled and clung to Harald's arm.

" Why comes he here to-night ? O my Harald ! is trouble yet brewing over our heads ? Is there no end, no limit to these storms that have swept over us ? Can he see us, think you ? "

" Nay, sweet one," said Harald. " Tremble not. He cannot harm us now. Listen ! He is singing ! "

It was true. Out over the Fjord rang a wild, fierce song. It broke the silence of the night with a pulsing that seemed to come from a heart that was torn with emotion. It grew furious and tender by turns; it raved and stormed; it prayed and besought; and ever was the singer's hand raised towards the north where two stars shone like angel's eyes amid the sapphire blue.

There was something hidden within that singing which made Persea shiver and grow faint.

" What means it, Harald ? What is in the soul of the priest that wrings my heart with fear and sorrow ? "

" Hush ! dear one," answered Harald, his voice low and tense. " Hush ! Speak not ! The great heart of the priest is breaking. He is singing his death-song ! "

Even while Harald spoke the song ceased. The rider seized the bridle, drew back the horse's head, and leaning forward, pressed his spurs into the animal's side. It snorted, reared, plunged, tried to draw back, — then in maddened obedience leaped sheer from the cliff.

To Persea and Harald came an instant's vision of a distorted, turning, twisting mass dropping from a terrible height — the waters of the Fjord opened and closed, and Iron Beard, last priest of the ancient gods, sank into a Norseman's grave.

Ere the waves rolled smoothly over that grave, out of the northern sky shot a falling star. Straight across the heavens it flew, and dropped out of sight behind the distant mountains, leaving a long trail of quickly disappearing light.

Persea cried out and buried her face upon Harald's breast, sobbing. Tenderly he spoke to her :

" Nay, grieve not. He has died as he lived, true to the mysteries and beliefs of the old gods. Christ will understand and be merciful. The falling of the star was as Iron Beard would have had it. It fulfilled the old belief that Valhalla opens when a light falls from the sky. See ! only one of those twin lights is left in the northern heavens ! "

Persea looked up. The light of one of those stars had truly gone out. Harald continued:

"Knowest thou, my Angel of the Dawn, that my soul is thrilled with the meaning of what we have seen to-night? The past is dead, buried in depths where the human cannot reach."

"Yea," answered Persea, with tear-wet cheeks and burning heart, "and out of the sky of Norge has vanished all the ancient superstition and ignorance. It has fallen into unfathomable space, and high in heaven above us shines a brighter, purer faith. Behold the Northern Star! Seems it not to quiver and glow with my words? Let us call it the Star of Christ the White!"

She rested her head on Harald's breast. He looked into her pure face and saw the burning soul-light in her eyes. Her beauty, her purity, her faith, overpowered him. Love, reverent and immense, possessed him. He thought of all that she had been to Norge and to him. Folding her closely to his heart, he said in voice choked with intense emotion:

"Tell me not to look to the skies! Thou, and thou alone, art the Star of Christ the White!"

EPILOGUE

GREAT prosperity came to Norge under Olaf Tryggvve-son's wise ruling. Temples were erected to Christ the White throughout the country. The Thrandheim, true ever to its claim of supremacy among the Northland Districts, built to the honour of the White Christ a temple fairer and better than any erected elsewhere.

Olaf moved among the people with none of the old steely glitter in his eyes. Strong was he in purpose and will; but that purpose no longer considered self alone, that will no longer strode relentlessly over the wishes and happiness of others. Tamed was his wild nature; conquered were his will and selfishness. His people loved and reverenced him as few Kings of Norge were ever loved and reverenced.

One day a woman of noble birth came to beseech protection from brutality. The King's heart went out to her in loving sympathy, and he took her to wife.

But ever he seemed to live under a cloud. He smiled rarely, and men shook their heads and said the King could not forget his first love.

Finally he buckled on his sword and went forth to the battle-field, striving to escape from that shadow which seemed ever resting upon his life.

Then came a dark day in the history of Norge. Trusting to false promises, led by false friends, he was betrayed into a conflict with foes so innumerable and strong that there was naught for Olaf Tryggvveson to do but to lash ship to ship and fight to the death.

Far below the foam-wreathed waves he sank in his kingly armour. Yet men so loved him that marvellous stories were told of his miraculous escape from death, and of the hermit in the far-distant Holy Land who was once King of Norge.

Was it true? Did he, by penitence and renunciation of the world, rise above the curse of Heid? Who knows?

Persea and Harald lived their Christian lives amid peace and plenty and richness of happiness, — helping, lifting, teaching.

High on the precipice overlooking the Fjord they built a

huge cairn in memory of the loved ones who slept afar off under and near the strange waves that lapped the shores of Christ's Land. Here they often came to talk of those sad days, — now rapidly drifting into the past.

Gradually all thought of the ancient worship faded from the minds of the people. The dark days were forgotten. The majestic stones that guarded the dom ring stood amid eternal silence and solitude. The huge, discoloured sacrifice rock knew no more the burning flesh nor the trickling of warm blood. Over all that wide land the White Christ reigned supreme.

Yet the glamour of the past still lingers on those fjelds and fjords and mountains sublime. Still do men raise high the cup of honour and say with mighty beating of the heart:

"Skal! Skal to Gamle Norge!"

FINIS

GLOSSARY

GLOSSARY

ASAR—Odin and his kin, worshipped as the gods of the north.

ASGARD—The abode of the Asar.

AURAR—A piece of money, eight of which made one gold mark.

BALDR—One of the Asar, called "The Good." He was killed through Loki's treachery.

BAUTASTONES—Grave stones.

BERSERK-RAGE—A fanatical anger which made those possessed with it rage and fight with unusual strength.

BIRTH-SPRINKLED—A sacred rite of great antiquity, consisting of sprinkling water over a new-born child.

BLOOD-EAGLE—A mode of dealing the death penalty. To inflict this punishment the flesh was cut on the back from each side of the spine in the shape of an eagle, and the lungs drawn through the exposed ribs.

BOER—Group of buildings composing a homestead.

BONDER—Freemen who owned land.

BRAGI-TOAST—A vow to perform some great deed.

BRIDAL-FALD—A white head-dress worn by brides.

BRIDGE OF ASAR—The rainbow, over which souls were supposed to pass to Valhalla.

BRYNJA—A ring coat of mail.

DOM-RING—A circle of twelve large stones surrounding the sacrifice stone.

DVERGAR'S MEAD—Wine of Dvergars, who were supposed to live under the earth and to have the power to give the gift of song.

DYNEJA—A separate building for women's use.

EGIR'S BROTHER—The Wind God.

FENRIS WOLF—Son of Loki, the evil god.

FIBULA—A fancy buckle or clasp.

GAMLE NORGE—Old Norway. An expression used with especial patriotic earnestness and feeling, even up to the present day.

GESTIR—One of the king's guard.

GIGJAR—A kind of fiddle.

GINUNGAGAP—A gaping void, which before creation, separated Nifl-heim, the world of cold from Muspelheim, the world of heat.

GOI—The sowing month.

GORNNANUD—Gore month. Named from the slaughter of cattle which took place in the first month of winter.

HAMMER OF THOR—Thor's especial weapon of great strength and virtue.

HELGA POOL—The first hell.

HIRDMAN—An attendant on the King.

HLAUT-BOLLI—A huge bowl, usually of copper, which caught the blood of sacrificed animals.

HLAUT-TEIN—A bundle of twigs used to sprinkle the temple and people with the blood of sacrifice.

HOSUR—A kind of light breeches, covering the feet and resembling high boots.

HUGIN—One of Odin's ravens which was supposed to bring messages from him.

KYRTLE—A long, wide garment made with long sleeves and a train and confined by a belt at the waist.

LOKI—One of the Asar, who was evil in all his thoughts and deeds.

LUR—A long horn.

MICKLEGARD—An ancient name for Constantinople.

MINIR'S WELL—The well of wisdom, about which the gods assembled to give their judgments.

MUNIN—Odin's Raven (See " Hugin ").

NECKLACE OF THE EARTH—The ocean.

NIDHÖGGU—A serpent which was Loki's son, and which lived in Helga Pool.

NIFL-HEL—The second hell.

NITHING—Considered the most insulting epithet one Norsemen could use against another.

NIORVASUND—The Straits of Gibraltar.

NOREG's-VELDI—Meaning Norway.

NORNIR—The three fates who decided men's lives.

PELL—A rich cloth similar to velvet.

RAGNARÖK—The end of the world. Literally the " Twilight of the Gods."

RAN—The wife of Egir, god of the sea.

Rett—A value on body and honour, varying with the person's position and wealth.

Seid—A kind of witchcraft performed with songs and incantations at night.

Shifting Lights—The Aurora Borealis.

Shirt of Gunnar—Coat of mail.

Sigrblót—A sacrifice for luck and victory held in the spring.

Skal—To your health.

Skali—The main building of the Norse homestead.

Skemma—A building for women's use only.

Skroelingi—Indians.

Stalla-ring—A large ring worn on the priest's arm and upon which oaths were sworn.

Thing—An assembling of the people for the purpose of law-making, settlement of difficulties, declaration of war, etc., etc.

Thing-bod ⎫
Thing-token ⎬ An arrow for war, — a stick for other causes, sent out from farm to farm, calling upon all men quali-
Thing-summons ⎭ fied to be present at the Thing plain on the fifth day after the issue of the summons.

Thori—The month of declining winter.

Tolle-kniv—A short knife for general use, worn in the belt.

Var—A goddess who listened to oaths between men and women and punished any violations of such oaths.

Vetrablót—A sacrifice which took place in the early fall.

Volva—A witch or sibyl who could foretell the future.

Well of Sacrifices—A well outside of the temple into which the bodies of the sacrificed were thrown.

Ymir—The first human being formed from the melting rime of Niflheim.